too Scot to Handle

GRACE BURROWES

piatkus

PIATKUS

First published in the US in 2017 by Forever,
an imprint of Grand Central Publishing, a division of Hachette Book Group, Inc
First published in Great Britain in 2017 by Piatkus

3 5 7 9 10 8 6 4 2

A CIP catalogue record for this book
is available from the British Library.

ISBN 978-0-349-41545-1

Printed and bound in Great Britain by
Clays Ltd, St Ives plc

Papers used by Piatkus are from well-managed forests
and other responsible sources.

MIX
Paper from
responsible sources
FSC® C104740

Piatkus
An imprint of
Little, Brown Book Group
Carmelite House
50 Victoria Embankment
London EC4Y 0DZ

An Hachette UK Company
www.hachette.co.uk

www.littlebrown.co.uk

To Devin W.

ACKNOWLEDGMENTS

I am having a wonderful time frolicking with my Windham friends again, but this joy wouldn't be possible without a lot of hard work and support from the good folks at Grand Central/Forever. My editor, Leah Hultenschmidt, has been particularly kind and patient as I navigate waters both new and exciting. To Michelle Cashman, Lexi Smail, and the rest of the crew, many thanks, and now I wish Uncle Anthony and Aunt Gladys had had more children!

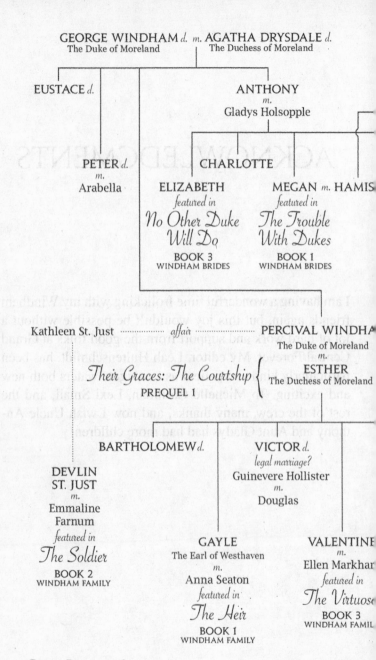

GEORGE WINDHAM *d.* *m.* **AGATHA DRYSDALE** *d.*
The Duke of Moreland — The Duchess of Moreland

EUSTACE *d.*

ANTHONY
m.
Gladys Holsopple

PETER *d.*
m.
Arabella

CHARLOTTE

ELIZABETH
featured in
No Other Duke
Will Do
BOOK 3
WINDHAM BRIDES

MEGAN *m.* **HAMIS**
featured in
The Trouble
With Dukes
BOOK 1
WINDHAM BRIDES

Kathleen St. Just ⋯⋯⋯ *affair* ⋯⋯⋯ **PERCIVAL WINDHA**
The Duke of Moreland
m.

Their Graces: The Courtship
PREQUEL 1

ESTHER
The Duchess of Moreland

BARTHOLOMEW *d.*

VICTOR *d.*
legal marriage?
Guinevere Hollister
m.
Douglas

DEVLIN
ST. JUST
m.
Emmaline
Farnum
featured in
The Soldier
BOOK 2
WINDHAM FAMILY

GAYLE
The Earl of Westhaven
m.
Anna Seaton
featured in
The Heir
BOOK 1
WINDHAM FAMILY

VALENTINE
m.
Ellen Markhar
featured in
The Virtuose
BOOK 3
WINDHAM FAMIL

GRACEBURROWES.COM

WINDHAM *Family Tree*

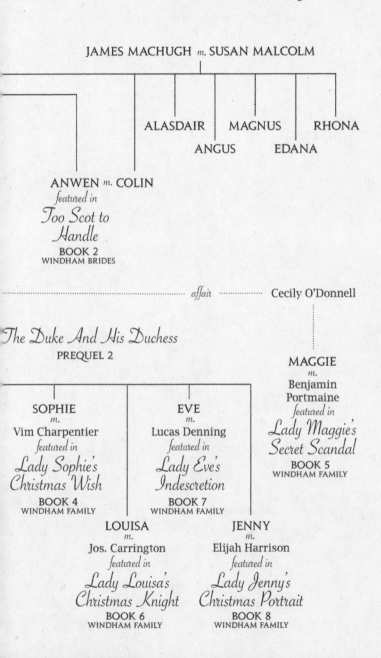

JAMES MACHUGH *m.* SUSAN MALCOLM

ALASDAIR

ANGUS

MAGNUS

EDANA

RHONA

ANWEN *m.* COLIN
featured in
Too Scot to Handle
BOOK 2
WINDHAM BRIDES

.... *affair* .... Cecily O'Donnell

The Duke And His Duchess
PREQUEL 2

MAGGIE
m.
Benjamin Portmaine
featured in
Lady Maggie's Secret Scandal
BOOK 5
WINDHAM FAMILY

SOPHIE
m.
Vim Charpentier
featured in
Lady Sophie's Christmas Wish
BOOK 4
WINDHAM FAMILY

EVE
m.
Lucas Denning
featured in
Lady Eve's Indescretion
BOOK 7
WINDHAM FAMILY

LOUISA
m.
Jos. Carrington
featured in
Lady Louisa's Christmas Knight
BOOK 6
WINDHAM FAMILY

JENNY
m.
Elijah Harrison
featured in
Lady Jenny's Christmas Portrait
BOOK 8
WINDHAM FAMILY

too
Scot
to
Handle

Chapter One

"IT IS A TRUTH universally acknowledged that a single gentleman in possession of a great fortune— Damn it, woman," Winthrop Montague bellowed, "where's my ale?"

"And in possession of a title!" somebody called from across the tavern's longest table.

"And damned fine looks!" his mate added.

"And a strapping bay gelding I'm keen to win over a hand of cards!"

Much rapping on the tabletop ensued, along with by-joves and hear-hears, until Lord Colin MacHugh's head throbbed to the beat of all this gentlemanly bonhomie.

"As I was saying," Montague went on, gesturing grandly with his tankard and sloshing ale on the floor. "It is a truth universally acknowledged, that a single gentleman in possession of a great fortune, must be in want of a passionate, beautiful, inventive, affectionate…"

"Mistress!" the company yelled.

"Two mistresses, so he don't wear 'em out too quick!"

"When you have as much good fortune as Lord Colin does, you should hire entire brothels and invite all your friends along as a gesture of charity toward the less fortunate!"

When you had as much good fortune as Lord Colin, you apparently were expected to hire the equivalent of entire public houses.

The harried young woman serving the dozen men who'd accompanied Colin and Montague from the club emerged from the kitchen for the hundredth time in two hours. She ferried a set of full tankards over from the bar and swiped aside a lock of dark hair with the back of her wrist.

One of Montague's friends pulled her into his lap. "I can't afford a mistress, my lovely, but I can show you a very fine time for tuppence."

"D'you suppose that's why they call it tupping?" Baron Twillinger asked. He'd reached the philosophical stage of inebriation while his companion, Lord Hector Pierpont, was still in the amorous phase.

Colin was not inebriated, though he was profoundly *bored*.

"If your lordship don't mind," the tavern maid said, wiggling against Pierpont's hold, "I'm not that sort of girl."

"You're all that sort of girl if the price is right," Pierpont replied, chasing her chin with the puckered lips of a hungry mackerel. "Am I right?"

"You're right," Twilly replied. "I'm foxed."

"My lord, please let me go," the girl said, struggling in earnest.

"I'll let you go, as soon as you let me come," her gin-Romeo retorted, groping her breast.

"Pierpont." Colin tried for that blend of condescension,

good humor, and command that came so easily to the true aristocrat. "If she's busy accommodating your prodigious appetites, she can't very well tend to the rest of us, can she? And we will provide her much more than tuppence to keep the ale and port flowing."

"He's got you there, Pointy," the baron said, raising his tankard. "A round to Lord Colin's superior intellect!"

Pierpont let go of the girl, and from across the table, Montague acknowledged a competent display of authority—or wealth—with a slight smile.

Colin signaled the serving maid with a tilt of his head, and that gesture—perfected in cantinas and public houses all across Portugal, Spain, France, and the Low Countries— earned him her cautious approach.

Smart woman—smart, exhausted woman. This impromptu drinking party had started a good two hours ago, and so far, Colin had found it a waste of time, coin, and decent ale. One didn't say that, of course, not when one was a newly titled Scottish lord learning to keep company with English aristocrats.

"Have the stable boy bring my horse around," Colin said, keeping his voice low. "I ride a blood bay, about seventeen hands with two white socks. Tell your master that Lord Colin MacHugh would rather the proprietor served us himself from this point onward."

"I'll get a cuff on me 'ead for telling me master—"

"Pierpont will get you a babe in your belly," Colin said, slipping the girl a few coins. "My brother is the Duke of Murdoch, and the publican will want to remain in my good graces."

"The Duke of *Murder*?"

How Hamish hated that sobriquet, but Colin would use it to keep this serving maid from ruin.

"The very one, and if anything happens to him, that title becomes mine. Away with you now, love."

She curtsied and moved off, and because Colin was a newly titled Scottish lord in the company of his English peers, he pretended to watch her backside as she sashayed away.

Then he yawned—the first expression of genuine sentiment on his part since he'd sat down with Montague and his friends.

* * *

Mr. Wilbur Hitchings heaved a sigh of such theatrical proportions, Anwen Windham suspected he'd rehearsed it.

"A lady of your breeding and refinement shouldn't be bothered with financial matters," he said, shuffling papers on the lectern before him, "though the general conclusion is simple enough: Charities need benefactors. Your good intentions are helpful and commendable, et cetera and so forth. Nevertheless, good intentions do not pay the coal man or keep growing boys in boots and breeches."

Anwen refused to sit quietly and be condescended to as if she were a recalcitrant scholar. She set about straightening the rows of desks and chairs before Hitchings's podium because the headmaster of the Home for Wayward Urchins couldn't be bothered to restore order in the empty classroom.

"You were hired by the board of directors for your expertise in managing charitable establishments for children," Anwen said. "How do you propose we address the shortage of funds?"

Hitchings peered at her over gold-rimmed half-spectacles. "Madam, I was hired because I have a firm grasp of the curriculum necessary to shape useful young men from brats and pickpockets. Financial matters are the province of the directors."

Hitchings had a firm grasp of the birch rod and the Old Testament. At meal times, he had a firm grasp of his bottle of claret.

"Your efforts with the boys could not be more appreciated," Anwen replied. "I had hoped, based on your years of experience, you might have fundraising suggestions for a lady who'd like to see the House of Urchins thriving well into the future—under your guiding hand, of course."

She let that sink in—if the House of Urchins failed, Hitchings's livelihood failed with it. A *simple enough* conclusion.

"Charity balls come to mind," Hitchings said, flourishing a handkerchief with which to polish his spectacles. "Subscriptions, donations, that sort of thing. To be blunt, Miss Anwen, funding endeavors are the only reason the directors bother having a ladies' committee. Your feminine endowments allow you to charm coin from those who enjoy an excess of means. If you'll excuse me, I have lessons to prepare."

Anwen's uncle was a duke, and her sister had recently married a duke. This preening dolt would not leave her to wrestle desks and chairs while implying that she should flaunt her breasts and hips to keep a roof over his head.

"I'm sure the lesson preparation can wait a few more moments, Mr. Hitchings. How much longer will our present funds last?"

He tucked the handkerchief away and rolled up the papers from the lectern, as if a nearby puppy might require swatting. "Weeks, two months at best."

In other words, as the social season neared its conclusion, the orphanage would approach its end as well.

"Have you applied for other positions?" Anwen gave him her best, most saccharine blink. "I'd be happy to write you a character."

Hitchings stopped halfway to the door. "A character for *me*, Miss Anwen?"

"Your salary is one of our greatest expenses." Hitchings's remuneration, in addition to his allowance for ale, candles, and a new suit, exceeded the budget for coal by a handy fourteen pounds eight per year. "In the interests of economy, the directors could seek to replace you with a lesser talent."

Hitchings might have been handsome in his youth. He had thick brown hair going gray at the temples, some height, dark eyes, and the rhetorical instincts of a classroom thespian. Middle age had added a paunch to his figure, though, and Anwen had never seen him smile at a lady or a child.

He smiled at the directors. Every time he saw them, he was smiling, jovial, and briskly uncomplaining about the social alchemy he claimed to work, turning society's tattered castoffs into useful articles.

"Replace me with a lesser talent?" Hitchings smacked the rolled papers against his open palm. "That would hardly result in economy, Miss Anwen. Instead of budding felons learning the straight and narrow under the hand of an experienced master, you'd be feeding and clothing little criminals for no purpose whatsoever."

Other than to save their lives? "I take your meaning, Mr. Hitchings, but the directors are men of the world, and they deal in facts and figures more effectively than I ever hope to. While you could easily find a post that more appropriately rewards your many talents, the boys will starve without this place to call home. I expect the directors will see that logic easily enough."

Especially if Anwen reminded them of it at every meeting.

Hitchings's mouth worked like a beached fish's, but no sound came out. He doubtless wasn't offended that his salary might be called into question, he was offended that Anwen—diminutive, red-haired, well-born, young, and *female*—would do the questioning.

"I cannot be held responsible for the poorly reasoned decisions of my betters," he said. "This organization is in want of funds, Miss Anwen, and what is the purpose of the ladies' committee, if not to address the facility's greatest needs? You can embroider all the handkerchiefs you like, but that won't keep the doors open."

French lace edged Hitchings's cravat, his coat had been tailored on Bond Street, his gleaming boots were fashioned by Hoby. Anwen wished she had the strength to pitch him and his finery down the jakes.

"Thank you for putting the situation in terms I can grasp, Mr. Hitchings," she said, adding a smile, lest he detect sarcasm flung in his very face. "Please don't let me detain you further. You have lessons to prepare, and we must not waste a day of whatever time you have left to exert your good influence over the children."

Anwen marched for the door, pausing to surreptitiously snatch up Hitchings's birch rod and tuck it into the folds of her cloak.

"You should probably finish tidying up the chairs and desks," she added. "I have always admired your insistence on order in the boys' dormitories. What better place to set that example than in your own classroom?"

She made a grand exit, ignoring the birch rod tangling with her skirts. Not three yards down the corridor, she ran smack into Lord Colin MacHugh and nearly landed on her bum.

* * *

Colin MacHugh liked variety, and not only regarding the ladies. Army life had offered a version of variety—march today, make camp tomorrow, ride into battle the day after—and just enough predictability.

The rations had been bad, the weather foul at the worst times, and the battles tragic. Other than that, camaraderie had been a daily blessing, as had a sense of purpose. Besiege that town, get these orders forward to Wellington, repair the axle on the baggage wain, report the location of that French patrol.

Stay alive.

Life as a courtesy lord, by contrast, was tedious as hell.

Except where Anwen Windham was concerned. Her sister Megan had recently married Colin's brother Hamish, and of all Colin's newly acquired English in-laws, Anwen was the most intriguing.

She crashed into him with the force of a small Channel storm making landfall.

"Good day," Colin said, steadying her with a hand on each arm. "Are you fleeing bandits, or perhaps late for an appointment with the modiste?"

She stepped back, skewering him with a glower. "I am deloping, Lord Colin. Leaving the field of honor without firing a lethal shot, despite all temptation to the contrary."

The pistol of her indignation was still loaded, and Colin did not want it aimed at him. "Is that a birch rod you're carrying?"

"Yes. Mr. Hitchings will doubtless notice it's missing in the next fifteen minutes, for he can't go longer than that without striking some hapless boy."

They proceeded down the corridor, which though spotless, had only a threadbare runner on the floor. No art on the walls, not even a child's drawing or a stitched Bible verse. The windows lacked curtains, and the sheer dreariness of the House of Urchins conjured memories of Colin's years at public school.

"Sometimes a beating assuages a guilty conscience." Colin had dabbled in the English vice, and had quickly grown bored with it. He was easily bored, and the idea that the boys in this orphanage had only beatings to enliven their existence made him want to exit the premises posthaste. "I don't suppose you've come across Lady Rosalyn Montague? I was to meet her here for an outing in the park."

Miss Anwen opened a window and pitched the birch rod to the cobbles below. The building had once been a grand residence, the back overlooking a mews across the alley. A side garden had gone mostly to bracken, but the address was in a decent neighborhood.

The birch rod clattered to the ground, startling a tabby feasting on a dead mouse outside the stables. The cat bolted, then came back for its unfinished meal and scampered off again.

"Lady Rosalyn has a megrim," Miss Anwen said, "and could not attend the meeting. Her brother was not among the directors in attendance either."

"It's a pretty day," Colin said, rather than admit that being stood up without notice irked the hell out of him. "Would you care to join me for a drive 'round the park?"

Colin knew better than to tour the park by himself. Far too many debutantes and matchmakers ran tame at the fashionable hour.

Anwen remained by the open window, making a wistful picture as the spring sunshine caught highlights in her red hair.

"I wish we could take the boys to the park. They get out so seldom and they're *boys*."

Long ago, Colin had been a boy, and not a very happy one. "Instead of punishing the miscreants with beatings, you should reward the good fellows with outings. For the space of a day at least, you'd see sainthood where deviltry reigned before."

"Do you think so?"

"I know so. Will you drive out with me?" Winthrop Montague had all but begged Colin to take Lady Rosalyn for a turn. Alas, a gentleman obliged his friends whenever possible, even when the requested favor was infernally boring. Lady Rosalyn Montague had a genius for prosing on about bonnets, parasols, and reticules until only the promise of strong drink preserved a man's wits. No wonder Win wanted to get her off his hands.

An hour with Anwen would be a delight by comparison.

"I shall enjoy the air with you," Miss Anwen said, taking Colin by the arm. "If I go back to Moreland House in my present mood, one of my sisters will ask if I'm well, and another will suggest I need a posset, and dear Aunt Esther will insist that I have a lie down, and then—I'm whining. My apologies."

Miss Anwen was very pretty when she whined. "So you will join me because you need time to maneuver your deceptions into place?"

She shook free of his arm and stalked off toward the end

of the corridor. "I am not deceptive, and insulting a lady is no way to inspire her to share your company."

Colin caught up with her easily and bowed her through the door. "I beg your pardon for my blunt words—I'm new to this business of being a lord. Perhaps you maneuver your polite fictions into place."

"I do not indulge in polite fictions."

The hell she didn't. "Anwen, when I see you among your family, you are the most quiet, demure, retiring, unassuming facsimile of a spinster I've ever met. Now I chance upon you without their company, and you are far livelier. You steal birch rods, for example."

She looked intrigued rather than insulted. "You accuse me of thievery?"

"Successful thievery. I've wanted to filch the occasional birch rod, but I lacked the daring. I'm offering you a compliment."

If he complimented her gorgeous red hair—more fiery than Colin's own auburn locks—or her lovely complexion, or her luminous blue eyes—she'd likely deliver a scathing set down.

Once upon a time, before Colin's family had acquired a ducal title, Colin had collected both set downs and kisses like some men collected cravat pins. Now he aspired to be taken for a facsimile of a proper lordling, at least until he could return to Perthshire.

"You admire my thievery?" Miss Anwen asked, pausing at the top of the front stairs.

"The boys will thank you for it, provided the blame for the missing birch rod doesn't land on them."

Miss Anwen had an impressive scowl. "Hitchings is that stupid. He'd blame the innocent for my impetuosity and enjoy doing so. Drat and dash it all."

She honestly cared about these scapegrace children. How...unexpected. "We'll have the birch rod returned to wherever you found it before we leave," Colin said. "Hitchings merely overlooked it when he left the schoolroom."

"Marvelous! You have a capacity for deception too, Lord Colin. Perhaps I've underestimated you."

"Many do," Colin said, escorting her down the steps.

He suspected many underestimated Miss Anwen too, because for the first time in days, he looked forward to doing the lordly pretty before all of polite society.

And before Miss Anwen.

* * *

"What news, Tattling Tom?" Dickie asked, pushing his hair out of his eyes.

As far back as they'd been mates, Rum Dickie had been asking for the news, and as best as Thomas could recollect, the news had always been bad.

"Hitchings will leg it in June," Thomas said, which came close to being good news.

"So we're for the streets by summer?" Dickie used a length of wire to twiddle the lock on the door, then hid the wire among the books gathering dust on the shelves.

Wee Joe kept his characteristic silence. He was a good lad, always willing to stand lookout. Because of his greater size, he was also willing to take on the physical jobs such as boosting a fellow over the garden wall or putting up with Hitchings's birchings.

"Miss Anwen is worried," Tom replied, trying to condense what he'd overheard outside the classroom. "Not enough funds to keep us fed, and Hitchings hasn't got any useful ideas about where to get more blunt."

Wee Joe remained by the window—the detention room had the best view of the alley, proof that Hitchings was an idiot. If you wanted to shut a boy in so he'd sit on his arse and contemplate his supposed sins, you didn't provide him a nice view from a window with a handy drainpipe two feet to the right.

"Joe, come away from there," Dickie said. "We're supposed to be memorizing our *amo, amas, amat*s."

Joe pointed out the window, so Tom joined him.

"Cor, Joey. That's a prime rig." Not only did the phaeton have spanking yellow wheels, the couple on the bench looked like they came straight off some painting of Nobs Taking the Air.

"Miss Anwen got herself a flash man," Dickie marveled.

Joe scowled ferociously.

"That's Bond Street tailoring, Joe," Dickie said, "and the best pair in the traces Tattersalls has seen this year. Spanish, I'd say, not Dutch nags."

The gent got the phaeton turned about in the alley—no mean feat—and the team went tooling on their way.

"Haven't seen him before." Tom was the designated intelligence officer in the group—Miss Anwen's description of him—and he prided himself on keeping track of names and faces.

"He's Lady Rosalyn's beau," Dickie said. "Saw them at Gunter's last week with Mr. Montague."

That earned another scowl from Joe, who took a seat on the floor beneath the window. Joe was blond, blue-eyed, and not a bad-looking boy, but he got cuffed a lot because he spoke so little. One of those blue eyes sported a fading bruise as a consequence.

"I know I shouldn't have been out on me own," Dickie said, "but I go barmy staring at these walls, sitting on me feak, listening to old Hitchings wheezing hour after hour. If Miss Anwen would come read to us more often, I might not get so roam-y."

Restlessness affected all the boys, the longing to be back out on the streets, managing as best they could, free of Virgil and Proverbs—and Hitchings.

"What do you suppose Hitchings will do when this place runs out of money?" Dickie asked.

Hitchings wouldn't last two days on the streets, but he certainly did well enough as the headmaster of the orphanage. Very well.

"He'll go for a tutor to some lord's sons," Tom said, "pound them with Latin and his damned birch rod, or kick them with his new bloody boots." What would it feel like to put on a boot made for your own very foot?

Joe swung his open hand through the air, mimicking a slap delivered to a boy's face.

"That too," Dickie agreed. "Thank the devil we're too big to be climbing boys."

Joe motioned jabbing the earth with a shovel.

"The mines are honorable work," Tom said, an incantation he'd overheard down at Blooming Betty's pub.

"The mines will kill us." John climbed in the window as he spoke, making one of his signature dramatic appearances. "I had uncles who went down the mines. They were coughing their lungs out within a year."

He leapt to the floor as nimbly as an alley cat. The skills of a born housebreaker went absolutely to waste in this orphanage, as did Dickie's ability with locks, and Joe's pickpocketing.

"Who wants a rum bun?" John asked, withdrawing a parcel from his shirt.

Joe shook his head.

"C'mon, Wee Joe," John said, holding out a sweet and

folding cross-legged to the floor. "It's a cryin' damned shame when a man can't work his God-given trade. Me own da often said as much."

"Before the watch nabbed him," Dickie muttered, snatching the bun. "You'll get us all flogged to bits, John."

"I'll get us all a fine snack," John said around a mouthful of bun. "What was that gent doing here?"

"Same thing we all do," Dickie said. "He was falling in love with Miss Anwen."

"Lady Rosalyn won't like that," Tom said, tearing off a small bite of his bun.

"Lady Rosalyn won't care," John countered. "She's so pretty, all the gents want her. I should have stolen more buns." He eyed the window longingly but remained where he was.

"Don't leave crumbs," Tom cautioned. "Hitchings will see them, and we'll be locked up in the broom closet next time."

The broom closet stank of dirt and vinegar, and the boys were never incarcerated there all together, the space being too small.

"Hitchings claims we're running out of money," Tom said, tearing off another tiny bite.

"Hitchings has to say we're nearly broke," John replied, dusting his hands. "He has to keep them pouring money into his pockets whether or not there's money in the box."

Tom studied his next bite of bun. "We could check. See what's in the box. It's been nearly a month. Never hurts to know the facts."

Nobody contradicted him, though sometimes it hurt awfully to know the facts. Tom had been the one to find his mum dead in her bed after the baby was buried. That fact still hurt a bloody damned lot.

"I don't mind it here, so much." Dickie stuck his feet out straight in front of him. His trousers had no holes or patches, though the hems were a good three inches too short. His boots fit, and they almost matched. "For once, I didn't spend all winter fighting for a place to shiver my nights away. That gets old."

"Nobody coughing himself to death here," John conceded. "Damned consumption gets hold of a place, next thing you know, everybody's being measured for a shroud."

"I say we should see how much blunt's in the box." Tom got to his feet and slouched against the wall near the window, not hanging out the window for all to see like some boys would.

"Shite," he whispered, pulling the window swiftly closed. "Hitchings is off somewhere."

"Whyn't he go out the front door like usual?" Dickie asked, crowding in on Tom's right. "Likes to be seen strutting down the walkway, showing off his finery, does our Mister Hitchings."

Joe snatched up his Latin grammar. Tom, Dickie, and John did likewise—Joe's hearing was prodigious good— and a moment later, footsteps sounded in the corridor. By the time the door swung open, all four boys were absorbed in the intricacies of *circum porta puella stat*...or *portal*. Possibly *portam*.

What did it matter, unless the *puella* was *pulchra* and *amica*?

"He's gone," MacDeever said, holding the door open. "You have an hour of liberty, but don't let Cook see you. One hour from now, you're to be back here, looking sullen and peckish."

"Thanks," Tom muttered, hustling through the door.

John and Dickie followed him, Joe left last, bringing his grammar.

MacDeever looked fierce, and he had the most marvelous Scots growl to go with his white eyebrows and tidy mustache, but he frequently foiled Hitchings's worst excesses, probably risking his own post in the process.

"One hour," the groundskeeper said. "And if I see anybody climbing down the drainpipe in broad daylight again, I'll deliver him in to Hitchings myself. What would Miss Anwen think if one of her boys were to break his head on the cobbles, eh?"

What would Miss Anwen think if she knew that, every so often, her boys broke into Hitchings's strongbox and took a detailed inventory of the contents?

Chapter Two

ANWEN LOOSENED HER BONNET ribbons and nudged her millinery one inch farther back on her head, the better to enjoy the beautiful day.

"Why don't you take off your bonnet?" Lord Colin asked.

He drove with the subtle expertise of one who knew his cattle and his way around London. Both horses were exactly the same height, build, and coloring, and they moved with the unity of a team raised and trained together.

Anwen's cousin Devlin St. Just, a former cavalryman who'd come into an earldom, would say these horses had an *expensive* trot. Muscular, rhythmic, closely synchronized, and to a horseman, beautiful.

"A lady doesn't go out without her bonnet, Lord Colin."

"Balderdash. My sisters claim to forget their bonnets when they want to enjoy the fresh air without wearing blinders. I have a theory."

"Are you the scientific sort, to be propounding theories?"

He was the fragrant sort, though his scent was complicated. Woodsy with some citrus, a hint of musk, with a dash of raspberry and cinnamon. Parisian would be Anwen's guess. Her sister Megan claimed Lord Colin was quite well fixed.

"I'm the noticing sort," he said, lowering his voice conspiratorially. "I suspect you are too. A younger sibling learns all the best ways to hide and watch. My theory is that women wear bonnets so that men cannot be certain exactly which lady they approach unless the gentleman is confronting the woman head-on."

He halted the horses to wait at an intersection before turning onto Park Lane, so heavy was the traffic. For a moment, Anwen simply enjoyed the pleasure of being out and about on a sunny day. Helena Merton and her mama passed them, and Helena's expression was gratifyingly dumbstruck.

Anwen wiggled gloved fingers at the Mertons, the grown-up equivalent of sticking her tongue out.

"Maybe, your lordship, the ladies wear their bonnets so they are spared the sight of any men but those willing to approach them directly."

Lord Colin gave his hands forward two inches and the horses moved off smoothly. "You would not have made that comment if any of your sisters were with us. Your sister Charlotte would have offered the same opinion, but you would have remained silent. If you were to pat my arm right about now, I'd appreciate it."

"Whyever—oh." Anwen not only patted his arm, she twined her hand around his elbow. "Helena fancies you?"

"That is the question. Does she fancy me, my brother's title, my lovely estate in Perthshire, or any man who will get her free of her mother's household? Your uncle is a duke, you've doubtless faced a comparable question frequently. How do you stand it?"

Even for a Scotsman, Lord Colin was wonderfully blunt. "I love Uncle Percy. There's nothing to *stand.*"

That was not quite true. The social season was an exercise in progressive exhaustion, and each year, Anwen wished more desperately that she could be spared the waltzing, the fortune hunters, the at homes, the fittings, the...

The boredom.

"So every fellow who bows over your hand and professes undying devotion means it from the bottom of his pure, innocent, financially secure heart?"

Anwen had not endured a profession of dying devotion from a bachelor for at least three years, thank heavens.

"The gallant swains are merely being polite, as am I when I accept their flattery. You have younger brothers, am I correct?"

"Three, each one taller, louder, and hungrier than the last. The French Army at its plundering worst couldn't ravage the countryside as thoroughly as those three when they're in the mood for a feast."

What would that be like? To have younger siblings? People to condescend to and look out for?

"You miss them, Lord Colin. I can hear it in your voice and see it in your eyes."

The MacHughs whom Anwen had met—Hamish, Edana, Rhona, and Colin—were red-haired and blue-eyed. Anwen's hair wasn't red, it was orange. Bright, brilliant, light-up-the-night-sky, flaming, orange.

Her male cousins had dubbed her the Great Fire when she was six years old.

Lord Colin's hair was darker than his brother's, shading toward Titian, and his eyes were a softer blue—closer to periwinkle than delphinium. Helena Merton would fancy herself in love with those eyes, while her mama was likely enthralled with the family title—a Scottish dukedom, no less—and the settlements.

"I miss my siblings," Lord Colin said. "I miss home, I miss wearing clothes that don't nearly choke a man if he wants to exert himself beyond a plodding stroll. I miss tramping over the moors with my fowling piece, and I sorely miss the smell of the wort cooking in the vats."

Did he miss a young lady who remained back in Scotland longing for him?

"Be patient another two months or so, and you can return to your Highlands, your distillery, and your sheep, or whatever else you're pining for."

To look at Lord Colin, Anwen would never have suspected he was homesick. He had a ready smile, and his manner was a trifle flirtatious. A dimple cut a deep groove on the left side of that smile and made his features interesting. Everything else was in gentlemanly proportion, though his nose was a touch generous, while that dimple pulled his expression off center, in the direction of roguish.

When Frederica and Amanda Fletcher wheeled past, their brother at the ribbons of their barouche, Anwen lifted her hand in a more extravagant wave.

"My thanks," Lord Colin muttered, as he guided the horses to the leafy beauty of Hyde Park in springtime. "Those two hunt as a pair, and a man can't dance with just the one sister, he must stand up with each in turn. Now that Hamish has gone off on his wedding journey, I'm the only escort Edana and Rhona have, so I'm always on picket duty."

A military term, though Mayfair's ballrooms were hardly battlegrounds. "You served in Spain."

"And in Portugal, France, the Low Countries. War is in some ways quite simple. Your equipment is a gun, a bedroll, and a few cooking implements, all of which you keep in good repair. You shoot at the fellows wearing enemy uniforms. You don't shoot at anybody else. Makes for a pleasing sense of order. London in springtime is a regular donnybrook by comparison. I considered it my job to guard Hamish's back, but now your sister has taken that post."

Lord Colin reminded Anwen of herself in her third season. The first season was all excitement and adventure. Even if marriage wasn't an immediate objective, it was at long last a possibility. In her second season, she'd enjoyed *not* being a debutante, not being so giddy and nervous.

In her third season, she'd started dressing for comfort instead of display, and learned that sore feet, a megrim, a head cold, all had their places on a young lady's spring calendar.

Now, she simply endured, but for her work at the orphanage, which might soon close its doors for want of coin.

"You abhor idleness," Anwen said as the press of carriages required the team to slow to a walk. "Is that because you're in trade?"

The question was bold, but not quite rude between inlaws.

"I am, indeed, in trade." Lord Colin sounded pleased about it too. "I gather some people expect me to sell my distillery and pretend I'm content to raise sheep. Hamish was given to understand that his breweries are also not quite the done thing for a duke. Good luck getting him to give up profitable enterprises."

"Orphanages are not profitable."

Lord Colin turned the phaeton onto a less crowded path, and the relative quiet was bliss. Anwen loved the boys, loved taking a hand in running the House of Urchins, but her time there today had left her frustrated.

And worried.

"Regarding profitable enterprises, I am in favor of wee hands doing wee tasks," Lord Colin said, "but using children for the production of coin on a significant scale will never meet with my approval."

His burr thickened when he spoke in earnest. When he and his brother had a difference of opinion, Anwen could hardly understand them.

"You don't employ children?"

"Of course I employ children. The tiger, the boot boy, the scullery maid—"

"No, I mean in your whisky-making business. Do you employ children in your business?"

"Nobody under the age of fourteen, and not in quantity. Why?"

Drat the luck. "One doesn't speak of financial matters."

Lord Colin laughed, a hearty sound at variance with the stillness and greenery around them. In two hours, the park would be as busy as the surrounding streets, but the fashionable hour had yet to arrive.

"Financial matters are what make the world go 'round, Miss Anwen. You can bet that your uncle the duke and his duchess discuss financial matters, everything from the news on 'Change, to the budget for candles, to the latest attempt by Parliament to fleece the yeoman of his profits."

Anwen had thought to enjoy a pretty day, but if she didn't raise the topic of the orphanage's finances with Lord Colin, then with whom could she have that discussion?

The Windham ducal heir, the Earl of Westhaven, was the family accountant, but he was also ... Westhaven. If Anwen brought up a financial matter with him, he'd smile sweetly, ask after her health, and admire her bonnet.

Oh, to be six years old and once again regarded as the tempestuous Great Fire of the Windham family.

"You've gone silent," Lord Colin said. "I hope I haven't given offense."

"I'm thinking. My orphanage is in want of funds. I'd like to propose a means of addressing that problem to the directors, for they'll tut-tut and such-a-pity while my boys are turned out onto the streets again. The Lords will dash off to their house parties in July and their grouse moors in August, and the children will never know safety or security again."

Some of the boys were eager for that fate to befall them, especially now that spring had arrived.

"You are asking me how an orphanage might raise funds?"

How refreshing. Lord Colin wasn't laughing or peering down his nose at her.

"Indeed, I am. Mr. Hitchings advised me to hold a charity ball, bat my eyelashes, and hope the attendees are motivated to part with coin on the basis of my flirtation."

"Many would be happy to part with coin if you held a charity ball." Lord Colin didn't come right out and say it: If you held yet another boring, predictable, dull, barely endurable charity ball.

Anwen wouldn't want to attend, much less organize, such a gathering.

"Say I hold a ball. Then what happens next year when the funds are again exhausted? I repeat my performance? What if something happens to me? What if my simpering isn't convincing enough? The children still have to eat, and they have nothing and no one without that orphanage."

Anwen surprised herself with the vehemence of her response, but when both Lady Rosalyn and her brother had failed to attend today's meetings, Lord Derwent, the chairman of the board of directors, had declared that without a quorum, he could only preside over an informational meeting.

Hitchings had informed them funds were running short. Fifteen minutes of throat-clearing and paper-shuffling later, the meeting had broken up with nothing decided and no plans in train.

"Has anybody told you that you're fierce?" Lord Colin asked.

"Not since I was six years old."

"Well, you are. Give me a moment to think, because in your present mood, only a well-thought-out answer will do."

He'd not only taken her question seriously, he'd paid her a compliment. "Take as long as you need, Lord Colin. If the topic were easily addressed, every orphan in London would have a secure future."

* * *

Silly and Charming—Scylla and Charybdis—were on their best behavior, suggesting Miss Anwen met with their approval. The geldings also liked Hamish and Edana, and they positively purred when Rhona accompanied Colin.

For Miss Anwen, they'd gone beyond purring to perfectly matching their steps, and spanking along at a trot Colin could have set his watch to. More than a few horsemen stopped to gawk, though in all eyes, Colin could see the question: *Wonder what he paid for that pair?*

"Has anybody explained the concept of interest to you?" Colin asked the lady beside him.

"As in, small boys have an interest in sweets?"

All boys had an interest in sweets of some sort. Miss Anwen had no brothers. No wonder her urchins fascinated her.

"Not quite," Colin said. "If you wanted to borrow your sister Charlotte's blue parasol, and she agreed, but said in return, you had to lend her your green parasol for an outing in two weeks, that would be an exchange without the financial version of interest."

"We'd be trading favors, which we do all the time."

"Correct. If Charlotte instead said that yes, you could borrow her parasol, provided that in two weeks' time, she could borrow both your parasol and your favorite reticule, that would be a transaction where she was said to charge you interest."

"The extra cost to me for borrowing her parasol is interest?"

"Exactly. You had better desperately need her parasol now, to be willing to give up your best reticule for a time in addition to your own parasol."

Colin expected Anwen to change the subject, though he couldn't make the explanation any simpler.

"How does this work with money, Lord Colin?"

Perhaps Miss Anwen had some Scottish blood back a few generations, though she'd lowered her voice on the word *money*.

"The same concept applies. Let's say you know of a highly profitable shipping venture, but you haven't any capital to invest at the moment—all of your money is committed. You come to me and agree that if I lend you a hundred pounds for a year, you'll pay me back a hundred and ten pounds because you expect to make a hundred and fifty."

"But you haven't *earned* that extra ten pounds," she said. "You simply made money off my ambitions."

Colin turned the team for another circuit along the quieter paths. "Or I lost the entire sum as a result of your dodgy venture."

"Hardly that. You'll toss me into debtor's prison if my scheme comes to nothing, have my goods seized, and probably know to the penny what I'm worth before you consider lending me a farthing."

"What if you're a titled lord," Colin countered, "and I can't toss you into debtor's prison?"

"Then you'll find some other way to protect your investment, or you won't lend me the money. My orphanage cannot borrow money, Lord Colin."

Miss Anwen had an intuitive grasp of how a loan worked, as did Edana and Rhona.

"Your orphanage can *lend* money," Colin said, steering the horses to the verge and bringing them to a halt.

"The House of Urchins hasn't money to lend. I haven't any either."

"Take the reins," Colin said, passing them to her. "We'll let the boys blow for a moment." He climbed down and loosened the check reins enough that his geldings could steal a few mouthfuls of grass.

"You're encouraging naughty behavior," Miss Anwen said, passing Colin back the reins. "Horses aren't supposed to graze while in work."

"Did your cousin Lord Rosecroft the cavalry genius tell you that?"

"And my first equitation instructor, and every instructor, groom, stable lad, and cousin since."

What a bloody lot of people she had telling her how to go on. "Ever stood at attention for three straight hours, Miss Anwen?"

She took off her gloves, untied her bonnet ribbons, and peeled the hat from her head.

The hat snagged on a hairpin, or a combination of hairpins. Colin intervened, carefully untangling silky locks from satin ribbons, and passing Miss Anwen several hairpins when she'd set her bonnet on the bench beside her.

"My thanks, sir." She used the hairpins to secure a loose curl. "I've passed years tied to a posture board, spent hours with three books piled on my head. My finishing governess laced me so tightly I once fainted at the top of the steps. Papa discharged her, but she'd been with me six months at that point. When she left, all of my dresses had to be to let out."

Miss Anwen turned her face up to the sun, though the phaeton sat in a quiet patch of dappled shade. She had a profile to make cameo artists weep, and the line of her throat was elegance personified.

She also had freckles. Faint, visible only if a man sat right beside her, and they could have easily been disguised with a touch of rice powder, but Anwen Windham had freckles.

Also a keen mind, and experience with physical tribulations Colin would never have suspected.

"When you took off your bonnet just now, how did it feel?"

She regarded him steadily. "Heavenly. It's Elizabeth's bonnet, and a touch snug when I do my hair as I have. I grabbed it by accident but didn't want to be late for my meeting. If you weren't sitting here, I'd...well. I will brush out my hair before changing for supper tonight."

Colin wrapped the reins around the brake and used his teeth to pull off his right glove. He reached over to Miss Anwen's nape and gently massaged her neck.

"How does that feel?"

She dropped her head forward, a soft sigh joining the afternoon breeze. "You ought not to touch me like that, even if we are practically family and no one is watching."

They were not practically family. To emphasize his point—not to enjoy the exquisite feel of smooth female flesh beneath his fingers—Colin persisted for another moment.

"That's what it feels like for my team when I release the check rein, and let the horses know that for a short time, they're off duty. For five minutes, they can relax, grab a snack, rest mentally and physically, before getting back to work."

Miss Anwen raised her head, but didn't put her bonnet back on. "I tell Mr. Hitchings the boys need to get out. They can't sit in a classroom hour after hour and be expected to attend much of anything. They're children, not monastic scholars training to be anchorites."

Colin withdrew his hand—he'd made his point. "And if the boys don't get out, they'll become querulous, and then Hitchings will punish them for squabbling *and* for lack of attention to their studies. Where did you find this old besom? He sounds like every grown man's worst boyhood nightmare."

"Mr. Montague said Hitchings was quite a bargain, for the salary we're paying him."

"Winthrop Montague?"

"He's the vice-chairman of the board, and Lady Rosalyn serves on my ladies' committee."

This interconnectedness of all parts of polite society

was something like the army, or Highland clans. Everybody knew everybody, and that was sometimes a good thing.

Though not always. "I'm acquainted with Win Montague," Colin said. "If he claims Hitchings was a bargain, then Hitchings was a bargain."

Miss Anwen set her bonnet back on her head, and Colin wanted to snatch it away and toss it into the bushes.

"How do you know Mr. Montague, Lord Colin?"

"We served together, both captains." Though that was years ago. Colin had passed through London a few times since mustering out, and once even called on Win, though Win hadn't been home at the time. "Montague has been helpful, acquainting me with what's expected of a titled gentleman of means."

Miss Anwen tied her bonnet ribbons and slipped on her gloves. "And acquainting you with Lady Rosalyn?"

Colin wanted to pitch her knowing smile into the bushes too. "Yes."

Lady Rosalyn Montague was a vision in blonde, blue-eyed pastels. Her movements were elegant, her laughter warm, her dancing made a man feel as if no one had ever partnered a woman more gracefully.

Colin liked to watch her, but he didn't enjoy watching other men fawn over her. She expected the fawning, which brought Anwen's earlier comment to mind: *You simply made money off my ambitions.*

Lady Rosalyn earned smiles off a man's ambitions, though to be fair, she dispensed smiles as well—with interest of a sort Colin didn't quite grasp but knew he would never pay.

"Lady Rosalyn is a friend," Miss Anwen said. "She made her come out two years after I did, and is in every way an estimable individual. You would make a very attractive couple."

That remark should be sent not into the bushes, but rather, tossed straight into the depths of the Serpentine.

"Don't do that," Colin said, passing the reins over and climbing down again. "Don't treat me as if I'm some orphan bachelor because I'm wealthy and new to polite society. I like Lady Rosalyn well enough, but if it came down to a night of waltzing with her, or cards with my brothers..."

"Yes?"

He fiddled with the check reins, leaving them a few holes looser than was strictly fashionable.

"I'd leave the ball early. I'm not looking to get married, Miss Anwen. Not yet. Someday, of course. But not...Hamish has been a duke for a matter of weeks, and I can assure you, until the title befell him, I wasn't considered half of an attractive couple. I was a presuming Scot, in trade, with airs above my station. Now I'm a lord. It unnerves a fellow."

It also predisposed a fellow to babbling. Colin climbed back into the phaeton, mindful that his tone of voice had caught the attention of his horses.

"Now you know what the ladies put up with year after year," Miss Anwen said. "We're seen as nothing more than half of an attractive couple, good breeding stock, decent settlements. Nobody refers to us as gorgeous settlements, even if a lady is an heiress. The highest praise she'll garner is 'decent settlements.' Be patient with the ladies, Lord Colin, for they are very patient with the gentlemen."

Colin gave the horses leave to walk on, when he wanted instead to offer some teasing, charming remark.

And yet, he could not make light of Miss Anwen's observation.

He'd watched his sisters over the past few months. Edana and Rhona had looked forward to enjoying the London social season for the first time, thinking to be more spectators than participants. Hamish had stumbled into a ducal title, Edana and Rhona were ladies by association, and enthusiasm had turned from glee, to wonder, to bewilderment, to disappointment.

Was anybody enjoying springtime in London?

"You were explaining to me about interest," Miss Anwen said, "and about how that could make the orphanage solvent. Please do go on."

"Right. Interest," Colin said. "If you're borrowing money, interest is a cost. If you're *lending* money, that interest is a benefit, and that brings us to the topic of endowments."

Miss Anwen listened to him as he prattled on, truly listened. One of *her* endowments was a keen mind, apparently, in addition to brilliant red hair, the airs and graces of a lady, and the heart of a lioness where her orphans were concerned.

Also skin so soft, Colin could recall the feel of it beneath his fingertips even as he waxed eloquent about the Rule of Seven.

* * *

"And here you are," Lord Colin said, alighting from the phaeton. "Delivered to your very own doorstep."

Anwen didn't correct him, though this was not her doorstep. Did a lady ever have her *very own* doorstep, short of widowhood?

She wasn't even alighting at her papa's doorstep, for Mama and Papa were again off cavorting in the wilds of

Wales, while Anwen and her sisters bided with Uncle Percival and Aunt Esther.

Lord Colin came around to assist her from the vehicle. Her descent was a precarious undertaking involving the use of several tiny metal footrests, and much gathering of skirts, until his lordship muttered something under his breath and swung her to the ground.

"My thanks," Anwen said, stepping back. "Was that Gaelic?"

His smile was bashful and a bit naughty. "It wasn't French. Allow me to see you inside."

"What about the horses?" For he hadn't a tiger to hold them or walk them.

"They will stand until the first snowfall."

"Unless somebody comes along to steal them." What was this propensity she'd developed for contradicting a gentleman?

He patted the offside beast. "They won't budge for anybody but me or their grooms, not without creating a riot first. One learns a few useful skills in the army."

Apparently, one did. Not even Devlin St. Just drove about without a tiger.

Lord Colin did the pretty for Anwen's sisters, Charlotte and Elizabeth, then went on his way before they could inveigle him into staying for tea—thank goodness. Anwen needed to think, to work some figures, and to gather more information.

"Anwen Heather Gladys Windham, where have you been?" Elizabeth demanded, before his lordship had even climbed back into his conveyance. "Her Grace was about to send out the watch."

The watch was Anwen's three male cousins—

Westhaven, St. Just, and Lord Valentine—all of whom were in Town for the season.

"I went to my meeting at the House of Urchins, exactly as I said I would," Anwen replied as Charlotte led her by the wrist to the family parlor.

"That was three hours ago," Elizabeth retorted, from Anwen's other side. "We were afraid you'd been struck with a megrim, or a fever, or turned your ankle, or come to harm. Are you sure you're all right?"

Any other time, Anwen might have admitted that a pot of peppermint tea would be welcome, because the day had been tiring. When peppermint tea became too much to bear, chamomile and lemon soothed the nerves. Ginger settled an upset belly. Lavender and valerian tisanes could quiet worry.

She had an entire apothecary of ploys with which to treat her family's need to cosset her.

Anwen shook free of Charlotte's grasp. "Do either of you understand compound interest?"

Charlotte and Elizabeth were both several inches taller than Anwen. They exchanged a dismayed look over her head that she nonetheless felt, and had been enduring intermittently since the age of seven.

"Were you out without your bonnet?" Elizabeth asked. "The sun was strong today, even though it's not yet summer. Too much sun for yo—for a redhead is ill-advised."

"I'll take that for a no," Anwen said, stopping outside the family parlor. If they got her in there, she'd be questioned until dinnertime, plied with tisanes, swaddled in three shawls, her feet up on a hassock.

"You don't know how your settlements are invested," Anwen said, continuing down the corridor, "and neither do I, but that's about to change."

"Anwen Windham, *where are you going?*" Charlotte nearly bellowed.

"I am going outside. It's a beautiful day, and if you want to interrogate me about my afternoon, then you will have to come outside with me."

The look bounced between them again. They pursed their mouths at the same moment and to the same degree.

"Those children at the orphanage are not healthy company," Elizabeth said. "I know you think they can do no wrong, but their upbringing exposes them to all manner of foul miasmas, and without intending you any harm whatso—"

Anwen ducked through a pair of French doors and let them swing closed behind her. The resulting *bang* felt lovely, until she spotted Aunt Esther already occupying the bench in the folly.

"Come join me," Aunt said. "It's a marvelous day to escape for a moment into the garden."

Behind the door, Charlotte and Elizabeth were looking concerned and keeping their voices down. Anwen crossed the garden with more haste than grace.

"How was your meeting?" Aunt asked as Anwen tossed herself onto the opposite wooden bench. The folly was latticed on two sides with roses not yet blooming, and Aunt made a pretty picture against the greenery. She was a duchess, but also a mother, political partner to Uncle Percy, a pillar of society, and a genuinely gracious person.

Anwen ought not to bother her, but the idea of returning inside . . . She couldn't. Not today.

"My meeting mostly didn't happen," Anwen said. "We lacked a quorum, which I suspect is a polite way to say, the directors would rather frolic at their clubs like truant schoolboys than worry about orphans."

"Your uncle would understand your frustration. Those same lords and honorables are equally cavalier about their parliamentary duties. Drives poor Moreland to shouting and pacing and all manner of colorful language."

"*Colorful language?*" Uncle Percy was the doting, jovial complement to Aunt Esther's grace and gentility. They were the perfect mature couple, the perfect duke and duchess.

Though at present, Aunt's slippers were tidily arranged beneath the bench, her feet up in a pose more reminiscent of a Grecian goddess at her leisure than a proper duchess.

"Your uncle Percy was once an army officer, you know," Aunt said. "A third son with limited prospects. A man of that ilk doesn't raise ten children without infusing some variety into his vocabulary."

Charlotte and Elizabeth were apparently content to let Aunt Esther deal with Anwen—for now. There would be questions over the last cup of tea in the parlor this evening, or over breakfast.

Or both. "Did you acquire a colorful vocabulary, Aunt?"

Aunt Esther snapped off a green tendril intruding into the folly. "Me?"

"You raised the same ten children, and you contended with Uncle." Anwen's papa was Uncle Percy's younger brother, and Papa, while ever loyal, was occasionally exasperated with the duke, as were His Grace's own offspring.

Delicate blonde brows swooped down. "I see your point. I resorted to German. My grandmother's English was never very good, so my German is excellent. It's a capital language for strong emotion."

Anwen's mother resorted to Welsh, and as a consequence, her children had a grasp of Welsh that exceeded their Latin and French.

"Perhaps I need to learn German," Anwen said. "I'm much afraid my orphanage will close its doors this summer, and all because I don't know how my settlements are invested."

Maybe she *did* need some chamomile tea.

"Your settlements are in the cent-per-cents," Aunt said. "The same as your sisters' are, the same as my widow's portion. I can have Westhaven explain the details, but you will not walk up the church aisle without first gaining a clear grasp of your finances."

Why had Anwen's own mother not explained this—why hadn't *her father*?

"The orphanage is running out of money, and nobody seems bothered by this but me. As Lord Colin and I toured the park today, he explained to me that if I can raise money for the orphanage, I can invest that money, and use the interest rather than principle to look after the boys."

"You would need a very great deal of money, my dear."

"So you see the magnitude of the problem? If all I can earn is five percent interest, then ten thousand pounds is necessary to yield the five hundred I need for the boys. That is a fortune, and it's a very small orphanage."

Aunt was quiet for a long moment. "You always did enjoy maths."

"I did?"

"Yes, which is why your maths tutor was the same fellow who'd worked with your male cousins. He'd done such a fine job with those five—and neither Devlin nor Valentine were naturally studious—that we brought him back from the north for you girls. Your uncle is not mathematically inclined, so it's fortunate Westhaven shares your proclivity."

The day had been unusual, with the meeting that didn't

happen, Lady Rosalyn's absence, an unscheduled outing in the park, and now this conversation. By rights, Anwen should have been in her room, having a short nap—of two hours' duration—before dinner.

She had neither time nor inclination to nap when the fate of children was at stake. "I want to hold a charity ball, Aunt. These boys matter to me, and yet, everybody holds charity balls."

The duchess snapped off two more vines. Anwen braced herself for a lecture about God's will, and the resilience of the lower orders, a woman's place, or some such rot.

"Your cousin Devlin could easily have been one of those boys," the duchess said. "His antecedents aren't a secret among the family, and what if his mother had fallen ill shortly after his birth? What if one of her protectors had taken the boy into dislike? What if Percival had gone back to Canada instead of falling in love with me? I have worried similarly for our dear Maggie."

"Precisely!" Anwen said, bolting to her feet. "Tom's mother died in childbed, and there he was, eight years old, nobody to look after him. He'd done nothing wrong. Joe barely speaks, but he's a good lad and quick, and quite sturdy for his age. John has man of business in his very blood, and Dickie really needs to be a valet, he's so taken with fashion. They are good boys, and they'll go back to picking pockets and housebreaking for want of money that so many could easily spare."

"My dear young lady," Aunt said, patting the bench beside her, "radical notions put roses in your cheeks. It's quite becoming, though your uncle will despair of your politics."

Anwen settled beside her aunt, soothed by the duchess's

fragrance. Aunt always smelled good—not sweet, fragrant, or feminine, exactly, though she was all those things—but virtuous, kind, *good*.

"Will Uncle let me hold a ball for my orphans?" The idea of planning a ball ... The duchess held only one formal ball a year, and every woman and half the men in the family were required to assist with the planning.

Her Grace stroked a hand through Anwen's hair. "It might surprise you to know that Westhaven keeps me on a strict budget for the season's entertainments."

No ball, then. Drat and blast.

"I'll use my pin money, but it won't go far." While the directors got drunk over endless hands of whist behind the stout walls of their—

A little shiver skipped across Anwen's nape as an *idea* tugged at the hem of her worries.

"Aunt, what if we held a charity card party instead of a ball? A percentage of everybody's winnings could go to charity. We'd be asking people to while away an evening as they often would, though chance would favor the orphans at every game, rather than smiling exclusively on the winners."

Aunt swung her feet down and sat back against the cushions. "I've never heard of a charity card party. Even high sticklers have no issue with a mention of coin when it relates to a friendly game of piquet."

And by all means, the sensibilities of the high sticklers should be foremost when children were threatened with a starvation.

"Gentlemen control the wealth in this realm," Anwen said. "An entertainment that caters to gentlemen has more chance of raising funds."

Aunt toed her slippers on, studying the satin bows adorning them. "I am expected to contribute to the tone of the social season, and for years, my farewell soiree has been a landmark on polite society's calendar. Perhaps it's time to change landmarks."

She rose, an impressively tall woman who carried herself with unfailing elegance, even in the confines of a folly.

The duchess began a slow circuit along the benches. "If I point out to Westhaven that my nieces need a project to distract them from Megan's departure for Scotland, he should allow me to divert the funds I'd typically spend on the farewell soiree to your card party."

The shiver had turned warm and hopeful. "This must be *your* card party, Aunt."

"The Windham card party, then," Her Grace said, staring off across the garden. "We have charity balls all the time, subscription balls, musicales...A card party will be novel, and attendance will be limited. We won't have the expense of an orchestra or the headache of errant debutantes and drunken bachelors."

The duchess resumed pacing. "We must be shrewd about the invitations, but not exclusive. Wagers should be capped at one hundred pounds, I think."

Anwen began doing math. "How many tables?"

"If we set this up in the ballroom, we can easily have twenty-five tables, which means one hundred people seated at play and perhaps another eighty wandering the terraces, listening to Valentine's music, or enjoying punch and a buffet."

As the duchess considered ideas, dates, and potential guests, Anwen added her thoughts and listened to a pillar of society throwing herself into a charitable cause.

Would any of this have happened if Lord Colin hadn't spent more than an hour explaining to Anwen how to put the House of Urchins on solid footing?

No, it would not. Anwen would be in the family parlor, her feet up, swilling chamomile tea, and thanking her sisters for their concern.

Much more of that concern and she'd go mad.

"What about Lady Rosalyn?" the duchess asked. "Shall she help us manage this affair? Her brother is a director, isn't he?"

"Winthrop Montague is the vice-chair, so he'll certainly be in attendance, but I think Lady Rosalyn would rather enjoy the play than involve herself in yet another committee. She's as much in demand as a partner at whist as she is on the dance floor."

Very much in demand, and Anwen wished her the joy of both undertakings.

"She'll be invited, but not involved." Aunt rang for a lap desk, and a pot of stout China black along with a plate of sandwiches. As the shadows lengthened across the blooming garden, and honeysuckle perfumed the air, the card party took shape.

Anwen stuffed herself with three sandwiches—they were small, and no helpful sisters appeared to remind her to eat slowly—and pondered a question she did not put to her aunt.

Lord Colin had been expecting to meet Lady Rosalyn at the House of Urchins, and he hadn't quibbled at Anwen's explanation of a megrim. Megrims happened, as did monthlies, bad fish, and all manner of ailments, but Lady Rosalyn had apparently made a rapid recovery.

As Lord Colin had gone off on a flight about compound interest—making money on making money, as he put it—Anwen had spotted Lady Rosalyn up beside Lord Twillinger in a fetching red-wheeled gig. Anwen had ignored her friend, for her friend had seemed intent on ignoring Lord Colin.

Had Lord Colin ever stripped off his gloves and caressed the back of Lady Rosalyn's neck, and did it mean anything if he had?

Chapter Three

"SO PAYING THE EXCISE man has helped our profits?" Colin asked.

Thaddeus Maarten removed his glasses and offered Colin a rare smile. "Your product is seen as higher quality. Paying the excise is apparently comparable to giving it a lordly title. Only the finest whisky can afford to turn up its nose at all the mischief most distillers consider a part of their trade."

That mischief included arrests, searches, explosions, incarcerations, fines, and bribes. Colin had watched his various cousins and competitors play fox and geese with the excise men for years. One cousin had lost a hand when a still had been blown up, another had emigrated to Boston one day ahead of an arrest warrant.

Colin's involvement in whisky-making had started with an uncle's urgent request to assist with repairs to a still the excise men had disabled.

"Ironic, that paying taxes should give my whisky respectability," Colin said, coming around the desk to take a seat by Maarten. "I started paying the government tithes out of youthful pigheadedness. I was determined that my business operations would go forward without the drama my relations seemed to thrive on. One wants a challenge, not a constant threat of annihilation."

Even as a soldier, the threat of annihilation had been only intermittent. Wellington had lost as many soldiers to disease as to enemy fire, and those who gave their lives in battle had done so for a reason more lofty than some yeoman's dram of the day.

"No argument there," Maarten said, tucking his glasses away. "I was determined to gain my freedom."

Maarten had been born in Georgia, the offspring of a wealthy landowner and a house slave. How he'd arrived to Britain and acquired the education of a man of business was a mystery. Quakers had been involved, and violations of various laws, in addition to determination, luck, and a prodigious intellect.

"You wanted your freedom, and I long to leave the most civilized city in the world as soon as may be," Colin replied, getting to his feet. "Here in London, I spend my evenings with men who sit in one place, never stirring for hours except to piss, and then they might go no farther than the chamber pot in the corner to relieve themselves—aiming badly because that's hilarious, I might add.

"They jeer at each other like schoolboys," he went on, "and call themselves witty, bother the tavern maids, and label themselves dashing, while soldiers who gave a limb or an eye for the safety of the realm sit cold and dirty in the street, begging for alms. I miss Scotland, where I was merely expected to work hard and keep my younger brothers out of trouble."

Oddly enough, Anwen Windham had made that plain to Colin on yesterday's outing in the park. In a moment, she'd clearly seen his longing for home, while Colin had only been able to identify a restless discontent.

"You spend some evenings waltzing," Maarten observed. "And flirting."

"I'm expected to escort my sisters, and flirting is part of what a titled gentleman does." The flirting was easy, except Colin preferred to flirt with women who were free to *flirt back*. Ennui was fashionable among the ladies aspiring to sophistication, and the debutantes...

They were the recruits to the ranks of society, the foot soldiers living in fear of a stain on their new uniforms or a blunder on the battlefield. Thank God and Scottish governesses, Eddie and Ronnie were made of sterner stuff.

So was Anwen Windham, for all her soft skin and clipped English diction.

A tap sounded on the door.

"Enter," Colin called, for his meeting with Maarten was concluded, and the sensitive information safely stowed in Maarten's satchel.

"Mr. Winthrop Montague has come to call, my lord," the butler said. "Shall I inform him that you're not at home?"

Colin wasn't at home—Perthshire was home, not this dwelling that was at once stuffy and much too big for three siblings and some staff.

"Send him up," Colin said. "He'll probably expect a tea tray, or lunch on the terrace, or some sort of free food and drink."

"Very good, my lord." The butler—a venerable relic by the name of MacGinnes—bowed.

"I should become seasick in his position," Colin said, when MacGinnes had silently withdrawn and silently pulled the door closed. "All that bobbing and bowing."

"How did you stand the army?" Maarten asked. "All the saluting and shooting?"

"Every job has its challenges." Colin extended a hand. "My thanks for the report, and for all you do to make my enterprise successful. I'll see you again, Tuesday next."

"I'm planning to return to Scotland by the first of May," Maarten said. "One doesn't like to leave the distillery unattended for too long."

Maarten was being delicate. Scottish law did not recognize slavery in any form, but English courts had dodged the matter, ruling only that former slaves could not be forcibly removed from England. Maarten could easily be snatched from some quiet London street and sold for a pretty penny in the West Indies.

"Maybe by the first of May, Eddie and Ronnie will have reached the limit of their fascination with fashionable society," Colin said. "I'd love to travel north with you."

"We won't tap the '89 until you're back home where you belong." Maarten buckled his satchel closed. "I already sent word that the duke is to be gifted with a barrel of the '93."

"The Duke of Moreland?"

"Your brother—the Duke of Murdoch."

"Right." And wrong too, somehow. Hamish was Hamish, and no more enamored of having a title than Colin was.

MacGinnes's tap sounded on the door again.

"Come in!" *For God's sake.*

"No need to announce me," Winthrop Montague said, dodging around MacGinnes. "Oh, sorry. I didn't realize you had company."

Montague peered at Maarten as if not quite sure Colin's man of business was animate.

"Mr. Maarten and I were finished with our meeting," Colin said, rather than subject Maarten to an introduction. "Maarten, my thanks, and please do start on your travel arrangements. The '93 for His Grace is an inspired notion. Perhaps we'll name the '89 for the duchess."

Maarten bowed and withdrew, never so much as making eye contact with Montague. MacGinnes drew the door closed, and Colin wrestled with a longing for a wee dram.

Not the '89, which would be lovely beyond imagining.

Not even the '93, a whisky worthy of a duke.

Any damned whisky would do, provided it took the edge off his restlessness.

"That's your man of business?" Montague asked. "He's different."

"Try to entice him away from my employ and I'll call you out," Colin said. "Maarten is shrewd, honest, hardworking, good with the men, and not prone to consuming my inventory."

Montague took the seat behind Colin's desk, because where else would a lordling choose to sit? "You're not joking, are you?"

"I found him working in one of my warehouses. He brought to my attention a discrepancy between items on hand and items supposedly delivered from another of my warehouses."

Montague opened the drawer to his right—even Edana and Rhona wouldn't have been so bold. "Have you any snuff? I'm in need of a dose. Going a bit short of sleep these days."

"I don't partake. Shall we be off?"

They were to ride in the park at the fashionable hour, there being safety in numbers, according to Montague.

"You don't fancy a late luncheon before we go? The weather is fair, meaning this won't be a short outing."

Typically English of the weather to be so disobliging. "A footman can lay out a tray for us in the garden. If you fancy ale, I'll have that served instead of tea."

"Please, God, some decent ale," Montague said, lounging back in the cushioned chair. "Just how many warehouses do you own?"

"Six, and I trade shares in six others."

"Twelve—? You own shares in twelve different warehouses?"

"I have a theory," Colin said, heading for the door. "Where the whisky ages has a lot to do with its flavor. A cask stored high in a warehouse near the sea will have that scent, that freshness and brine. One tucked away in a Highland glen will bring the mountains into the nose or the finish. Sometimes, the sherry or port previously stored in the barrel overpowers the palate, but before and after, that's where the subtleties sneak in."

"One can hardly understand you when you wax poetical about your barbarian libation," Montague said. "You put me oddly in mind of the temperance ladies when they're on about demon rum and blue ruin."

He gave a mock shudder as they emerged onto the back terrace, though the English temperance society hadn't been convened that could outdo its Scottish cousins for zeal.

"Are you sure we have to idle about in the park this

afternoon?" Colin asked. "I have some correspondence to see to."

Montague had taken pains to instruct him on this point. A gentleman did not announce to even his friends that he craved to work on estimates for pricing and distribution of his finest whisky yet. A gentleman tended to correspondence.

Just as a gentleman was home when he wasn't home, and was not home to certain callers when he was perched on his rosy fundament within earshot of his own front door.

All very confusing, this gentlemanliness. Colin wondered if his sisters, in their private moments, found being ladies equally trying.

"Of course we must be out and about this afternoon," Montague said, clapping Colin on the shoulder. "If you are to take your proper place in society, you must acquaint yourself with the leading lights of that same body. Most of them are to be found in two places."

Colin could recite this lecture by heart, but instead gestured to the table in the shade of a balcony.

"A gentleman," Montague went on, "enjoys the company of the fairer sex on social occasions, and the carriage parade is a highly social occasion. He enjoys the company of his fellows at the clubs and sporting venues. Have you let it be known you'd like to join Brooks's yet?"

Colin took a seat, though he wasn't hungry. "You're not a member. Why should I become one?" At great expense and bother, when he was already a member at three other clubs. Then too, Colin could easily be blackballed, and his failure to gain membership would become the subject of talk.

Polite society seemed to exist primarily to talk about itself.

"You must join," Montague said, appropriating the chair at Colin's right and flipping out his tails with enviable panache, "so that I can take my proper place with you there. Your brother is a duke, therefore you should have no trouble gaining access. If you aspire to Whig politics, and I suspect you do, then Brooks's is *de rigueur*, old chap."

Colin did not aspire to Whig politics, though Montague did. Younger sons stood for the House of Commons, or became vicars, diplomats, or military officers. Montague wasn't interested in serving in Canada or India, and Colin couldn't see him managing in a parsonage.

"I adore a rare roast of beef," Montague said, tucking into the offerings on the tray. "Let's have some ale, shall we? No rule says a pair of bachelors can't wash down an afternoon repast with ale."

Colin caught the eye of the footman standing in the sun near the door. "Ale, if you please, and have Prince Charlie brought around."

"Of course, my lord."

"Montague, if you're not interested in socializing with a particular lady, why bother with the carriage parade? We ran that drill on Monday." And the Friday before that, and the Tuesday before that.

Montague paused with a quarter of a sandwich halfway to his mouth. "Do you or do you not have a grasp of what marital relations entail?"

"Don't be insulting."

"Right, so. One marries, and the immediate benefit therefrom is obvious even to Scottish courtesy lords with more warehouses than I have fingers. If one marries shrewdly, then one acquires a papa-in-law who might finance a political campaign, tuck a little estate or two into the settlements, or include a doting son-in-law in his more lucrative investments. If one sires an heir to the family title, then the emoluments proliferate along with spares. It's all quite lovely."

To Colin, it all sounded damned boring. He'd go along on this scouting mission in Hyde Park because Anwen Windham might be among the ladies taking the air, and he had some potentially useful ideas regarding her orphanage.

"I have a business to run," Colin said as the rest of Montague's sandwich met its fate, "in addition to two estates, and no political aspirations. I have no need of a doting papa-in-law."

Eating, drinking for free, and scheming to eat and drink for free seemed to be the measure of an aristocratic young man's ambitions—with the occasional stupid wager, idiot horse race, or mindless tup thrown in for variety.

Oh, and waltzing. Mustn't forget the waltzing.

"MacHugh, I'm sure in Scotland you're justly proud of your accomplishments and wealth, but here, you must temper your pride with some—ah, just in time, my good man, just in time."

The footman set a tray with two foaming tankards before Montague.

Montague lifted one, blew the head off, and managed to spatter the footman's slippers with flecks of ale.

"You're excused," Colin said. If any force of nature equaled an English lordling's quest for meaningless diversion, it was the English servant's quest for decorum.

"You're not drinking?" Montague asked, patting his ale mustache with his serviette.

"Not if we're to leave for the park straightaway. You're welcome to mine, of course."

"Don't mind if I do," Montague said. "Now, see here, MacHugh. You're looking a bit down in the mouth, and that won't serve. I know all this socializing and smiling is tedious, but this is how you gain entrée where it matters. You can count on me to ease your way up to a point, but then the work falls to you, my friend. You've made great progress, and I daresay having your ducal brother away from Town can only benefit you. He was a bit of an original."

And that was a bad thing? That a man didn't toady to society, or jeopardize his honor for any reason? That he married for love, not for...*emoluments* in exchange for stud services?

"Win, I'm bored." The admission felt both pathetic and brave.

Montague patted his arm. "We all are. Boredom is marvelously fashionable. Justifies all manner of extravagance. We'll have a bit of sport at Mrs. Bellingham's tonight. That will put you back on your mettle. I fancy that new blonde gal, though she comes dear, as it were."

"My sisters require my escort tonight," Colin said, rising. "I'll tell the grooms to bring your horse around, and I'll meet you out front."

"MacHugh, a moment."

Montague looked very much a lord about his leisure, the pewter tankards at his elbow, the afternoon sun glinting off his stylishly curled hair.

He also looked a bit desperate.

"Yes?"

"If you're truly in want of a diversion, perhaps it's time you took on a charity or two. Twelve warehouses is rather a lot."

"I own only six, but what does that have to do with anything?"

Montague took a gulp from the second tankard.

"*Noblesse oblige*, to whom much has been given, that sort of thing. You should sit on a charitable board of directors, dole out some coin, do your bit for the deserving poor. The ladies admire a man with some charity in his heart—suggests he has coin in the bank, if you get my drift."

Anwen Windham was much interested in one charity in particular. "You think I should take up the cause of a few charities?"

"Please, MacHugh, let's not be extravagant. Start with one—the House of Wayward Urchins will suit you wonderfully—pay it some mind, and you'll acquire a nice philanthropic patina on your new title. If you overdo, or are too generous, people will say you're trying to buy your entrée into polite society."

Colin had merely to glance in the direction of the house, and a footman—a different footman—came bustling forth to take the trays.

"I'm to buy my way into at least four clubs, buy every round of drinks or joint of beef ordered by your friends, buy—"

"Our friends."

"—buy vouchers for Almack's, buy independent quarters that are fashionable but not too ostentatious, keep every tailor or bootmaker on Bond Street in business, do my bit at Tatts even though I already have six horses here in London alone, have a coach made as well as my perfectly functional phaeton, and tithe to the bordellos and gaming hells as well, but I mustn't be seen to spend too much on *charity*?"

Montague saluted with his ale. "MacHugh, you restore my faith in public school education. My efforts have not been in vain, and your grasp of the challenge you face is commendable—for a Scot."

He was serious, or as serious as a man could be when half-foxed well before sundown.

"Meet me out front," Colin said. Montague's advice was well intended, and the idea of taking an interest in Anwen's orphanage had appeal.

The boys mattered to her. They weren't a stupid wager or an afternoon spent debating the merits of red wheels on a conveyance as opposed to yellow.

By the time Colin reached the garden gate, Winthrop Montague had wandered beneath a shady oak, the tankard of ale held with his right hand. With the left, he undid his falls and waved his cock over the heartsease, an arc of lordly piss spattering the hapless flowers.

* * *

"I am so sorry I missed our meeting yesterday," Lady Rosalyn said as her barouche rolled into the park. "Devilish bad megrim, probably from drinking too much ratafia at Lady Beresford's card party."

"Save your breath, Ros," Anwen replied, unfurling her parasol. "I saw you out with Lord Twillinger. Our meeting hadn't a quorum because neither you nor Win attended, and nothing was decided."

Lady Rosalyn Montague could only look lovely— adorably lovely, sweetly lovely, mischievously lovely. Her version of contritely lovely was fairly convincing too.

"I am sorry, Anwen. I thought to have a lie down, then Twilly came calling, and Win suggested fresh air might clear my head. He was right, as usual. Yesterday was too beautiful to spend entirely cooped up, much less at a dreary meeting."

Meaning Winthrop Montague could easily have attended that meeting without his sister.

Not that one could *say* that. "I've come up with an idea—or rather, Her Grace of Moreland has—for the House of Urchins."

"Do tell. There's that dreadful Flora Stanbridge. I must have a word with Pierpont's wife about the company her husband is keeping."

Rosalyn could do it too. She dispensed blunt advice with a sympathetic, winning smile, and such a gracious touch of humor that taking offense at her words was impossible.

"Pierpont's wife might be grateful to Miss Stanbridge. About my idea?"

"Your aunt's idea?"

Well, yes. Anwen had made a mere suggestion. The final creation would be entirely Aunt Esther's.

"Her Grace is planning a charity card party in lieu of her final soiree this season, with a portion of everybody's winnings going to the House of Urchins."

The full blue-eyed glory of Rosalyn's stare fixed on Anwen. "A *charity* card party? That is…Anwen, that is *brilliant*. That is…everybody will wish they'd thought of it. If we must entertain ourselves with silly wagers, why not benefit the children while we do? The bachelors will be in alt—excellent punch, no standing up with the wallflowers, no guilty conscience for hiding in the card room for the entire evening. Oh, I would hate you for being so clever, except your dear aunt thought of this idea, and one can't hate a duchess."

Rosalyn paused to nod graciously at the Duke of Quimbey.

"I'm so glad old Quimbey took a wife," Rosalyn went on when the duke's cabriolet had rolled past. "My aunts had plans for me where His Grace was concerned, plans a young lady shuddered to contemplate."

"With *Quimbey*?" He was a dear old fellow, but a dear *old* fellow.

"A duke is a duke. Your sister Megan found the backbone to accept when the Duke of Murdoch offered, did she not?"

One could never be entirely certain when Rosalyn was teasing. "They are a love match. I'll thank you not to imply otherwise."

"My goodness, you can be prickly." Rosalyn beamed at Miss Stanbridge and Lord Pierpont as the carriages passed. "Let's not quarrel, for there's Winthrop and Lord Colin. We must tell them about our card party."

Lord Colin had called Anwen fierce, rather than prickly. He and Win sat their horses a dozen yards along the path, chatting up an entire vis-à-vis of parasols and bonnets.

"No, Ros, we must not disclose the duchess's plan." And it wasn't *our* card party. "Her Grace was very clear that until the guest list has been decided, we must be circumspect about the details."

"But just a teeny, tiny—"

"No."

Surprise registered, followed by Lady Rosalyn's endearing smile. "Oh, very well. One doesn't contradict a duchess."

Not a single duchess was to be found in the carriage. "I mention the party to you only because you are a supporter of the orphanage and you love a spirited hand of cards."

"That I do. Whist and hazard, hazard and whist, piquet for variety. At the card table, we are the equal of the gentlemen in every regard save recklessness, most of the time."

The carriage inched forward, bringing them closer to Winthrop and Lord Colin.

"Rosalyn, have you been wagering again?" Anwen had made more than one "little loan" to her friend. Friends did that—preserved one another from embarrassment.

"My maid is selling my castoffs," Rosalyn said. "I've three beautiful reticules that will fetch fine prices. I'll come right in time for the party, never fear. What can you tell me about Lord Colin?"

Lord Colin had a lovely command of economics, and a sweet touch upon a lady's nape, while Lady Rosalyn was nigh addicted to large, fancifully embroidered reticules.

"Lord Colin is charming and he dances well. He'd die for those he cares about." He also took an escort's responsibilities seriously, and made sure any who approached Lady Edana or Lady Rhona knew it.

Lord Colin had stood up with the Duke of Murdoch at the wedding, and if Hamish MacHugh had been dignified, his younger brother had been positively regal with family pride.

"The dying for one's friends part doesn't sound very nice," Lady Roslyn murmured, "and I already knew about the charm and the dancing."

The day grew slightly less sunny, slightly less interesting. "Do you fancy Lord Colin, Ros?"

"I might," she said as the carriage moved two entire yards forward. "Depends on the settlements. He's the ducal heir now, but I can't expect that to last. Win says Lord Colin is well fixed."

Lady Rosalyn expected Anwen to reveal facts relevant to Lord Colin's financial situation, because the evidence—his fine team, his lovely conveyance, his family's title, his exquisite tailoring—might suggest enormous debt rather than solvency.

"I'm not in a position to say, Rosalyn. Lord Colin owns

a distillery business, and his family has land in Perthshire and the Borders as well as other commercial interests."

Rosalyn wrinkled her nose, and even that looked lovely. "You'll warn me if I'm wasting my time, I trust. No harm in being friendly, but the gentlemen so easily get *ideas* if one is too friendly."

With that she beamed at her brother. Win and Lord Colin touched their hats to the ladies, and came trotting right to Lady Rosalyn's side.

Chapter Four

"LORD COLIN! WHAT A lovely surprise!" Lady Rosalyn offered a gloved hand, which Colin was supposed to bow over, despite being on horseback. Fortunately, Prince Charlie was a Town horse, sedate in the face of noise, traffic, or close quarters.

Colin grasped her ladyship's hand. Miss Anwen apparently didn't expect him to ride around to the other side of the carriage and extend a similar courtesy to her.

"I trust your ladyship has recovered from yesterday's megrim?" Colin asked.

"Yesterday's—? Oh, quite! I am so sorry to have missed our outing. My heart nearly broke with disappointment, just ask Win."

"Poor creature was desolated," Win said, "distraught, nigh hysterical. I have seldom seen her so upset short of being unable to find her new bonnet or reticule when we're late to the opera."

Lady Rosalyn laughed sweetly, and several other gallants along the line of carriages cast Colin envious glances. Would they envy Colin as much if they'd known her ladyship had stood him up to go tooling about with Lord Twillinger?

"Miss Anwen, I trust you are well?" Colin asked.

"I am in the pink of health, thank you. That is a very handsome gelding. May I ask how you came by him?"

"Won his dam in a card game," Colin said, "and didn't know she was in foal. Best surprise of a young officer's life. I left the dam at the estate of a Portuguese officer, and the second best surprise was when I came to fetch her two years later, this little fellow was gamboling happily in the next paddock, as handsome a creature as ever cantered a fence line."

And the Portuguese officer, having a bone-deep love of the equine, had given Prince Charlie an ideal start in life.

"He has some progeny," Colin went on. "I didn't geld him until—"

"I've asked Lord Colin to consider involving himself in the House of Urchins," Win announced. "A gentleman of means does what he can for the less fortunate, after all."

In mixed company, a gentleman apparently didn't raise the topic of gelding his horse, even though Lady Anwen, at least, could discern the horse's present reproductive limitations easily.

A lack of balls on a man was harder to spot.

"Lord Colin is taking an interest in the House of Urchins?" Lady Rosalyn cooed. "My prayers have been answered, your lordship. I was so vexed to be unable to attend yesterday's meeting, precisely because an orphanage without benefactors soon becomes a precarious proposition. Anwen, I'm sure you agree that his lordship's generosity could not have a better recipient."

"I don't think Lord Colin has made up his mind yet, my lady."

Lady Rosalyn sent Colin an arch look and twirled her parasol. "I have faith in Lord Colin's ability to discern a deserving charity. I also have faith in my brother's ability to convince his lordship that the House of Urchins is such an institution."

Anwen stilled her friend's parasol. "You're unsettling your brother's horse, my lady."

"Gracious, Win. Get the beast under control before he provokes my team," Lady Rosalyn said.

Without the parasol whirling in its face, the horse calmed, though it might have done so sooner had Win not been two sheets to the wind.

"Shall we move up?" Miss Anwen suggested.

The coach rolled on at a funereal pace, and Colin maneuvered Prince Charlie to Miss Anwen's side of the vehicle. His place near Lady Rosalyn was immediately taken by Sycamore Dorning, a gangly youngster who ought to be at university learning how to hold his drink.

"Are you truly in the pink of health?" Colin asked quietly. "I know you're concerned for your orphans."

"I have some plans in train where the House of Urchins is concerned. Don't involve yourself solely because Win Montague suggested it."

"I thought you might welcome my involvement." Had expected she would, after yesterday's discussion. His involvement, not merely his money.

"I like Mr. Montague," Anwen said, patting Charlie's glossy neck. "He's good company, a fine dancer, a cheerful partner for whist."

"His interest in my situation has been invaluable," Colin replied. "One cannot insinuate oneself into polite society, one must be sponsored, like an orphanage. Without the right patronage, doors are mysteriously closed, invitations don't materialize."

Anwen twiddled the dark hair of Charlie's mane, a sure way to get her gloves dirty. "My aunt and uncle would be only too happy to—"

Charlie turned a large, poetic brown eye on the lady. Gelded he might be, but a fool he was not.

"Some doors can only be opened by another young fellow, my dear."

"Oh." She left off petting the horse. "My cousins, Lords Westhaven, Valentine, and Rosecroft, would surely be willing to—"

"I talk horses with Rosecroft, business with Westhaven, and music with Valentine, but Miss Anwen, they are married." Moreover, they had become extended family, by virtue of Hamish's marriage to Megan, and Colin didn't want family at his elbow when he called on Mrs. Bellingham's establishment.

Not that he had.

"About the House of Urchins," Colin said. "If you'd rather I find another charity to polish my gentlemanly credentials with, I'll ask Win where else I might—"

"Don't *ask Win*. He's the vice-chairman of our board of directors. His motives for involving you are not entirely disinterested."

Winthrop Montague knew everybody, and more to the point, got along with everybody. Colin had relied on Montague to provide advice on everything from which clubs to join to how often to stop by Tatts, to which tailors were in fashion. So far that advice had been mostly sound.

Colin leaned nearer the coach. "I owe Win Montague, Anwen. If he invites me to take up a charitable cause, I'm inclined to do it."

She wasn't wearing a bonnet per se, more of a decoration in her hair. Silk flowers, pearls, feathers...Her nape was exposed, and Colin itched to take off his gloves and touch that soft skin.

With his tongue, God help him.

"Don't take up a charitable cause simply to polish your gentlemanly halo," Anwen shot back. "They are *children*, Lord Colin. I know you have a passing acquaintance with the species because at some point, you must have been one."

Laughter came from the group on the other side of the coach, and Win gave Colin a slight wag of the head. *Get back over here and join the party.*

"You're angry," Colin said, fascinated with his own conclusion.

"I am frustrated, though now is not the time to air this topic."

Had she also seen Win's signal? "Do you ever hack out in the morning?"

"Lord Colin, you must give us your opinion!" Lady Rosalyn called. "We are debating the benefits of shade cast by the maple versus the oak, and Mr. Pettyfinger claims to favor the oak."

"The maple lacks acorns," Colin replied, tipping his hat to Pettyfinger, "and thus does not attract squirrels as readily as the oak. For quiet, the maple will do. If one wants the diversion of squirrels overhead, the oak will oblige."

Montague clapped, joined by several other fellows who'd flocked to Lady Rosalyn's side of the coach.

"I can ride out tomorrow," Anwen murmured. "At dawn,

I'll meet you at the foot of the Serpentine, weather permitting."

Colin extended a hand toward the lady, which earned him a smirk from Pettyfinger. A gentleman did not presume to take a lady's hand, but Miss Anwen offered him her gloved fingers, nonetheless.

"Until tomorrow," Colin said, softly enough that only Anwen would hear.

He resumed his place at Montague's side and let the laughter and inanities swirl about him. When Lady Rosalyn directed her coachman homeward, claiming a need to prepare for the evening's entertainments, the other gentlemen melted away to flirt elsewhere.

"Shall we be off to Mrs. Bellingham's?" Montague asked. "Her doors open at mid-afternoon, so a fellow can fortify himself for an evening of waltzing and looking harmless."

Colin could see the nape of Anwen's neck as Lady Rosalyn's carriage wheeled toward a bend in the path. Maybe that's why young ladies wore bonnets, to prevent presuming young men from—

"If you're gazing adoringly after my sister like that in public," Montague said, "then I think a visit to Mrs. Bellingham's becomes mandatory. Speaking of which, you *are* joining the House of Urchins board of directors, aren't you?"

"I'm considering it. I'll not be accompanying you to Mrs. Bellingham's."

"What if we went later in the evening? Not good for the manly humors to get out of balance."

Colin turned Prince Charlie back toward Park Lane. "A touch of the French disease is far worse for the manly humors than a bit of abstinence."

Win tipped his hat to another wagonload of muslin, not a one of the ladies looking above seventeen years old, save the chaperone.

"Do you know how the Scots got a reputation for a dour disposition, MacHugh?"

By putting up with the English for neighbors. "I'm sure you'll tell me."

"Of course, because I am your friend and your welfare concerns me utterly. The Scots are notorious among all races for a lack of cheer because they have become afflicted with too much religion and not enough sport."

The conversation, however manly, struck Colin as ungentlemanly. "What would my responsibilities be, if I became a director on the House of Urchins board?"

Montague took out a flask, uncapped it, and tipped it to his mouth. "One attends the meetings, unless a handy excuse materializes. Old Derwent, as chairman, does the parliamentary bits, and Hitchings sees that the minutes are kept. You really ought to give it a go, MacHugh. If you take a seat on the board, then I can step back, having done my part to find a successor. Then too, should you ever stand for a seat in the Commons, charitable work along the way won't hurt, dull though it is."

Colin couldn't see how any of the foregoing qualified as work. "So you're asking me to replace you on the board?" The idea appealed, because it went beyond tagging along at Montague's exquisitely tailored elbow.

"One isn't expected to chain oneself to these projects in perpetuity. I'd hand you the reins eventually. I'll be off to the house parties in July, the shooting in August. The little season requires a gentleman's attention, hunt season comes along, the holidays, and then it's back to Town."

Montague's attention was drawn to a gig driven by none

other than Mrs. Bellingham. A house cat didn't watch a caged nightingale any more closely than Winthrop Montague attended the stately brunette.

"You asked earlier why we had to make this outing," Montague said. "There's my reason, right there."

Not a hint of banter infused his tone, and his gaze was solemn rather than adoring. The lady passed with the barest tip of her chin in Montague's direction. His flask was back in his hand before the sound of her carriage wheels had faded.

"A very pretty reason," Colin said.

"I haven't the blunt to make that reason mine," Montague said. "Such are the tribulations of a younger son, but I can worship from afar. Word in the clubs is she doesn't tolerate advances from anything less than a duke."

His gaze followed the retreating vehicle, and Mr. Jonathan Tresham—a duke's heir—turned his horse to accompany her.

"I'm for home," Colin said. "I've some correspondence to tend to before my sisters demand my company for the evening. Will I see you at the Pendleton musicale?"

Nobody approached Mrs. Bellingham's vehicle as long as Tresham rode beside her. He was known to be infernally wealthy and of a surly disposition. A mastiff trotted at his horse's heels, every bit of sixteen stone and much of that teeth.

"Win?"

"I'm sorry?"

"Pendleton's, this evening. Violins, punch, sandwiches, a soprano or two?"

"Of course. Rosalyn will expect it of me. Until then." He turned his horse to follow in the wake of Mrs. Bellingham and her escort.

Rather than watch Winthrop Montague worship from a distance of about ten yards, Colin steered Prince Charlie in the opposite direction.

Montague was in love with an ineligible *parti*, and all he could think to do in the face of that problem was drink, pine, and pretend not to care.

Maybe the lot of a society gentleman wasn't so easy after all.

* * *

Anwen hadn't dragged herself out of bed to ride in the park at dawn for at least two years. The last time she'd attempted to start her day with a hearty gallop, two sisters, three grooms, dear cousin Valentine, and the duchess herself had all mysteriously taken a notion to greet the morning in the same fashion.

What was the point of seeking the splendor of a solitary sunrise when half the family came along to prevent the ride from progressing any faster than a trot?

This morning Anwen had prevailed upon Lord Rosecroft for his escort. Cousin Devlin was so thoroughly enamored of horses that if Anwen asked him to go riding with her, he took that to mean athletic activity on the back of a horse, not an exchange of gossip at an idle walk.

The two grooms were several yards back from Anwen's mare, while Cousin Devlin had a gallop beside the Serpentine and Anwen dawdled along, wondering if Lord Colin would oversleep.

"Halloo, Miss Anwen!"

"Lord Colin, where is your hat?"

He'd cantered in from the direction of St. James, his hair windblown, his cheeks ruddy. The picture he presented was altogether attractive, but the leap in Anwen's heart was simply because he'd kept their appointment.

"My hat is sitting safely on the sideboard at home. I can't tell you how many have gone sailing into the undergrowth when Prince Charlie gets to stretching his legs. Some urchin is always the richer for my folly because I can never find the deuced things when I come back to hunt for them. You look fetching in that shade of blue, Miss Anwen, especially when you start a fellow's day with such a gorgeous smile."

He was smiling too, his dimple shamelessly in evidence.

The words 'Oh, this old thing?' were on the tip of Anwen's tongue, exactly what Lady Rosalyn would have said.

"Thank you, but flattery at this hour isn't necessary, my lord. Shall we ride on?"

"Flattery ought never to be necessary, but sincere compliments are always appropriate. Tell me something you admire about me."

Was this flirtation? Before the sun had even gained the horizon? "I'd rather discuss the House of Urchins with you."

"Now," he said, petting his horse's neck, "there you go being tenacious and devoted to your cause, which I admire about you. I'm determined to practice my social discourse this morning, so you will please oblige me with a compliment."

Anwen was tempted to argue that the orphanage was more important, but she sensed Lord Colin would only turn that to more banter—while he gently stroked his horse's crest.

Where to start? He was a kind and genial escort to his sisters.

He thought for himself when it came to training horses

rather than accepting sermons handed down since Xenophon had been a boy.

He was loyal to his friends.

He didn't idle about waiting for a quarterly allowance when he could instead apply himself to gainful occupation.

He was patient, deft, and gentle when untangling bonnet ribbons and hairpins.

"You apply commonsense to the business of whether to wear a hat for a morning gallop."

"Do you hear that, Charlie?" The gelding's ears swiveled at the use of his name. "I'm a sensible fellow, at least where my hat is concerned. That is a unique compliment, Miss Anwen, and I shall treasure it. Is that Rosecroft showing off at such an early hour?"

Cousin Devlin's horses were taught classical airs, and this morning he was schooling his gelding in *passage*.

"Rosecroft makes a dashing picture, wouldn't you agree, my lord?"

"He's dashing, but I'm sensible. I prefer the compliment you gave me to the one you gave him. How bad is the shortage of funds at your orphanage?"

Anwen told him, told him at length how ineffectual the directors were at addressing the problem—how unmotivated.

"I suspect the problem isn't a lack of motivation so much as a lack of imagination," Lord Colin said when they'd been riding for thirty minutes. "These are not people who've ever had to earn coin, much less manage it to the penny. They are out of their depth."

"But they are from the best families, all of them claiming significant wealth. Imagination won't feed my boys."

"At the risk of contradicting a lady, I humbly suggest you're wrong. The building that houses your orphanage is enormous, and yet, you don't have it filled nearly to capacity."

"We can't afford to fill it to capacity," Anwen shot back. "Every extra boy means more food, more candles, more laundry, more—"

"So rent out the nicest rooms to young gentlemen, and provide them breakfast trays, laundry service, and a stall in the mews for a horse. The boys can learn to be valets, footmen, and grooms. Moreover, the children will hear proper diction from young toffs every day, as well as earn coin from the occasional vale.

"The gentlemen get safe, affordable accommodations with all the amenities," he went on, "and the cachet of aiding a worthy cause without spending any extra to do it—while spending less, in fact, than they'd pay at the Albany or many of their clubs."

The sun chose that moment to break through the trees, which surely qualified as an omen from on high. Anwen turned the scheme over in her mind—the empty accommodations at the House of Urchins could generate coin, staff on hand could provide services for hire, and the paying boarders could teach the boys skills.

She could find no fault with it. *None at all.* "How did you come up with this idea, Lord Colin? Have you read about it in some book or seen it done in Scotland?"

Like many brilliant notions, this scheme had *why didn't I think of that* written all over it, not that anybody would have listened to Anwen if she'd suggested it.

"If Hamish hadn't opened up the townhouse, I'd be one of those young gentlemen, looking for a quiet, modest place to retreat to when being useless, drunk, and merry paled. Such lodgings are nearly impossible to find during the season, though we've missed the opportunity for this year."

"But it's an idea, and the little season attracts some young men to Town, at least until the hunting starts. The holidays are the same, and as soon as Parliament sits again..."

Anwen had been out of bed for well over an hour, but Lord Colin's casual suggestion woke her up in a way tea and toast, and even fresh morning air, had not.

"You don't think we could start this scheme anytime soon?" she asked.

"To do this properly, you'd need to fit out the rooms, advertise, interview the gentlemen to ensure the proper sort joined the household, train the boys, work out the budget for such an undertaking. All of that requires time, and the season is, thankfully, half over."

Yes, but by autumn, Anwen could manage every task on the list. "Lord Colin, I fear I must pay you another compliment."

He brought his horse to the halt, his expression solemn while his eyes danced. "Do your worst, Miss Anwen. I'm braced for the ordeal."

"You have given me hope."

She expected him to laugh, to fire off a witty rejoinder. Cousin Devlin would hear that laughter and come passaging over, and this magical sense of *possibility* would fade like the mist over the Long Water.

"I have given you hope," Lord Colin repeated softly. "Tell me more."

Could she? He wasn't laughing, he was *listening*. "I am so worried for those children, and it's tempting to yield to that worry, to be paralyzed by it. I could ignore the whole problem, and pretend wiser heads than mine will solve it. Any head is supposedly wiser than a single young woman's. Sometimes, a problem is not solved by wisdom of the head, but by wisdom of the heart. I can aspire to wisdom of the heart, to imagination, to a charity card party because that's what I *can* do."

Prince Charlie walked on, and Anwen's mare fell in beside him.

"I want to hear about this charity card party, but if the sun gets any higher, this park will become too crowded for a good gallop. Shall we?"

They'd come to a straight stretch of the bridle path, and Lord Colin was inviting her to gallop, to feel the wind in her hair, the horse pounding along beneath her, the greenery going by in a blur.

Without warning, Anwen cued her mare into the canter, then snugged her knee to the horn as Prince Charlie leapt forward.

"Go, girl!" Anwen shouted. "Show 'em your heels!"

The mare was exquisitely trained, but she was also a healthy creature confined to Town rather than enjoying her home pastures in Kent. She burst into a thunderous gallop, and with a whoop, Lord Colin let his gelding stretch out as well.

The gallop became a race, Anwen tucked like a highwayman over her horse's withers, Lord Colin's gelding puffing heartily at her elbow. By the time she pulled up three hundred yards on, she'd had a full length on Lord Colin.

The grooms were cantering some yards back, so Anwen permitted herself to raise her whip in the air.

"We beat you! Good girl, Baronessa! You showed them who's faster." She patted the mare's shoulder, and the horse responded by curvetting about on the path, her form worthy of one of Cousin Devlin's finished mounts.

"Well, of course you beat us," Lord Colin said. "You had all the advantages, not that I'm complaining."

He wasn't complaining, he was smiling, his feet kicked out of the stirrups, his horse on a loose rein.

"What advantages?" Anwen retorted. "I'm riding aside, I haven't galloped for ages, and I lack your athleticism. I'm also wearing a hat." Which had more or less stayed affixed to her hair.

"That is not a hat. That is feathers and flowers intended to call attention to your glorious red hair. Your advantages are numerous, but let's start with you surprised me with a fast start. You are smaller and lighter, your horse was fresher while this poor fellow was out until all hours last night. Most of all, you were determined to win, while I..."

"Yes?" If he said he'd let her win, the day would lose much of its glory.

His smile faded. "I was determined to win too. I simply underestimated you. Ungentlemanly of me, but it's the truth. Shall we walk for a bit? I still want to hear about your charity card party."

"Don't feel bad. People have been underestimating me since I was seven years old." Anwen unhooked her knee from the horn, and arranged her skirts so she could dismount. "I was supposed to die on several occasions, but failed to oblige the physicians. Mama would not let them bleed me, and sent them packing when their quackery only made me more ill. I didn't die, though my recovery took months and featured several relapses."

Lord Colin swung off his horse and came around to put his hands on Anwen's waist. "I'm glad you didn't die, glad your mama was as fierce as you are, though I suppose this is part of why you're so protective of your boys."

"Maybe."

"No maybe about it," Lord Colin said, easing her to the ground. "Our early experiences can shape us profoundly. Yours has made you indomitable."

A goose honked a greeting to the day out across the water, and the moment imprinted itself on Anwen's mind. She could smell horse sweat and fresh grass, cedar with a hint of honeysuckle. Beneath her gloves, the muscles of Lord Colin's arms were firm and vital.

She woke up yet again, to her own indomitable nature, to the beautiful day, and to the fact that she wanted to kiss the first man to admit he'd underestimated her.

Chapter Five

HIDING BENEATH DEMURE MANNERS and modest tailoring was a stunning young woman. Colin stood a touch too close to Anwen Windham, counting the shades of blue, gray, agate, and indigo in her eyes.

Would their children have blue eyes and red hair?

He stepped back and handed off the horses to the grooms. The mare flicked her tail at Charlie—she knew she'd won the race—but let herself be led down the path.

"We'll stay in view of the benches," Colin said, winging his arm. "Or perhaps you'd like to sit for a moment?"

"That bench," Anwen nodded in the direction of the placid water sparkling in the morning sun. "Let's take that bench, and I'll tell you of my boys."

She knew the entire dozen by name, knew their strengths and weaknesses, their personalities, and some of their stories.

Colin knew what it felt like to touch the nape of Anwen's neck, which might explain why he stuffed his riding gloves into his pocket.

"I worry most about the four oldest," Anwen said when they'd been ensconced on the bench for fifteen minutes. "They are restless, and they need direction, not a constant round of birchings because they can't sit still."

Colin was trying to listen to Anwen's recitations, but the elegant curve of her cheek, the definition of her jawline, the hint of lace at her throat distracted him endlessly.

The distraction was not unusual—he adored women on general principles—but his irritation with himself was. He wanted to attend her words, but he also wanted to brush his thumb over the exact arch of her russet eyebrows.

"Your boys would be well suited to work in the mews or as footmen," he said. "You say they need activity and those are busy jobs."

All boys needed activity, as did girls. Edana and Rhona were an asset to any cricket team and could drive a golf ball nearly as far as any of their brothers could.

"What I say doesn't matter," Anwen replied softly. "I'm merely a member of the ladies' committee, I've never raised a boy. I knit scarves by the hour, but that doesn't deserve anybody's notice."

She'd also taken off her gloves and folded them finger-to-finger, then rolled them together.

"Many a soldier would have kissed your feet in exchange for a warm scarf, madam. We can't take in gentlemen boarders at the House of Urchins this season, but you could set the boys to doing some of the housework instead of lessons."

Anwen stared at the water as if expecting Triton to rise from its depths. "Hitchings won't like that. He says they're so far behind in their schooling, every spare moment must be spent with the books."

"Then Hitchings is an idiot who's trying to make his own post seem more necessary than it is."

Colin had met such men all over the army. Self-important idlers who'd always found a way to be moving prisoners or carrying orders when battles were fought.

Anwen offered Colin a sidelong glance that carried a hint of the girl who'd refused to die. The highlights in her hair were countless. Golden white, fiery brandy, copper sun—and those freckles. Exertion had made them more apparent, and brought the color to her cheeks.

Portraitists would line up to paint her, and her smile...

Colin looked away rather than study her mouth. Anwen Windham had a capacity for mischief and mayhem, whether she admitted it to herself or not.

"I think Hitchings means well," she said, "but all he knows how to do is teach. He lacks imagination, in the words of a wise gentleman. If we set the boys to some of the lighter jobs, we wouldn't need to spend as much on domestics."

"True. Start with simple tasks—bringing up the coal, setting the table, footman's work, and each boy gets an allowance if his tasks are done right and timely. If that goes well, then work in the stables and yard will be the reward for the boys who distinguish themselves."

Anwen unpinned her hat, or whatever the thing was. A toque, maybe. Her wild gallop had set it askew.

"Grounds work is a reward? I thought house servants ranked above the outdoor servants?"

Colin took her hat from her, examining the collection of pheasant feathers and silk roses that had probably cost a footman's monthly wages.

"I think we do best that which we enjoy most." He enjoyed kissing and that which often followed kissing he enjoyed *exceedingly*. "If a boy is to spend his entire life at a job, it had better be a job that he has some aptitude for. Let the fellow with a passion for horses work in the mews, and the young man who delights in a perfectly starched cravat become a valet. It's all honorable work."

He was being a Scottish commoner with that sentiment.

"That's sensible," Anwen said. "Sense is what the orphanage needs. Not good intentions or idle talk. Common sense. What are you doing with my— Lord Colin?"

He'd pitched the thing with feathers into the bushes five yards off, so it hung from an obliging branch of the nearest maple.

"Come," he said, taking her by the hand. "The squirrels have no need of such fetching millinery, and the grooms are busy with the horses."

"Right," Anwen said, rising. "Enough serious talk for now. I'm full of ideas and can't wait to put them into action."

"Exactly so," Colin said, leading her into the deep shade beneath the tree. "Time to put a few well-chosen ideas into action."

Also a few foolish ones.

He made sure they were safe from view, drew the lady into his arms, and kissed her, as a snippet of her earlier words settled into his imagination. She'd claimed he'd given her hope.

She'd given him hope too.

* * *

"We can't find Anwen," Elizabeth announced, Charlotte nodding vigorously at her side. "She's not in bed, she's not in the garden, she's not in the mews."

"My dears, good morning," Percival Windham, Duke of Moreland, replied. "Please do join me. Her Grace has abandoned me to break my fast in the dubious company of the newspaper, and that's enough to turn any duke's digestion sour."

He smiled his doting uncle smile—Esther said it was one of his best—and rose to hold chairs for a pair of worried nieces.

"But *we can't find Anwen*," Charlotte said, refusing to be seated. "She's gone, not in the house, not on the grounds. We checked the library, the music room, everywhere she might be, even the conservatory."

"You neglected to check Hyde Park," Percival replied, patting the back of the chair. "The day is beautiful, and your cousin Devlin was without company for his morning ride. Anwen took pity on him."

God forbid these two should learn that Anwen had ridden out on her own initiative. Their feelings would be hurt, and they'd worry as only a Windham could worry about another family member.

"Rosecroft took her riding?" Charlotte muttered, subsiding into her seat. "At this hour?"

"You know how he is." Elizabeth snapped a serviette across her lap. "When he rides, he *rides*. He's not visiting, taking the air, or showing off his tailoring. Anwen wouldn't expect him to be sociable. Pass the teapot, Charl."

Charlotte served herself first. Breakfast at Moreland House was enjoyed without servants in attendance, though maids and footmen waited by the kitchen bells should the toast run low or the tea grow cold.

"How will Anwen keep up with Rosecroft? She's nowhere near his caliber of equestrian." Elizabeth poured out for herself, running short after half a cup. "Thank you once again, Charl."

Charlotte saluted with her tea. "If I'd known Anwen was up for an outing to the park, I might have joined her. Dawn is chilly this time of year, and it's easy to overdo."

Easy to overdo the sibling concern too. "Charlotte, you insult your cousin," Percival said. "His lordship would never allow Anwen to come to harm. The butter, please, before Bethan requires that I add to the dairy herd for want of same."

All of Tony and Gladys's girls had good appetites—including Anwen. Only Percival referred to these young ladies by their childhood names, and Elizabeth—Bethan, once upon a time—glowered at him for his consideration.

"Rosecroft is a dear," she said, rising to give the bell pull a single tug. "But he's Rosecroft. If his gelding starts going unevenly, Anwen could fall into the Long Water or be kidnapped by brigands, and Rosecroft wouldn't notice. Who ate all the raspberry jam?"

"Her Grace." Abetted by Percival himself. "Did you two know the duchess is planning a charity card party?"

"She's *what*?" they asked in unison.

Percival was permitted to share the news within the family, and the longer he kept this pair at the table, the more time Anwen would enjoy at liberty. The girl needed to get out more, and to somewhere besides that dreary orphanage.

"A charity card party instead of our farewell soiree as the season nears its end," Percival went on. "Her Grace has a kind heart, else she would never have married the undeserving soul you see before you. She's—"

"A handsome, undeserving soul," Elizabeth interjected.

"Who we're told was an accomplished flirt," Charlotte added.

Lord Colin, who might well chance upon Anwen in the park, was also an accomplished flirt. Percival kept that observation to himself, lest two nieces bolt for the mews before he'd put his serviette down.

"Windham menfolk are gallant," Percival said, passing Elizabeth the butter, as the footman arrived with a fresh pat. "Thank you, Thomas. Have we any more raspberry jam?"

"Of course, Your Grace. I'll bring some up straight-away, and a fresh pot of tea."

"Compliments to Cook on the eggs," Charlotte said. "Nobody gets them as light as she does."

"I'll tell her you said so, Miss Charlotte. Do you need anything else from the kitchen?" Thomas was a handsome lad, as footmen were supposed to be. Tall, sandy-haired, blue-eyed, and cheerful without being obsequious.

"That will be all," Percival said. "Be off with you, and don't waste too much time flirting with the tweenie."

Thomas bowed and withdrew in diplomatic silence.

"Her Grace has him in mind for the underbutler's job at Morelands," Percival said. "I think the poor tweenie will go into a permanent decline if young Thomas removes to Kent." Better a decline than an untimely occasion of moth-erhood, in Esther's opinion.

"The tweenie is Evans," Elizabeth said. "If I were al-lowed to set up my own establishment, I could provide employment for them both."

This again. Under protest, Percival had allowed his old-est daughter, Maggie, to have her own household when she'd turned thirty. Now the precedent had been set, and Elizabeth was determined on the same path.

"Elizabeth, you'd leave us desolate should you defect to your own household," Percival replied, "and don't bother haranguing me on the topic because your parents must be involved in any discussion of such an arrangement. As your devoted uncle, I seek only to keep you safe and happy."

"Were you safe and happy wintering in Canada as a cavalry officer?" Charlotte asked.

"Oddly enough, I was, for the most part, but if you continue along these contentious lines, my dears, I won't tell of your aunt's card party. I believe she's making up the guest list while you bring acrimony to my breakfast table."

The sisters exchanged a look: *Fall back and retreat.* Perhaps they were hatching a plot to establish a spinster household together, which would break dear Tony's heart.

"You say the card party is to be in place of the farewell soiree?" Elizabeth asked. "Let me guess. This charity will benefit Anwen's urchins, and next year Mayfair will see a half-dozen charity card parties every Friday evening."

Not a bad idea.

"Charity card parties will have caught on by the little season," Charlotte rejoined. "If we inspired the gentlemen's clubs to set aside one table each for charity play, even one night a week, London would soon run out of urchins."

"You must suggest these ideas to your aunt," Percival said. "You have the Windham genius for turning a situation to its best advantage. The Second Coming will arrive before the Church of England or my friends in Parliament address the issue of London's poor children."

He'd got their attention, which was the point of the digression.

"I thought you were firmly in the Tory camp on this issue," Elizabeth said. "Let the poor humbly accept the will of the Almighty or work to better themselves, that sort of thing."

Percival humbly accepted the will of his duchess, on most matters. Let the Almighty bear the challenge of arguing Her Grace around, for only He was equal to the task when that good woman was convinced of her position.

"Those are reasonable, even kindly sentiments," Percival said. "To inflict expectations on the lower orders that they have no way of realizing only damns them to greater disappointment." Or so his cronies in the Lords would argue. "However, your aunt points out that your cousins Devlin and Maggie were born very much among the poor." To Percival's mistresses, before he'd met his dear duchess. "When transplanted to a household where abundant love, nourishment, and education were available, they thrived magnificently."

The duchess, born to wealthy if common stock, had made those arguments in the privacy of the ducal apartment. In all honesty Percival couldn't offer a suitable response from the Tory side of the aisle. His children—illegitimate and born into relative poverty—were now of the peerage, despite their maternal antecedents.

And Percival could not be more grateful.

While Charlotte and Elizabeth debated the divine right of kings like a pair of ambitious back benchers, Percival sipped his tea and pretended to read the paper.

He hoped Anwen had galloped over every acre of Hyde Park with some handsome gallant at her side. Rosecroft would of course be absorbed with schooling whatever mount he'd taken for the outing, but he was also a former intelligence officer.

Nothing would transpire in the park without Rosecroft

to bear witness and report the goings on back to his papa. Nothing.

* * *

Nothing penetrated Anwen's awareness except *pleasure*.

Pleasure, to be kissed by a man who wasn't in a hurry, half-drunk, or pleased with himself for appropriating liberties from a woman taken unawares by his boldness.

Pleasure, *to kiss Lord Colin back*. To do more than stand still, enduring the fumblings of a misguided fortune hunter who hoped a display of his bumbling charms would result in a lifetime of security.

Pleasure, to feel lovely bodily stirrings as the sun rose, the birds sang, and the quiet of the park reverberated with the potential of a new, wonderful day.

And beneath those delightful, if predictable pleasures, yet more joy, unique to Anwen.

Lord Colin had bluntly pronounced her slight stature an advantage in the saddle—how marvelous!—and what a novel perspective.

He'd *listened* to her maundering on about Tom, Joe, John, and Dickie. Listened and discussed the situation rather than pontificating about her pretty head, and he'd offered solutions.

He'd taken care that this kiss be private, and thus unhurried.

Anwen liked the unhurried part exceedingly. Lord Colin held her not as if she were frail and fragile, but as if she were too precious to let go. His arms were secure about her, and he'd tucked in close enough that she could revel in his contours—broad chest, flat belly, and hard, hard thighs, such as an accomplished equestrian would have.

Soft lips, though. Gentle, entreating, teasing...

Anwen teased him back, getting a taste of peppermint for her boldness, and then a taste of *him*.

"Great day in the morning," he whispered, right at her ear. "I won't be able to sit my horse if you do that again with your tongue."

She did it again, and again, until the kiss involved his leg insinuated among the folds and froths of her riding habit, her fingers toying with the hair at his nape, and her heart, beating faster than it had at the conclusion of their race.

"Ye must cease, wee Anwen," Lord Colin said, resting his cheek against her temple. "*We* must cease, or I'll have to cast myself into yonder water for the sake of my sanity."

"I'm a good swimmer," Anwen said, peering up at him. "I'd fish you out." She contemplated dragging a sopping Lord Colin from the Serpentine, his clothes plastered to his body....

He kissed her cheek. "Such a look you're giving me. If ye'd slap me, I'd take it as a mercy."

"I'd rather kiss you again." And again and again and again. Anwen's enthusiasm for that undertaking roared through her like a wild fire, bringing light, heat, and energy to every corner of her being.

"You are a bonfire in disguise," he said, smoothing a hand over her hair. "An ambush of a woman, and you have all of polite society thinking you're the quiet one." He studied her, his hair sticking up on one side. "Am I the only man who knows better, Anwen?"

She smoothed his hair down, delighting in its texture. Red hair had a mind of its own, and by the dawn's light, his hair was very red.

"No, you are not the only one who knows better," she

replied, which had him looking off across the water, his gaze determined.

"I'm no' the dallyin' kind," he said, taking Anwen's hand and kissing it. "I was a soldier, and I'm fond of the ladies, but this is... you mustn't toy with me."

Everlasting celestial trumpets. "You think I could *toy* with you?"

"When you smile like that, you could break hearts, Miss Anwen Windham. A man wouldn't see it coming, but then you'd swan off in a cloud of grace and dignity, and too late, he'd realize what he'd missed. He wouldn't want to admit how foolish he'd been, but in his heart, he'd know: I should ne'er have let her get away. I should have done anything to stay by her side."

I am a bonfire in disguise. "You are not the only one who knows my secret. *I* know better now too, Colin." She went up on her toes and kissed him. "It's our secret."

A great sigh went out of him, and for a moment they remained in each other's arms.

This embrace was lovely too, but different. Desire simmered through Anwen, along with glee, wonder, and not a little surprise—she was a *bonfire*—but also gratitude. Her disguise had fooled her entire family, and even begun to fool her, but Lord Colin had seen through all the manners and decorum to the flame burning at her center.

"I'll guard your secret," Colin said, "but if we don't get back on our horses in the next five minutes, I'll be guarding your secret as the late, lamented Lord Colin. Your cousins have a reputation for protectiveness."

Anwen stepped back and plucked her millinery from the branch above. "We were looking for my hat, which was blown into the hedge as I galloped past." Along with her wits, her heart, and her worries.

Most of her worries.

"Just so." Lord Colin took her hat and led her past the bench and back to the bridle path. "Hat hunting, a venerable tradition among the smitten of an early morning in Hyde Park. That excuse will surely spare my life."

By the time Rosecroft trotted up on a handsome bay, Anwen was back in the saddle, her skirts decorously arranged over her boots, her fascinator once again pinned to her hair. The grooms trundled along at the acceptable distance, and the first carriage had rolled by, the Duchess of Quimbey at the reins.

"Anwen," Rosecroft said. "My apologies for losing track of the time. Denmark here was going a bit stiff to the right, so a few gymnastics were in order. Lord Colin, good morning."

"My lord," Colin said, bowing slightly from the saddle. "That's a beautiful beast you have, and it's a glorious day for enjoying nature's splendors, isn't it?"

Rosecroft's mother had been Irish, and when he wasn't being an overbearing big brother and meddlesome cousin, he claimed a portion of Gaelic charm. His smile was crooked, his pat on the horse's shoulders genuinely affectionate.

"I'd rather be admiring nature's splendor back up in the West Riding," he said, "but I can report to my superior officers that today's outing was in every way a success."

He turned his smile on Lord Colin, who smiled right back.

Anwen had been raised with four male cousins in addition to Rosecroft, and grasped that some sort of masculine communication was in progress, though a commotion closer to Park Lane caught her eye.

"Somebody's in trouble," Rosecroft said as a boy shot across the green at a dead run.

"Somebody's mighty fleet of foot," Lord Colin observed as a corpulent man pursued the boy, shouting words snatched away on the morning breeze.

"Somebody's chasing my Johnnie," Anwen retorted, driving her heel into her mare's side and taking off at a gallop.

Chapter Six

"BUT WHY, JOHN?" TOM asked, for the third time.

They were all back in the detention room, because Dickie had failed to appear for breakfast before grace had begun. Dickie said in front of all the little ones that he'd been in the jakes, waiting for Nature to pay a call.

Hitchings had delivered him a proper smack for that, though Dickie had spoken the God's honest truth. Even the bowels seized when a boy sat for too long, day after day.

John had barely made the breakfast bell. His knees had been grass stained and his palms smeared with dirt, but Hitchings had been too busy ringing a peal over Dickie's head to notice that John had been taking the air again.

"Why, if you have to roam, did you nick some half-drunk nob's purse?" Tom pressed.

"Nick 'em when they can barely stand," Dickie said. "Didn't our da teach you anything? When the nobs are wandering home at dawn, after they've been at the cards, the drink, and the whores all night. Never an easier time to lift a purse than at daybreak, unless you choose the wrong cull."

John sat, back braced against the wall beneath the window. Joe, who'd said nothing thus far, had his nose in a French dictionary somebody had forgotten from a previous incarceration.

Or maybe Joe had left it here on purpose, because he was that canny.

"I go crazy here," John said. "It's spring. Winter's over, the air is clear for a change, and outside, I can breathe."

Tom knew all too well what he meant. Being cooped up like laying hens all night was bad enough, but then the sun came up, the birds sang, and a boy felt the urge to move, to ramble, to see what was afoot at the docks, maybe set a snare for an unsuspecting rabbit in the park...

Life was meant to be more than grammar, sermons, and birchings.

Tom leapt up to catch the top edge of the enormous empty wardrobe in the corner of the room and swung himself atop it. The high vantage points helped with the restlessness, though nothing made it go away entirely.

"Orangutan," Joe said, without looking up from his dictionary.

He got a laugh for that observation.

"Tom likes to climb things," Dickie said. "John likes to steal the occasional purse from them as can afford it."

"Robin Hood's going to end up in Newgate." Tom rolled to his back and studied the stain spreading from a corner of the ceiling. The mark was old, suggesting somebody had long ago patched the leak causing it. The shape put him in mind of Hitchings's fat arse.

"I ditched the purse," John said. "I won't be taken up,

because Miss Anwen was ready to tear a strip off the cull for calling me a guttersnipe."

"Ooooh, a guttersnipe!" Dickie smacked his forehead and pretended to stagger against the table. "Our darlin' young Johnnie, a guttersnipe!"

John ignored his brother's humor. "If you'd seen Miss Anwen with that sidesaddle whip, you'd not be making sport of her. Cull shut his gob and started bowing on the spot. Miss Anwen's flash gent were with her, and some other cove who looked like the god with the hammer."

"Thor," Joe said, turning a page.

"Not him, the blacksmith one," John went on. "Miss Anwen came galloping across the grass, dirt clods flying out behind her horse, the two gents bringing up the rear. She put her mare between me and the cull, and I have never been so glad to see that woman in all my life."

They were all, always glad to see Miss Anwen.

"Then what?" Dickie asked.

"Then her flash gent flipped the cull a sovereign. The cull winked at me, bowed to the lady, and charged off as if he'd landed a whole pot o' gold."

"He nearly did." Most of Tom's acquaintances would go their whole lives without holding one of the recently minted sovereigns.

"How'd you get back here?" Dickie asked.

Joe stopped turning pages and aimed a look at John, just as John might have launched into what Miss Anwen called an embellishment on the truth.

"The flash gent brought me back."

"Miss Anwen wouldn't even talk to you," Tom guessed. "D'you think she'll tell Hitchings?"

John drew his knees up and hung his head. "She looked like she wanted to cry. She told Lord Colin—that's the red-haired gent with the smart phaeton—to get me back here as soon as may be, before my adventure became common knowledge."

"Your adventure was stupid," Tom said. "You can be hung for stealing, or transported, and that's assuming enough of you survives a couple of weeks in Newgate. Newgate is no place for a pretty boy, John Wellington."

The horrors awaiting such a boy were easy enough to imagine, not so easy to endure. Tom was fairly certain Joe could describe them firsthand, and Tom had had a few narrow escapes himself.

"This place is making us soft," John said, raising his chin. "The cull knew I'd nicked his purse only because I've lost my touch. I was clumsy, and he wasn't as drunk or tired as I'd thought. Stupid and clumsy, I was, because of this place."

Tom waited for Dickie to chime in, because brothers were loyal and talk cost nothing. Tom was tempted to sing out the usual chorus of frustrations and indignities that went along with life at the House of Urchins too, but Joe's steady stare stopped him.

If John was a clumsy, stupid thief, that was nobody's fault but his own.

"Miss Anwen deserves your thanks," Tom said. "So do the gents who were with her. We get locked in detention together, but you'd go to jail—or Van Diemen's Land— alone. I'd hate that."

"You're going soft," John shot back. "I can't wait for this place to close, so I can have my freedom back. Dickie and me will—"

Joe rose and opened the window. He bowed and gestured to John, then crossed his arms.

Freedom awaits.

John was on his feet, nose to chin with Joe. "I can't just up and leave. I promised Lord Colin I'd not pike off again until he and I had a talk. That's all he said. *No more larks for you until you and I talk, young man.* I gave my word and I don't go back on my word."

Joe appeared to consider this, then offered a come-get-me-little-man gesture, and tousled John's hair. John knocked his hand aside, and Dickie leapt up onto the table, which would give the combatants room to air their differences. John had just spit in his palms and put up his fives when the door swung open.

The flash gent stood there, looking like the thunderbolt god with red hair.

"Gentlemen, using the term loosely, good day. Come with me."

Joe shot a longing glance toward his dictionary, but Dickie was already off the table, and John had pulled the window closed—but not locked it.

"You too," the gent said, aiming a glance at Tom's perch atop the wardrobe. "There will be some changes around here, starting now, and you will either learn to accommodate them, or leave so another boy wise enough to take advantage of his good fortune can have your place."

Like it or lump it, as near as Tom could translate. This fellow sounded like MacDeever, but sharper, more dangerous. Tom leapt down from the wardrobe and fell in behind Joe as his lordship took off down the corridor.

"Master John and I have an errand to see to later today," Lord Colin said. "I happened to find a gentleman's purse in the undergrowth at the park, and I require John's assistance to return it to its rightful owner. Before he and I can undertake that task, you will assist Mr. MacDeever to clean the mews. I expect to hear nothing but good cheer and excellent manners from you all for the duration."

Lord Colin drew up at the back door. "Do I make myself clear?"

"Yes, sir," Dickie said, though he'd smirked, the stupid git.

Lord Colin smoothed a hand gently over Dickie's hair, but Dickie had ducked—too slowly. The blow would have landed had the gent been in a smacking mood, and his lordship's point had been made.

"Do I make myself clear, gentlemen?"

"Yes, sir," John said, elbowing his brother.

"Yes, sir," Tom echoed.

Joe nodded and pulled his forelock.

"Joey don't talk much," Tom said, lest his lordship get to using his fists on poor Joe.

Lord Colin peered down a whacking great nose at Joe. "I admire a man who can keep his peace. You'll be in charge for the morning, Joseph."

Joe stood taller, though how he would be in charge when he couldn't give orders was a mystery.

"In charge of what, sir?" Tom asked.

"In charge of what recruits do best, which is shovel shite, of course. I'm ashamed to stable my horse in yonder mews, lads, and a gentleman always takes good care of his cattle. Do you agree?"

Many a gentleman couldn't afford a donkey, much less a horse, but that didn't seem to matter at the moment.

"Yes, sir," Tom said, as Dickie and Johnnie muttered their assents.

"Then you will all do your bit as gentlemen of the House of Urchins, and take up pitchforks and shovels until that stable is the cleanest in the neighborhood."

Tom knew nothing about tidying up a stable, but he

knew he'd rather muck out stalls, get dirty, and take orders from Joe than spend another minute in the detention room. Trying to keep peace, preventing John from going to jail, and dealing with his own temptations was doomed to failure when the drainpipe sang its siren song.

Because John had a point. Winter was behind them, the streets were full of culls, and Latin conjugations had never kept a boy fed, clothed, or safe.

* * *

The British army worked surprisingly well, given that its officers were mostly drawn from the ranks of those with means. Means, however, generally resulted in an education that included some military history, and in social rank sufficient that ordering subordinates about was a part of everyday life. Means also—Colin accorded this quality the greatest weight—should have resulted in a sense of responsibility, such as an officer bore toward his men, his superiors, and the noncombatants affected by the hostilities.

Somebody had to take Anwen's boys in hand or the orphanage was sure to fail. The wealthy would open their purses to support a worthy charity, but a charity that produced no results, or worse, became tainted with scandal, would collapse overnight.

A boy transported for theft was scandal enough to bring the whole institution down. More to the point, Anwen would never recover from the child's disgrace and would hold herself accountable.

"You take the muck wagon," Colin said, gesturing to the mute boy, because he was the largest. "You two take up the pitchforks," he said to the next largest two. "And you," he said to the smallest. "Your first job is to dump, scrub, and refill all the water buckets, then pitch each horse another two forkfuls of hay, and the pony one forkful. When that's done, you join the mucking out. Questions?"

Mucking a stall efficiently was an art—start in the back corners, never dig too deeply into the straw on any one pass—but that wasn't the point of the exercise. The point was to exhaust the boys, give them a chance to work together, and get them outside doing something useful.

"Will we get lunch?" John asked. He was the clever one of the bunch—if the initiative to snatch a man's purse was clever—but also impetuous, would be Colin's guess.

"We didn't get breakfast," Tom added. "Hitchings sent us to detention instead." Wee Tom was nimble as a goat, and Colin pegged him for the regimental aide-de-camp, the fellow who was always thinking things through, anticipating problems, and weighing options. He'd be brave, but he'd tend to worry.

"You will have lunch," Colin told the boys, "but you'll have to eat it in the garden. Cleaning a stable is miserably dirty work, and Cook would have an apoplexy if you tramped through her kitchen in all your dirt."

Then too, Hitchings might spot the boys and devise some way to ruin their day out of doors. The dark-haired lad, Dickie, would be outraged at an order countermanded before a task was complete. Colin had shared the same affliction for his first two years in the army.

Mention of eating in the garden had Tom studying his boots, though the boy was grinning.

"Sandwiches and ale will have to do," Colin said, improvising. "No hot soup for you today. Can't be helped. I'll be back this afternoon, and this stable had better be spotless."

Colin stifled the urge to salute the lads lined up with their pitchforks. By sundown, they'd have blisters on their blisters. Their backs would ache as if burned, and one or two might have a smashed toe, courtesy of the orphanage's aging team and cantankerous pony.

But they'd sleep soundly tonight, and they'd sleep in their own damned beds until the sun came up.

More to the point, Anwen would sleep well too.

Colin left orders in the kitchen that the boys were to be fed, and fed well, in the garden at midday. The next stop was Winthrop Montague's bedroom, where Win was lounging about in slippers and a blue silk robe.

"Shall we start the day with coffee?" Win asked, tugging a bell pull. "My evening ran rather late."

Not at the musicale, it hadn't. "You were enjoying the company at Mrs. Bellingham's?"

Win yawned and scratched his pale chest. "One takes consolation where one can find it."

Or afford it? The room was handsomely appointed, with blue velvet hangings swathing an enormous white bed, and gold-flocked wallpaper highlighting blue and cream appointments. The windows, mirrors, lamps, and candlesticks gleamed, the carpet was more blue and cream softness beneath Colin's boots. Win's robe became the moving center of the decorative scheme.

The whole impression—wealth, grace, and elegance without limit—made Colin want to climb out a window. He propped himself against a bedpost rather than sit and risk getting a stray horse hair on the upholstery.

"If you're in love with Mrs. Bellingham, then doesn't seeking your consolations under her very nose present something of a contradiction?"

"I'm flaunting my wares, making her jealous," Win said,

running a hand through blond hair and examining his teeth in the vanity mirror. "I'm not sure it's working, but my mood benefits nonetheless, despite the cost to my exchequer."

Win's wares were soon entirely on display. Part of a gentleman's morning might well be spent watching another fellow dress. To lounge about half-naked, swilling chocolate and coffee, being shaved and washed by a valet, could all become a social encounter for a young man and his closest friends.

The very same friends he'd probably spent the evening with, ridden in the park with, and met at entertainments—genteel and otherwise—available during the season.

Win's valet had come along to shave him, brush his hair, and tie his neckcloth before Colin asked the question that had been plaguing him for three straight hours.

"Have you ever kissed a woman and meant it, Win?"

Win was experimenting with various angles to his top hat, admiring himself in a cheval mirror.

"Kissing is quite personal," he said, tipping his hat up an inch. "I tend to avoid it, though on occasion, I make exceptions. I've kissed Mrs. Bellingham's hand, for example. Truly kissed her hand, like the daring rogue I wish she'd take me for. What do you think, left or right?"

For pity's sake. "Right," Colin said. "Bit more dashing. Everybody's hat slouches off to the left, because most fellows are right-handed."

"Good point. I tend not to do much kissing unless I'm drunk. Have you been kissing somebody I should know about?"

"A gentleman doesn't kiss and tell." Colin had known that before he'd turned twelve years old.

"No matter, Rosalyn tells me everything, even when I wish she wouldn't. You're brother to a duke, so I'm sure your liberties will be well tolerated, just don't— Why are we expected to wear both rings and gloves? That has never made any sense to me." Win tossed a ring from his smallest finger onto a tray on his vanity.

"I haven't been kissing your sister." Hadn't even speculated about kissing Lady Rosalyn.

"Of course you haven't, and that you're willing to involve yourself in the same pointless charity she supports is purely a coincidence. Is the boutonniere too much?"

Win's ensemble was a blue tailcoat, cream breeches, blindingly white linen, and a sapphire cravat pin. The proffered boutonniere was white rosebuds.

"It's not enough," Colin said. "Pink would be more interesting, or violet, or even red."

Red was a very fine color. Memories of Anwen Windham's rosy lips and her brilliant hair sent Colin into Win's dressing closet, where he could examine the soles of his boots for dirt and grass.

The air in the dressing closet was heavy with lavender and bootblack. The only furniture was a cot upon which Win's valet presumably dozed while waiting for Win to return from his evening revels. The cot had been made up, so rather than take a seat, Colin inspected his soles as best he could standing.

He used a handkerchief to wipe a smudge from the right boot. "How many suits do you own, Winthrop?"

"Haven't a clue. You really think pink would add the right dash to this outfit? Cranston might be offended, though I suspect you're right."

Cranston being the valet.

"The ladies notice us when we take a little extra effort

over our appearance," Colin said, wondering if his hair needed a trim. Anwen had seemed to like mussing his hair.

"Have you given any more thought to taking my place at the House of Urchins?" Win called from the bedroom. "Or at least sitting in on a few meetings?"

Colin tucked his dirty handkerchief away and left the dressing closet, which had been as cramped and utilitarian as the bedroom was spacious and opulent.

"At some point, I must return to Scotland," Colin said. "But until then, I will take a hand in the goings-on at the orphanage. Where are you off to?"

"The tailor's," Win said, shooting his cuffs. "You'll come with me, I trust? I'm being fitted for a new pair of riding breeches. We'll send out for some viands and port, round up Pointy and a few others, make a day of it?"

All of this sartorial splendor was to impress the tailor? Or perhaps to impress Mrs. Bellingham, should she chance to drive down Bond Street.

"I can't join you today," Colin said. "I'm behind on my correspondence, and the rest of the week will be busy."

Win pitched his pretty white boutonniere into the ash bin. "You're bored, aren't you? You mentioned something about that. Sorry to impose the House of Urchins on you when you're already dying of ennui. I don't think the place will last much longer."

Not if one of the boys was convicted as a cutpurse. "Why do you say that?"

"Coin of the realm is in short supply according to Hitchings, which is no secret, but then, we're housing a dozen little pickpockets and housebreakers." Win drew on a pair of pristine gloves. "How long would you expect a business to remain viable, with a nest of juvenile criminals dwelling on the premises?"

This same thinking labeled every Irishman a drunk, and every Scot a brawler—and inspired the drinking and brawling too.

"They're children, Montague, most of them barely breeched. You're supposed to assist them to find the right path in life, not consign them to the hulks as a result of unfortunate birth."

Win led the way from his apartment, down a carpeted hallway to the ornate front stairway that opened onto the oak paneled foyer.

"You think me coldhearted, I know," he said, accepting his walking stick from a silent butler. "And I admit their years are tender, and they aren't entirely to blame, but the older boys drive Hitchings to distraction. They're dull-witted, and they seem to spend as much time in detention as they do at their studies."

Which reflected unfavorably on Hitchings, in Colin's estimation. "When you were given detention, how did you spend it?"

Win's smile was naughty. "If I was alone, I indulged in the sin of Onan, of course, and sometimes if I wasn't alone. You never got detention, I'm guessing."

All the bloody time. "Detention has its place, but so do fresh air, hard work, and rewards for jobs well done. Enjoy your day at the tailor."

"I shall, and you see to your correspondence. You can't spend every waking moment writing letters, you know. Rosalyn likes some liveliness in a fellow, not that you'd be interested in her likes or dislikes."

Win winked and strode off in the direction of Bond Street, while Colin retrieved Prince Charlie from the mews.

"I'm not interested in Lady Rosalyn's likes or dislikes,"

he informed his horse as they trotted on their way. "I'm interested in Miss Anwen."

Actually, that wasn't quite true. Colin was *taken* with her, and part of his interest in her charity was because it was important to her. Then too, he thrived on a challenge, and what could be more challenging than putting an institution on sound financial footing when, as Winthrop Montague had pointed out, a dozen potential thieves dwelled on the very premises?

* * *

"The two of you are peeved with me," Anwen said. "I'm sorry, but I had business to conduct with Lord Colin relating to the orphanage. A ride in the park seemed the best way to do that."

Anwen *wasn't* sorry, not truly. She'd had a lovely outing, and her older sisters would have ruined it.

Charlotte, who cared little for fashion, turned a page of the latest copy of *La Belle Assemblée*.

"So you weren't actually *riding* in the park?"

For the first time in years, Anwen had galloped *madly*. "I was on my mare, but for the most part, I was discussing the orphanage with Lord Colin. Rosecroft was nearby at all times, though he focused more on his horse than on the discussion." Nearby being a relative term, of course.

"Lord Colin is family, more or less," Elizabeth said, adding a line to a sketch of the parlor cat, a lithe gray tabby by the name of Bluebell. "You wouldn't need an escort to amble down a bridle path or two with him, but why take the air at all? You could have his lordship over to tea or luncheon. If you grew fatigued, we could send him on his way and he'd have to understand."

Anwen was very fatigued of her sister's protectiveness. She took a pile of blue spun wool from her workbasket and began winding it into a ball. Colin's eyes were a deeper blue than the yarn, but this color would look very nice on him.

"Has it occurred to either of you," Anwen said, "that you have required the services of a physician more often than I have in recent years?"

"You needn't thank us for taking such good care of you," Charlotte said, peering over the top of her magazine. "You're our baby sister, and we'd do anything for you."

Except leave me alone. The truth was, if Anwen caught a sniffle or a cold, she hid the symptoms as best she could and soldiered on, lest she be put to bed for six weeks, her hair cut short, and her feet wrapped in noxious plasters by the hour.

Bluebell rose from her hassock and padded along the sofa to bat gently at Anwen's yarn.

"Blue says you should leave your workbasket and have a lie down," Elizabeth said. "It's not every day you get up at the crack of doom to risk the damp and fog in the park."

Anwen mentally tossed the ball of yarn at her sister's sketch pad. "The sunrise was beautiful, and Lord Colin has agreed to take an interest in the House of Urchins. I consider the outing, in every way, to have been a success and well worth my time."

"I'm glad to hear that." Lord Colin stood in the parlor doorway, still in his riding attire. He was early for a morning call—it was barely past luncheon—but Anwen could not have been happier to see him.

"Your lordship, welcome," she said, when he'd offered bows to each sister. "Please join us."

"Did nobody offer to announce you?" Elizabeth asked, setting her sketch aside.

"Your butler offered, and I declined. No need to stand on ceremony, as I'm only here for a moment. Miss Anwen, I thought you'd like to know that Master John and I paid a call on a certain unfortunate gentleman who'd lost a personal item in the park earlier today. I chanced upon that item after we parted this morning."

"Anwen, *what unfortunate gentleman*?" Charlotte demanded. "You *said* you and Lord Colin merely chatted about charitable business."

"Miss Anwen and I had a very pleasant encounter," Lord Colin replied. "We came upon this fellow in passing. I've been thinking, though, about the House of Urchins, and I wonder if Miss Anwen will spare me a turn about the garden while I share my ideas with her?"

That the gentleman's purse had been found was bad news, because it suggested John had stolen the purse and tossed it aside to be retrieved later. That Lord Colin considered the morning's encounter *very pleasant* nearly caused Anwen to leap from the sofa and dance a hornpipe.

"The garden is a fine idea," she murmured, rising.

"I'll get your bonnet," Charlotte said.

"You'll need a shawl," Elizabeth added.

They flung curtsies at Lord Colin and were gone in the next instant.

"Please be honest," Anwen said. "John stole that man's purse, didn't he?"

"Yes, John stole that man's purse," Colin replied, taking Anwen by the hand, "and I'm stealing you. Where can we go that we'll have peace and quiet?"

He wanted privacy with her, thank the celestial choirs. "The conservatory. It's the last place they look for me, because of the damp."

Colin's grasp of her wrist was warm and firm, and for a

moment, Anwen simply beheld him. Lord Colin MacHugh was *calling on her*.

Then he was kissing her, the worst, most unsatisfying little press of his lips to hers, before he led her from the parlor.

"I ought not to have done that," he said as they hurried off in the direction of the conservatory. "I apologize. Anybody could have come by, bearing a tea tray, a bonnet, a lecture. Your reputation is precious to me. I want you to know that."

Riding out early had tired Anwen, and she'd ache in inconvenient places tomorrow, but she'd be damned if she'd ask Lord Colin to slow down.

"I'm more concerned about John than about my reputation," she said as they turned down the corridor leading to the conservatory. "Theft is a very serious matter."

"Theft is a stupid matter," Colin retorted. "The boy has no need to steal. He's fed, clothed, housed, and being educated, after a fashion. He wasn't stealing out of necessity."

Colin held the conservatory door, and Anwen crossed the threshold into warmth, shadows, and the rich scent of earth and greenery. Would she forever associate that scent with being kissed?

She likely would, because as soon as Lord Colin closed the door, Anwen wrapped her arms around him, sank her fingers into his hair, and recommenced kissing him. He smiled against her mouth, settled his arms around her, and joined in the kiss.

His kissing included *tactics*. He got Anwen interested in the stroke of his tongue over her lips, until she realized his hand was sliding down ever closer to her bum. Anwen tried the same caress, finding the terrain wonderfully muscular. There was so much of Colin to explore, so many textures and contours, and yet she was worried about John too.

She broke off the kiss and remained in Colin's embrace. "I like kissing you."

"I rejoice to hear it, madam, though I long for the day when you love kissing me."

"Do you love kissing me?"

His blue eyes held not a hint of teasing. "I do, Anwen. I hadn't foreseen this, it's not convenient, when I must leave for Scotland at the end of the season. I'm sure you could have more impressive beaus by the dozen, but you have...I feel..."

He smelled faintly of leather and horse, good smells, but his expression was not that of a man who'd just shared a lovely kiss.

Anwen brushed her fingers over his hair. "Yes?"

"I *feel*," he said. "I'm not used to having sentiments of any significance where kisses are concerned. Shall we leave it at that?"

No, we shall not. "You typically kiss women for whom you feel nothing?"

"I typically kiss women for whom I feel desire, passing affection, and mild liking, and hope they feel the same for me. I do not accost decent young ladies beneath the maples, and then look forward to accosting that same young lady again within hours."

Anwen drew away, the better to conceal an odd pleasure. Lord Colin could be flirtatious, unlike his older brother who was serious to a fault. Colin was charming and had a light, friendly manner socially.

His expression was neither light nor friendly, because Anwen had kissed him. *I am a bonfire, and Colin MacHugh is not the will-o'-the-wisp he wants society to think he is.*

She kissed him again, a solid smack. "Tell me about John."

He touched his fingers to his mouth, as if to make sure his lips were still affixed to his countenance.

"John took terrible risks. I expect all of the older boys go for the occasional stroll without supervision, but John spotted a potential mark, pursued him with malice afore-thought, stole the gentleman's purse, then fled with the contraband. That's about eight felonies, and the victim—exhausted, portly, and half-seas over, would likely have tired of the chase if we hadn't come along."

Anwen paced away, lest she spend the next thirty min-utes staring at Lord Colin's mouth, when she ought to be considering how to deflect young John from the path of ruin.

"The boys are bored," she said, "and John is their leader in mischief. If he had made off with that purse, he would have crowed about it to the others. The next time, Dickie would have gone with him."

"There can't be a next time," Colin said, remaining by the door. "If word gets out that the House of Urchins is not only pockets to let, but harboring cutpurses and thieves, you won't raise a single groat from your wealthy friends."

"It's worse than that," Anwen said, though what could be worse than consigning a dozen boys to prison? "I've involved my family in the effort to raise funds, and any stain on the reputation of the House of Urchins will reflect on my family's consequence. If I bungle this, they'll never again let me involve myself in a similar project and they won't involve themselves either."

And that she could not allow. The boys mattered, and having something to do besides waltz, embroider, swill tea, and rest her feet mattered too.

Colin propped a hip on a potting table, palm fronds and a lemon tree framing him with greenery.

"I gather one of the four oldest boys tarried too long before breakfast this morning, and all four were sent to detention. I set them to cleaning the stable, and they did a creditable job. My objective is to tire them sufficiently that they haven't the energy to wander, and to give them a job they can take pride in."

"I would never have thought to do that," Anwen replied, "and yet, it's perfect. The stable is a disgrace. MacDeever has too much work to do, and Hitchings seems oblivious to anything but the scholarly curriculum. You have younger brothers, is that how you knew what to do?"

"I was a captain, a lowly enough officer that I had to actually supervise my men. They were mostly humble young fellows more interested in getting up to mischief than routing the French."

Anwen knew how that felt—to be interested in getting up to mischief—thanks to Lord Colin. She scooted onto the potting table six inches from where he stood.

"So you started the boys off with cleaning the stable, a punishment that's in fact a relief from their miseries. What else do you have in mind, and how soon can we meet with Hitchings to explain that his approach requires modification?"

Lord Colin leaned closer. "*We* are meeting with Hitchings?"

"The ladies' committee should be represented, in the event there's some capacity in which we could be of aid. If John's stealing purses, the situation is dire, and no resource should be spared to put it to rights."

"The situation is dire," Lord Colin muttered. "Very well, join us at the meeting. I suspect I'll have an easier time talking old Hitchings around if we bring Winthrop Montague along and the chairman of the board as well."

"Excellent suggestions," Anwen said, hopping off the table. "Now I suggest we do repair to the garden."

Lord Colin crossed his arms. "Because?"

"Because Charlotte and Elizabeth will be finished searching for us there, and we can continue this discussion without their helpful interference. I'd as soon keep the conservatory as my hiding place of last resort for as long as possible."

She was out the French doors in the next instant, Lord Colin following with gratifying alacrity.

Chapter Seven

"YOU'VE APPARENTLY ENJOYED THE longest ride in the park in the history of Hyde Park," Lady Rhona MacHugh said.

Colin stopped at the foot of the garden steps. "And a fine day to you too, sister."

"Don't start acting like a brother." Edana used her foot to push out a chair at the table they occupied beneath a stately oak. "We worry about you."

They made a pretty picture on a pretty afternoon, two lovely redheads at their leisure in the MacHugh back garden. But then, Colin had kissed Anwen Windham farewell not an hour past. He'd be in a sunny mood even if rain were coming down in torrents and a foul miasma had wafted in off the river.

He took the proffered seat. "What have you two been up to while you were so worried about me?"

"We got a letter from Hamish." Rhona passed over a

single folded sheet of paper. "Married life agrees with him."

The letter had been addressed to Colin. "Reading my mail, are you?"

"It was from Hamish," Edana said, filling a teacup for Colin. "If there was trouble, we'd want to know." She added milk and sugar, gave it a stir, put four biscuits on the saucer, and passed it over.

"If there was trouble, you two would be in the thick of it. My day got away from me."

"We called on Cousin Dougal," Rhona said, arranging three sandwiches on a plate and setting it beside Colin's teacup. "He and Patience are in anticipation of a blessed event. As laird, you should settle a sum on the child."

The tea was strong and hot, the biscuits buttery and sweet. Colin would get to the sandwiches.

"Ham's the laird." Hamish was also the duke, poor sod. Now that he'd snabbled Megan Windham for a duchess, the duke part doubtless rested more lightly on his broad shoulders.

"The clan counsel met," Edana said, waving at Hamish's letter. "They decided that because Ham's the duke, you should take up the responsibilities of laird, at least until Hamish gets his dukedom sorted out."

Meaning, until a ducal heir or three was on the way.

"I'm the laird now?" Colin considered the third sweet. "I'll have a wee word with Hamish over this nonsense. It's a dirty damned trick to play on me, when I'm stuck here in London and can't speak for myself at the counsel. They want free whisky at their gatherings. Excellent, free, *legal* whisky."

Though Colin was pleased. Being laird these days was

mostly a matter of attending weddings and christenings, presiding at games, and settling squabbles.

"It was my idea," Rhona said. "Hamish has enough to do, learning to be the duke. You're next in line, and if you didn't take the job, I might have been stuck with it."

"You might still be," Colin said, demolishing the last biscuit. "I've better things to do than listen to the women argue over which red dye to use in the hunting plaid."

Edana kicked him under the table—an affectionate blow, from her. "We got Hamish married off. Behave yourself or you're next."

A fly had the temerity to buzz near Colin's sandwiches. Edana flicked her serviette, and the insect was either killed in mid-flight or inspired to disappear into thin air.

"*You* got Hamish married off?" Colin countered, starting on the sandwiches. Chicken with a dash of French mustard, his favorite. "To hear the Windhams tell it, a certain English duke was involved, along with a bloody lot of meddling cousins."

Good fellows, those cousins. One of them had escorted Anwen in the park that morning—more or less.

"Who dragged Hamish the length of the Great North Road?" Rhona asked. "Who endured his muttering and pouting the whole way? Who argued with him for the duration of a Highland winter to take us to London? Who made him bring his formal kilts, in which he looks so very fine despite being the shyest man ever to call Perthshire his home?"

"In which he looks verra fine," Colin mimicked, "despite bein' the shyest mon ever to call Pairthsher his hame? You get very Scottish when you're on your dignity, Ronnie mine, and in answer to your questions, *I did*. Hamish and I nearly came to blows several times."

Rhona smiled, snatched Colin's sandwich, took a bite, then set it back on his plate. "I am verra Scottish, and that's Lady Ronnie to you, laddie. *We* got Hamish married off. Our work here is done, unless you've a notion to stick your dainty foot in parson's mousetrap."

"Now you sound daft and English," Colin said, picking up a locket sitting by Rhona's plate. A cameo brooch was suspended on a gold chain, and the links had become knotted up. "It's you two who should be looking over the eligibles."

"We have," Edana said, "and they're more eligible than interesting. Don't break that locket, please. Your friend Mr. Montague isn't a bad sort."

Colin considered Edana's casual tone, considered her absorption with the top of the garden wall thirty yards away. He also considered the knotted-up chain, lest she kick him for simply looking at her. The gold was delicate, but the locket was unwearable in its present condition.

Damn Hamish for running back home with his duchess. He was the eldest, the brother who ought to deal in awkward truths.

"You could do worse than attach Win Montague's interest," Colin said, rolling the knotted links gently between his fingers. One did not describe one's best friend as a lazy tomcat, and yet what did Win do but make wagers, lay about at the tailor's, pine for Mrs. Bellingham, and swill spirits at his clubs?

"I suppose he has a ladybird," Edana muttered. "English gentlemen do, before they take a wife. I know that."

And in pragmatic Scottish fashion, she was prepared to accept reality. "Eddie, Win hasn't one special ladybird," Colin said. "I can't see that he has much of anything to support a wife with either."

The chain was loosening, as chains often did when patience, light pressure, and warmth were applied.

Edana snapped her serviette at another pesky fly. "I have funds of my own."

Ronnie was taking half the day to consume the remains of Colin's sandwich. No help there.

"Those are *your* funds." Colin unclasped the necklace so he could more easily untangle it. "That money is for you, and for your daughters should their father die before making provision for them." Not for supporting the lazy younger son of an English lord.

"I have to marry somebody," Edana retorted, balling up her serviette and pitching it at Colin's face. "If I don't marry, I'll turn into Auntie Eddie, the old lady all the braw half-drunk lads stand up with at the *ceilidh* when they lose a bet. Some toothless crofter will offer for me when I'm too old to have children, and I'll accept him just to get away from the pity of my siblings."

"Eddie," Rhona said, holding out a biscuit. "Cease your dramatics. Colin will take us home, and we can be done with this London nonsense. One brother's a duke, the other's a laird, we've our own funds. We'll not want for dances."

Edana slapped the biscuit from her sister's hand and dashed into the house.

Colin eased the knot from the golden chain and finished his tea—cold now. Crumbs littered the paving stones as a result of Edana's tantrum.

He passed the necklace over to Ronnie. "Is Eddie that taken with Win Montague?"

"She fancies him. Mr. Montague has been insinuating himself into your good graces, and that means he pays attention to me and Eddie. She fancied that dreadful Sir

Fletcher when she first met him, and next week she'll fancy somebody else. You've saved me a trip to Ludgate Hill both by provoking her temper and by repairing her jewelry."

"Win is being gentlemanly," Colin said. "He's the reason I'm a member of the right clubs, and my custom is accepted at the right establishments. When he stands up with you and Eddie, he's being a friend."

Rhona patted Colin's hand, and abruptly he wanted to send his teacup to the flagstones along with Eddie's biscuit. Was this how Anwen felt when her family cosseted and fussed despite her roaring good health, fierce heart, and active intellect?

"Eddie and I are a pair of hags," Rhona replied, "and Mr. Montague is so kind as to spare us a dance here and there, but when was the last time he bought you a drink?"

He'd bought Colin a drink to celebrate Hamish's succession to the title weeks ago. "The English don't pinch pennies the way we do, Ronnie. They don't keep track."

"Yes, Colin, they do," Rhona said. "They know who has a title, who has money. Who has a title but no money, and who has both. Hamish and you have both, now Eddie and I have both too. Your Mr. Montague isn't stupid."

"He's quite bright." That much Colin could honestly say. "He also takes an interest in the less fortunate."

"You are not the less fortunate, Colin MacHugh, and neither are Eddie and I."

God help the man who thought so. "I meant that Winthrop Montague sits on the board of the House of Urchins, and soon I shall as well."

So that Win could spend more time slobbering over Mrs. Bellingham's hand?

And yet, Win wouldn't know what to do with young

John or his friends. Anwen had listened to Colin's ideas and added a few of her own. Between them, they'd not let John slip away to a life of crime without a fight.

"You're to take up a charity?" Rhona mused. "Isn't that what the church is for?"

"I think it's like being a laird, Ronnie. If you have a title, even a courtesy title, then certain expectations come with it."

"You have sisters. Edana wanted to see a London season, I wanted some new frocks. Now, we want to go home, Colin, and we expect you to escort us."

He couldn't tell them he had more kissing to do, though he hoped he did—a lot more kissing. "Turn tail now, will you? Edana stomps her foot and we all pack up and leave? I think we owe Hamish and Megan a little more of a honeymoon than this, Ronnie. Eddie is thinking only of herself, but when she's staring wedded bliss in the face day after day back home, when she's Auntie Eddie in truth, she'll wish she'd tarried another few weeks in London."

Rhona rose and dusted off her skirts, then dropped the locket into a pocket, where it would doubtless get all tangled up again.

"We're without witnesses," she said, "so I can admit you have a point. Then too, you won't be the one shut up in the coach with Eddie the whole way home. I can put that pleasure off for another few weeks. Mr. Maarten came by while you were flirting in the park, and he asked that you attend him at your earliest convenience."

Colin stood as well. If he was expected to escort his sisters that evening, he needed a damned nap, not another meeting with Maarten.

"How do you know I was flirting?"

Rhona patted his cheek. "You're always flirting. Hamish was the brooder, you are the flirt, though you're a dab hand at fixing jewelry too. Magnus is the hothead, Angus the scholar."

She was right. "What about Alistair?"

"The dreamer. I'm beginning to dream of home, I suspect you are too, Colin. Maarten said he'll be leaving by the first of May."

"Any idea why he came by?"

"He left you a note in the library. Does Win Montague really have no ladybird?"

What did a friend say to a sister? Rhona might be able to talk sense into Edana.

"Montague can't afford a mistress, Ronnie, and he's drawn to a woman who's both beyond his means and beneath his station."

"He's neither eligible nor interesting, then, not in any meaningful sense. Time to widen your circle of friends, Colin, lest Eddie and I grow bored."

The last time Ronnie and Eddie had grown bored, they'd sold Hamish's cigars on the sly to other young ladies.

Colin offered his sister his arm, which had become a habit over the past weeks. "Where are we off to tonight?"

"Lady Pembroke's rout. The talk will be political and artistic. You should be bored witless."

A week ago, even a day ago, Colin would have consoled himself with the knowledge that as a widow, Lady Pembroke would have other widows in attendance. Widows were among the friendliest exponents of polite society to young, single men of good birth and better fortune.

"You're right—I'll be bored witless." Unless Anwen Windham were there.

If she was among the guests, Colin wouldn't be bored at all.

* * *

"We value your scholarly abilities exceedingly, Hitchings," Winthrop Montague said. "But these are not typical English schoolboys, amenable to the values of polite society."

"Blood will tell," Hitchings replied, folding his hands across his paunch. "I can't argue that, though I took this post intending to treat these children the same as if they were the sons of decent families."

Anwen shot a look across the table at Colin, for that was the very problem. The boys had more or less raised themselves. Why say grace three times a day if there's nothing to eat? Why learn Latin when you'd never own a bound book from which to read it?

"You are to be commended for your generosity of spirit," Colin said, "but the oldest boys are reaching a dangerous age. A somewhat more military approach with them might yield faster results. As it happens, I'm familiar with how the army shapes boys into men."

"The lads are running out of time," Hitchings said, "just as we are running out of money."

Lord Derwent, who'd been notably silent throughout the meeting, sat back. "Just so, Hitchings. Out of time and nearly out of money." He was a thin, older man, with a nasal voice that carried even when he spoke quietly. "This is as good a moment as any to inform the assemblage that the press of business requires that at month's end, I must regretfully resign my post. With Lord Colin joining the board, we'll maintain a quorum, if only just. I wish you gentlemen every success with the House of Urchins."

While the men rose and shook Derwent's hand, wishing him well, claiming they understood, and thanking him for his *leadership*, Anwen silently reviewed a litany of Welsh curses. Missing half the meetings and citing rules intended to squeeze legislation out of three hundred drunken members of the House of Commons was not leadership.

"Miss Anwen, thank you for attending on behalf of the ladies' committee," Winthrop Montague said. "Always a pleasure when a pretty face can grace a gathering, no matter how dreary the agenda."

He was the chairman of the board of directors now, else Anwen would have made a comment about a handsome face being an equally pleasant addition to the decorative scheme—despite all the noise gentlemen typically generated.

"Thank you, Mr. Montague. I appreciate the chance to learn more about how the institution is managed. Lord Colin's involvement gives me great hope for our continued success."

Mr. Montague aimed a twinkling smile at her. "You believe housing a budding cutpurse is the path to success?"

Colin appeared at her side, her cloak over his arm.

"I believe," Anwen said, smiling right back, "that when children have been cooped up for months, bored witless, beaten for the smallest lapses, without anyone to love them or remark upon their frequent good behavior, one minor slip is the behavior of a saint."

If she'd kicked Mr. Montague's ankle, he couldn't have looked more surprised.

"A refreshingly optimistic point of view," Colin said. "Somewhere between that outlook and complete despair lies a reasonable way forward, I hope."

Hitchings had ushered Lord Derwent to the door, though the headmaster had clearly overheard Anwen's outburst.

"Madam, I commend your faith in these children," Hitchings said, "truly I do, and no one will be more pleased than I if Lord Colin's attempts prove successful."

Colin wrapped Anwen's hand over his arm, as if he knew she was two heartbeats away from interrupting Hitchings's lecture.

"But," Hitchings went on, "if John's adventure were to be mentioned in the newspapers, eleven other children would find themselves again homeless, friendless, and starving. When you advocate for giving John another chance, for seeing the good in him, remember those other children, and all the children who might someday benefit from this institution if we can overcome the present difficulty. A lark for young Master Wellington could have tragic consequences for many."

He shuffled out, his birch rod for once nowhere to be seen.

"He has a point," Mr. Montague said. "You must admit he has a point."

So do I. "He's had nearly a year to impress upon the boys the opportunity this place can be for them," Anwen said. "Hitchings has tried, I'll grant him that, but his efforts with the older boys have not been successful."

"They haven't entirely failed either," Colin said, holding out her cloak. "And now it's my turn to see if I can inspire the boys to more responsible scholarship. Montague, thanks for attending, and I'll see you here Tuesday next."

Mr. Montague consulted his pocket watch. "What's Tuesday next?"

"The regular board meeting," Anwen said. "And you are now the chair."

Montague snapped his watch closed. "'Fraid that won't do. I have a standing obligation on Tuesday afternoons, and until I can rearrange my schedule, Lord Colin will have to chair the meetings."

Colin shoved Anwen's bonnet at her when she would have reminded Mr. Montague that without him present, they'd not have a quorum, and thus no business could be transacted.

She snatched the bonnet from his lordship. "If you can spare me a few minutes, Lord Colin, I'd like to look in on the boys before I leave."

"I'll be on my way." Mr. Montague sketched a bow and sauntered out the door, gold-handled walking stick propped against his shoulder.

"I can't close the door," Colin said, very softly, "though if you curse quietly, nobody will hear you."

"I can curse in Welsh," Anwen said. "But foul language won't change a thing. That prancing bufflehead can't be bothered to miss a card game for the sake of these children."

"Is bufflehead the worst appellation you can think of?"

"Imbecile, buffoon, dandiprat." She lapsed into Welsh, a fine, expressive language for describing what anatomical impossibilities a man might perform with his infernal consequence.

"I caught most of that," Colin said. "Gaelic and Welsh being kissing cousins. Let's take a look at the ledgers Hitchings left for us in the chairman's office."

Oh, dear. "You can understand Welsh?"

"When you speak it," he said, leading the way down the corridor, "about as well as you can understand my Gaelic, I'm guessing. I'll ask my man of business to take a look at these ledgers when he and I meet this afternoon."

All over again, Anwen was furious. "Won't approving such a review take a resolution by the board, discussion, a motion, a second, half the afternoon wasted debating a commonsense suggestion that will cost the institution not one penny?"

She'd seen the board pull that maneuver any number of times, only to table the motion because somebody was late for an appointment with his bootmaker.

"You raise an interesting point," Colin said, pausing outside the office door. "If the board can't gather a quorum, we can only have informational meetings, and as acting chair, we'll do pretty much what I say we'll do."

"Oh." Anwen's anger evaporated into a pressing need to wrap her arms around Colin and hug him for sheer glee. She lifted the latch and pushed the door open, for the chairman's office would afford them some privacy,

She stopped short on the threshold.

Four boys were gathered about the table, one of them—Dickie—wielding a tool that looked like a chisel with the narrow end flattened.

"That's the strongbox," Anwen said. "John, Dick, Thomas, Joseph, what are you doing with the strongbox?"

Lord Colin snatched the tool from Dickie's hand. "They were breaking into the strongbox, and judging from the wear on these fittings, it's not the first time they've stolen from the very hand that's trying to keep them fed, clothed, housed, and out of jail."

* * *

Esther, Duchess of Moreland liked to go barefoot.

Percival had learned that about his wife before they'd even wed. She also liked to have her feet massaged—no tickling allowed, unless a husband wanted to lose his foot-massaging privileges for at least a fortnight. Why those thoughts should occur to him as he peeked in on his wife at midafternoon, he could not have said.

She looked up from addressing invitations, a niece arranged on either side of her at the library table. Percival silently blew her a kiss rather than disturb her, and drew the door closed.

"Thomas," he said to the footman on duty at the end of the corridor, "please send a tray of bread and cheese to the ladies, and include a bottle of hock with my compliments."

"Of course, Your Grace. Some lemon biscuits too?"

They were Esther's favorites. "Good thought, and a few forget-me-nots if we have any on hand." Esther said they were the same blue as Percival's eyes.

Thomas bowed. "Very good, sir."

A commotion in the foyer below signaled the arrival of the duke's oldest son, Devlin St. Just, Earl of Rosecroft. Percival's view from the floor above meant he could see that his son's dark hair was still thick even at the very top of his head.

Esther worried about the boys going bald when their father had not, and Percival knew better than to make light of her concern, though what did a man's hair have to do with the price of brandy in the bedroom?

"Greetings, my boy!" the duke called, halfway down the stairs. "You are without reinforcements?"

"Bronwyn remained in the mews, petting cats, talking to horses, and getting dirty," Rosecroft said. "I'm sure she'll come inside to polish a bannister or two before my business is concluded."

A duke maintained a decorous household. A grandpapa had all the best bannisters.

"She will pay her compliments to me and to the ladies in the library," Percival said. "You'd think the women were planning to invade France, the way they've gone about preparing for this card party. How is your countess?"

Rosecroft was taller than the duke by perhaps two inches, and whereas Percival's coloring was fair, his first-born was Black Irish to the bone.

"Emmie thrives, despite all challenges."

And because the countess thrived—Rosecroft devoted himself to that very objective—the earl thrived and their children thrived as well.

"The library is occupied by Her Grace and the nieces," Percival said. "Why don't we join Bronwyn in the mews?"

Rosecroft passed his hat, spurs, and riding crop to Hodges, the butler. Not by a flicker of an eyelash did the earl react to the duke's request for privacy.

"We will be called upon to name kittens," Rosecroft observed, "and reminded that kittens and puppies make fine playmates."

"So they do," the duke said. "In fairy tales."

Percival's true motive for choosing the mews was that Rosecroft loved horses the way young grandchildren loved a smooth, curved bannister. The equine was Rosecroft's familiar. When he'd been a shy, tongue-tied boy trying to fit into a bewildering array of brothers and sisters in the ducal household, the horses had given him solace and room to breathe.

Also a place to excel beyond all of his siblings.

"Tell me of your outing in the park with Anwen earlier this week," the duke said as they crossed the garden. "She appeared quite invigorated by her excursion."

"We met Lord Colin, as she'd told me we would. Man knows how to sit a horse."

No higher praise could flow from Rosecroft's lips. "Good to know. What else?"

"His riding stock has some Iberian blood, but I wouldn't be surprised to find Strathclyde draft a generation or two back. Fascinating combination, the hot and the cold, the light and the heavy. The Clyde horse is a magnificent beast, but so are the Andalusian breeds. The result of a cross is a beast that's both—"

"Rosecroft." The result of Anwen's dawn ride was a son trying to prevaricate at a dead gallop.

Interesting.

"Anwen's hat, if that's what it's called, came loose. Lord Colin was compelled by gentlemanly concern to help search for it."

The old hat in the bushes ploy. "Not very imaginative."

"They found the hat, as it were, after diligent searching."

"You are smiling, Rosecroft. Does one conclude you are proud of your cousin for losing her millinery?"

Percival was. Anwen spent too much time in her sisters' shadows, too much time being quiet and agreeable. For a Windham—much less a Windham with flaming red hair—that simply wasn't right.

"Her hat was very small, Your Grace. Locating it likely took determination on the part of both parties."

A mutual hunt for the hat, as it were, the only acceptable variety. "What do we know about Lord Colin, besides that he rides well, has excellent horseflesh, and a keen eye for a stray hat?"

"He owns a distillery—a legal distillery—and the product is considered exceptionally good quality. He's particular about the barrels he uses to age the whisky. He doesn't bottle a young whisky."

"Something of an innovator, then. What was his military record?"

"Brave on the battlefield, excellent record as an artificer, and a first-rate strategist. He'd leave his campfires burning and one man behind playing fiddle tunes, while the rest of his company sneaked off to go raiding. The French fell for that ruse repeatedly. He bothered to learn Spanish and French, and he stayed out of trouble with his superior officers, for the most part."

Lord Colin's older brother had kept him out of trouble.

"And with the ladies?" Percival asked.

They'd reached the back of the garden, and a shriek of childish laughter echoed from across the alley.

"Lord Colin was with the ladies rather a lot," Rosecroft said. "No bastards, that I could find."

That would matter to Rosecroft, given his own irregular antecedents. It mattered to the duke as well. Many a fine gentleman had illegitimate offspring, but in the estimation of polite society—and the Duke and Duchess of Moreland—those children deserved their father's support.

"So Lord Colin has nothing scandalous lurking in his ancient history," Percival said, though a man not yet thirty didn't have ancient history. "What about recent history? Is he keeping a ladybird? Playing too deep? Making stupid wagers, or hunting for a different hat every day of the week?"

A half-grown orange cat skittered over the garden wall in a panicked leap and dodged off into the heartsease beneath the nearest balcony.

"The ladies seem to pursue Lord Colin," Rosecroft said, as flowers bobbed in the cat's wake. "The merry widows and bored wives."

"And his lordship, being young, newly titled, and freshly sprung on polite society, does anything but flee over the nearest garden wall. I don't like it, Rosecroft."

Percival unlatched the garden gate, which opened on a shady alley. The Moreland mews and coach house sat across the alley, ranged around a small courtyard, where young Bronwyn was using a leafy twig to entertain a tomcat.

"I see you are charming Galahad," Percival said. "Hello, princess."

"Grandpapa!" Bronwyn abandoned the cat and pelted up to the duke, arms outstretched.

Percival caught her up in a tight hug, bussed her cheek, and set her down—with the older children, it was important to set them down quickly. Bronwyn would soon be too dignified for such exuberance, but Percival would steal a few more hugs before then.

"Galahad was taking a nap, but he woke up when he saw I had come to call. I've inspected the horses, Papa. They are all present and accounted for."

"You inspected the hayloft too," Rosecroft said. "That pinafore used to be white, Winnie."

"It will be white again," she said, rubbing a finger over the dust streaking her apron. "Just not today."

Rosecroft ruffled her dark ringlets. "As long as you've already ensured the employment of the laundresses for another week, I don't see any harm in a few more trips up and down the ladder."

Bronwyn was a climber. Trees, attics, haylofts, the garden folly... She'd be atop any of them in a blink. An odd quality for a little girl, but her early years had lacked supervision. Rosecroft likened her aerial predilections to manning the crow's nest, a safe observatory above all the fighting.

"Will you come up with me?" she asked, grabbing Rosecroft's hand.

"Afraid I can't," Rosecroft said. "I must pay my respects to Sir Galahad."

The cat was back to napping in the sun, a splendid orange comma of a feline, resting from his endless bouts in the romantic lists.

"He likes to play," Bronwyn said, dropping her papa's hand and scampering off.

"Does Lord Colin like to play?" Percival asked.

Rosecroft knelt to pet the cat, and stentorian rumbling filled the afternoon quiet. "His lordship doesn't gamble to excess, he doesn't chase the lightskirts overtly, I've never seen him drunk, nor found anybody who has."

"My boy, you can either tell me what it is you're reluctant to share, or you can tell Her Grace. I'd rather you told me and I hazard the duchess would rather you did as well."

Rosecroft stood with the cat in his arms. The beast lolled against the earl's chest, not a care—or shred of dignity—to its name.

"Lord Colin has debts," Rosecroft said, scratching the cat's chin.

"We all have debts," Percival snorted. "Particularly at this time of year. You would be well advised to start saving now for Bronwyn's come out, my boy. The undertaking can cost more than a military campaign, and Lord Colin has likely assisted in the launch of both sisters."

"Something isn't adding up," Rosecroft said. "I mean that literally. Lord Colin is a single gentleman of means and new to Town, but for a fellow who's never half-seas over, he has an enormous bill for liquor at every one of his clubs."

Well, drat and damn. "You're suggesting he has the very hard head of the former soldier?"

"He has bills all over Bond Street. Tailors, bootmakers,

haberdashers, glove makers and more. His dressing closet must take up an entire wing of the house."

"A dandy with a hard head."

"Many a dandy has a hard head, and fine cattle, and some commercial revenue quietly supplementing his agricultural income, but I've never seen a single gentleman run up anything like the sums Lord Colin owes the trades after mere weeks in Town." Rosecroft named a total that topped the annual income of most vicars and not a few barons.

"And the season's only half over," Percival muttered.

Esther would be unhappy with this development. She'd had hopes where Lord Colin was concerned. Anwen, however, would be devastated. No Windham daughter or niece could be permitted to develop expectations where a spendthrift younger son was concerned, no matter how he excelled at finding missing hats.

Chapter Eight

TWO ASSETS HAD SERVED Colin well in the military. The first was a certain natural soldiering ability. His aim was excellent, he rode well, he didn't need much sleep, and what had smoothed his way more often than not was a capacity for a soldier's jocular charm.

He'd instinctively known the *right sort* of humor, the *right sort* of warmth, to apply to any situation. He'd been able to jolly his superiors out of their tantrums and sulks, and cheer his men through the worst mud-marches. He'd defused arguments among the laundresses as easily as he'd broken up fights between the men, usually with a joke or some commiserating.

When detailed to the artificers, he'd known how to repair canteens, muskets, or haversacks without having been given instructions.

Perhaps being second in line among seven children had

given him an ability to see what was wanting in a situation and to provide it.

His other asset, though, which surprised most who'd known him in the military, was a cold temper.

He fought, as his men and commanding officers had both said, in cold blood. The fury he directed at his enemies was as lethal as it was calculating, enhancing his aim, his stamina, his grasp of a strategic advantage. When the fighting ended, he was once again good-natured, friendly Captain MacHugh, but in battle, he was formidably detached from tender sentiments.

Staring at four little boys, their eyes glittering with defiance, their little chins tilted in stubborn pride, Colin's temper flared like an arctic storm.

"Explain yourselves," he snapped. "You—" He aimed the screwdriver at the biggest boy, Joe. "What are you about here?"

Silence, while Colin's temper billowed to gale force.

"I want an explanation, gentlemen. The funds in this box are all that stand between you and starvation. Did you think to steal them?"

Anwen had gone as pale as Win Montague's linen, though the boys still said nothing. They shuffled their feet, darted glances among themselves, and squared their shoulders.

Colin jabbed a finger at Joe's chest. "Speak to me, or it's my open palm that will be—"

"You leave our Joe alone!"

The smallest boy, Dickie, had spoken—shouted, rather.

"Joe can't tell you anything," Thomas added. "Joe can talk, but he doesn't like to, and there's nothing to tell."

Anwen's dismay was palpable, as was her inability to grasp that these children had betrayed her trust.

John, the most daring of the group, remained quiet. Shrewd he might be, but his loyalty to the others didn't include taking blame for a shared crime.

"I cannot believe you'd steal from the younger boys," Anwen said. "I know you, I know you to be gentlemen in your own fashion and you're not greedy, not mean."

John stared at the window as if he were contemplating a leap to the cobbles below.

"Why shouldn't I summon the magistrate?" Colin snapped. "Why shouldn't I have the lot of you charged with theft, conspiracy, lockpicking—?"

"We didn't take nuffink," John muttered.

"You took the screwdriver," Colin said, brandishing the stolen item. "MacDeever will doubtless be looking for it. Another five minutes, and that box would have been empty as well, and apparently not for the first time."

Anwen wiped a tear from her cheek, and the sight of her distress boiled through Colin as battle lust never had.

"My boys would not steal from their own home," she said. "I will never believe it of them. They are good boys, and if you summon the magistrate, I will never speak to you again, Lord Colin."

The boys goggled at her, as did Colin.

"Madam, we caught them red-handed. To ignore the matter only tempts them to steal yet again. Do you know what word of this mischief would do to the reputation of the institution? Bad enough we have a cutpurse putting his feet under the dining table three times a day. Now we have embezzlers multiplying in our midst."

"All the more reason you cannot summon the magistrate. The details of this situation—of whatever has transpired here—cannot leave this room."

Well, damn. She had him on that one. "Miss Anwen, I

cannot in good conscience champion the cause of an organization that ignores criminal behavior twice in the same week." He aimed a glower at John. "This is not a matter of first impression."

Her chin came up at the same angle as young Tom's. "Then don't. Resign from the board before you've been officially appointed. Go back to making stupid wagers by the hour, waking up every day with a sore head, and *playing whist* until dawn. The boys and I will manage."

Charm wouldn't put this moment right, and Colin hadn't any to command in any case. "These children have disgraced themselves. You ignore that not only at the peril of the rest of the organization, but at the peril of the boys themselves. They've done wrong, and they know it. To allow their behavior to go unpunished is not in their best interests."

His point wasn't moral, it was purely practical. The boys had no respect for authority, and if ever a situation called for an exercise of authority, this was it. To let them go merrily stealing and lockpicking on their way was unthinkable.

"Lord Colin, I admire your sense of justice," Anwen said with terrible dignity, "but I cannot ignore what I know about these young men. They've had thousands of opportunities to steal, hundreds of chances to take what doesn't belong to them. Why would they choose to break into a strongbox in broad daylight, and by the time-consuming method of dismantling the hinges rather than picking the lock? Why take something Hitchings is absolutely certain to note has gone missing? Accuse the boys of many things, but they are intelligent young men. Stealing from this strongbox wouldn't be smart."

Tom's nose twitched. John's gaze had gone thoughtful.

Dickie was frowning mightily while Joe regarded Anwen as if she'd sprouted a halo and wings.

"Bloody hell." Logic, ruthless and unassailable, cut through Colin's temper. To snatch a purse from an exhausted, half-drunken reveler as he staggered home was simple. Breaking into a strongbox with Hitchings one floor down, taking money that would be missed by sundown...

"Language, Lord Colin."

"Somebody had better tell me exactly what's going on here," Colin said, "or my language will grow much more colorful."

More silence, more shuffling. Anwen put an arm around Joe, and his bony shoulders slumped.

"Count the t-t-take," the boy said.

"Bollocks," John muttered.

"Now you done it," Dickie added.

"Now I've done what?" Colin asked.

"If you get Joey bletherin' on, we'll be here all night," Tom said, "but he's right. You never finish a job without counting the take."

"What job?" Anwen asked, and Colin let her question hang in the air, because the boys might talk to her when they'd die rather than peach on one another to him.

"When you toss a house," John said. "You never split up the haul before it's counted. Everybody reports back, and you count up the take all fair and square before you decide what to do with it."

"So nobody drops anything on the way home," Dickie added. "Can get a man killed, dropping a bauble or two on the way home."

"We were counting the take," Tom said. "We do it regular, to make sure old Hitchings isn't dipping his fat fingers in the till."

"How would you know?" Colin asked, propping a hip on the table.

"'Cause he runs this place on a budget," John said. "That's when you don't spend more than the same amount each month. Winter is more dear because of the coal, but we allow for that."

Anwen retrieved a pencil and paper from the desk across the room. "Show us."

What followed was...Prince Charlie bursting forth into a horsy rendition of a Mozart aria would have been less dumbfounding.

"You have the finances more or less to the penny," Colin said, running a finger down a long list of figures. The boys had guessed high in some places, low in others, but by virtue of watching what went on in the kitchen, the mews, the classroom, and elsewhere, and by monitoring expenditures month by month, they'd come very close to auditing the orphanage's finances.

Auditing, not embezzling.

"So why not simply pick the lock?" Colin asked, setting the figures aside. The boys were ranged around the table, and Anwen sat directly across from Colin. The unopened strongbox at the end of the table.

"You can bust a lock if you pick it too often," Dickie said, shrugging. "You can also make it harder to pick next time. We figured there might come a day when we were in a hurry, and we'd need to pick the lock. Until then, unscrewing the hinges worked well enough, and old Hitchings would never notice a stray nick on the metal."

They were boys—children—and capable of thinking more clearly than many grown men.

"How did you know how much cash was coming in each month?" Colin asked.

"Hitchings labels the packet when he puts it in there," John said. "We can show you."

"Be quick about it," Anwen said.

Dickie brushed his knuckles over his sleeve, grinned at his fellows, and put his fingers on the lock. In less than a minute, the tumblers clicked and the box was open.

Tom was deep into an explanation of how much longer the available money would last when Joe grabbed Colin's sleeve and pointed toward the door.

"Hitchings," John whispered, putting the contents back into the box in the same configuration they'd occupied earlier.

Dickie slapped the lock into place just as footsteps sounded outside the door.

Anwen went to the door, while Joe and Tom silently repositioned the strongbox on the chairman's desk across the room.

"Oh! Mr. Hitchings," Anwen said, opening the door a few inches in response to Hitchings's sharp rap. "You startled me. I beg your pardon. I don't suppose you've come across my parasol? I'm almost certain I brought a parasol with me, but I don't recall having it at the meeting. I grow scatter-brained when I'm peckish. Does that happen to you?"

She effectively blocked Hitchings's view of the office for the few instants necessary for the boys to arrange themselves around Colin, peering over his shoulder at the budgets Hitchings had prepared.

"Um, er, yes," Hitchings said. "I do tend to get a bit foggy when I'm hungry. I came to retrieve my—what are you lot doing here?"

Colin could feel the tension in the children, could feel them wondering how much of their behavior would be disclosed and with what consequences.

"Hitchings," Colin said, shuffling the papers. "You write a very thorough budgetary report. The boys are developing a fine grasp of our financial posture as a result. You have my thanks."

"But they're supposed to be...Oh, never mind. I'm late for class. Miss Anwen, good day. Boys, I'll expect to see you at dinner."

"Yes, Mr. Hitchings."

He withdrew, his footsteps faded, and a beat of silence went by, then Colin heard a snicker at his elbow. A chortle started at his right shoulder, a guffaw on his left. Anwen began laughing, and Joe—silent, stuttering Joe—joined in, until Colin was surrounded by merriment.

* * *

"I think his lordship was scared," Dickie said, grasping a handful of greenery and yanking. "Ouch—blast it!"

"If it has thorns," John observed, "it's probably a rose or a raspberry. Something that belongs in a garden—not like us. Best leave it."

"Never tasted a raspberry." Tom sat back on his heels. "Lord Colin wasn't scared of Miss Anwen. I think he was impressed."

Every male in the room at yesterday's odd gathering in the chairman's office had been impressed. Miss Anwen had torn a strip off his lordship, when his lordship had been busily tearing strips off all four boys.

A fine sight, that. A fancy gent agog at the little miss, unable to argue with her *because she was right*, not only because she was a lady.

"I'm impressed," John said, jabbing at a tangled mess of lily roots. MacDeever said they were lily roots, but Tom hadn't been on the property long enough to know what might bloom along this wall.

They'd been at the books all morning, but after their luncheon, they were cast upon MacDeever's mercy. He'd consulted a list Lord Colin had made, and declared the boys were to establish order in the garden.

Not in a day they wouldn't. Not in a week, though when did a week pass in London without rain? Possibly not in a month.

"What do you suppose this is?" Dickie asked, holding up a sprig of greenery. "Smells good, and it's tough."

"Like Miss Anwen," John said.

Dickie threw the plant at his brother, sending a shower of dirt from the roots. "If it weren't for her, we might be at the Old Bailey instead of poking about in this dirt. Show some bloody respect."

The four of them were poking about in the dirt, *outside*, beneath the sun, free from Hitchings's lectures and glowers. The day was beautiful, and Tom was pleased as *bloody hell* to not be sitting on his arse in the detention room.

Joe looked up from spading a bed farther down the wall. His glance was enough to quell the bout of fisticuffs that might have erupted between John and Dick.

"Dickie's right," Tom said. "After what Miss Anwen did for us yesterday, I'll not insult her."

John sniffed the plant. "Saying she smells good and she's tough is an insult?"

"Are ladies supposed to be tough?" Tom asked, taking a whiff of the plant and passing it to Joe.

Joe rubbed his fingers over the silvery green leaves and brought them to his nose. "L-lavender. F-french lavender. For soap."

"We should change your name to Encyclopedia," John said. "Do I put it back in the dirt?"

"I will," Dickie said, retrieving the plant. He tore off a leaf, stashed the bit of greenery into his pocket, and gently tucked the roots of the lavender into a patch of soil Joe had spaded free of weeds.

"Think it will grow?" The poor thing looked lonely to Tom, all on its own in a garden that was otherwise rioting with weeds.

"If it's as tough as Miss Anwen," Dickie said, "I don't think anything can stop it. It's been growing here for years, without any attention from a gardener, and Joe says it's a useful plant."

Now that Joe had identified the shrub, Tom recognized it. In back gardens all over Mayfair, lavender grew in great billowy borders. Ladies made sachets out of it, and biscuits, and dried bouquets.

Tom fetched the watering can from near the downspout at the corner of the building and gave the lavender a drink.

"I think we should each take a wall," he said, "once we get rid of the damned weeds. If it's your wall, then you keep after the weeds and the watering and the whatnot." He had no idea what else was involved in caring for a garden besides weeding and watering, but gardening was an occupation, so there must be work involved beyond the initial effort.

"That's not fair," Dickie said, getting back to his weeding. "The garden is a rectangle, not a square, so two fellows would have short walls, and two would have long walls."

"Dickie's right—for once," John said, "and the short walls have either the door to the house or the back gate in them, so they're even less work."

Joe was turning over turf in a slow, steady rhythm, as

if he'd done it many times before, though Tom didn't see
how that could be.

"Trade off."

Leave it to Joe. "Take turns, you mean?"

Joe nodded.

"How about we put in a proper garden before we decide
how to manage it," John suggested. "It's not like we'll be
here much past June."

Dickie pitched a clump of weeds so hard against the
stone wall that dirt exploded in every direction. "We might
be here. Lord Colin has ideas."

"We need blunt," Tom said. "We could last through
summer, but once the coal man starts coming around again,
we'll need money, not ideas."

They all fell silent, and got back to work, when for once,
Tom wished the other three would try to argue with him.

* * *

"Think of it as a jest," Winthrop Montague said, sighting
down the barrel of a Manton dueling pistol. "Officers were
always getting up to pranks, you no less than anybody else.
So the lads charged a few items to your accounts, or a few
toasts to your health. That is a gentleman's version of a
prank."

He aimed and fired. Birds flew from the surrounding
trees in a cloud of indignation, but the clay pot he'd tar-
geted remained sitting on a lower branch.

"Win, what sort of prank costs a man a fortune?" Colin
retorted. "I'm not laughing, and I am considering pressing
charges."

He took aim with the second of Win's matched pair of
pistols, pictured the laughing, half-drunk pack of jackals

Win called friends, and blasted the pot into a million pieces.

"Nice work, MacHugh."

They passed the firearms back to Win's groom, who reloaded while another groom set up more targets among the branches of the surrounding trees. Richmond Park was quiet this late in the afternoon, a good place for Colin to let his temper loose.

"Win, who did this to me? Or are the names too numerous to recall?"

Montague gestured for the groom to fetch him a drink. "Pointy was probably a ringleader. Pierpont is bored, his missus is lately a mother and likely hasn't any time for him, and he's none too bright. I confess I agreed to go along with the tavern bills." He named ten other young men, exactly the crowd Colin would have suspected of such larceny.

The bill for drinks at the tavern was enormous. In Colin's absence, the lordlings and younger sons he'd thought to make his friends had cheerfully directed the publican to put one drinking orgy after another on Lord Colin's bill.

And why wouldn't the tavern owner oblige them? Colin himself had given the man similar direction on at least three occasions.

The same game had been effected at a tailor's, a glove shop, a bootmaker's, and—thank God, only the once—at Tattersalls, among other places. Maarten was still sorting out the situation at Colin's clubs, but more damage had been done there. If Colin had followed the typical English habit of paying the trades annually rather than monthly, he could well have ended up in real difficulties.

"You don't buy a horse on another man's credit," Colin

said. "If that's how being a gentleman works, then I want no part of it."

Win accepted a glass of wine from the groom, took a taste, and nodded. "That might be the point, MacHugh. You either pay up, or your entrée among the fellows will evaporate overnight. They won't stand up with your sisters, won't sit down to cards with you. Nobody will be rude, but you'll have been weighed in the scales and found wanting. Have some wine."

Colin did not want wine. He wanted a wee dram of the water of life, and he wanted to break some heads. Even in Spain, with the bloody French intent on murder, he'd not been this infuriated. The French had been doing what soldiers did—fighting, trying to hold territory for their commander, attempting to keep France's borders secure.

While Win's cronies were little better than well-dressed pickpockets. "The horse must be returned, with Pierpont's apologies. A misunderstanding, a wager gone awry. I don't care what story he concocts."

Horses were bloody damned expensive, and if a man couldn't afford to buy one, he might well be unable to properly keep the beast.

"I can't recommend that course," Win said, passing Colin a glass of wine. "Twenty years from now, when your daughter is making her come out, you'll hear whispers that her papa has no sense of humor, that he values a penny more than the goodwill of those gracious enough to accept him into their ranks. The offers she'll get, if any, will be colored by how you behave now."

Rage and bewilderment racketed about in Colin's mind, along with a sense of betrayal. The young men to whom Win had introduced him had seemed like good fellows. They were polite to Edana and Rhona, and greeted Colin with open good cheer on the street, in the clubs, and in the ballrooms.

Now this. Now dozens of fingers sneaking coin from Colin's pockets, and he was supposed to call it high spirits, a lark, a joke.

"I feel as if I've intercepted a message in code." Colin tossed back the entire glass of wine, though his behavior caused Win to wince. "The words seem to say, 'Welcome to polite society, Lord Colin. Congratulations on your good fortune.' The true message is, 'Welcome, Lord Colin. How much can we fleece you for? We're lazy, greedy, completely without honor, and you're a Scottish fool who was better off mending harness or tending to his whisky.'"

Win refilled Colin's wine glass. "May I ask how much you're expected to pay?"

Colin named a sum that had sent him into a twenty-minute swearing orbit about the library desk that morning. Thank God that Maarten had insisted on tidying Colin's affairs in anticipation of departing for Scotland.

"That is"—Win took another delicate sip of wine—"rather a bit of coin. If you pay off the sums owing, I'll put a word in a few ears. A jest is one thing, but I hadn't realized how far it had gone." He passed his wine glass to the waiting servant. "I trust you can manage the sums due?"

The question was carefully casual.

"I'm tempted to not pay the damned bills," Colin said, exchanging his wineglass for a reloaded pistol. "I'm tempted to remind the good tailors, haberdashers, glove makers, horse traders, and publicans of Mayfair that what a customer does not order or sign for, he is not obligated to pay for, gentlemanly pranks be damned."

Win sighted down the barrel of the second reloaded pistol. "Again, MacHugh, such a tantrum would have repercussions you'd regret. Not only would those in on the joke learn of your parsimony, but the third parties involved would be bilked of needed coin. You can't gather up the dozen men who might have drunk a few toasts to you, and assign each of them a portion of the resulting expense."

Colin had been considering that very approach. Spread over twelve quarterly allowances, the amount in question was extravagant but manageable.

The grooms were busily arranging crocks and jars along a single branch, though the targets were small this time—jam jars from the looks of them.

"So what do you advise, Win? I'm to pay these bills, smile, and pretend it's all quite amusing to have been robbed by your friends?"

That solution was so nauseatingly English, Colin considered scooping up his sisters and leaving the entire problem behind him. He could be sued for debt—he was a commoner—but these were not debts he'd incurred. They were debts landing in his lap because the tradesmen and merchants had no choice but to trust their betters.

Reneging on the bills would, as Win pointed out, simply widen the circle of victims to include people less able to bear the burden than Colin was.

"You not only pay the bills, smile, and pretend it's all amusing," Win said gently, "you publicly stand the perpetrators to a round in honor of their boldness."

Good God, this was schoolyard politics. "Is that before or after I call them out, and dim their arrogant lights, one by one?"

The pistol was double-barreled, two shots being standard in most contests of honor. The weight was exquisite, the workmanship so elegant, the result should have been art rather than weaponry.

"MacHugh, your Scottish temper will not serve you in this instance. Take it in stride, smile, and consider it the cost of membership in a very worthwhile club. By June, you'll be sorry to part from the same men you want to call out now."

Colin had not expected to remain in London until June, and the delights of a London season had apparently paled for Ronnie and Eddie too. But he had the House of Urchins to consider, and the surprising realization that Anwen Windham had been willing to forego Colin's kisses—his very company—to stand up for the boys.

She'd amazed him, and probably amazed the lads as well.

She'd amazed him *again*. Ladies didn't kiss Captain Colin MacHugh and send him on his way. He kissed them and left them, usually smiling but not always.

Anwen had been in absolute earnest when she'd told him, in so many ladylike words, to either drop his accusations against the boys or take himself back to Scotland. She'd meant to send him packing, and he'd have had no choice but to go.

She'd been right too.

"Stand back," Colin said, taking Win's pistol from him. "I'll pay the damned debts this time, but let your friends know that if this happens again, I'll get up to a few pranks of my own, and they will not like the results."

"Come now, MacHugh. There's no need for drama. What could you possibly be planning, when none of the fellows have the—"

Colin took aim and fired all four barrels. The entire branch dropped amid a crash of clay and glass.

"I'll think of an amusement that will give the lot of them nightmares, Win. I'm grateful you've been on hand to talk sense to me, and Pierpont and his cronies should be grateful too—very grateful."

Colin passed the smoking pistols to the servants handle-first.

"These fellows are your friends too," Win said. "Or they will be after this."

"No, Win. They will not be my friends. Not ever."

He left Win standing before his coach, sipping wine, while Colin climbed aboard Prince Charlie and headed back to Town at a smart canter.

Chapter Nine

ALL DAY, ANWEN HAD waited for Lord Colin to call. She'd knitted, she'd embroidered, she'd tatted lace, and woven fancies by the hour, until Charlotte had asked if she was sickening for something.

"As it happens, I *am* sickening for something," Anwen said, stuffing her embroidery hoop back in her workbasket.

Charlotte's hand was already on the bell pull before Anwen could continue.

"I am dealing with a case of self-reproach," she went on, getting up to pace. "The affliction is novel, at least in terms of severity."

Charlotte's hand drifted back to her side. "You addressed just as many invitations to the card party as we did. Why reproach yourself?"

"We thought you might have overdone, riding in the park earlier this week," Elizabeth added. "Fatigue always puts me out of sorts, and the whole blasted season is an exercise in staying up too late, imbibing bad punch, and enduring the wandering hands of—"

Charlotte gave the bell pull a tug. "I did fancy the hock Uncle sent to the library. I'm in the mood for raspberry cordial, as it happens."

Two years ago, for the ladies to order their own bottle of cordial during daylight hours would have caused somebody to notify the duchess. Two months ago, eyebrows would have been raised belowstairs at least.

"Tell us about this self-reproach," Elizabeth said, patting the cushion beside her.

Anwen ignored the invitation to perch beside her sister. If anything, she wanted another headlong gallop down a bridle path.

"I've considered Lord Colin just another handsome face," she said. "I thought he was charming, a good dancer."

"He's all of that," Elizabeth said, going to the door when a soft tap sounded. She instructed the footman regarding the cordial and closed the door. "He's quite dashing in his kilt, a man of means, and from a titled family. I like him, to the extent I know him."

"Do you see what I mean?" Anwen asked, stopping before a bust of Plato sitting on a windowsill. "We do it too."

"Do what?" Charlotte asked. "Wennie, did you skip luncheon?"

"She didn't," Elizabeth said. "She ate her soup, the fish, not much of the potatoes but then she never does, a serving of fruit tart—"

"Stop."

"—and she had two servings of tea, but also some lemonade. Aunt prefers a very tart lemonade. Perhaps that didn't agree—"

"You will both cease fretting over me this instant!" Anwen shouted.

If old Plato had spoken, Charlotte and Elizabeth could not have looked more surprised.

"Not a word," Anwen said. "You will listen to me, and you will hear me. I am well. I am probably in better health than either of you, because I go outside. I must, to escape your carping, and managing, and discussing me as if I were no more animate than he is."

She slapped Plato on his marble crown.

Elizabeth looked over at Charlotte, who was staring at her slippers. Plain, comfy house mules that might once have been pink.

Elizabeth drew in a breath. "We mean only to safeguard—"

"Wennie's right," Charlotte murmured, toeing off her slippers. "We're getting worse. If we clucked and fussed any more, we'd need beaks and feathers. This season feels longer than all the previous ones put together."

For Charlotte, that was quite an admission—also, in Anwen's opinion, the God's honest truth. The quality of the next silence was both sad and thoughtful.

"I want my own household," Elizabeth said. "I want to plan my own garden, my own menus, my own social calendar, not limit myself to choosing which bonnet I put on when Aunt drags us about on her endless social calls."

Elizabeth had hinted, she'd implied, she'd occasionally alluded to this wish, but she'd never stated her preference so plainly.

"Then you go to Westhaven," Anwen said. "You enlist Rosecroft's support, and you consult Valentine, who is regarded by our lady cousins as the most sensible of their brothers. You stop treating our cousins as if they are simply

handsome lads with a fine command of small talk, and enlist their aid dealing with our elders. That's what I meant."

"You'll have to spell it out for us," Charlotte said, going
to the door to retrieve the cordial. She poured three generous
servings. "Here's to the rest of the season galloping by."

They touched glasses. Charlotte resumed her place on
the sofa, while Anwen stayed on her feet.

"You were saying?" Elizabeth prompted.

"We resent that to the gentlemen, we're just pretty faces,
pretty settlements, a connection to this title, or that landed
family. The men don't see us."

"They touch us," Charlotte said, taking another sip of
her drink. "I hate that. 'I beg your pardon, Miss Charlotte,'
when they stumble on the dance floor, and their hands acci-
dentally slip before half of polite society. My knee has had
to slip a time or two, despite my vast quantities of ladylike
restraint."

"Mine too," Elizabeth said, "and I've learned the knack
of stepping on my own hem. I've practiced this, in case I
need to repair to the retiring room, which is unfortunate."

"It's ridiculous," Anwen snapped. "Why don't we simply tell the miserable blighters we don't waltz with presuming bumpkins? We know who they are."

"Because a lady doesn't pick and choose between her
partners. She stands up when invited to or sits out the
evening," Charlotte recited.

"Why?" Anwen asked.

"So as not to offend the gentleman's sensibilities." Elizabeth sounded unimpressed with her own answers.

"But they can offend us without limit, groping, stum-
bling, nearly drooling on our bodices. We aren't people to
them, and I could strut about in high dudgeon on the strength
of that vast insult, except I've been guilty of it too."

"One develops a certain detachment," Charlotte said, draining her glass. "If it's a cattle auction, and we're the heifers, then we do our best to make them into bullocks."

"Bulls," Elizabeth said, saluting with her drink. "Every one of them regards himself as the most impressive champion bull ever to make a leg. I hate it."

"But some of them aren't like that," Anwen said. "I have taken a fancy to Lord Colin, and even permitted him a small liberty or two. At the meeting earlier this week, we had a disagreement."

"Have some more, Charlotte," Elizabeth said, topping up her sister's drink. "This cordial is quite good, and I want to hear all about your disagreement, Wennie—and these liberties you permitted. Every detail, please."

Anwen took the hassock before the sofa. "His lordship and I came upon the oldest boys at the orphanage where they ought not to have been, and Lord Colin accused them of wrongdoing. I didn't believe the evidence warranted those accusations, and we quarreled."

"I hope he apologized," Charlotte said, topping up Elizabeth's drink. "A gentleman doesn't argue with a lady."

"But friends are protective of one another," Anwen said. "Lord Colin was concerned not only for the four oldest boys, but for all the children, and for me, and even the Windham family reputation. He's not simply a charming smile and a fine dancer."

"He wears the kilt to perfection," Elizabeth said.

Charlotte touched her glass to Anwen's. "To kilted laddies."

"But that's just it. He's not a lad. He's a man. He's commanded soldiers, he manages his business, and he owns two estates."

"He's not a boy," Elizabeth said softly. "His older

brother had the same quality. They're men who have better things to do than leer at debutantes, amuse the merry widows, and exchange remedies at the club for their sore heads."

"Aunt calls that bunch handsome idlers," Charlotte said.

"Uncle calls them much worse than that," Anwen observed, "but Colin isn't among their number. He can save the orphanage, and I'm not sure another gentleman in all of Mayfair has either the ability or the motivation to take on that challenge."

She had no delusions that it would be a challenge. The card party must go off flawlessly and become an annual event. The House of Urchins must maintain a spotless reputation, and something had to be done about the board of directors, most of whom couldn't be bothered to perform their duties.

"Do you fancy Lord Colin, or fancy his ability to save the orphanage?" Elizabeth asked.

"Both," Anwen said. "I like that he can argue with me, and that he can listen to me. He doesn't treat me like I'm about to expire with every sniffle or megrim."

"Do you have a sniffle?" Charlotte asked.

Elizabeth snatched up a pillow and cocked her arm. "Take that back, Charl. Wennie's being serious."

Charlotte downed her cordial in one gulp. "Fire away, Bethan, because I'm guilty as charged, but Wennie, we nearly lost you. You don't know how that changed Mama and Papa. All you know is they took turns reading to you, telling you stories, playing cards with you, when you weren't asleep for days at a time. We nearly lost them too. It was terrifying."

Charlotte offered not a reproach but an explanation.

"I recall Aunt Esther moving in for a time," Anwen said,

"and then Aunt Arabella. Mama wouldn't listen to anybody else, and even Uncle Percy had to remonstrate with her."

"But she wouldn't let the physicians bleed you," Elizabeth said. "She told Papa that she'd steal you away herself before she'd lose you to quackery, and he'd never find her."

"What did Papa say?"

"That he'd not lose two of the people he loved most in the whole world, and that as sick as you were, you weren't getting worse, so Mama's decision would stand." Elizabeth, as the oldest, probably had the clearest recollection. "You started to improve from that day forward."

"You heard Mama and Papa quarreling?" Anwen had no memory of her parents' disagreement. She recalled crying as Mama had cut her hair, and being so sick of her bed, that Mama had the servants set up beds for her all over the house. She recalled the scent of straw wafting in the windows, for Papa had carpeted the whole drive with straw the better to muffle the noise of coach wheels.

"The entire shire would have heard them arguing," Charlotte said.

Maybe it was the cordial, maybe it was the conversation, but warmth welled from Anwen's middle.

"Lord Colin and I can have a difference of opinion, a fair donnybrook, and he still listens to me. I think I'm in love."

Charlotte beamed, which had to be at least partly attributable to the cordial.

"Is Lord Colin in love?" Elizabeth propped her feet at the edge of Anwen's hassock. "Westhaven would call that a material consideration."

"Rosecroft would call it a tactical concern," Charlotte added, tucking her feet at Anwen's other side. "He'd be right."

"Lord Colin seems enthusiastic about my company, he doesn't need my settlements, and he argues with me. He might not be smitten, but he's interested."

Anwen hoped. But if he was interested, why hadn't he paid her a call and reported on the doings at the orphanage?

Stopped by to ask her to save him a dance at the next ball?

Sequestered himself with her in the conservatory again?

"I'm interested." Elizabeth studied her drink. "I'm interested in paying a call on Ladies Rhona and Edana."

"Bit late in the day for that," Charlotte said.

"We'll bring them a bottle of Her Grace's cordial. Anwen, will you join us?"

Oh, they were the best of sisters, when they weren't hovering and fretting over her. "I'll be at the front door in five minutes, but two bottles of cordial, I think. One for each sister."

"Fine notion," Charlotte said, "and I'll just take the rest of this one up to my room for safekeeping."

Her tone was so like Her Grace's that Anwen was provoked to giggling, Elizabeth followed suit, and Charlotte soon joined in.

Five minutes later, though, they were assembled at the front door, prepared to go calling.

* * *

The ride back to London did nothing to improve Colin's mood. He'd been robbed, plain and simple, by a lot of indolent, arrogant English lordlings, and—damn them all to the bottom of Loch Ness—he hadn't seen this betrayal coming.

He'd believed he was developing the right associations, more fool him.

Worse yet, in a few hours he'd be expected to don his dress kilt and go out socializing in company with his sisters. Probably not a fancy ball—those were preceded by bickering between Edana and Rhona, last-minute trips to the modiste, and the occasional slammed door—but a soiree, a musicale, or that worst torment ever devised by woman, the dinner party.

In every case, he'd be confronted with men who'd spent his coin without his permission. The urge to flee to Scotland, where a thief was a thief and a laird was a laird, nearly overwhelmed him.

And yet, the whole business with the misappropriated funds was Colin's problem—not his family's, not his commanding officer's, his. A result of *his* bad judgment and no other's.

If Colin spent the evening at home, his sisters would be without an escort, which meant he could not remain home if he valued his continued existence.

Every path before him was unappealing, and yet, he must go forward.

He handed Prince Charlie off to the grooms, charged across the garden, and prepared to storm the family parlor. Tonight he'd be home by midnight, come fire, flood, or French foot patrols.

Feminine voices sounded from the other side of the parlor door. Ronnie and Eddie were likely stirring a cauldron of gossip or deciding with which of their fourteen thousand friends he must stand up and in what order later in the week.

Colin swung open the door. "I don't care which infernal waste of time ye think yer dragging me to this evening, I'm leaving at midnight with or without ye."

Five female pairs of eyes turned to him. Five pairs was

too many, and two of those eyes—a lovely blue pair—belonged to Anwen Windham.

Shite. Colin managed to not say that aloud, but only just. He was delighted to see her. The joy of beholding her coursed through him the way the fragrance of heather could grace even the dreariest of rainy afternoons.

He was not delighted to have made an arse of himself in the space of a single sentence.

"I beg everybody's pardon. I am tired and out of sorts." He bowed—even a complete dunderhead bowed before retreating—and headed for the door.

"Lord Colin, please don't feel you must change your attire to accommodate company," Anwen said. "We called late in the day and time has got away from us."

The ladies had been conspiring. Their smiles and three open bottles of some potation confirmed it, as did Colin's sense that he'd interrupted a strategy meeting of senior officers. And yet, he was loath to turn on his heel and give up a chance to spend time with Anwen.

They'd had a fair fight at the orphanage—his first with a woman other than Edana or Rhona—and he wanted to do a fair bit of making up with her.

"You should stay," Rhona said. "We're considering the guest list for Anwen's card party. Who among your circle of acquaintances can stand to lose a substantial sum of money for a good cause?"

"A substantial sum?" Colin asked, because the fellows Win had introduced him to were for the most part younger sons on allowances or half-pay officers dangling after banker's daughters.

"The substantial-er the better," Miss Charlotte said. "The money is all for Anwen's orphanage, you know."

Her smile was a trifle lopsided.

"A very good cause," Edana said, then hiccupped.

Rhona winked at Colin, or maybe she had something in her eye.

Anwen rose. "Lord Colin, let's adjourn to the library, so I might make a list of the names you suggest. I'll pass them along to Her Grace."

"Fine idea," Miss Elizabeth Windham said. "I am a firm believer in making lisht. Lists, rather."

Rhona emitted a delicate *burp*.

A good brother would stay and monitor the consumption of whatever was in those bottles, for clearly, the ladies were having a genteel drinking party.

Well, let them. A *very* good brother trusted his sisters to be moderate in their indulgences. "Perhaps we should all adjourn to the library?" Colin suggested. For him to be alone with Anwen under her family's roof with doors open and relations nearby was one thing, but elsewhere...

"Run along, you two," Charlotte said, grabbing a bottle by the neck. "We'll be fine."

Anwen made for the door, her stride confident—and steady. When they reached the corridor, she took Colin by the hand and pushed him up against the wall.

"I'm about to kiss you," she said, "unless you object now."

"I object."

Russet brows drew down.

Colin brought Anwen's hand to his lips. "As badly as I've missed you all night and all day, as much as I have to discuss with you, and as urgently as I long to wrap my arms around you and whisper sweet indecencies into your ear—"

"Sweet indecencies?"

"For starts. I'll progress to the bold sort if you allow me

to. Regardless, the privilege of initiating this kiss belongs to me."

Colin didn't simply initiate the kiss, he gave all his frustrations and longings the order to charge headlong into pleasure he could share with Anwen. The hour was such that servants were belowstairs enjoying a cup of tea, guests would not call, and even the front door was unmanned.

He shifted, so Anwen's back was to the wall, and he could envelop her in an embrace that included arms, hands, body, mouth, *everything*. The feel of her clutching at his hair, pressing closer, eased some of the day's tension, and the taste of her—raspberry, both tart and sweet—drove him to growling.

Arousal joined the conflagration and Colin was glad for it. Money problems, sororal expectations, the situation at the orphanage—those were all messy, tangled, and unappealing. Desire for Anwen Windham was real too, though, and so very lovely.

She subsided against him and patted his chest. "That's better."

Better and worse. "I've missed ye." The words of a callow swain, but also the truth. Colin had missed the feel of Anwen in his arms, the sound of her voice, the delicate scent of her lemony perfume, and even the way her hair tickled his cheek.

"You're upset about something," she said.

"How can you tell?"

"I can sense it, taste it. Are the boys all right? Don't protect me from truths you think I'm too delicate to handle, Colin."

"You're formidable as hell." Also precious. To hold Anwen like this did more to bring Colin right than all the hard galloping and harder cursing he'd done throughout the day. "I need your advice."

He'd never said those words to anybody. In some way, they were more intimate than a kiss.

"I need yours as well. Shall we to the library? Napoleon mounting an invasion wouldn't part our sisters from the remaining half bottle of cordial."

"Bless the cordial, then," he said, leading her to the library three doors down the corridor. The room was modest compared to its Windham counterpart, though what books the MacHughs owned had been read—every page cut— and much appreciated. Hamish had used this room as his estate office, and Colin was doing likewise.

The calculations Maarten had brought remained on the desk, a stack of foolscap weighted with a silver pen tray embossed with the MacHugh crest. A single white rose graced a vase on the windowsill.

"The boys are putting the orphanage grounds to rights this week," Colin said. "If the weather's fair. If the weather's not fair, I was hoping you could teach them to knit."

"Knitting is easy, needles cost nothing, and I would love to teach them all I know. I'm sure Lady Rosalyn would be willing to help me. The boys are not what troubles you." Anwen picked up a book of poetry from the desk. "Poetry, Colin?"

"Robert Burns. Hamish favors him. Did you attend finishing school?"

She set the book aside. "Yes, for two years, though the school was only two hours' ride from the Moreland family seat in Kent. I spent many holidays with my cousins, as did my sisters."

A pair of straight-backed, utilitarian chairs sat in front

of the desk, and a capacious reading chair was angled before the hearth. Colin scooped Anwen up and settled with her in the reading chair.

"This is friendly, Captain Lord MacHugh."

Colin kissed her nose to help quiet his thoughts. Or something. "I've been made the butt of a prank, a very expensive prank."

She nestled about, like a cat circling before settling to the exact most comfortable spot on a cushion.

"Is the worse hurt to your pride or to your purse?"

"The hurt to my purse is considerable." He named the sum, lest she think him exaggerating the situation, and explained the jest, if a jest it was.

"They spent *that much*? In less than a month?"

"I know who did it, between recollection, Maarten's research, a few pointed discussions with the trades earlier today, and Win's confirmation. A dozen men conspired to empty my pockets. I'm supposed to make light of it, pay every penny, and stand the perpetrators to another round."

That Win had joined in the joke rankled badly, though he'd seemed remorseful at how far matters had gone.

Anwen sat up and peered at Colin. "You're supposed to pretend this is humorous, and merrily hand over a small fortune? That makes no sense. You said it yourself: If our boys had stolen from the orphanage, then letting their misdeeds go unpunished was tempting them to steal again. That would have made us nearly complicit in their next theft."

Our boys. They were her boys, not Colin's.

"Winthrop Montague isn't a former cutpurse. He's my friend." On the ride back to Town, Colin had figured out the true problem. He could leave Win's cronies to pay the expenses they'd incurred, meaning the trades would be unreimbursed.

That in itself was wrong.

The true problem, though, was that Win would also be held responsible for Colin's decision to not play along. Win would be subtly excluded, whispered about, and treated to small indignities, because Win had tried to open doors for Colin.

Colin could not allow his friend to be treated thus over a prank.

Anwen subsided against Colin's chest, and if he had been capable of purring, the feel of her in his arms would have inspired him to it. She felt that right, that sweet, and perfect in his lap.

Also that desirable.

"Winthrop Montague spent two years marching about in Spain," Anwen said. "Though if you question him about the battles, he has little to say. I gather he was more of a secretary than a soldier. Other than that, I don't think he's worked a day in his life. Most of his friends can't claim even a stint in the army. If they stole from you, it's because they have no sense of what it takes to earn money."

"They stole from me. They stole my dignity and my coin, and I want both back, but not at the cost of what friendships I have."

Colin wanted Anwen too. More with each passing moment, which she had to be aware of. She fiddled with his cravat, with his hair, and with the buttons of his waistcoat, while desire fiddled with Colin's wits.

"Can you pay the debts?" Anwen asked, kissing his cheek.

"Easily, though it will mean moving money from Edinburgh to London. That's not the point. Win suggests I do nothing in retaliation, and if anybody grasps how gentlemen go on with each other, it's Winthrop Montague. His advice thus far has been sound."

A delicate warmth tricked across Colin's throat.

She'd undone his cravat. "Anwen, I didn't lock the door."

"I did. What has Win advised you about?"

Should Colin be dismayed, terrified, or pleased that she'd locked the door? "Win has told me which clubs to join, which tailors to patronize, when to drop in at Tatts. God, that feels good."

Anwen had wound her hand around Colin's neck and was massaging his nape. He'd touched her in the same fashion in the park, making the caress all the more intimate.

"My cousins could have told you the same things," she said, "and done a better job of it. Their friends would not have set you up for penury and called it a jest. Had Win advised you regarding investments, which entertainments to avoid, or whose sister had taken an extended repairing lease in the north last year, I might see your point."

Anwen made sense, even as she made a muddle of Colin's ability to think. Hamish was a shy man, not given to even brotherly displays of affection. Edana and Rhona expected Colin to offer his arm at their whim. The men in the clubs might slap Colin on the back or shake his hand.

Nobody offered this, this bliss, this warmth, this combination of affection, pleasure, friendship, and desire.

"If you keep that up, madam, I will become incoherent."

She kept it up. "I caught Uncle Percival rubbing Aunt's feet once. I'd forgotten my workbasket in the music room. They didn't see me."

Colin would adore having his feet rubbed, among other places. "You're not the least bit tipsy, are you?" He'd have to return her to her sisters if she was.

"I am drunk on the pleasure of your company," she said, quite briskly. "You argued with me at the orphanage, Colin. Went figuratively toe to toe with me. Nobody has paid me that compliment since I was six years old. You don't treat me as if I'm a porcelain shepherdess perched too near the edge of the mantel, and that makes me happy."

He had no idea what she was going on about, but she was either able to hold her cordial, or exercise restraint around an open bottle. Regardless, he approved. A wife who was too fond of drink, no matter how lovely, sweet, delightful, and passionate, would always cause a man worry.

Colin kissed Anwen, and the closeness necessitated by that liberty meant he caught a whiff of her, up close, where she was warm and well-endowed. Her lemony fragrance acquired a spicy undertone, much as Colin's falls acquired a snugness.

A wife who greeted her husband like this, who listened to him, who saw him honestly, who took his troubles to heart, such a wife would be...

Wife.

Husbands had wives. For the first time, Colin envied them that good fortune. "Hamish and Megan are happy with each other," Colin said, "and I know they had their differences. He's deliriously happy. I've never seen Hamish so happy. He glows with it. He laughs, he—"

Anwen's fingers had gone still. "Megan too. I watched her walk up the church aisle on her wedding day, and I wondered, what fools, what blind idiots, said my sister was plain? She's never been plain, and to Hamish MacHugh she never will be."

A certainty took possession of Colin's heart, a knowing born of instinct, but also of sense and experience. Anwen

Windham was different, special, and precious. For a long moment, he simply held her, savoring a sense of peace where all had been frustration and tumult before.

"I'd like to ask you something, Anwen."

She rested her head against his shoulder, the weight of her in his arms exceeding even perfection, and achieving a sense of completion.

"Ask me anything. I'll argue with you if we disagree."

That pleased her, so it pleased Colin. "Would you think me very forward if I requested permission from Moreland to pay you my addresses? Please be honest, because with you, I want no posturing, no prevaricating to spare me embarrassment. I'm known to be precipitous, but that's not truly my nature. I can be patient, it's just that—"

"Yes, I would think you forward."

Well, all right, then. Colin's heart sank, but he couldn't blame her. They hadn't known each other long, and her family had much more consequence than his. He'd bear up, somehow, under a disappointment that made his earlier foul language look like casual remarks in the church yard.

"I would think you forward," Anwen said, "and I would approve heartily of your initiative. I am so blessed sick of wasting each spring on the company of men I cannot esteem, and I esteem you ferociously, Colin MacHugh."

That was...that was a yes. That was permission to court, and a lady did not grant permission to court unless she was mightily impressed with a fellow.

"Are you sure, Anwen? Are you very, very sure?"

She scooted around, so she was facing him. "I'm very, very sure, and the door is very, very locked."

Chapter Ten

IN THE WORDS OF countless gentlemen, Lady Rosalyn Montague was *lovely*, not merely pretty. The matchmakers had bestowed the usual appellations upon her— diamond of the first water, incomparable, jewel of the *haute ton*—but Rosalyn secretly preferred the *nom du guerre* given to her by the wallflowers.

The Problem. As in, "There goes the Problem," and, "If it weren't for the Problem."

Rosalyn had never meant to be a problem, but when she'd decided Christian charity required her to befriend the merely pretty, the poor dears had resented her. The gentlemen had flocked to Rosalyn's side as she'd whiled away dance after dance among the potted palms. The wallflowers had apparently felt even more ignored with the Problem in all her loveliness sitting in their very midst.

One could but try.

"You have that look about you," Win said as he entered

the library at Monthaven House and went straight to the sideboard. "As if you've been too good for too long. Care for a tot?"

He was the best of brothers. "I'll have a sip of yours." The housekeeper would know who'd drunk out of the second glass otherwise, and a lady didn't partake of strong spirits for any reason save medical necessity.

In theory.

Win tossed back a brandy, then refilled the glass and brought it to Rosalyn. "You could have come shooting with Lord Colin and me. Your gracious presence might have spared me an awkward dressing down—an awkward, undeserved dressing down."

Rosalyn laid out another card, the knave of clubs, which was of no help at all. "Have you been naughty, Winthrop?"

Poor Win fancied Mrs. Bellingham, according to Rosalyn's maid, who'd gleaned that tidbit from the first underfootman, who'd heard it from Win's valet. Mrs. Bellingham would be a very expensive frolic.

"How could I be naughty when I am ever a paragon, sister dear?" Win cast himself onto the library sofa and propped his boots on a hassock. "Come sit with me."

Even the best of brothers did not deserve Rosalyn's attention whenever he snapped his fingers, and yet, Win had been out with Lord Colin, who was the brother of a duke, not bad-looking despite his red hair, and rumored to be well off.

Rosalyn tidied the deck—how she loved the feel of a stack of cards in her hands—put it back into the hidden drawer, took another sip of her drink, and joined Win on the sofa.

"You're in a mood," she said. "I have whiled away a perfectly lovely day, practicing the pianoforte, writing to

Aunt Margaret to inquire about the weather in Italy this time of year, and otherwise avoiding Papa's notice, while you went off to Richmond. One of us has to behave some of the time, Winthrop."

He leaned his head back and closed his eyes, the picture of young manhood at his oppressed leisure. Perhaps his new boots had given him a blister or he'd lost a particularly vexing wager.

"Lord Colin presumed to remonstrate with me." Win's tone was slightly bewildered and definitely peevish.

"He outranks you. He's a duke's heir, you're merely an earl's spare. I don't pretend to understand the nuances of gentlemanly posturing, but why shouldn't he remonstrate with you?"

"We fellows don't posture, Roz. We are honorable, civil at all times. We are gentlemen."

They were a lot of hypocrites, professing to honor women while making sport half the night with soiled doves; tut-tutting in their clubs about a climbing boy's death—climbing boys were always meeting horrible fates, given the number of chimneys in London—while doing nothing to amend the laws affecting the poor little wretches.

"You are merely human," Rosalyn said, "though I suspect Lord Colin has chosen the wrong time to turn up human himself. His circumstances aren't easy, Winthrop."

"Must you be so good, Roz? I'm embarking on a fit of the dismals, and you're helping all too effectively."

Rosalyn took another swallow of brandy and passed the drink over to Win. Half a glass resulted in an agreeable glow, and Win would pour more for her if she asked it of him.

"I'm good only because it annoys you. Tell me about Lord Colin."

Rosalyn had considered attaching the affections of the new Duke of Murdoch, Lord Colin's older brother. His Grace was a brute of a man. His past, rife with rumors of scandal and disgrace, had quelled her enthusiasm for his company. While she'd been steeling her nerve to endure his suit despite the gossip—he was a duke, and rumored to be quite wealthy—Miss Megan Windham had stolen a march on her.

These things happened, though Rosalyn would rather they didn't happen to her. Young, single, wealthy dukes were scarcer than sober university students.

"About Lord Colin," Win said, making even the name an ode to long-suffering. "A few of the fellows decided to play a prank on him. We thought we'd lighten his pockets by putting a convivial evening or two on his account. He can stand the expense, believe me, Roz."

And Win could not. Rosalyn well knew how financial constraints could pinch worse than an overlaced corset.

"He failed to see the humor?"

"I gather Scottish humor is an oxymoron." Win finished the drink and held the glass up to the light. "I can't entirely blame him for his pique."

"Blame him a little. He's put you out of sorts, and that I cannot abide."

Rosalyn took the glass from Win and refilled it at the sideboard. She helped herself to another sip, brought it back to Win, and settled next to him.

"What's the rest of it?" she asked, because in the normal course, Win would have lifted a handsome eyebrow at his lordship, six other lackeys would have lifted their eyebrows—a Greek chorus of manly condescension—

and Lord Colin would have fallen into an embarrassed silence.

He was not a stupid man, even if he was red-haired and Scottish.

Though his lordship had let Win entangle him with the House of Urchins—not the most shrewd decision, that.

"The prank got out of hand, which I should have anticipated. Pierpont has never known when to leave well enough alone. He had the tailors bill a new morning coat to Lord Colin, who, thanks to me, patronizes the same establishment. Pointy told them it was in settlement of a wager."

"For Hector Pierpont, that verges on genius."

"Exactly. Who would have thought Pierpont, of all the dim candles, could have aspired to such cleverness? Not to be outdone, Twillinger decided to try the same tactic at Tatts, and came away with one more horse for his stables, a fine gelding. I gather a pair of boots is on order, a dozen pairs of gloves, three gold-tipped walking sticks, and who knows what else has been put in train."

Tatts dealt with only top quality horseflesh, and English law took anything relating to an exchange of equine stock very seriously.

"You are not concerned for Lord Colin," Rosalyn said. "You are in a pet because your scheme has taken on a life of its own. Your dearest friends have placed you in an awkward position, though all of them would reciprocate by claiming you put them up to it."

And the claims would doubtless be justified. Winthrop had a devious streak, which when combined with his gift for bonhomie could look a lot like manipulation.

"I hate you." Said with sincere, if reluctant, brotherly affection. "I very nearly hate old Pointy, Twilly, and the lot of them." He drained half the glass and passed it to her. "At least it wasn't entirely my idea."

Rosalyn knew an attempt to shift blame when she heard it, for she'd talked herself around many an awkward position.

"The initial idea was yours, Win. I'd wager your example at the public house was not subtly rendered, nor was it a single instance."

Rosalyn could not recall the evening Win had ended entirely sober, and regarding drink, he was a Methodist spinster auntie compared to most of his friends.

"I might have been a trifle sozzled when the inspiration first came to me," Win said, studying his brandy. "Not at my best when I'm sozzled."

"None of us are, dear heart. I hear your affections are attached in an unfortunate direction these days too."

"Rosalyn, you are a lady. I'll thank you not to venture into corners best kept private, or I won't escort you to Lady Dremel's whist party tonight."

"You must be violently in love." Which was unusual for Win and probably bewildering. He was utterly selfish regarding intimate matters, as far as Rosalyn could tell. What man wasn't? "Can you apologize to Lord Colin, Win?"

"That's the difficult part. A man apologizes when he's not wrong, as a polite gesture, a sop to appearances. When he *is* wrong, the matter becomes more complicated."

Pure masculine balderdash. "Is that what you learned at Oxford?"

"Don't be a shrew."

Rosalyn very much wanted to attend the evening's card party. No entertainment appealed to her as much as gathering around a table with a deck of cards and three other people, all equally skilled, and equally at the mercy of chance.

"I can tell you what works for me," she said, because Win was a prince when sober, but he could be a brat when he imbibed. He'd plead a headache and deny her the only outing she'd looked forward to all week.

"Do tell," he muttered, finishing his drink.

"I throw myself on the other person's charity," she said. "If it's an IOU I can't pay timely, a comment I shouldn't have made that was overheard, a bit of confusion regarding who was supposed to dance with whom for the supper waltz. I apologize, I explain why I was not at my best, and I ask them to forgive me. Works a treat every time."

Especially with the gentlemen. Other young women were generally tolerant as well, but Rosalyn was careful with the older ladies and with a few of the older gents.

"You think I should turn up sweet with MacHugh," Win said, sniffing at his empty glass. "Bat my eyes, simper, and look helpless?"

"More or less. Has he agreed to pay the shot?"

"He'll do it, but it was a near thing. The Scots are so tightfisted."

"Then you thank him effusively, tell him you'll never forget his magnanimity, and assure him you're in his debt."

Win was on his feet, heading back to the sideboard. "A bare-kneed, upstart Scot, and I'm in his debt. I thought merely to curry favor with a new title, and now I'm saddled with a mess, though I suppose you're right."

A mess of Win's own making. He'd taken aim at Lord Colin's friendship with the same calculation Rosalyn chose her dancing partners and her reticules, which was entirely understandable.

Win poured another half a glass, downed it, and set the empty glass on the tray. "I could cut Lord Colin. He's grown prodigiously tiresome."

Good heavens, drink made men imbeciles. "You'd have to deal with him at the orphanage, and Anwen Windham wouldn't appreciate your change of heart toward her in-law. You should court her, by the way."

For the first time, Win smiled, and my, he was a handsome devil when he truly smiled. "Court Anwen Windham? She's meek, retiring, red-haired, and nowhere near next in line to be fired off."

Those same attributes hadn't stopped her sister Megan from becoming a duchess. "Anwen wouldn't give you any trouble, and she's desperate to get out of that household. I like her, when she isn't being passionate about her orphanage. She's not catty, even though I'm much prettier than she is."

Beauty really could be a burden. So few understood that.

Anwen was also willing to make a discreet loan to a friend when a loan was much needed, and she didn't fuss about it. She didn't tattle, she didn't put on airs, she never mentioned the favor, and she was genuinely kind.

Too bad when it came to marriage, she wouldn't do any better than an earl's younger son, not with two older sisters left to marry off first and a personality about as colorful as a winter sky.

"Miss Anwen strikes me as a woman who'd expect her husband to be *involved* in the marriage," Win said. "She has a seriousness that bodes ill for a lighthearted fellow like myself. Besides, I'm not ready to get married."

"So few of us are. You won't cut Lord Colin, will you? Snubbing a member of a ducal family, especially a wealthy ducal family with two marriageable daughters, will create endless awkwardness."

Winthrop picked up the decanter and headed toward the door. "I won't cut MacHugh, much as I wish I could. He likely has money coming out his arse, but even more than money, he's wallowing in honor, and Scottish honor can take a violent turn. He warned me that the joke is over, or else."

"Or else what?" Win couldn't control a dozen drunken fools, no matter how he might flatter himself to the contrary. If the joke wasn't over for them, no telling who might end up calling out whom.

"That's why I won't cut him," Win said, one hand on the door latch, the other wrapped around the brandy decanter. "He more or less threatened to lay about with his claymore if the fellows don't stop their nonsense. I'll start putting the word out tonight that the joke has run its course, else you'd not get me to move from my bed."

Win sauntered on his way, decanter at the ready, and Rosalyn let him go.

He was a fine brother, but his version of friendship was mercenary even for Rosalyn's tastes. No wonder Lord Colin was disappointed. Friends were for borrowing from, not stealing from. If one had to steal, better to steal from strangers.

Even the little pickpockets and housebreakers at the orphanage would know that much.

* * *

The door to the MacHugh library was locked, and Anwen's heart was opening in a way that had nothing to do with a glass of cordial, and everything to do with the man she was kissing. Colin not only argued with her when the situation called for it, he confided in her, and he sought her counsel.

The physical intimacy he offered in addition was like the fragrance enveloping a colorful bouquet, another dimension, more subtle, and apparent only in close proximity. Precious, but by no means the only important attribute of the whole.

"Anwen Windham, you know how to start off a courtship."

"Who swept me off my feet, Colin MacHugh?" Physically and emotionally. Colin had shifted, so Anwen lay across his lap, her back and legs supported by the arms of the chair. The posture was novel, also cozy and—with him—comfortable.

"I chose a chair for us. How would you like to be courted, Anwen, my dear?"

"Briefly."

His expression turned fierce. "I'm no' intent on dallyin'. I'm intent on making a proper fuss complete with all the nonsense. Walking you home from the kirk, sitting down to dinner with your family, callow swaining at its handsome best." He leaned closer. "I want your supper waltzes, woman. Every one of them."

He wanted her waltzes. She wanted to have his babies. "We have only a handful of weeks remaining to the season, Colin. Most people announce an engagement before polite society departs for the country at the end of June."

His brushed the pad of his thumb over her lips. "We'll be getting engaged, then?"

He clearly didn't assume so.

"I hope we will, or I wouldn't have agreed to let you court me."

Colin cradled her closer, his cheek against her temple. "The English do things differently. Kiss me."

What had he expected? That she'd lead him a dance for the next eight weeks, then flounce off for the dubious pleasures of the house party circuit?

The Scots apparently did things differently. Perhaps permission to court was a more tentative undertaking with them, but Anwen had made up her mind. No man—not her cousins, not their friends, not the endless procession of handsome bachelors or halfhearted suitors—had ever taken her concerns to heart the way Colin had.

He trusted her, he talked his frustrations over with her, he—

He kissed like Anwen's every fantasy made real, like a raspberry cordial love potion, so Anwen was both bonelessly relaxed and increasingly restless. She scooted close and became abruptly aware that their kisses had *affected* him.

"I'm stirred up." His smile would stir up a saint. "I hope you are too."

"A lady doesn't... that is... Whatever do you...?" Anwen had no idea what he meant. A glimpse of frisky livestock every so often hardly educated a woman about the *details* of courting intimacies. "I'm *bothered*."

"Bothered is a fine start. I can show you how to get unbothered. I'd like to, if you'll let me."

His smile had muted to an expression both tender and determined.

"I can't think, not when you insist on being so handsome."

"Close your eyes, bonnie lady. You tell me to cease, and I will, but I won't want to."

Anwen trusted Colin MacHugh. That was what lay beneath all of this marvelous intimacy, beneath their ability to air a difference, to share cares and worries. She trusted him to be honest and honorable, and to offer her marriage in a very short time.

Anwen closed her eyes, and Colin brushed kisses to her eyelids. "You excel at this callow swaining business, sir."

"I'll excel at the courting too, seeing as we're off to such a fine start."

Anwen's skirts whispered about her ankles and a warm caress glided up her calf. Colin's touch was callused, slow, and novel, but not unpleasant.

"Your mind is busy, lass. I can't imagine we're supposed to think our way through a courtship."

No witty or even coherent reply occurred to her, so she occupied herself with the interesting task of kissing Colin. He tasted of mint. His tongue brushed her lower lip, and Anwen devoted herself to learning the contours of his mouth.

Megan had said that being courted had been wonderful beyond description. She had been right.

"Spread your knees a wee ... aye, like that."

How bold he was, though Anwen didn't feel rushed or presumed upon. She felt cherished and *curious*.

"Do I get to touch you like this some time?" she asked.

"Whenever ye like."

She slid a hand inside his shirt, felt the beat of his heart beneath her palm, the exact texture of the hair dusting his chest.

His fingers slid higher, and Anwen went still, focused on the sensations Colin created as he stroked her knees and thighs. Her breasts ached, and frustration entwined with pleasure.

"This isn't working," she said. "I'm getting more bothered." So was he, if the solid ridge of flesh pressing against her hip was any indication. Impressively bothered.

"It's working."

They were arguing again, which reassured Anwen that Colin knew what he was about. His caresses drifted higher, to ruffle the curls at the juncture of her thighs.

She turned her face into his shoulder and surrendered herself to his expertise. His touch was at once careful and bold, reassuring and daring.

"Are you sure this is part of courtship, Colin MacHugh?"

"It's part of our courtship. A significant part, if you enjoy it. Or I can stop."

Colin's fingers glossed over intimate flesh, and sensation streaked through Anwen like the *ignis fatuus* that glowed in wild places deep in the night. Like those elusive lights, the pleasure flickered and faded on the instant.

"Don't stop, but don't..."

His touched slowed.

"Colin MacHugh, tease me at your peril."

"How I adore a woman who knows what she wants."

Anwen didn't know exactly what she wanted, but she trusted Colin could find it for her. A feeling like vertigo stole over her, so that instead of gravity, Colin's touch was what kept her oriented. All of Anwen's awareness focused on his caresses, on the rhythm of his breathing, on the heat and longing he generated.

"Don't chase it," he said, kissing her brow. "Let it light upon you from within."

Colin's breath whispered across her cheek, just as the pleasure caught, ignited, and burst forth into feelings too intense to qualify as mere sensation. Anwen clung to Colin, shuddered against him, bucked up into his touch, and shuddered yet more.

Nothing about the moment was dignified, but everything about it was precious. Colin's hand rested over her sex as her body quieted. His heat and strength sheltered her, while a maelstrom of tenderness buffeted her from within.

"I had no idea," she said. "No earthly notion. No inkling. No suspicion. Mother of God."

If Colin had told her that colors existed she'd never perceived, or there were lands beneath the earth, and kingdoms in the sky, she could not have been more dumbfounded.

Or pleased.

"I'm still bothered, in a sense," she said. "I could not bear for you to touch me like that again just now, but I'm still stirred up too." In a complete, golden muddle, in fact.

"Now comes a wee cuddle, while you get your bearings."

"What about your bearings?"

"I didna lose them, this time. We will speak of comfortable things and ease away from the fire. When we leave this library, you will be a woman with a devoted suitor, assuming your uncle doesna object."

She loved the feel of his speech when his burr became pronounced. Words rumbled out of him, like water down a burn after a rain, rather than some placid little trickle meandering through a pasture.

"Uncle will approve," Anwen said. "He accepted your brother, whose reputation was tarnished by gossip. Why do I want to close my eyes?"

"Because you've earned a rest."

He kissed her eyelids again, as if putting a parenthesis of caresses around this extraordinary interlude. For a few luscious moments, Anwen drowsed. As a child, she'd watched butterflies emerging from their cocoons. The process was gradual, and the new butterfly was hardly recognizable until it had taken time to rest, unfold its wings, and bask in the sun.

Anwen basked in new sensations, in revelations, and in Colin MacHugh's secure embrace.

Her last thought before nodding off was that she'd acquired a devoted swain, and their courtship was off to a glorious start.

Chapter Eleven

"MISS ANWEN SUGGESTED I might prevail upon you for some assistance." Colin liked how that had come out. Not a question, not a demand. A statement. He liked the look of Lord Rosecroft's stable too, tidy and utilitarian. Horses contentedly munched hay in their loose boxes, a cat napped in a heap of straw at the end of the aisle.

No piles of horse droppings left about to draw flies, but no engraved brass name plates on the stall doors either.

The rhythm of Rosecroft's currycomb on the gelding's quarters was the steady, unhurried touch of a man who knew his way around the equine.

"You are granted permission to court a woman one day, and you're importuning her cousins for favors the next? Fast work, MacHugh."

After the encounter with Anwen the day before yesterday, Colin had wasted no time scheduling an interview with Moreland. The discussion had been brief, jovial on

Moreland's part, and terrifying as hell for Colin. Moreland had cheerfully promised to call him out if he broke Anwen's heart.

The duke had not been jesting.

"I had a *private* interview with His Grace yesterday, and Anwen's personal business is being discussed by her cousin in the mews today?"

Rosecroft paused in his currying and banged the brush against the sole of his boot. Horse hair, dander, and dust cascaded to the raked floor of the stable.

"What sort of assistance do you seek, MacHugh? I refuse to come within fifty yards of that orphanage. By June, my womenfolk and I are for Yorkshire."

Tactical retreat, both in the conversation and the travel. Rosecroft's reputation in the army had been effective prosecution of any task he'd been given. He'd delivered orders against long odds, fought ferociously and often, and had been well liked by his subordinates.

He'd also been more than fair to Hamish when Colin's brother had been courting Miss Megan.

"I need ponies," Colin said. "Four healthy, sane, welltrained ponies who will mind their manners in traffic and for outings in the park."

Rosecroft kept a hand on the horse's quarters and walked around to the beast's other side. "You'll look damned silly on a pony, MacHugh."

"As would you. The ponies aren't for me, they're for the orphanage."

Rosecroft leaned over the horse, one arm draped across the animal's croup, the other across the withers.

"You love her, don't you?" The question was rendered with sympathy rather than menace.

"Hamish warned me that the Windhams are very much

in each other's pockets." Colin prevaricated not only because his sentiments toward Anwen were private, but also because they were hard to describe.

Complicated, which was unnerving.

"If you don't love Anwen, you're an idiot," Rosecroft said as the horse cocked a hip and sighed. "Because if she wants you for a husband, you're as good as married, MacHugh. I don't care if your brother is a duke and your mother plays whist with the archangel Gabriel. Anwen deserves to be happy."

"We are agreed on that priority. About the ponies."

"Ponies are the equine equivalent of fairies," Rosecroft said, giving the horse a scratch about the withers. "Not to be trusted, always busy about their own ends, and deceptively adorable. I much prefer horses when there's a choice."

The gelding was a big, raw-boned chestnut, its musculature not yet caught up to its size. For a young animal, it was calm and patient with the grooming routine, and its conformation promised smooth, ridable gaits.

"I'd put this fellow at about five," Colin said. "Possibly six, if he was started late. Needs hill work to strengthen the quarters, which is hard to accomplish in London."

"That is the bloody damned truth," Rosecroft said. "I have plans for this one that will have to wait until summer. Until then, boredom is his greatest foe. What do you have planned for four ponies?"

Rosecroft wouldn't deal well with boredom either.

"The orphanage has one pony to pull Cook's trap when she goes to market, and a team for when Hitchings takes the coach about town, a pair of bays who are mostly idle. When they're in the traces, they're cross and Hitchings requires a coachman to harness them and drive them. Keeping those horses costs a small fortune, and around ill-tempered equines of that size, boys just learning to groom won't be safe."

If a pony stepped on a boy's toes, the boy could shove the wee beast off. A coach horse might break the boy's foot and still not be inclined to move away.

"Ponies bite," Rosecroft said. "They kick, rear, strike."

"And are more manageable than coach horses when they do. These boys have weathered London winters without shelter, lost their families, and endured hours of detention day after day. They need to learn useful activities through which to support themselves or they'll revert to lives of crime and chaos when they weary of the orphanage's rules."

Rosecroft exchanged the curry for a soft brush and started at the top of the horse's neck. "They need to be boys, but if the orphanage is in want of funds, why take on four more mouths to feed?"

And stalls to bed, feet to trim? Hitchings had asked the same question.

"We'll get rid of the coach horses and the coach. The pony trap has a bonnet, and Hitchings can time his few errands for fair weather. The boys can learn to groom, maintain harness, hitch and unhitch, and even ride and drive while the House of Urchins saves money."

The chestnut's coat glowed as Rosecroft worked his way all over the horse. Rosecroft knew what he was doing too, knew where the horse was more sensitive, and where a firmer touch was in order.

"You're daft, replacing a proper team with demon ponies," Rosecroft said. "What will you do if the orphanage has to haul something substantial? Say, a lot of desks donated by a patron? A piano or two?"

"I'll borrow a team from my brother's London brewery," Colin said. "I'll prevail on MacHugh the publisher to lend me his team. MacHugh the saddle maker could probably oblige me as well, and MacHugh the fishmonger has a huge wagon, though it reeks of fish. You know what it costs to maintain a coaching team."

"That I do," Rosecroft said, taking a comb to the horse's mane. "What about when the boys outgrow these ponies?"

"Then the boys will be old enough to start in some fine gent's stables, and younger boys can take their places. If you're not interested in helping, Anwen suggested Lord Westhaven can be relied upon—"

Rosecroft glowered across the horse's neck. "Don't be bothering his lordship. His youngest is teething. The man gets no peace, and I suspect he's to be a papa again. Don't tell him I said that. Your idea is unconventional."

Rosecroft had the look of the duke about the chin and nose. He also had a green smear of horse slobber across his cravat.

"Adhering to convention has left the orphanage facing penury. The four oldest boys all slept in one bed last winter because it was the only way to keep warm. They heaped all their blankets together, dove under, and shivered until morning. They organized the smaller boys' dormitory in the same fashion, else half the children would likely have perished of lung fever."

Colin hated that the children had had to make shift for themselves, but he delighted in their ability to solve a serious problem on their own—and convention be damned.

"So you'll give them ponies, the finest guilt offering any parent ever made. Four ponies, not just one or two. Heaven help you if your union with Anwen is fruitful. Don't say I didn't warn you."

Did every Windham have this compulsion to argue? "Rosecroft, what are you doing?"

"Combing my horse's mane. He likes it, and he's a handsome lad when properly turned out, if a bit stiff to the right and lacking in courage."

"You're an *earl* in your own right. Your father is a duke, and here you are, your fingernails dirty, your boots in need of a serious shine. *What are you doing?*"

Every hair of the horse's mane lay tidily against its neck. "I'm caring for my cattle."

"Exactly. Even the son of an English duke is taught how to look after a horse, not because that boy will need employment someday, but because horsemanship builds character. Work in the stables also builds the physique, self-discipline, and organizational abilities.

"Ponies are a way for the orphanage to offer the boys all of that," Colin went on, "while cutting costs. What's unconventional is that I want those children to have access to at least one of the lessons considered indispensable for every gentleman's son. Not Latin, not philosophy, not ancient history that they'll never use, but simple horsemanship. Even an English earl ought to understand that much."

"Half-English," Rosecroft said, fishing a lump of carrot from his pocket. "My mother was an Irishwoman who had an irregular relationship with Moreland before he met his duchess."

Colin knew that Rosecroft cared greatly for Anwen, that he admired her and wanted to protect her. When Colin had asked to court her, he hadn't quite bargained on her bringing such a lot of family to the undertaking.

Hamish had married into the Windham family less than a month ago, and Colin was still not entirely sure where his brother had found the courage.

"Rosecroft, why would I give a pig's fart about what Moreland got up to more than thirty years ago? You're here, you're part of Anwen's family, and I need four good ponies."

The earl unfasted the crossties on both sides of the horse's headstall, and still the animal stood as if rooted.

"Glad to know Anwen is being courted by a man of sensible—though unconventional—priorities. If I catch you frequenting dark balconies with merry widows, though, you will learn the pleasure of flying headfirst into a bed of roses."

"That must be the Irish half of you threatening violence, because I have it on good authority English gentlemen never stoop to acknowledging bad behavior."

Rosecroft fed the horse another lump of carrot. "Good boy, Malcolm. Come along."

Without Rosecroft touching the headstall, the horse followed as meekly as an elderly pug, straight into a stall at the end of the row. Rosecroft said a few more words to the horse, then slid the half door closed.

"You named your horse Malcolm?"

"My daughter names all the horses," Rosecroft said. "Who told you English gentlemen don't acknowledge bad behavior?"

"No less personage than Winthrop Montague assured me that if I remark ill usage by some of his associates, I'll be considered ungentlemanly. The repercussions will be endless and severe."

"What in the hell are you going on about?"

Hamish had said that of the three male cousins—Westhaven, Lord Valentine, and Rosecroft—Rosecroft was the one most sympathetic to an outsider. He was also the oldest of the ducal siblings, and Anwen liked him.

"I've been made the butt of a joke," Colin said. "An expensive joke."

He explained, and the retelling left him angry all over again. He'd arranged to borrow from Hamish's brewery while funds were being transferred between Edinburgh and London because he wanted the debts paid in full immediately.

"I'm not to even the score," he said, "but I can't abide the notion that twenty years from now, these prancing ninnies will snicker into their port because Colin MacHugh was an easy mark. Then I tell myself, twenty years from now, I'll have much better ways to occupy myself than with what a lot of overgrown English schoolboys think of me."

He offered that bit of manly philosophizing while the barn cat stropped itself against his boots.

"Winthrop Montague is a philandering sot who can barely afford his tailor's bills," Rosecroft said. "Pay the trades, MacHugh. Not because you need Montague's approval, but because he's not worth your aggravation. You will join my brothers and me for cards on Tuesday, and let that be known among Montague's little friends."

Colin picked up the cat, a sleek tabby that had likely been the doom of many a mouse. "Montague fancies himself quite the arbiter of gentlemanly deportment, the heir apparent to Brummel."

"The Beau is kicking his heels in Calais because he has no funds to go elsewhere. He's a charity case. If Montague doesn't marry very well and soon, he'll end up likewise."

Colin scratched the cat behind the ears. Hearing Rosecroft's assessment of Win's situation should have been unsettling rather than reassuring.

"You forgot to pick out the gelding's hooves." Even if a

horse was put up without being groomed, a conscientious owner picked out the feet, lest a stone lodge against the sole and cause an abscess.

Rosecroft subsided onto a tack trunk. "I leave that to the lads, because nobody cares if they get dirt on their breeches. Montague is not your friend, MacHugh."

Colin took the place beside him and let the cat go free. "I should tell you that Win Montague isn't responsible for the behavior of a lot of drunken fools, and he means only to preserve me from more mischief."

Except, Montague had been *in on it*, very likely an instigator, and he'd done nothing to monitor the situation or stop it, until Colin had been on the verge of calling somebody out.

Anwen had certainly been angry.

"A friend should have told you immediately what was afoot if he couldn't prevent it," Rosecroft countered. "I take it you will be in attendance at Anwen's card party?"

The Windham family was like a Highland village. News traveled faster than pigeons, and in all directions at once.

And that was more unexpected reassurance.

"I am on the board of directors at the orphanage now, so yes. I'll be in attendance at the card party, prepared to gracefully lose a decent sum. You?"

"Oh, of course. I can hardly contain my enthusiasm for hours of polite society pretending it gives a damn about the poor children it ignores starving in the streets."

No wonder Rosecroft longed for his Yorkshire acres, if he was always plagued by such honesty.

"I can't do anything for the whole of London's poor," Colin said, "but these children matter to Anwen. I'll be at the damned card party."

"You're in love," Rosecroft said, whacking him on the

back. "If it's a matter of first impression, sometimes a fellow isn't sure. The proof is in the suffering. Wait until you're reading *Gulliver's Travels* to your children yet again, or forgoing the pleasures of the marriage bed because a thunderstorm descends in the same hour you find yourself private with your wife for the first time in a fortnight. Then there's teething, and—"

"Rosecroft, are you daft?" Though if the earl was daft, he was cheerful with it.

"I am in love," he said, rising. "Meet me at Tatts tomorrow at nine."

Thank the winged cherubs. "It's not a sale day."

"Only dandiprats and nincompoops buy from Tatts exclusively on sale days. Those are the horses they want to get rid of. The very best stock never goes on the block. What have you heard from your brother the duke?"

Colin rose and dusted the cat hairs off his breeches. "Not much. He's honeymooning with your cousin."

"Marital bliss takes a toll on a fellow's correspondence. You'll never get that cat hair off your breeches."

Colin flicked his lordship's cravat. "You're giving me fashion advice?"

Rosecroft peered at the green stain adorning his linen. "Malcolm's still learning his manners. Join me for an ale, and I'll tell you what I know about surviving a courtship. Takes strategy and stamina, but a man fixes his eye on the prize and endures. I suspect a woman does too."

Colin could believe that. The other evening, he'd sent Anwen back to her sisters and locked the library door behind her, lest he go blind with thwarted desire. Five minutes later, he'd buttoned up, drained his flask, and rejoined the ladies in the parlor, though he'd taken care not to sit within six feet of Anwen.

Rosecroft was deep into an analysis of the benefits of a special license—and halfway through a tankard of very fine summer ale—when Colin realized that Rosecroft had been right.

Winthrop Montague was not Colin's friend. Around Win, Colin had always felt subtly judged and wary of making a wrong move. Around Rosecroft, who shrugged at a stained cravat and admitted easily to being in love, Colin could relax.

His instincts had been trying to warn him that Win's crowd wasn't where he belonged. Why had he ignored his own instincts, and should he heed them when they prompted him to find some way to even the score?

* * *

Megan, Duchess of Murdoch, passed the whisky glass back to her husband without taking a drink.

"The scent is fruity," she said, "in a good way. Oranges and limes, rather than lemons. An odd note of cedar too." Her condition had made her palate and her nose extraordinarily sensitive, and her husband extraordinarily attentive.

She'd also become extraordinarily eager to reciprocate his attentiveness, even for a newlywed Windham.

"By God, you're right," Hamish muttered, taking a sip of the whisky. "I would have missed the cedar. Colin would have too."

As the days since the wedding had turned into weeks, Hamish mentioned Colin more and more. The three youngest MacHugh brothers were off enjoying Edinburgh's social season, but they'd never served in battle beside Hamish, hadn't stood with him at the front of St. George's, hadn't been his second on the field of honor.

"Write to him," Megan said. "Tell Colin you miss him, and that his business needs him."

"Bloody correspondence," Hamish muttered, setting the glass down. "I don't suppose a wee note could hurt." He took a seat at Megan's escritoire, a delicate Louis Quinze item of fanciful inlays, tiny drawers, and shiny brass fittings.

Hamish should have made an incongruous picture seated there. He was tall, broad-shouldered, and far from handsome by London standards.

They weren't in London, though. Megan and her spouse were lazing away a morning in her private parlor, which she'd chosen because it had both south- and east-facing windows. While London townhouses favored fleur-de-lis and gilt, Hamish's Perthshire estate tended more to exposed beams, plaid wool, and comfort. This parlor, however, was Megan's domain, and thus the wallpaper was flocked, the desk French, and the carpet a vivid red, gold, and blue Axminster.

The chair creaked as Hamish settled to his task. Megan took off her slippers, tucked her feet under her, and fought off a wave of drowsiness.

"Are you having a wee nap, Meggie mine?" Hamish asked sometime later.

She stretched and yawned, for indeed, she'd curled up on the sofa, and some considerate husband had draped his coat over her.

"Is this my second or third nap today?" Megan asked.

"Third, but it won't be your last. May I read you this letter?"

Hamish read to her frequently. Her eyesight was poor, and he sought to spare her visual effort. Megan indulged him, mostly because she loved to hear his voice.

The note was chatty by Hamish's standards, describing various weddings and birthings among the local gentry and tenants, and ending with a stern admonition to "mind the tailors don't bankrupt you."

"A very fraternal letter," Megan said as Hamish sprinkled sand over the page. "Might I add a line or two?"

"I can write them for you, Meggie mine. Use wee words, though, for the sight of you asleep in the morning sun befuddles a mere Scottish duke. What would you like to say to our Colin?"

Very little befuddled Hamish MacHugh. "I had a letter from Anwen yesterday."

Hamish stroked the goose quill with blunt fingers. Not a gentleman's hands, but how Megan loved her husband's touch.

"What did Anwen have to say?"

"She prosed on about her orphanage, which is in dire financial straits, and some card party that she hopes will rescue it. She mentioned that Colin has taken an interest in the orphanage."

Hamish folded his arms. Without his coat, Megan could see his biceps bunching and flexing. Her next nap would be in the ducal bed and would involve her husband's intimate company.

"Colin has about as much interest in orphans as I have in the quadrille, Meggie."

"Anwen would have me believe Colin's doing his gentlemanly bit for charity."

Hamish rose and joined Megan on the sofa. He tucked a blanket over her lap and bare feet, which necessitated several near-caresses to her ankles.

"Colin does plenty for charity," Hamish said, shrugging back into his coat, "though mostly he supports wounded veterans who reported to him. He can't ignore a situation that needs fixing, which is why he served much of his time as an artificer. Tinkering with temperamental stills is apparently fine training for keeping an army in good repair."

"My sister is not in want of repair." Though Anwen was lonely, and as the youngest, she tended to be overlooked. Colin might notice that.

And Anwen had definitely noticed Colin.

"I think we should nudge Colin and Anwen in each other's direction," Megan said. "Encourage them."

"Meddle, you mean? Are you trying to make a Windham duke of me, Meggie? Moreland is doubtless keeping watch. If there's matchmaking to be done, he's the fellow to do it."

Hamish crossed to the desk and resumed writing without taking a seat.

"Are you warning Colin about Moreland's tendency to matchmake?"

"I'm trying my hand at meddling. I'm a duke now, and mustn't shirk my responsibilities." He waved the paper gently and brought it to Megan along with one of her six pairs of spectacles.

At the bottom of the page Hamish had added a postscript. "Get your handsome arse home where you belong, and don't forget to bring Ronnie and Eddie with you. If you're not back by Mid-Summer's Day, I'm tapping the '01."

"But I don't want him hurrying home," Megan said. "Anwen will never leave London if her orphans are imperiled, no matter how many times I invite her to visit."

"Done a bit of meddling yourself, have you, Duchess?" Hamish removed her spectacles and tucked them into his pocket, for they were the spare pair he always carried for her. "I know my brother. If I order Colin home, he'll remain in London out of sheer contrariness."

Having been born a Windham, and having married a MacHugh, Megan had a fine appreciation for the contrary male.

"I suspect you have the right of it, Hamish."

"Between the orphanage being in trouble, and a bit of high-handedness on my part, Colin will not budge from Mayfair until he's good and ready to. Maybe by then, Anwen will have fixed whatever is ailing Colin."

Hamish followed up that observation with a kiss.

As it happened, Megan's fourth nap of the day did not take place in the ducal bedchamber, but rather in the duchess's private parlor, after a thorough loving on the sofa.

Her second of the day, and not her last.

* * *

Anwen's life had acquired a sense of direction that combined getting the orphanage on sound financial footing with marrying Colin MacHugh. In the three weeks since he'd asked to court her, the board of directors had met weekly, and on the one occasion when they'd had a quorum, Colin had pushed through motions to acquire ponies, sell the coach and team, get estimates for fitting out a wing of rooms as gentlemen's quarters, and advertise for an assistant headmaster competent in French, music, and drawing.

Not to *hire* an assistant headmaster—Win Montague had bestirred himself to make that point—but to advertise and interview candidates.

"You want me to ask other ladies for their spare yarn?"

Lady Rosalyn said, when the directors had left the meeting room. Two other ladies on the committee had pleaded various excuses, though Anwen couldn't be bothered to care.

"Yes, I want you to ask your friends for their spare yarn." Rosalyn had helped to teach the boys to knit, though Anwen detected a cooling of relations between Winthrop Montague and Colin. "Everybody has yarn they've set aside for a specific project, and then didn't or couldn't use. I want that yarn."

Lady Rosalyn blinked slowly, twice. "Then shouldn't *you* ask them for it?"

"I will ask my acquaintances, and you will ask yours, who are far more numerous than my own. Extra yarn just clutters up a workbasket, and the boys will put it to excellent use. And while you're about it, please ask your friends to ask their friends, and I'll do likewise."

Her ladyship's pretty chin acquired an unbecomingly stubborn angle. "We have only twelve boys here, Anwen. How many scarves do you think they can wear? Are they knitting scarves for their ponies?"

"Rosalyn, they are knitting the scarves to sell and to donate to other orphanages. The orphanage needs to earn money where it can, and even small hands can knit competently. Then too, the boys need to learn that giving ennobles the giver. Consider how something as minor as one of your smiles brightens a gentleman's entire evening, and how you are gladdened to have cheered him."

As flattery went, that should be sufficient to make the point.

Her ladyship wrinkled a nose about which poetry had been written, albeit bad poetry. "Charity is one thing, Anwen, but once coin is exchanged—you mentioned selling the scarves—the matter veers perilously close to *trade*."

Joseph tapped on the door. He still didn't say much, but he was more animated, and time in the garden agreed with him.

"Yes, Joseph?"

He passed Anwen a note. *"The ladies are invited to join me for an inspection of the garden. Lord Colin MacHugh."*

"Is that a naughty note, Anwen Windham?" Rosalyn asked. "Your smile suggests you've received correspondence from a gentleman, and though I would never criticize a friend, even you must admit that certain lines, once crossed—"

Anwen passed over the scrap of paper. *"We* have received an invitation, nothing more. Joseph, thank you. We'll be down in five minutes."

Joseph bowed—the older boys were becoming quite mannerly—and withdrew.

"I must confess that child makes me uneasy," Rosalyn said. "I'm never certain what he comprehends."

"Joe is very bright." Anwen rose and straightened the chairs around the table one by one. "I assume he understands anything said in plain English. I left my bonnet in the chairman's office. Let's fetch it and join his lordship in the garden."

Lady Rosalyn had assembled her reticule, pelisse, and parasol, but didn't move until her gloves were on and smoothed free of wrinkles, and the most elaborately embroidered side of her enormous reticule was showing.

"Am I presentable? One wishes a mirror were available, though encouraging the children in vanity would be unkind."

"You are far beyond presentable. You'll put the flowers to shame." Assuming her ladyship arrived in the garden before autumn.

Lady Rosalyn moved at a decorous pace, as if giving all and sundry time to admire her. When she and Anwen arrived at the chairman's office, she peered around, running her gloved fingers over the desk surface and lifting the lock on the strongbox.

"Is there anything inside, or is this for show?"

Anwen plunked her bonnet on her head—a comfy old straw hat that fit perfectly. "Colin says at least three months' worth of coin should be on the premises at all times. Banks can be robbed, flooded, and burned to the ground, while Hitchings can haul that box out of the building in all but the most dire emergencies."

Rosalyn twiddled the lock's tumblers. "So the exchequer yet contains three months' worth of funding?"

Barely. "It does. Has Win said something to the contrary?"

"How does one open this? It looks quite secure."

"There's a combination, probably under some candlestick or blotter. Win would know. Shall we be off?"

Rosalyn had started to lift the candlesticks on the mantel, one by one. She reminded Anwen of a small child in new surroundings.

"You referred to Lord Colin as Colin, Anwen. You seem quite friendly with him."

"His brother is married to my sister. I should hope we're friendly. Do you know not a single invitation to the card party has sent regrets so far?"

Rosalyn promenaded down the corridor, her arm linked with Anwen's. "You fancy him, don't you?"

The last three weeks had been the happiest of Anwen's life. Colin called almost every day, danced with her at least once at each social gathering, and had twice sent her a note that purported to deal with business at the orphanage.

And on two magnificent occasions, they'd found the privacy to renew the intimacies Colin had introduced Anwen to in the library.

"Would it create awkwardness if I said yes, I do fancy him?" Anwen congratulated herself on a diplomatic understatement, not only because her friend's sensibilities should be spared, but also because Rosalyn could pitch a fit of pique like no other.

Her ladyship stopped at the foot of the stairs. Beyond the doorway, the boys were lined up along the steps leading to the garden, and Anwen heard Colin holding forth about...slugs?

"I had considered Lord Colin," Rosalyn said. "He's modestly good-looking, and his brother is a duke. His lordship owns a distillery, but I understand that's not unusual in Scotland, rather like owning a mill in more civilized environs."

Rosalyn was serious, or as serious as she ever was.

"Are you still considering him?"

The moment became fraught as Anwen realized that she *pitied* Rosalyn. Her ladyship had no idea that Colin more or less tolerated her. True pity was not a comfortable emotion, including as it did the knowledge that nothing Rosalyn could do, promise, say, or become would render her more attractive to Anwen's intended.

Colin could not be tempted by Rosalyn, because he was Anwen's.

As Anwen was his.

And Lady Rosalyn Montague of the beautiful perfection was in some way pathetic.

"The red hair puts me off," Rosalyn said, "meaning no insult to you, of course. If you married him, he couldn't blame red-haired children exclusively on you." She shot a glance toward the side door and leaned closer. "I think *you* should consider him. Your sister will bide in Scotland, and she might need the moral support. You're inclined toward charity by nature, after all."

She patted Anwen's arm, clearly pleased with having found a solution to the problem of Anwen's red hair.

"No need to thank me," she said, swanning off toward the door. "I'm good at managing delicate subjects, and at least until your sister increases, you'll be married to a duke's heir. Let's get this garden tour out of the way, shall we? Win is taking me to a musicale tonight, and one does want to dress carefully when most of the evening consists of sitting about, looking beautiful and gracious, hmm?"

And hiding one's general lack of usefulness, and the anger that likely engendered. Anwen suspected Rosalyn hid the frustration of being ornamental even from herself.

"I'll be along in a moment," Anwen said. "I forgot my spare knitting needles."

Lady Rosalyn snapped open her parasol. "Don't tarry, please. I've no wish to hear about noxious weeds and burrowing rodents. The company of small boys is trial enough for a lady's delicate sensibilities."

As Rosalyn made her way out to the garden, Anwen scampered back up to the first landing, where she tried to decide whether she ought to laugh, ignore the entire exchange with Rosalyn, or say a prayer for the poor fellow her ladyship eventually married.

Anwen did laugh quietly, and was still trying to compose herself into a semblance of ladylike decorum when Mr. Hitchings passed her on the landing five minutes later.

Chapter Twelve

Chapter Twelve

"SHE WON'T KNOW YOU'RE keen on her if you're always so serious-like," Tom said, because clearly, Lord Colin was not the brightest of fellows when it came to the ladies.

"Tom's right," Dickie said, sniffing at his fingers. He liked to brush them over the lavender bushes and then not wash his hands until supper. "Miss Anwen likes you. She says any question we have about manners that we don't want to ask her, we're to ask you because you are a *very fine gentleman.*"

Lord Colin propped one boot on the upper step of the garden terrace and swatted at his toes with a handkerchief. He managed to look gentlemanly doing even that, which in Tom's opinion was damned unfair.

"You lads are giving me advice on how to woo a lady?" his lordship asked, dusting off the second boot.

"Somebody had better," John said. "When I brought in the lemonade for your meeting upstairs, you were acting like Miss Anwen wasn't even sitting at the same table. You're not supposed to ignore the girl you like. Only utter gudgeons and Methodists think like that. The ladies can ignore us, but not the other way 'round."

Lord Colin straightened and put his handkerchief away. Joe watched him, expression thoughtful. "Wrinkles."

"Because I didn't fold my linen? Joseph, you will become a scientist, so closely do you monitor your environment." Lord Colin withdrew the handkerchief, folded it so his initials were visible, and tucked it in his pocket. "Better?"

Joe smiled, something that had begun to happen about two weeks ago. The first time he'd smiled was when Dickie and John had got into a manure battle in the mews, horse droppings being ever so well suited to serving as missiles. Dickie had ducked behind the muck wagon, lost his footing, and nearly pitched into a day's worth of manure.

"The ladies will join us in a few minutes," Lord Colin said. "If any man has a suggestion for how I ought to improve my standing in Miss Anwen's eyes, let him speak now."

"He means, if we have advice so she'll be sweet on him," Tom said. "Joe, what do you think?"

Joe studied Lord Colin, who cut a murderous fine figure in his riding attire. He'd promised to teach them all how to drive the ponies, but first each boy had to learn how to hitch up and unhitch. John had figured it out on his own, but Tom never seemed to get all the straps and buckles right so John was trying to show him, step by step.

At Lord Colin's request for advice, a smile started in Joe's eyes, then caught at the corners of his mouth and spread over his whole face, like the smell of baking bread fills a house on a rainy day. He puckered up his lips and made a kissy sound, and got a good punch in the ribs from Dickie for his suggestion.

"Miss Anwen's a lady," Dickie cried. "You show some respect."

Dickie was reminding everybody to show respect lately. He followed up his scold with a shove in John's direction, and John, of course, shoved him back.

"I do respect Miss Anwen," Lord Colin said, mussing Dickie's hair, "and I would never presume on a lady's person, but do you suppose she might be tempted to presume on mine? I would treasure her kisses."

"She likes you," Tom said, because this point had apparently not sunk into his lordship's handsome skull. "And you're an idiot if you don't like her back."

"Bring her flowers," Dickie suggested. "Something that smells good, not like John."

"Everybody brings the ladies flowers," Tom scoffed. "Just like everybody pities orphans. Miss Anwen doesn't just pity us and go on her way, she pays attention to us."

"She taught us to knit," John said. "Lady Rosalyn mostly scolded us for not knowing how."

"Perhaps Miss Anwen would teach me to knit," Lord Colin said.

Joe shook his head, which meant pounding some sense into his lordship was up to Tom.

"You can do the flowers and the flirting bit, just like everybody else, or you can *pay attention* to her. She likes you, she's pretty, and she cares a lot more about us than Mr. Montague Moneybags does. If you want her respect, you make sure she has yours first. The kissing part can come later."

"Tom will throw you in the honey cart if you hurt Miss Anwen's feelings," Dickie said. "John, Joe, and I will help him."

Lord Colin's smile faded. "Thank you, gentlemen, for sincere and wise advice, and a truly impressive threat. I like Miss Anwen exceedingly and esteem her greatly."

Lord Colin might have had more to say, except the side door opened and a parasol appeared. When the hand on that parasol turned out to belong to Lady Rosayln, no Miss Anwen at her side, any fool could have figured out which lady his lordship was *not* sweet on.

Lady Rosalyn came down the steps, her parasol in one hand, her skirts clutched up in the other, as if good green grass was so much pony poop.

"Your lordship, I'm afraid this tour will have to be brief. Miss Anwen will be along directly, but I must soon take my leave of you."

Her ladyship was beautiful, in a golden, perfect way, and she smelled good, and she acted as if four hardworking boys weren't standing right there ready to show her where the kitchen spices grew, and where the Holland bulbs would go.

Those decisions had been made by committee, which meant Tom and the other boys had had jolly loud arguments over damned sunlight, sodding drainage, bloody soil quality, and other particulars.

Tom was considering wishing her ladyship a cheerful bloody damned good day, when Joe gave a slight shake of his head.

A gent never takes offense when a lady's manners slip. Lord Colin had assured them on many occasions that gentlemanly manners were a matter of behavior not birth, so Tom considered himself a gentleman in training.

He wasn't at all sure Miss Anwen's pretty friend was a lady, though. He'd put that question to Lord Colin when Lady Rosalyn was no longer clinging to his lordship's arm like manure stuck to the bottom of a fellow's best Sunday boots.

* * *

Colin's happiness had blossomed along with the garden at the orphanage. Between hard work, stock donated from the vast Moreland gardens, and the benign weather of an English spring, weeds and bracken had been replaced with flowers, herbs, and medicinals.

Chaos had been replaced not only with order, but also with beauty.

And in Colin's life, warmth and hope had replaced duty and busyness. Hamish had sent along news from home, and *almost* admitted to missing Colin, but the pull of Perthshire was balanced by the satisfaction of progress at the orphanage.

And by Anwen's kisses. Respect was all well and good—the boys were right about that—but Colin also treasured Anwen's affection.

"You fellows should be ever so proud of this accomplishment," she said, after she'd admired each plant and flowerbed. "You've reduced Cook's market expenses, enhanced the appearance of your home, and created potential for income if we have flowers and herbs to spare. Job well done, gentlemen."

Four notably clean faces beamed. Tom shoved Dickie, who kicked Tom's foot, and all was right with Colin's world.

Almost.

"I agree with Miss Anwen," Colin said, snapping off a white climbing rose from a trellis the boys had woven of sticks. "Job very well done, and I must think of a way to reward the fellows responsible. I'm open to suggestions, so consider what would be appropriate."

"A reward?" Dickie asked, scrunching up his nose. "Like for peaching on your mates?"

The boys occupied the garden's lone bench, a simple plank affair that had probably been a tree when Duke William had paid a call from Normandy.

"A prize," Anwen said, brushing Dickie's mop of dark hair back from his brow. "Just like the prizes given out for writing the best essay, doing all the sums accurately in the shortest time, or having the neatest dormitory."

Tom sat a little taller at the mention of yesterday's sums contest. He'd earned an extra helping of pudding for his talents, which he'd given to the smallest boys, claiming to be too full to enjoy it.

Anwen was brimming with ideas for how to motivate the children with benefits and rewards rather than the birch rod. Old Hitchings had grudgingly reported an improvement in scholarship over the last month, even as funds had dwindled and board meetings had become exercises in futility.

"Lord Colin wants us to think of the prize we'd like best." Tom frequently served as interpreter, whether for Joe's silences or Anwen's genteel flights.

Joe took the rose from Colin and held it out to Anwen. "H-home."

The sight of the young boy, gaze hopeful, offering a single word to go with his blossom did queer things to Colin's heart.

"He's got that right," John said. "We'd like for this place to stay open."

"Aye," Dickie said. "We'd manage, but the little 'uns would be up the chimneys and down the mines or worse."

"That wee Walter's too pretty by half," John said.

"The orphanage has plenty of funds for the present," Colin said, before John could expound on the risks a pretty boy faced in London's underworld. "But I think four ponies might need their stalls set fair before luncheon."

The day was lovely, and setting fair was a periodic excuse to get outside, away from the desks, lectures, and Latin. The boys were off the bench and down the garden path in the next instant, their farewells bellowed in Anwen's direction as they scampered away.

Colin propped a hip on the stone wall and realized he was more or less alone with his lady love, but in the location least likely to afford them privacy.

"Two things bother me of late," he said.

She plucked a sprig of mint and took a seat on the bench. "Your friendship with Mr. Montague has become strained."

Colin didn't dare sit beside her, because if he sat beside her, he'd want to take her hand, and if he took her hand, he'd have to kiss the sensitive spot on her wrist that smelled of lemon blossoms and memories.

"That is one bother. How did you know?"

"He's testy. You make a motion, he lets the discussion go on so long that there's no time to vote on it, and then he doesn't bother to show up at the next meeting. You offer a quip, he can barely bring himself to smile. I'd hoped the whole business with the mischarged bills was behind you."

"I paid the bills within the week. Moreland even complimented me on dealing promptly with my debts. I think that's part of the problem."

Anwen patted the bench beside her, clearly willing to hear whatever troubles Colin cared to share with her. This aspect of their courtship—the heart-to-heart friendship

Anwen offered—pleased him even more than her passionate nature.

"Madam, I don't dare sit beside you."

She twined the mint around her white rose. "Whyever
not? We're in full view of half the neighborhood."

"Because if I sit next to you, I'll want to sit too close.
If I sit too close, I'll want to take your hand. If I take
your hand, I'll want to kiss your wrist, and if I kiss your
wrist…"

She knew exactly where wrist-kissing could lead, because he'd shown her that destination an entire week of hot
dreams and cold baths ago.

"Tell me about Winthrop Montague, sir."

Colin took some consolation from Anwen's smile,
which assured him that she'd be happy to discuss wrist-
kissing *later*.

"The objective of the mis-charging exercise," Colin
said, "was to shame me. I was to go hat in hand to the
various tradesmen, and explain that I needed time to address the situation. To ask for forbearance from the clubs
within weeks of being admitted would have been galling,
to say nothing of my new tailor, my bootmaker, Tatts, and
so forth."

Not galling, but rather, impossible. Colin would have
sold his horses, borrowed from his sisters, and taken work
with MacHugh the fishmonger rather than let those bills
linger.

"This lark grows complicated," Anwen said. "I like it
less as time goes on, and I hated it to begin with."

"If I'd asked Win what to do about the money, begged
him for a loan he couldn't make, complained to him about
being in dun territory, then I would still have his
friendship."

"Such as it was."

Anwen was very clear that Winthrop Montague had behaved badly.

"Are you angry with him on my behalf, or because he's shirking here at the orphanage? He warned me I'd be replacing him eventually."

"That was before Lord Derwent dodged off for the race meets. I understand that these men don't take the orphanage seriously, Colin. The directors have never shivered through the month of January fighting for a place to sleep in a church doorway. Win has stopped even pretending to care."

Hitchings came out of the building, a sheaf of papers in his hand rather than his birch rod.

Colin lowered his voice. "Win's unlucky in love, and apparently getting unluckier. The ladybird he longs to call his own is considering the protection of a duke's heir, and Win's nigh mad with frustration."

Colin could tell Anwen such things. She wasn't easily shocked, and Colin, being very lucky in love himself, felt an awkward pity for Win.

"Mrs. Bellingham again," Anwen said. "Perhaps Winthrop should hold a card party to sponsor his aims where she's concerned. Surely half the club members in Mayfair would turn out to support that worthy goal."

She was furious with Win, and Colin couldn't blame her.

"Win will be at your card party, and so will his friends."

Hitchings was gazing about, as if he expected four boys to pop out from the hedges. In bright sunlight, the headmaster looked pale and tired, and yet, he was clearly intent on some goal other than allowing Colin more privacy with Anwen.

"Winthrop Montague is chairman of the orphanage's board," she said, untangling the mint from the rose's stem. "If he fails to attend the card party, my aunt will skewer his social aspirations for the next five years."

"I hadn't thought of that. That explains why all of his friends accepted their invitations. I asked the duchess to extend her hospitality to each of the men responsible for trespassing on my good nature and my exchequer. Your dear aunt agreed that such graciousness was appropriate under the circumstances."

Before Colin could draw his next breath, Anwen was off the bench, her arms locked around his neck. "Oh, that was diabolical, Colin! No wonder they hate you, and it's so...It's brilliant."

The scents of mint and rose blended with Colin's delight at gathering his lady close. He'd expected the joy of being affectionate with her to wane, to mute into something more dignified, but every time he wrapped his arms around Anwen—every time he saw her, or even thought of her—his heart leapt.

As did another part of his anatomy.

"You approve?" he asked, taking a half step back, but keeping hold of her hand. "It's not quite revenge, but it's a statement. Rosecroft pronounced it a gentlemanly rebuke."

As had Edana and Rhona, who'd found torn hems, pressing thirst, or sudden fatigue cropping up whenever Win's friends had asked them to dance. Rosecroft had had a word with his countess and his regiment of lady sisters and sisters by marriage.

Win's friends were sitting out quite a few dances, and they weren't exactly flooded with invitations either.

Such a pity.

Anwen's smile would have lit up a Highland sky on a

January night. "Your gentlemanly rebuke is perfect. The orphanage will be the better for their attendance at the card party, and their pride will be the worse. I love it."

A throat cleared in the direction of the terrace.

Colin released Anwen's hand as boots scraped on the stone steps.

"Hitchings, good day." Hitchings had been notably quiet at the board meeting earlier in the day. He looked positively glum now.

"My lord, Miss Anwen. I trust you are aware that the orphanage cannot endure the sort of talk that would circulate had any but myself witnessed your display of exuberance for one another's company."

This was one reason Colin was desperate to announce their engagement, so that pompous old fools had no grounds to pass judgment and pontificate.

"I do apologize," Anwen said, "but as you know, Mr. Hitchings, the Windhams and the MacHughs are very closely connected, and I hope my respect and affection for Lord Colin are obvious to all."

Oh, nicely done.

Hitchings blushed. He shuffled papers, he cleared his throat. The old boy was shy in the presence of a lady, and why shouldn't he be? The orphanage was a male preserve, but for the influence of Anwen and her committee.

How lonely Hitchings must be.

"You came out here with information in hand," Colin said. "Is the matter urgent?"

From the mews across the alley, some boy shrieked with laughter, and then a loud clatter followed, along with more laughter.

"They love those ponies," Hitchings said, his tone both bewildered and aggrieved.

"Who wouldn't love a pony?" Anwen replied. "They're very dear, much like the boys."

Hitchings sent Colin a look. *All boys are hooligans.*

Colin certainly had been. "Do your papers have anything to do with the ponies?"

Hitchings looked at the papers as if they contained a draft of Wellington's eulogy. "I'm afraid so, indirectly. Perhaps Miss Anwen should excuse us?"

Hitchings trying to be mannerly sent alarm skittering down Colin's middle.

"If it has to do with the orphanage," Anwen said, "then I'd rather know sooner than later." She twined an arm through Colin's, which Hitchings noted with a raised brow.

"His lordship has proposed a scheme to turn the empty wing into gentlemen's quarters," Hitchings said. "Unusual notion, but worth exploring. Desperate times calling for desperate measures, and all that. I took it upon myself to inspect the unused wing, something I haven't done in a year."

At some point in the last few weeks, Hitchings had lost his air of perpetual affront, and replaced it with a dogged weariness. He taught every day, he occasionally went out on private errands in daylight hours, and he sat quietly at board meetings unless called upon to recite.

The boys certainly weren't complaining at the change, though funding had to be troubling the headmaster, as did having his authority gainsaid on occasion by a board that had never taught a single Latin declension.

"The building is old," Anwen said. "We know that. What did you find?"

Hitchings's expression became downright doleful. "Rising damp. The unused wing of the house is far gone. Deuced blight is everywhere that fires aren't routinely lit.

I blame myself, but economies being what they are, and English weather being what it is, half of this building is not going to stand much longer without substantial, expensive repairs. I'm sorry."

* * *

The news got worse.

As Anwen trailed Colin and Mr. Hitchings about the House of Urchins, she made a list. The windows in the unused wing hadn't been glazed for some time, and thus rain had worked its way in and attacked the walls and sills.

The ceilings in some rooms were also suffering water damage, or had at one time. Numerous stains were apparent, but how recently they'd developed was not clear.

The lower floors, being more frequently heated, showed less damage from the damp, but they were far from presentable in the unused wing. The boys' wing was in better repair, and the cellars closest to the kitchen's heat looked mostly sound.

As Colin and Mr. Hitchings had tramped from one floor to another, the smaller boys had followed them with worried gazes.

"We don't have this difficulty as much in Scotland," Colin said as he settled beside Anwen on the seat of his phaeton. "We build with stone, and then haven't enough wood for the moisture to get into. Our weather is cold enough that we keep fires going year 'round, whereas here, you often let the parlor fires go out in summer despite the damp."

Anwen longed to lay her head on his shoulder and wail, but that wouldn't solve the problem.

"Will Hitchings keep his mouth shut until after the card party?"

A tiger rode behind them, which was a gesture on Colin's part in the direction of greater propriety. Anwen suspected Colin was also taking a precaution against any "pranks" that might involve his vehicle and team.

"Hitchings has become something of a puzzle," Colin said as he gave the horses leave to walk on. "It's as if when the boys began to apply themselves to their studies, Hitchings came unmoored from his birch rod and he's been drifting since. Do you have any idea where he goes on his periodic jaunts up the alley?"

"Ask the boys," Anwen said. "They miss nothing, and they might have followed him from time to time."

She hoped the children were making fewer unscheduled outings, but they were boys. In many ways they were more self-sufficient in their minority than a proper lady would ever be, even should she attain widowhood.

"You are a wee bit dispirited," Colin said.

"I'm despairing." Anwen and her beloved were honest with each other. No reason to depart from that policy now. "The building is huge and full of problems—expensive problems—that somebody should have spotted before the orphanage was established there."

When Colin might have offered reassurances—the difficulties weren't that great, the repairs weren't that expensive—he remained silent, and that was honest enough. When he handed Anwen down in the Moreland mews, she pitched into him and wrapped her arms about him.

"I don't want to go into that house and be interrogated about the meeting's agenda, what outlandish reticule Lady Rosalyn carried today, and whether heartsease or roses would make better centerpieces for the card party buffet."

Colin stroked a gloved hand over her hair. "You want to cry? I do, or get drunk. Home is a feeling in the heart, but it's also a place, and for those boys to lose the place they live will upset them, even if we can establish the orphanage in new quarters. For too long, they've had nowhere to call their own and moving will be hard on them."

Anwen had been so muddled, so *angry*, she hadn't figured out even that much. "You think we can move the orphanage?"

As the grooms led the team away, Colin turned her under his arm and walked with her across the alley to the garden.

"In some ways," he said, "starting over elsewhere would be best. The old building is hard to heat, drafty, and badly laid out for the function it now serves. I gather the premises was once a grand townhouse, or several fine properties built together, and thus we have no connecting corridor between the two dormitories, no stairs from the classrooms to dining hall, and so forth."

"I never noticed that."

"I've stuck my nose in parts of the building you haven't, and you notice the boys. They are what matter."

The Moreland House garden was lovely, as only a well-tended English garden could be, and yet the flowers and sunshine did little to cheer Anwen.

"Maybe we should cancel the card party," she said. "Maybe we ought not to be taking people's money for a doomed endeavor. We can find places for the dozen boys we have. They weren't supposed to spend the rest of their lives at the House of Urchins. I know that."

She also knew that without Colin at her side, she'd be upstairs in her bedroom, crying as quietly as she could.

Colin drew her behind a lilac bush that hadn't a single blossom. "Is that what you want to do? Admit defeat, care for the wounded as best you can, then retreat?"

He draped his arms over her shoulders and kissed her. The touch of his lips was tenderness itself, as gentle as his inquiry. That he'd ask Anwen what she wanted meant worlds, and gave her the purchase she needed to consider her answer as she leaned into his embrace.

"The building is ill, far gone, Colin, and bringing it back to health will mean resources are diverted to architectural matters that ought to go to the boys. Fixing that place up, even if we had the means, would involve all manner of disruption to the boys, as well as extra effort for somebody to supervise the project. I know you want to return to Scotland in a few weeks and the board of directors will do nothing without you wielding the birch rod."

"Interesting analogies—the illness and the birch rod. We don't need to solve the entire problem today, though. We have some time."

In the circle of Colin's arms, Anwen calmed. He was right. They had time to think—or to plan a different path for the boys. They had time to consider options.

"The card party is Friday," Anwen said. "I won't have an opportunity to get back to the orphanage before then. Somebody should tell Winthrop Montague what Hitchings found. Mr. Montague is still the chairman of the board."

Colin kissed her again, more lingeringly. "He's still a donkey's arse too. I'm keen to leave London if for no other reason than to get away from him and his ilk."

In Colin's embrace, Anwen found comfort. In his kisses, she found a reminder that this was the man she'd soon marry, and she hadn't had nearly enough privacy with him since making that decision.

"We had a note from Mama and Papa yesterday," she said, sliding a hand around Colin's hip. "They've begun their homeward journey."

"So have I," Colin muttered.

His kiss intensified, from the garden variety that might be quickly stolen behind the hedge, to the voracious, plundering passion that obliterated Anwen's awareness of anything but him. His warmth, his strength, his heathery scent, his taste.

"Mint," Anwen said against his lips.

"I prefer it to parsley."

For all the pleasure Colin's kiss brought, all the reassurance and desire, Anwen also sensed a question in his touch.

They had agreed to marry, and had become close, physically and otherwise. Anwen had assumed she'd end her social season with a wedding and a journey north to her new home. In his caresses and kisses and even his silence, Colin was asking a question:

Could Anwen travel hundreds of miles north on her wedding journey, making a new home with Colin in Scotland, when she knew the boys at the House of Urchins might soon have no home at all?

Chapter Thirteen

Before Colin started undoing his falls in the very garden, he broke off the kiss.

"I should be leaving, my dear. If I don't see you tomorrow, you may be assured I'll be at the card party. I'm prepared to lose a goodly sum, and I've secured a promise from no less person than Jonathan Tresham that he'll do likewise."

Tresham was a duke's heir, and a cold, quiet fellow. Colin liked him for keeping his own counsel, though he suspected Tresham's generosity toward orphans might be an effort to impress Mrs. Bellingham rather than a display of honest charity.

"I don't want to talk about the card party," Anwen said, taking Colin by the hand. "In fact, I refuse to air that topic further until after the occasion itself, and do you realize we've given no thought to our own wedding?"

Edana and Rhona had sworn that wedding preparations would distract Anwen from her anxiety over the orphanage.

Edana and Rhona had been wrong—thus far.

"I've been to a few weddings," Colin said. "They've mostly been modest affairs. The couple speaks their vows, signs the documents, enjoys a fortifying meal with friends, and goes on their wedding journey. What did you have in mind?"

Anwen's smile was sweet and naughty. "I've been more focused on the wedding night. Are you concerned that if the orphanage isn't sorted out, I won't want to join you in Scotland?"

Well, hell. "Should I be?"

Colin visually inspected the garden rather than see the hesitation in his intended's eyes. His gaze fell on the curved back of a wrought-iron bench, which bowed like the top of a symmetric, stylized heart—or like a lady's cleavage in a snug bodice.

Lately Colin had been seeing cleavage everywhere—in clouds, puddles, bowls of oranges, and most assuredly in his dreams. The center of a flower prompted even more erotic fancies, and he'd forbidden himself to even glance at Anwen's lips.

"Colin, look at me."

Not at her lips. He couldn't risk that, but he could look into her eyes.

"No matter what happens with the orphanage," she said, "I will marry you, and we will repair to Scotland. I care very much about the boys, but I have promised to marry you, and I keep my promises."

Colin didn't want his fiancée speaking her vows out of duty alone, and yet, that Anwen cared for the boys was important to him too.

"Anwen Windham, I promise you that whatever happens, I'll find a decent situation for each of the twelve boys we have now. MacHugh the publisher can use a few more newsboys. MacHugh the saddle maker will take on an extra apprentice. We won't turn your boys back out onto the street."

Not even if MacHugh the distiller had to take the four oldest into his own household.

Anwen studied him for so long, Colin did take notice of the perfect, pink bow of her lips. He'd caught a glimpse of her nipples once by candlelight eleven days ago. They were nearly the same pink as her mouth, one shade more pale perhaps, and the areolae one shade paler than that.

"Colin MacHugh, you are having naughty thoughts."

"Worshipful thoughts," he said, stepping closer. "Wedding night thoughts." He was having wedding night sensations too, directly behind his falls, at every damned hour of the day and night, especially if Anwen was in sight.

She tucked in closely enough that she had to be aware of his arousal. For him, desire had become a constant low hum, like honeybees in a flower garden, droning on and on, never satisfied.

This was different from the occasional flare of interest that in past years had had more to do with boredom and availability than any finer sentiments.

"I love you," Anwen said. "I'm not sure when this happened. Maybe when you were lecturing the boys about the pleasures of swearing in French, or maybe the first time you kissed me. Maybe it keeps happening. When you stare down Win Montague in a meeting, I love you. When you make grooming a filthy pony an exercise in gentlemanly deportment, I love you. When you hold me, I love you. When you listen to me and take me into your confidence,

I am so violently in love with you, I cannot find words to express my sentiments."

Doves took wing in Colin's heart, or something equally undignified. This was not the tolerant love of a sibling or the casual affection of extended family. This was passion, and a reassurance that he wasn't the only member of this couple nearly mad with tender emotion.

"Anwen, you...I love you too." Inadequate, considering the declarations she'd give him, so Colin tried again. "I will never betray the love you give me, or the trust you place in me. I'd sooner die than disappoint you."

She sighed in his arms, and he was coming to know what each of her sighs meant. That one had been pleased but weary.

Colin scooped her up and carried her down a short laburnum alley, dipping at his knees so Anwen could open the door to the conservatory.

"I adore the scent of this place," she said. "To me this is the fragrance of peace and privacy. Nobody has ever found me when I've sought sanctuary in here. I can read by the hour, or knit, or kiss you, and it's as if this is my kingdom, safe from any outside disturbance."

"Ye should no' be telling me that, my heart, not after what you said in the garden."

They hadn't even set a date, much less dealt with settlements, announcements, or wedding plans, but Colin had purchased a special license, because surely, surely, they'd be married in the next six months.

He settled Anwen onto a sofa tucked under the lemon tree and flanked by a pair of potted orange trees.

"If you run off now, Colin MacHugh, I will hunt you down and kiss you within an inch of your wits." She toed off her slippers and tucked her feet up beside her.

Colin permitted himself one peek at her ankles, though it was a lengthy peek, as peeks went. Perhaps more of a longing glance.

"You stole my wits three weeks ago, madam, and I haven't seen them since."

She twitched at her skirts so a hint of pale ankle showed below her hem.

Most women, especially in temperate weather, wore nothing beneath their skirts. That fact ricocheted around in Colin's mind as he studied a bunch of violets overgrowing their pottery three feet away. Violets symbolized modesty, but the soft, tangled greenery put Colin in mind of other soft, tangled textures in shadowy locations he ached to revisit.

"I kissed you within an inch of your wits three weeks ago?" Anwen asked. "Then what about last week, in the saddle room, and the week before, in the music room?"

Those memories had sprung up aching eons ago, and were as close as Colin's next daydream. He turned his back on Anwen, lest she notice that his breeches had developed an awkward fit.

"Those were lovely occasions. I have a special license, you know, in case you'd like to be married right here, in your conservatory."

In the next five minutes would have suited Colin wonderfully.

"That is a lovely, lovely thought. I've had a lovely thought too."

He risked a glance over his shoulder. The picture Anwen made on the sofa—another article of furniture designed to replicate female charms—was lovely, though with her feet bare, and one red curl brushing her shoulder, also erotic.

A man who found clouds, puddles, and sofa backs a trial was a pathetic creature.

"If your idea is about the card party," Colin replied, plucking a lone violet, "you said we weren't to speak of that for two days." A fine idea. He wished he'd thought of it himself.

"My lovely thought is this: We have not announced our engagement, though we certainly have an understanding in the eyes of my family. I'd like to consummate that engagement, Colin."

He had been dreaming of consummation for three straight weeks. He knelt before the sofa and tucked the violet into Anwen's décolletage.

"Couples do," he said, brushing the errant curl behind her ear. "Couples who are in love. It's not a step to be taken lightly." Oh, that sounded quite rational, quite awfully stupid. "Shall we plan an outing to Richmond next week, a wander in the woods? You'll notice I'm not capable of arguing with your suggestion."

She brushed a hand over his hair and Colin felt her caress in impossible places.

"I notice we have privacy right here, right now, your lordship."

He settled his arms around her and laid his cheek against her hair. "Right here, right now."

Colin searched his motivations for selfishness and found some. He desired Anwen in every way a man desires a woman, physically, madly, passionately. Another emotion crowded close behind the pawing of the male beast, though.

He wanted to please her, to cherish her, to give himself to her, in the most intimate way a man could surrender himself to his beloved. On that thought he rose, locked all available doors, pulled down three shades, and tugged off his boots.

He slipped the violet from Anwen's bodice, set the flower aside, tossed a cushion onto the rug, and resumed his place on his knees before her.

* * *

"Inviting all the lads to that infernal charity card game when MacHugh knows the lot of us are pockets to let was the outside of too much," Win declared.

Rosalyn should not have insisted that Win take her to the modiste's in his present mood, or perhaps—she liked this notion better—Win should not have been sulking when she had a new bonnet to pick up.

The thought of that bonnet had cheered her through the interminable purgatory of today's meeting at the orphanage.

Lately, nothing appeared to cheer poor Winthrop.

Rosalyn did so enjoy tooling about beside him in his phaeton, though. "You're the chairman of the House of Urchins board of directors. You have to be at this party even if you aren't my escort, which you most assuredly will be, Winthrop. What do you care if Twilly and Pointy lose a few more groats? They'll come around when they get their quarterly allowances."

Rosalyn never got a quarterly allowance. She received pin money, which dear Papa hadn't increased since her come out. Thank heavens she could sell last year's wardrobe and otherwise contrive on her own.

"You don't understand, Rosalyn. MacHugh paid every last bill immediately, and that's insult enough. He hasn't complained, he hasn't muttered, he hasn't so much as grumbled. Now he's rubbing all of our faces in his filthy lucre by insisting we turn out for this damned charity do. Even MacHugh grasps that one doesn't refuse an invitation from the Duchess of Moreland."

Lord Colin hadn't paid a call on Win or stood up with Rosalyn for the past month. She'd seen him turning down the room with Anwen Windham and her sisters, but that was to be expected, given the family connection.

Maybe Anwen had tried to win his lordship's favor and failed, poor thing.

"I'm confused, Win. When a man pays bills he doesn't owe and keeps silent about his ill-usage, that's not the done thing?"

She should not be baiting him, but really, somebody had to save Win from making a complete cake of himself.

"I don't expect you to understand the finer points of gentlemanly honor, but no, it's not the done thing as MacHugh has gone about it. He's insulted every one of us, and now we're to contribute to his infernal charity, regardless of whether we can afford such a pointless gesture. I've half a mind to let on to the others that MacHugh excused thievery by one of the boys."

Win had to pause in his diatribe to watch Mrs. Bellingham drive by. He couldn't acknowledge such a creature with Rosalyn sitting right beside him, but he could admire her.

And for what? Because Mrs. Bellingham had pretty ways, and had tossed her virtue into the ditch? Sometimes, Rosalyn wanted to smack all men with her parasol, though that would hardly be ladylike and might ruin a fine article of fashion.

"Win, I sympathize with your exasperation where Lord Colin is concerned, but you are the director. If one of the boys is committing crimes, might that not have unpleasant consequences for you as well as the other children?"

"Those boys will be back on the streets by Michaelmas. The sooner the orphanage closes its doors, the better. False hope is cruelty by another name."

"I agree entirely. If I didn't enjoy a good hand of whist above all things, I'd not be going to this card party either." Bad enough Anwen expected Rosalyn to beg yarn from her friends, bad enough Rosalyn had had to sell her favorite pink muslin from last year to afford the bonnet at her feet.

Life was full of trials.

"I confess I have an ulterior motive for being so tolerant where MacHugh is concerned," Win said as he turned the horses onto the quieter residential streets.

"Besides your inherent gentlemanly nature?" Which hadn't stopped Win from complaining at every turn, of course.

"Besides that. I'm considering offering for Anwen Windham. She has nothing better to do than fret and fuss over that silly orphanage, which has at least given me an opportunity to consider her attributes somewhere other than a ballroom. She's quiet, not at all troublesome, and not awful looking, if I can ignore that hair and the incessant knitting. I could give her babies, so she'd not be reduced to meddling in doomed charities."

Oh, dear. Roslyn herself had suggested this very possibility to him, though half in jest and weeks ago. Dear Winthrop's financial situation must be desperate.

"You'd overlook Anwen's unfortunate hair in the interests of getting your hands on her settlements, Win. I admire your pragmatism, so you needn't splutter about tender sentiments. You'd be doing Anwen a favor."

If Anwen accepted him. If she rejected him and brought

Lord Colin up to scratch, war would break out in the clubs on St. James's Street.

"She's already your friend," Win said, as if Rosalyn didn't know half the ladies in Mayfair. "Makes strengthening the connection between families that much easier. Too bad Anwen hasn't any brothers to take an interest in you. You're good to befriend her, Roz."

Because the streets were all but empty of traffic, Rosalyn spoke honestly. "I associate with some women because their company makes my own attributes more obvious. My favor does nothing to hurt the other young lady's standing, but I choose my acquaintances with a certain practicality. I like Anwen, and I think you would make her a wonderful husband, but one shouldn't contract marriage as a charitable undertaking, Win. Anwen's not at all your style."

Win would be an adequate husband until the money ran out.

Rosalyn did not envy a younger son his lot. Much easier to be a daughter, passed from papa to husband for care and cosseting until widowhood gave a lady the freedom to cosset herself.

And thank God that Winthrop was the sort of brother one could be honest with.

For the most part.

"A woman's lot isn't easy," Win said, propping a shiny boot on the fender. "Miss Anwen must be quite impatient to marry, waiting for her older sisters to dodder off to spinsterhood. I think she fancies me, to the extent such a creature is capable of fancying anything save her workbasket and her cat."

The Monthaven townhouse came into view, one of the few set back from the street enough to allow a shallow curve of a drive where coaches could pull over. All was swept walkways, and cheerful red salvia in symmetrically spaced pots. Rosalyn had made a game of hiding those pots as a girl, putting them where the gardener would never think to look for them.

The idea still tempted her, though her gloves might get dirty.

"Anwen hasn't the confidence to hold aspirations in your direction, Winthrop. I suggested to her the other day that Lord Colin might do for her. He and Anwen already have a familial relationship, and they share that unfortunate red hair."

Win sent her a peevish look. "You pushed her at Lord Colin?"

"I wouldn't say pushed. A woman in Anwen's position—without airs and graces, without a title, without much beauty—can't be choosy." A woman *with* those attributes could be choosy—lovely notion. "She wasn't singing his praises, mind you. I think the appropriate term would be, she is considering settling. Women do, I suppose some men must as well."

"Do we ever. Miss Anwen doesn't have to marry a damned presuming Scot. I can preserve her from that sorry fate."

"Very noble of you, though a bit of courtship might be called for. Anwen's uncle is a duke, and so is Lord Colin's brother."

"Why do you think I've bothered to maintain my place on the orphanage board? Why do you think I'll spend half the card party doting on her? I'll take her driving a few times, steal a kiss, go down on bended knee, the whole bit. Least I can do for my future wife. Besides, Lord Colin's brother is only a Scottish duke and they hardly count."

Except in the order or precedence, where any duke counted for rather a lot. "You'll steal from Lord Colin a chance to marry as well as his brother did. Very clever of you, Winthrop."

Win brought the horses to a halt before the house. "There is that. Can't be helped, if the lady prefers the better offer." He smiled beatifically, bringing out every aspect of his handsome visage—blue eyes, perfect teeth, and the aristocratic bone structure Rosalyn saw echoed in her own mirror.

"Go carefully," Rosalyn said as a footman emerged from the house. "I would hate to see anything bad happen to my favorite brother, and Lord Colin has foiled your schemes before."

"Fool me once," Win said as the footman aided Rosalyn to alight. "I'm off to the clubs. See you at supper."

How his mood had improved for contemplating holy matrimony—and revenge.

Rosalyn passed the hatbox to the footman and shooed him into the house. "Wellington will be at the card party, Winthrop. If you can manage it, I'd like a chance to play against him."

"I've been kept away from the details, sister dear. You be careful. His Grace can be quite competitive."

Rosalyn twiddled her fingers at her brother. "So can I. Until supper." She sashayed up the walk while Win rattled off in his fine equipage, though she spared a prayer for dear Winthrop and his friends.

They were commoners for the most part, and excessive debt could land any one of them in the sponging houses. Fortunately, Rosalyn's papa would never allow such a fate to befall her, one of the many benefits of being an earl's well-cared-for daughter.

* * *

In the leafy privacy of the conservatory, Anwen wrapped her arms around Colin and rejoiced.

This was right. This ultimate intimacy was what came next when two people were in love, committed to each other, and desired each other deeply.

And yet, Anwen hadn't a clue how to go on.

"Does this work like the other times?" she asked, scooting closer to the man on his knees before her. "You bring me rainbows first?"

Colin had other names for the pleasure he brought her, names in French, Gaelic, and naughty cant, but Anwen's description was as close as she could come in English to naming the experience.

"Ye'll have rainbows today," he said, tracing his finger over the swell of her bodice, "and we go on as we please. Perhaps you have a suggestion."

The fit with Colin on his knees before the low sofa was comfortable, provided a lady was willing to spread her knees.

Anwen unknotted Colin's cravat and used it to tug him closer. "Don't be nervous. Megan told me it gets better with practice. If my practices with you get any better, I will expire of bliss."

One corner of his mouth quirked up. "Thank you for those reassurances. I'd rather neither one of us expired just yet."

Anwen was nervous, and clearly Colin knew it. The warmth in his gaze, the way he scooped her closer, said she needn't be. He'd bring her rainbows, sunrises, and joys without number simply because she'd asked him to.

When she might have started babbling, he kissed her.

This kiss was different, both carnal and solemn, an odd combination that unsettled Anwen's insides. She worked at unbuttoning Colin's shirt, though one or two buttons might have got the worst of her haste.

"Ye'll not be rushing this," he said, untying the bow at the top of her bodice. "We'll make a race of it if ye like some other day, but I want this time to savor you."

Anwen had worn two shifts rather than jumps or stays, and both shifts tied at the front. Colin eased both bows open but made no move to touch her breasts. Instead, he wrapped a hand around each ankle, and nudged her skirts up with a caress to her calves.

The quiet became profound, as if the very trees were keeping silent in honor of the moment. Cloth whispered against skin as Colin kissed Anwen's shoulder, and a feeling close to panic gripped her.

"Hurry, please."

He cupped her jaw and kissed her, another openmouthed, possessive intimacy that gave Anwen a focus for the urgency uncoiling inside her. She kissed him back, tangling her tongue with his, fisting her hands in his hair.

"Enough of that now. Lie back, Anwen."

"I can't kiss you if I'm lying—"

Colin shoved a pillow behind her. "*Please.*"

Anwen flopped back, out of breath, out of sorts, out of patience. "I want rainbows, Colin MacHugh, big, colorful, rainbows with sparkly—"

He peeled aside the layers of silk and cotton covering her breasts.

"With my body," he whispered, "and with all the rainbows you can withstand, I thee worship."

With his mouth, he drove her barmy, kissing, nuzzling, drawing on her gently, caressing with a maddening sense of what was not quite enough, then not quite too much. These pleasures were new for Anwen, though she also sensed Colin was enjoying himself, indulging in fantasies long anticipated, and so she mustered the ability to relax into his caresses.

"That's better," he said, resting his cheek against the slope her of breast. "I didn't want to neglect the color pink, ye see. Part of every self-respecting rainbow."

Anwen flexed her hips in response to that nonsense and Colin drew in a sharp breath.

"Right," he said, straightening. "Now comes the sparkly part." He unbuttoned his falls and Anwen sat up enough to watch him.

"More pink," she said, glossing her finger over intimate male flesh. "Maybe this is where the color maiden's blush truly originates."

Colin's hands fell to his sides, and for a few quiet moments, Anwen explored his contours.

"If ye keep that up, lass, ye'll make me blush."

"I'll bring you rainbows." That her touch pleased Colin was a heady realization, for all the strangeness Anwen yet felt to see him aroused. "I've seen a replica of the Apollo Belvedere, and your proportions and his are very close— except here."

"Apollo didn't have you to inspire him, poor sod."

Anwen wrapped her hand around Colin's shaft. "Let's inspire each other." Wasn't that what a strong marriage should be? A source of mutual inspiration?

Colin kissed her back onto the pillow, and she let go of him. The next part was curious, sweet, and breath-stealing. Colin took himself in hand and teased at her sex. The sensations were similar to what he'd inspired on previous occasions, but...more.

"We'll take this slowly," he said. "Your word on it, Anwen."

"Slowly," she said, "and soon."

He pushed inside her, and her body eased around him. She was slick with desire, though Colin was maddeningly—excruciatingly—patient. Tendrils of yearning wrapped Anwen more tightly the more deeply he joined them, until she cast off into a pleasure so profound it nearly replaced consciousness.

"You've a short fuse," he panted, going still.

Anwen assembled his words into a fragment of meaning. "That was marvelous." More marvelous than anything they'd done previously. "Are we finished?"

"No, love. We're barely getting started."

Oh, my. "I'm not sure I have another rainbow in me." She felt as if light had burst through every part of her, as if she'd found a small piece of the sun to carry in her heart forevermore. The tenderness was as overwhelming as the joy and the pleasure.

"You've endless rainbows left," Colin said, moving as if to withdraw. "I'll prove it to you."

Anwen locked her ankles at the small of his back, certain that unjoining from him would kill her, but there was no need. He eased forward in a slow, sure thrust that made her want to laugh and weep—and *move*.

"Oh, you..." Colin whispered, as Anwen caught his rhythm.

She lost track of time, place, everything except Colin, and making love with him in her favorite place in the world. He was patient, inventive, and devious, and when he finally withdrew from her, Anwen wanted to call him back, rather than endure the sense of being parted from him.

He produced a handkerchief, rested his cheek against

her thigh, and in a few strokes, spent his seed. While Anwen sprawled in a heap on the sofa, Colin's breath warmed her leg, and green branches stirred minutely in the conservatory's unseen breezes.

He patted her knee. "All right, then?"

Anwen stroked her fingers over his hair, the only place she could reach him without moving.

"I feel different." Changed, exposed, enlightened, a trifle sore, but something lay beneath even those emotions.

Colin knelt up, righted his clothes, and joined her on the sofa, cuddling her against his side. "Tell me."

"How do you feel?" she asked.

"Like I could conquer the world for you, after a good nap. Thank you, Anwen. Under Scottish law, we'd be married by now, and in my heart, we are."

Oh, what a lovely man he was. "Mine too. Maybe that's part of how I feel—married."

"Is there more?"

This resting in each other's arms, talking quietly, marveling together, was so precious, and yet, Anwen still had to hedge her bets.

"You won't laugh?"

"I might laugh with you, never at you, at least not until we're married."

She smacked his arm. "I feel healthy."

He kissed her temple. "How d'ye mean?"

"What we did was physical, vigorous, wonderful. I made love with you. As your wife, I'll do that with you a lot, and bear your children, I hope. I feel ready for all of it, eager for it. I'm in excellent health and ready to enjoy being married to you."

She was doing a poor job of explaining to him the sense of bodily joy that making love had brought her. Irrespective of rainbows and cuddling, she felt good in her bones, and glad to be alive in a way she hadn't since early childhood.

That was her last waking thought, until Colin roused her from her nap by brushing a violet across her lips, and bidding her a reluctant and very affectionate farewell.

Chapter Fourteen

"OLD HOOKY'S TO BE at this damned card party?" Rudolph, Baron Twillinger cried—and he nearly was in tears. "Wellington himself? I could have pled a last-minute bilious stomach and sent along a few genteel shillings, but not if...Wellington, *himself*?"

Men who'd risk snubbing a duchess, even the Duchess of Moreland, could never treat the Duke of Wellington to the same slight.

"Can't be helped," Pierpont said. "If Wellington's attending, we're attending. I could call MacHugh out for this."

"Why don't you?" Twillinger countered, though he kept his voice down.

Win had tracked them to one of the more modest gentlemen's establishments—one of the cheaper ones—and found them both swilling ale rather than port or brandy.

One always drank ale near the end of the quarter, though that was a good six weeks away.

"Dueling's illegal," Pierpont rejoined, nose in the air. "I am a father, and must think of my progeny when the demands of honor weigh heavily upon me. Wouldn't do to make an orphan of the children so early in life. Not considering who they have for a mama."

"No orphans, please," Win said. "I cannot think of a drearier topic. Orphans are why we'll all flirt with penury tomorrow evening."

Though Twillinger's new phaeton had to have cost a pretty penny.

"I'm not above passin' a few farthings to the less fortunate," Pierpont said, "but Colin MacHugh is a problem. Just because his flamin' brother's a duke all of a sudden doesn't mean he's good *ton*. Quite the opposite, in fact."

"Hear, hear," Twillinger said, rapping on the table as if they were in the corner pub. "The next time some presuming Scot is plucked from obscurity and given a lofty title, his whole family will expect vouchers from Almack's delivered to their very doorstep. What is the world coming to?"

Pierpont licked the ale foam from his upper lip. "A bloody sad pass, I can tell you. 'Scottish duke' ought to be one of those what-do-you-call-'ems. Contradiction whatevers. I'm as titled as MacHugh is, and a damned sight better bred."

He belched, beery fumes wafting about the table.

"So you are," Twillinger agreed, patting Pierpont's hand. "Montague, why so silent?"

"I'm thinking."

Pierpont and Twillinger smiled and ordered another round of ale.

"I do so love it when you think," Twillinger said. "Spares me the trouble. Think me up a way to earn some blunt, would you? Not earn-earn it, but come into it, proper-like."

"Lord Colin would tell you to rent out your phaeton." Win was jesting, though Twillinger appeared taken with the idea. Twilly was half-seas over, as usual.

"I would tell Lord Colin to put Twilly's vehicle up his strutting Scottish—"

A waiter bearing three glasses of ale interrupted Pointy's musings. "Separate accounts, gentlemen?"

"Please," Winthrop said, before either friend could send him a hopeful look. They'd put their whole afternoon's drinking on his account, and that would not do.

When the waiter had gathered up empty glasses and departed, Win set his ale to his right, away from Pierpont. Pointy was notorious for drinking out of the "wrong" glass as his own grew empty.

"I've been thinking," Pointy said, using the back of his sleeve to wipe his mouth this time. "What if the card party is a failure? Not much blunt donated, for all we waste a fine evening at the tables?"

"Then the orphans go hungry," Twillinger said. "Which I thought orphans did most of the time anyway."

"Quiet," Win said as Jonathan Tresham walked by. The damned man had no title at all, not even a courtesy title, but he was some sort of nabob, and heir to the Duke of Quimbey. Worse, Mrs. Bellingham professed to *like* him.

"He'll be there," Pointy said, following Tresham with his gaze. "And if Tresham is there, Quimbey will likely be as well. With Moreland and Wellington, that's a three-duke card party. It can't fail. His Grace of Anselm will doubtless put in an appearance, and that's four dukes."

Win waited until Tresham had chosen a table across the room. "Pointy, I hadn't realized you'd been working on your counting skills. I'm impressed. The card party will be a great success, which can't be helped. It's not Lord Colin's card party, though, it's Miss Anwen Windham's, whom we all esteem greatly."

They drank to that sentiment.

"Lord Colin dances with Miss Anwen," Twillinger said. "M'sister has remarked it."

"Lord Colin dances with the lot of them," Pointy countered. "All the red-haired spinster Winsters. Windhams, I mean. Has to. Family, you know. I dance with my wife for the same reason."

"Or she dances with you," Win said. "The challenge is how to bring Lord Colin down without letting the scandal touch Miss Anwen. The card party itself must go smoothly."

"The Duchess of Moreland's affairs always go smoothly," Pointy said. "Spinster-winsters. I rather like that."

"We had a bit of trouble at the orphanage a few weeks back," Win said as ideas began to mix with excellent ale. "One of the boys got loose and pinched a purse."

Pointy took a sip of Twilly's ale. "Stole goods from a man's very person? That's a criminal act, plain and simple. Such a boy should have been bound over to Newgate, not given a soft bed, three meals, and a hymnal."

Win kept a hand on his own tankard, for the summer ale at the club was superb—for ale—and by no means free.

"Lord Colin, without any authority whatsoever, decided the matter could be informally resolved. The boy returned the purse, apologized, and has been a model citizen ever since. The headmaster keeps me informed of these things."

"Why did you ever involve yourself with that place?" Twilly asked. "Sounds like a cross between Eton, Bedlam, and Newgate."

"My father offered to increase my allowance if I undertook participation in management of a charity. Somebody suggested the House of Urchins, and I've been regretting it ever since."

"Paters are like that," Pointy said. "My own promised an increase when the wife dropped another calf. Pater forgot to remind me the little fellow would need a nurse, nappies, dresses, rattles... Sending my heir off to Eton will be a savings at the rate the boy runs through blunt now."

They drank to dear old Eton, where nobody had learned much of anything except how to drink, smoke, and commit the sin of Onan.

"You'll see that Lord Colin is ruined?" Twilly asked.

"Somebody should," Pointy agreed, taking a second sip of Twilly's ale. "Principle of the thing. Got well above himself, putting on airs and so forth."

"I may not be able to see him transported, but I can at least send him packing back to Scotland with his tail between his legs. He's quite possibly toying with a lady's affections, and taking advantage of her soft heart, but I can show her the error of her ways."

"We should always be looking out for the ladies," Pointy said.

"When we're not looking up their skirts." Twillinger lifted his almost-empty tankard. "Are they pouring the pints short these days?"

"You simply hold your liquor well," Win said. "I'm off to look in on the orphanage."

Win sketched a bow and left, though he wasn't about to set foot on the premises of the orphanage. Mrs. Bellingham's establishment was open, and a gentleman could drink ale there as well as anywhere else.

* * *

"You made Jonathan Tresham smile," Charlotte said beneath the soft lilt of a string quartet. "Anwen Windham, you've been working on your flirtation skills. Perhaps Lord Colin has assisted you in this regard."

Mr. Tresham had not only smiled at Anwen before the entire ballroom full of card players, he'd waxed congenial about donating a watchdog to the orphanage out of a mastiff litter much anticipated by his ducal relations.

Jonathan Tresham, *congenial*. The whole gathering was congenial, as if a chance to do something for the less fortunate was a relief rather than imposition.

"Lord Colin isn't half the flirt he's made out to be," Anwen said.

Charlotte leaned near and whispered, "Your evening is a success already, Wennie. You should be proud of yourself."

"I'm proud of *us*, Charlotte. You and Elizabeth pitched in, Her Grace lent her considerable expertise, Lord Colin has helped, and the cousins are here in force."

Charlotte took a sip of her lemonade, and waggled her fingers at Rosecroft who walked past in company with Baron Twillinger. If the two were discussing horses, Rosecroft probably hadn't seen Charlotte's greeting.

"We need family projects," Charlotte said. "Activities we can all support, and the brilliance of your card party is that we're doing something useful. If Her Grace doesn't turn this into an annual event, we sisters should. Lady Rhona and Lady Edana would help, and—his lordship does cut a dash in that kilt, doesn't he?"

Anwen had asked Colin to trot out his Highland finery. In full dress regalia he was formidably attractive, which might explain why Lady Rosalyn had been hanging on his arm rather a lot.

Poor dear—and poor Colin too.

A whiff of spiked fruit punch presaged Winthrop Montague joining them at the edge of the ballroom.

"My sister and Lord Colin make an interesting couple, don't they?" he said. "Not Rosalyn's usual style, but she is ever kind and Lord Colin knows better than to get ideas where her ladyship is concerned."

Win was in typical evening attire, and he looked like every other gentleman in the ballroom, with the exception of Cousin Valentine, who had the panache to wear more lace than most men favored.

"You think Lord Colin might entertain aspirations where Lady Rosalyn is concerned?" Charlotte asked.

"He'd best not, for it can't come to anything. Rosalyn is very discerning about the company she keeps, and while she can admire initiative in a man, a Scottish distiller whose family stumbled into a title is hardly likely to hold her interest in the matrimonial sense. I mean no insult to MacHugh—he's a friend, after all—but standards must be maintained."

Given her brother's example, Lady Rosalyn was unlikely to *recognize* initiative in a man, much less admire it.

"I esteem Lord Colin greatly," Anwen said. "He's taken the orphanage's situation to heart, and tonight is the result of ideas he sowed in discussions with me. If he's an example of the men you consider a friend, Mr. Montague, then your taste is to be sincerely commended."

Charlotte became fascinated with her lemonade.

"You have such a good heart," Mr. Montague said. "I've always admired that about you, Miss Anwen."

His compliment was accompanied by a peculiar contortion of his features. He lowered his lashes, pooched out his lips, peeked over at her, then lowered his lashes again. A moment later, Anwen realized she'd been the recipient of a *melting glance*.

"You two will excuse me," Charlotte said, holding up her glass. "Time to make sure the punch bowls are all re-filled."

She shot Anwen a you-can't-kill-me-unless-you-catch-me look and bustled away.

"Such a shame," Mr. Montague said, "when a woman of excellent breeding and decent looks can't find a man who appreciates her, don't you agree?"

"Of course, just as when a man of excellent breeding and decent looks endures a similar fate. Loneliness is a heavy burden, regardless of gender."

His nose twitched, as if he might have caught the scent of something overripe. "There's your kind heart in evidence again. Might I convince you to take pity on me, and join me for a stroll about the terrace?"

He gave her the portentous look again, and it occurred to Anwen that Winthrop Montague was attempting to *flirt* with her.

Oh, dear. Oh, gracious, oh, ye gods and little fishes. What on earth could he be thinking?

The quartet launched into a lively gigue, and the chatter in the ballroom swelled accordingly, as Mr. Montague escorted Anwen toward the doors to the back garden. Perhaps he sought to curry favor with Aunt Esther or Uncle Percy by paying attention to the most retiring Windham sister.

He'd do that. Think himself clever for flirting with a wallflower—the toad.

"I can't tarry outside too long," Anwen said. "I'd like to be on hand if Her Grace needs me for anything."

Aunt Esther could organize a function twice this size in half the time with half the help, and the evening would still be splendid.

"I am honored with whatever time you will spare me." Mr. Montague patted the hand Anwen had laced about his arm, and looked her squarely in the eye.

If this was what Mrs. Bellingham had to endure three nights a week, no wonder the woman had declined Mr. Montague's overtures.

Just before they left the ballroom, Colin shot Anwen a puzzled look across the buffet table. She winked and got a smile in return.

"You must know how much I respect your entire family," Mr. Montague said once they were on the terrace. "That they'd rally around an institution facing dire financial straits is indicative of the values I admire most. Sometimes, our pragmatism must be informed by a generosity of spirit and nobleness of gesture that defies the understanding of the less loftily situated."

Even young Tom would have difficulty translating that sermon. "Are you saying the orphanage is a lost cause, but a noble lost cause?"

He tilted head his up when they reached the terrace balustrade, as if striking a pose, "Handsome Swain Admiring Invisible Stars."

"More or less. This evening looks to be quite a success, though these funds will soon run out. The fate of the orphanage is sad but predictable, and we must comfort ourselves with the knowledge that our feeble efforts, temporary though they might be, have made a difference in the lives of a few unfortunate boys."

Some efforts had been notably more feeble than others. Mr. Montague was working very hard on his smile of manly regret, for example, far harder than he'd worked on behalf of the orphanage.

"I am pleased to inform you, sir, that this card party will likely become an annual event. Her Grace hosts many affairs at which four dukes are present. She mentioned she'd like to try for six next year."

A dozen dukes would not be beyond Her Grace's abilities, though she might have to summon a few from the Continent.

"That is... well." Mr. Montague rocked up on his toes, then settled back, like a nervous scholar who'd failed to memorize the day's recitation. "That is most kind of her, most charitable. Exactly the sort of dedication to worthy causes I've noticed in you, Miss Anwen."

He was working up the nerve to kiss her. This realization presented itself in Anwen's awareness as if her bodice ribbon had come loose in the middle of a reel. Discreet escape was both imperative and impossible.

"It's a shame your own inclinations are taking you away from the charity dearest to my heart," Anwen said. "We'll feel the lack of your wisdom and perspective once you leave the board, Mr. Montague. You have my thanks for all you have done."

She gave him her brightest, most brisk smile.

"I will eventually and reluctantly step aside from the House of Urchins solely so that Lord Colin can continue to associate with the place in my stead. He has much to learn about comporting himself as a member of polite society, but I'm doing what I can for him."

Mr. Montague's tone combined long-suffering and resignation.

"That's very humble of you," Anwen said. "Stepping back so those with greater native talent for administration have a chance to shine. Humility is one of the greatest virtues, don't you agree?"

His nose did that wrinkling thing again. "Moderation in all things, my dear, including moderation, right?"

Such brilliant wit. "If you say so, Mr. Montague. Perhaps you'd be good enough to escort me back to Lord Colin's side?"

"You're trying to keep an eye on him as well? I wish he'd have done with that Scottish nonsense when an occasion calls for formal attire."

So Colin would stop outshining all the dandies dressed exactly as Mr. Montague was?

"I very much enjoy keeping an eye on Lord Colin regardless of whether he's wearing his national dress or less imaginative attire. He's asked to pay me his addresses."

Mr. Montague came to a halt just outside the French doors. "I beg your pardon?"

"Lord Colin has asked to pay me his addresses." Small words and not too many of them. Even considering how much punch Mr. Montague had consumed, their meaning should be within his grasp.

His expression turned pensive. "I'm so sorry. That must be terribly awkward for you, given the family connection. I could have a word with him, but you mustn't blame Lord Colin too much. His brother did marry your sister, and subtleties such as lack of a ducal title might be beyond Lord Colin's notice."

What on earth to say to that? *You're a presuming dolt who's not fit to polish his lordship's boots?*

"He's put you in a very difficult position," Mr. Montague went on, patting Anwen's hand *again*. "As devoted as you are to the orphanage, you'll encounter him there, even aside from family gatherings. I'll simply tell him his overtures are a bit too late, shall I? And nobody will blame you if you take a repairing lease from the House of Urchins now that the coffers are in better health. I'll explain to Lord Colin that my own interest in you predates his, and he'll leave the lists as any gentleman should—any *honorable* gentleman."

"You'd lie to him, pretend you and I had an understanding, and suggest I step away from the orphanage?"

Mr. Montague drew himself up, which coaxed forth a burp from his belly, though he stifled it, probably from long practice.

"For you, Miss Anwen, yes, I'd take a small liberty with the chronology of the factual details, as it were. I do esteem you greatly, so greatly I might not be entirely misrepresenting the situation, if you take my meaning."

He peered down at her, one eyebrow arched in question.

"Your sacrifice is entirely unnecessary, Mr. Montague. Honesty is the best policy, provided it's tempered with kindness. In that spirit, I must tell you that I have not rebuffed Lord Colin's overtures. You'll excuse me now. I'd like to invite Lady Rosalyn to join me at the orphanage tomorrow morning. She'll doubtless be as eager as I am to tell the boys of the evening's success."

Anwen wiggled her hand free of Mr. Montague's grasp and marched into the ballroom. She'd rather have stayed with him on the terrace, giving him the setdown of his presuming, arrogant, useless life.

This was the Windham charity card party, though, and standards must be maintained.

* * *

"At the risk of approaching vulgarity," the Duke of Moreland said, as the clock struck twice, "that is a bloody lot of money, gentlemen. My duchess has much to be proud of."

Colin let the old boy preen, because Moreland was right, not because he was a duke. "My thanks, Your Grace, for making the party possible. The evening has been in every way a success. A dozen children will benefit and possibly many more."

"And I thank you as well," Winthrop Montague said from opposite Colin at Moreland's library table, "on behalf of the House of Urchins, and also on behalf of all who enjoyed themselves this evening thanks to your hospitality."

Moreland ran a finger down a long list of figures. "Her Grace was getting bored with the same soirée, year after year, and frankly so was I. My brother claims soirée is the French word for standing around making idle chatter at the expense of one's wits. This card party will be the talk of the town for the rest of the season, and one does like to do one's part for the less fortunate."

The difference in fortune between a child like Joe, and the card players who'd kept the Moreland staff busy into the small hours, was the difference between John O'Groats and Mayfair.

"If that's all, then," Montague said, reaching for the sack that held all of the cash and coins. "I'll take this to the House of Urchins and stow it in the strongbox until the banks open on Monday."

"We've yet to list the jewels," Colin said. *You never finish a job without counting the take.* The boys' advice seemed appropriate when Win Montague and a sum of money were involved.

"That will take another hour," Montague protested. "It's the middle of the damned night, MacHugh."

The duke paused in his ciphering. "You'll think me old-fashioned, Montague, but indulge me, please. In this house, we observe proper address when wearing our evening finery. Yonder Scot is Lord Colin until he's back in his riding attire. Her Grace put that rule in place nearly thirty years ago, and it's served us well."

What a splendidly gentle rebuke. Montague's ears turned an equally splendid shade of red.

Rosecroft spoke up for the first time. "We divide the jewels into four piles, each of us making a list of one pile, and each checking the work of the man to his right. We'll be done in fifteen minutes."

"Excellent notion," the duke said, which settled the matter without Colin having to call Montague out for attempting to abscond with the jewelry.

The lists were an impressive display of the generosity polite society was capable of. Rings, necklaces, cravat pins, even the occasional pair of cufflinks or earrings sat in glittering heaps about the table.

"We shouldn't sell all of this at once," Colin said, when the lot had been inventoried. "We'll get a better price if we parcel it out a little at a time."

"How do you propose we keep it safe while we're parceling it out?" Win retorted.

"The banks will keep it safe," Colin said. "And until we can get the lot of it to the bank, we have a strongbox at the orphanage, to which only you and the headmaster have the combination."

Colin did not, and wouldn't ask for it, not while Win was playing dandy in the manger as chairman of the board.

"I don't like having so many valuables stowed among those children," Montague said, collecting the jewels into another sack. "But I suppose it will have to do. Now might I take this lot to the orphanage, *Lord Colin?*"

"Don't be daft," the duke said, rising. "You will take his lordship and Rosecroft, as well as three of my largest footmen, and the Windham town coach. Half the thieves in London probably got wind of this party, and are lurking among Her Grace's hedges to waylay you. A man who's hungry enough will steal from orphans. We don't have to make that crime easier to commit."

The duke shook hands all around, and Colin was soon ensconced in a capacious crested coach with a small fortune and Win Montague's small-mindedness. Rosecroft had chosen to ride up on the box, and Colin might have joined him except for the covetousness he'd seen in Montague's eyes as the jewels had been counted.

"I had a private chat with Miss Anwen," Montague said as the coach pulled out of the mews.

Colin had seen them walking out to the terrace, and he'd seen Anwen return to the ballroom alone not ten minutes later. He hadn't found time to ask her about the conversation.

"Is your discussion any of my business?"

"I'm making it your business, MacHugh. The lady admitted that you've pressed her to accept your addresses. That is the height of bad form, and I expect better from even you."

Ach well, then. Whatever else was true about this private chat Montague was so fixed on, Anwen had let the fool live. Colin took his inspiration from her gracious example.

"I trust you will enlighten me regarding particulars of my bad form," Colin said, "as you have so generously done on many previous occasions."

Montague propped his foot on the velvet-cushioned bench opposite him. "Anwen can't put you in your place, you idiot, because of the family connection, and because she must face you across a conference table every time she attends one of our meetings. The orphanage means a lot to her, and her family means even more. If she tells you to pike off, as she ought, then she creates awkwardness on every hand. A shy little mouse like Miss Anwen can't do that."

A *shy little mouse*, who'd told Colin to pike off for the sake of the boys, the first time he'd threatened their well-being. Montague was lucky Anwen hadn't parted his cock from his cods.

"So you're running me off on her behalf?"

"I will make it plain to the lady that she has options, MacHugh, plainer than I already have. Let me make something else plain to you."

In the dim light of the coach lamps, Montague's complexion was sallow, and fatigue grooved his features. His golden good looks would soon give way to a saturnine countenance, if the French disease didn't do worse than that.

"Do go on," Colin said.

"I am chairman of the board of directors for the House of Wayward Urchins," Montague said. "The building is rotten with rising damp, and by rights should be condemned. The safety and comfort of the children must be my foremost concern, and if you continue to bother Miss Anwen with your rutting presumptions, I'll have the building razed to the ground. Every effort will be made to find other accommodations for the children, but the boys would be safer in the streets than at a ruin of an orphanage."

Montague was concerned with the safety and comfort of

only one person—himself. That he'd try to come between
Colin and Anwen was merely selfish and arrogant. That
he'd threaten the well-being of children to effect his claim
was vile.

"You'd put the children back on the street, if I paid my
addresses to Anwen Windham?"

"Go back to Scotland," Montague said. "She doesn't
want you, and neither does anybody else. I have tried to be
decent where you're concerned, but you don't fit in, you're
not welcome, and you impose on the good graces of your
betters every day you remain in London."

The cold, calculating temper Colin had relied on to see
him safely through battle rose, and stayed his hand when
he might have slapped a glove across Montague's face.

"Your advice, as always, bears consideration. I am
touched, Montague, at the tenderness of your regard for innocent children. I'm sure Miss Anwen would be too. I take
it you intend to offer her marriage?"

Winthrop expelled a gusty sigh that bore the rank scent
of overimbibing.

"One doesn't march up to a gently bred woman and haul
her off to the altar. Even you knew to start with a request
to pay the lady your addresses. I will observe every jot and
tittle of protocol, lest any think less of Miss Anwen for
seizing hastily on the first proper offer to come her way."

"And what about Mrs. Bellingham?"

"None of your bloody business, though you'll stay the
hell away from her too, MacHugh."

Colin had known the building was a problem, and he'd
given Anwen his word he'd keep the children safe. That
wasn't a new challenge. If Winthrop had the orphanage
condemned, then the time to ensure each boy was in a situation suited to him was being ripped away.

That was a problem because these boys had been tossed about too much already in their young lives. The idea that Winthrop Montague would pitch the children into the street if Anwen refused his proposal was arrogance of a magnitude that eclipsed mere sin and flirted with evil.

"You're not smitten with Miss Anwen," Colin said after the coach had rattled along for some minutes. "Why marry her?"

Montague smiled, and such was the smug self-satisfaction in his eyes that he should have been tasting the air with a forked tongue.

"The poor dear has to marry somebody, as do I. Our kind grasp what marriage is and is not about. I don't expect you to understand, but I'm doing you a favor, MacHugh. You'd make her miserable and regret the match within a year."

Colin let that masterpiece of self-deception remain unanswered. Montague had at some point come to believe his own handbills regarding the privileges of his station. Whatever he wanted, he was entitled to have, even a woman who'd shown no interest in him. Whatever he believed became fact, despite any evidence contradicting such a contention.

Were he not the son of a wealthy, titled Englishman, Montague would be a bedlamite.

But he was the son of a wealthy, titled Englishman, and enormously well connected in polite society. Until Colin—who was enormously without connections—had done proper reconnaissance, had at least a few hours' sleep, and had thought the matter through, he'd keep his own furious counsel.

* * *

"You are the sole defendant of the sideboard this morning?" Anwen asked.

Elizabeth sat alone at one end of the breakfast table, and a trick of sunlight had turned all the highlights in her hair to molten gold. Sipping her tea, she looked like a cross between the English spinster in training and some fantastical creature from one of Mama's Welsh fairy tales.

"I wanted to review the new invitations before Aunt got hold of them," Elizabeth said, eyeing a stack of correspondence near her plate. "The house parties are already trying to wedge themselves onto the calendar."

Soldiers probably volunteered to serve with a forlorn hope in the same brave, stoic tones.

Anwen pulled out the chair at Elizabeth's elbow, because Elizabeth had taken the place at the foot of the table—the duchess's seat—where the light was best at this hour.

"You could visit Megan in Scotland, Bethan. Charlotte would happily come with you."

Elizabeth poured Anwen a cup of tea and set the toast rack before her. "I could visit *you* in Scotland, you mean? And Megs, of course. Your card party was a smashing success, Wennie, and all that remains is for Lord Colin to speak his vows with you."

More bravery. Anwen was abruptly reminded that all might be coming right in her world, but Elizabeth and Charlotte would be left with not one younger sister married into a ducal family, but two.

"You might ask Megan about Perthshire's lending libraries," Anwen said. "If they are in anything less than excellent repair, you could put them to rights in no time."

Elizabeth was passionate about lending libraries, of all

things. Anwen had overheard Cousin Devlin remark that at least dear Bethan didn't crusade for temperance.

Cousins could be idiots.

Elizabeth tidied the stack of letters. "Was this how you felt when all and sundry prescribed plasters and nostrums for you when you weren't ill, Wennie?"

"I beg your pardon?"

"Don't forget to sugar your tea," Elizabeth said, setting the sugar bowl near Anwen's teacup. "To be unmarried is not an illness, such that desperate measures must be taken to stop its course. The tipsy bachelors haven't chased me through anybody's gardens for a good two years, and if I'm patient, I will eventually have my own household."

For the first time, Anwen heard not determination when Elizabeth spoke of her eventual independence, but more of the stoic bravery of the doomed infantryman.

"At least at the house parties," Anwen replied, "the ladies and gentlemen are present in comparable numbers. I've kept up with many friends that way."

One or two being many, some years.

"It could be worse. Nobody is throwing a house party for the sole purpose of getting me engaged. The Duke of Haverford's sister is apparently to endure that indignity."

Anwen applied a generous portion of butter to her toast. "I've wondered why Lady Glenys is yet unwed. She's a decent sort. Not prone to cattiness or gossip, and not silly. I've heard another theory about Haverford's house party."

Colin had passed this speculation along.

"Do tell, because I'll likely be forced to attend. Any pretext to journey into the wilds of Wales will meet with Mama's approval."

Most of Wales was wild, from what Anwen had seen of it. Also beautiful. "The gentlemen speculate that Haverford's sister is throwing the house party in hopes that His Grace will find a bride. Mama would be ecstatic if you caught the attention of a Welsh duke, my dear."

Anwen would be happy for her sister too. Elizabeth needn't marry the fellow to enjoy what ducal attentions might do for her spirits, after all.

Elizabeth took a slice of cold, plain toast from the rack. "A duke is the last sort of husband I'd accept. I've seen what a duchess has to put up with—no privacy, no rest, very few real friends, one political dinner after another. I'd go mad."

The right duke would be worth a little madness, so was the right Scottish lord.

"Do you know Haverford?"

"I cannot claim that honor. He votes his seat, I'm told, but other than that, he lurks in his castle. Why is it a man can lurk in his castle, but a lady isn't permitted the same pleasure?"

A castle in Wales sounded a bit lonely to Anwen, but then, anywhere without Colin would be lonely.

"Don't you want butter on that toast?"

Elizabeth stared at the toast from which she'd just taken a bite. "I forgot butter. Perhaps I'd best go back up to bed and try starting this day over. There are at least four house party invitations in this pile of mail. I've considered declining them and signing Aunt's name to the note."

"That is desperate talk." Though Anwen had been desperate to save the House of Urchins. Why shouldn't Elizabeth be desperate to save her freedom? "Do you suppose Haverford might feel as unwilling to marry as you do?"

Elizabeth took another bite of dry toast. "Dukes must marry. That's holy writ. He needn't be faithful or even loyal, but he must marry."

"Maybe he'd rather not," Anwen said, appropriating Elizabeth's toast and slathering butter on it. "Maybe he lurks like a dragon in his castle because he's not keen on finding a duchess. Maybe Lady Glenys has turned down all offers because she doesn't want to abandon her brother."

Elizabeth ignored the toast on her plate and regarded Anwen severely. "Listen to me, sister mine. You will accept Lord Colin's proposal of marriage, and you will waft away to the Highlands with him on a cloud of connubial bliss. You are not to prolong your engagement or put him off in hopes that Charlotte or I will bring some duke or other up to scratch. Megan is happy, beyond happy, and I want that for you too."

For a retiring spinster, Elizabeth could be ferociously dear. "Colin and I are agreed that a short engagement will be best."

Elizabeth picked up the toast. "Like that, is it? Anwen, you little hoyden. I'm proud of you."

Anwen was proud of herself, but wished her sister might have been just the smallest bit envious.

"Be proud of Lord Colin. He's not the average London dandy trolling for an heiress."

"While trolling dandies are about all I can look forward to if I let myself be dragged to these house parties."

"Say no. Refuse to go. We're no longer six years old, such that our cousins can scoop us up bodily and deposit us in the nursery when we're bothersome."

Elizabeth munched her toast in silence, while Anwen helped herself to eggs and ham from the sideboard. She was in good appetite this morning, and looking forward to sharing happy news with the boys.

While Elizabeth feared falling into the clutches of a Welsh dragon.

"I should return the mail to the library before Aunt rises," Elizabeth said. "You won't tell her I was spying?"

"Don't be daft. I'm on my way to the House of Urchins and you haven't yet left your bed."

"You are the best of sisters. I will miss you." Elizabeth rose, collected the letters, and left the parlor at a near rush. Her toast remained on her plate, so Anwen added jam and finished it in a few bites.

Elizabeth's situation was troubling—Anwen had rarely seen her eldest sister reduced to tears—but Bethan was the equal of any duke, and whatever else was true about Haverford, no scandal attached to his name. The only fact Anwen could dredge up about Julian St. David, Duke of Haverford, was that—like a dragon—he'd inherited a family tendency to hoard a certain object.

Perhaps Elizabeth had forgotten this about the St. David family. His Grace, like all the dukes of Haverford, was an avid collector of ... books.

Chapter Fifteen

ACCORDING TO COLIN'S NOTE, the sum that had been turned over to Hitchings in the dead of night had exceeded Anwen's most ambitious prayers. The Duchess of Quimbey had wagered an antique pair of rings given to her grandmother by the first King George, and a competition of sorts had ensued, involving all manner of small items of jewelry.

"At next year's event, I think we should try for more duchesses than dukes," Anwen said. "Her Grace of Quimbey might have started a tradition."

Lady Rosalyn lifted her skirts as they walked through the orphanage's garden. The day was chilly and damp, and yet, in Anwen's heart all was sunshine and roses.

"Her rings were hideous, weren't they?" Lady Rosalyn replied. "Winthrop said the whole heap of gewgaws was of inferior quality, but there was so much of it Hitchings wasn't sure where to stow it all. I have that problem with my bonnets and reticules. It's very vexing."

"The duchess's gesture was magnificent," Anwen replied, and the rings had simply been more ornate than present fashion favored.

"If your charity card party means polite society earns praise for discarding unattractive baubles, I will applaud you as a genius," Rosalyn said, snatching her skirts away from a thriving border of lavender. "I do wish I hadn't had quite so much of that delicious punch."

Her ladyship had lost heavily, and with a gracious unconcern that had earned her many compliments from her opponents.

"I wish we'd thought of a charity card party sooner. Uncle Percival said he'd mention the idea at his club as a quarterly event. The House of Urchins is only one small institution amid many that deserve assistance."

Rosalyn stopped and stared at the door as if, in the absence of a liveried footman, she wasn't certain how one opened such a thing.

"Must you be so relentlessly good, Anwen? I will drop you if you don't at least spill punch on your bodice or snort when you laugh."

She sounded half serious.

Anwen opened the door and let Rosalyn precede her through. "I'll do my best to spill strawberry punch all over my favorite fichu, but before you drop me, can we let the boys know they won't be freezing to death next winter?"

Anwen was in deadly earnest.

"By all means, let's put that chore behind us, and I can bid the boys farewell while I'm about it."

The orphanage smelled slightly mildewed on damp days, and today was no exception. Other scents blended with the damp—coal smoke, cooking, and something Anwen thought of as old books. Not a fragrance, but a unique scent she associated with this special place.

"What do you mean, you're bidding the boys farewell?"

Rosalyn stopped on the first landing, the image of pastel fashion, right down to a large, riotously embroidered reticule.

"Winthrop inveigled me into joining your committee, Anwen, but you clearly don't need me anymore. You have the coin you sought, and I've lent this place my cachet long enough that finding new committee members should be easy. You mustn't be greedy. You said it yourself: Many worthy charities deserve my support."

She glided up the steps before Anwen could fashion a suitably grateful reply that didn't also sound relieved. Rosalyn was a puzzle, one who looked lovely and sounded lovely, but didn't always act lovely, much less logically.

Before Anwen had framed her response, Tom came barreling up from the lower floor.

"Miss Anwen! It's Saturday. You never come to visit on Saturday."

"Lady Rosalyn and I bring good news, Tom. Can you and the other boys meet us in the study room?"

"Yes, ma'am!"

"Thomas." Lady Rosalyn's cool voice from above stopped him halfway down the stairs. "Aren't you forgetting something?"

Tom's face as he gazed up the stairwell was blank for an instant, then he flopped a bow. "Good day, your ladyship." He was off before Lady Rosalyn could excuse him, scold him for running, or castigate him for speaking too loudly.

His retreating steps echoed from the bowels of the house as Rosalyn descended to stand beside Anwen.

"I admire you so, Anwen, for your devotion to these

children, but if a boy can't even recall how to address a lady, or to keep his voice down indoors, his deportment is sadly lacking. My head has begun to pain me terribly, and I think I'd best wait in the coach. You'll wish the boys good-bye for me, and assure them I'll always think of them fondly, won't you?"

"Of course." If and when the boys noticed Lady Rosalyn was off *lending her cachet* elsewhere.

Anwen went up to the third floor. The former detention room had been turned into a space where any boy could find peace and quiet if he wanted to spend time at his studies. A fern taken from the Moreland conservatory sat in the windowsill, and the chairs around the table bore matching cushions. The hearth sported a fire, albeit a modest one, and the floor was covered with an old rug.

Luxurious it was not, but comfortable was a vast improvement over its previous incarnation.

The boys joined her a moment later, all four looking anxious and trying to hide their worry behind eager good manners.

"Please have a seat," Anwen said. "I'm bringing wonderful news."

Her words did not appear to reassure them. They took chairs around the table, and Anwen seated herself at the head. She would ask Colin to teach the boys how to hold a chair for a lady, now that more pressing concerns had been tended to.

"The card party was last night," Anwen said, "and I'm overjoyed to tell you it was a rousing success. The guests were very generous, and my family will likely have a similar event every year. We can keep the doors to the House of Urchins open, gentlemen. Your home is secure."

The words brought a lump to her throat, and maybe the

boys were touched as well, because none of them would meet her gaze.

"Th-thank you," Joe said, elbowing Dickie in the seat next to him.

A chorus of thanks went around the table, and still, Anwen had the sense her message hadn't sunk in.

"We'll have all the coal we need this winter, all the hot potatoes, all the blankets. We'll be able to afford a physician if the younger boys take sick, and—is there something you're not telling me?"

Somebody kicked somebody else under the table.

"What about the building?" John asked. "Hitchings says it's falling down around our ears."

The unused wing had problems. "What else did Hitchings say?"

"Tell her," Dickie said, glowering at Tom. "You're the one that heard 'em."

Tom was a sensitive soul—with sensitive hearing. Charlotte had the same gift. She could pick out conversations from across the room and catch every word.

"Mr. Montague said no amount of money would set this place to rights, and the whole card party was a waste of time. We'll close by Michaelmas."

"Just in time for cold weather," Dickie added.

"Just in time for hunt season, Mr. Montague said," John went on. "We'll be hunting, all right. For every meal and groat we can beg or steal."

The faces that had become open, even hopeful over the past several weeks were again pinched with worry and bitterness. These boys were one sunny day away from scooting down the drainpipe, and into the vast sewer of the London stews. Nothing—not the promise of hot meals, an education, eventual employment, even safety—could keep their faith in the House of Urchins alive in the face of Win Montague's pronouncements.

Rage such as Anwen had never experienced flooded her. What could she say that would make a difference to four children whose ability to hope and trust had been trampled too thoroughly and too often? What did she have to offer, when she'd been raised with every privilege?

Only Joe would meet her gaze, and the longing she saw in his blue eyes was unbearable. The boys wanted what every child should be able to take for granted—hope. Hope for a life of meaning, for some security and comfort in a world where wealth was flaunted before them every day.

She had nothing, no great speeches, no charming wit, no significant wealth of her own.

Despair touched her, an old enemy, one she'd battled when she was even younger than these boys. This was what sat beneath the rage—the firsthand knowledge of how badly a child could be overwhelmed by life's worst challenges. This was why her heart had been captured by homeless children with no one to champion them.

Anwen Windham knew the temptation to give up. To slip out the window and down the drainpipe, never to be seen again.

"I almost died," she said, shoving to her feet. "I was younger than the lot of you, and I almost died, several times."

Whatever the boys had expected her to say, it wasn't that.

"But you didn't die," John said. "You're here, and you're fine."

He was asking a question, bless the boy. "I am fine, I'm better than fine. I'm in the pink of health, my family loves me, and I'm full of plans and dreams, but the fevers nearly took me. For weeks I could barely get out of bed to use the chamber pot. I couldn't eat, I had to force myself to swallow even beef tea, and I was so tired of being sick I wanted to give up. I'd rally a bit, then relapse. The priest was summoned more than once."

"You wanted to die?" Tom asked.

Joe stared at the fire, and his silence spoke volumes.

John hunched his shoulders. "Every winter, it feels like that. Then you see some poor gin drunk who's so far gone he's not even shivering anymore, and it's all you can do not to steal his coat. But you don't—not yet—not until you're as bad off as he is."

Oh, God, what these children had endured. All over again, Anwen wished she'd publicly humiliated Win Montague before all of polite society.

"I did not die," Anwen said. "I wanted to give up, to be where it didn't hurt anymore, where I wasn't tired anymore. I wanted the illness to let go of me, any way I could make that happen. I'd open my eyes, though, and my mother would be beside the bed, ready to spoon more tea into me or read me a story. I'd open my eyes again, and my papa would be there, playing solitaire on the counterpane. I'd not even open my eyes, but I'd know one of my sisters had broken the rules again and was napping beside me. I could not let them down. I had to try, and keep trying, and try some more after that."

As a child, she hadn't been able to name that sense of obligation, but she could name it now, and be endlessly grateful for it.

"You had family," Tom said, not quite making it an accusation.

"And you have me, and Lord Colin, and all the people who gave their diamonds, and emeralds, and pearls so you'd be warm this winter. You have each other, and if you're ready to give up, I'm not. I'm far from ready to give up on children who deserve just as much love and care as I had."

She'd taken a risk, mentioning love, but honesty was the best policy, and nothing short of love had saved her life. Call it determination, devotion, familial loyalty, or any less intimidating term, but the motivating force had been love.

Across the room, Joe, all alone at the end of the table, sniffed and swiped at his eyes with his sleeve.

Anwen didn't dare go to the boy, or she'd lose what little composure she had left, and forever embarrass him. Instead she passed him her handkerchief.

"Keep that for me, Joseph, and I'll keep a promise for you. You will not lose your home. You've worked too hard to make the House of Urchins an institution to be proud of, and Winthrop Montague is a horse's arse."

John snickered, Dickie hooted, and Tom smiled.

"He is that," John agreed. "A lame horse's arse. Sounds better when you say it."

"A spavined, lame horse's arse," John said, "and he has cow hocks."

They'd become quite the horsemen since the ponies had come to bide in the mews. While Anwen wondered who'd top John's insult, and where the insults might end, Joe darted to the window and Tom followed him to peer around the fern.

"Lord Colin's here! I wish he'd draw Mr. Montague's cork."

So did Anwen, and a bloody nose was the least of the damage she'd like to inflict on Winthrop Montague.

"Will you tell him, Miss Anwen?" Dickie asked. "Tell him what Mr. Montague said?"

"I will, though I'd ask you not to alarm the younger boys. There is rising damp in the unused wing, but the rest of the building seems sound enough. There's rising damp in half the homes in London, and yet those houses still stand."

For a time, but rotten beams, crumbling plaster, and peeling wallpaper were inevitable results, and just the start of the decay that dampness in the walls caused. Win Montague was the social equivalent of rising damp, encroaching on the basis of arrogance and birth where he'd done nothing to earn a proper introduction.

And he was frequently less than fragrant in close quarters too.

"I'll greet his lordship," she said. "I think you boys should see how much generosity has been sent your way. We have enough gold and jewels to make any self-respecting pirate swoon."

An exaggeration, but not by much. Anwen left four smiling boys in the study, and sailed out the door, only to once again run smack into Lord Colin MacHugh.

* * *

"My lord, good morning!" Anwen's greeting was cheerful but her eyes were suspiciously shiny.

"Has somebody made you cry?" Colin asked, hands settling on her arms. "I'm not in a very tolerant mood, and I'd relish an opportunity to break a few heads."

The door behind her eased open. Tom, Dickie, John, and Joe peered out from the study room, their gazes carefully blank.

"Mr. Montague made Miss Anwen cry," John said. "More or less."

"He's right," Dickie said. "You should draw his cork."

"Plant him a facer," Tom added, and Tom was usually the soul of diplomacy.

Joe pantomimed a knee to the stones, which Anwen couldn't see, because the boys were behind her.

"I gather there's trouble in paradise?"

Anwen whirled away, back into the study. "I am so angry, trouble is a polite term. Please tell the boys the building isn't going to be demolished over their very heads. Winthrop Montague said as much to Mr. Hitchings, and was overhead by one of the boys. Now they're convinced no amount of coin can keep the House of Urchins afloat, just when our finances are surely coming right."

Him again. "Winthrop Montague is making all kinds of a plague of himself, isn't he?"

Anwen worried a nail, and nodded. *Not in front of the boys.*

"Listen, ye wee scamps," Colin said. "You have a home, no matter what. There's rising damp all over the other wing, but that's not unusual in an old building that's been neglected. This wing is sound. Even if it's not sound, you're hard workers, well-mannered, good at most any-thing you turn your hands to, and done with a life on the streets. My word on that as a gentleman."

He added a glower worthy of his sainted papa so the children would know he meant business.

"We weren't worried," Tom said. "We were mad at Mr. Montague. Bloke ought to be looking out for the little ones, not scarpering off to his house parties and hunt balls."

Mutters of assent sounded from John and Dick, while Joe maintained his characteristic silence.

"I told them you wouldn't let them down," Anwen said. Such faith she had. "If you boys will excuse us, Miss

Anwen and I have a few things to discuss regarding the card party. I know you'll worry, but don't do anything foolish because of it. I'll get Mr. Montague sorted out."

"Sort 'im out with your fives," Dickie said. "He upset Miss Anwen."

Anwen tousled Dickie's hair, and for once the other boys kept their elbows to themselves.

"Madam, if you could spare me a few minutes?" Colin asked.

"We'll be back," Anwen said. "I want to show the boys the pirate's treasure that resulted from the card party."

A good idea, because what the children could see, they'd believe.

Colin stole a quick kiss in the corridor, and Anwen stole a not-so-quick kiss too.

"We have to talk," Colin said. "I gather Montague made a pest of himself last night?"

"Not here," Anwen said, "and I left Lady Rosalyn waiting in the coach. She's quit the committee, by the way. I'll get around to telling the boys that if they bring it up."

"She is the least of our problems," Colin said, leading Anwen across the corridor into an empty classroom. Not a single lamp had been lit, so the space was gloomy, chilly, and quiet. "I sent her on her way, and told her I'd take you home. What happened between you and Montague last night?"

"He acted very oddly," Anwen said, rubbing her arms and pacing between the desks. "He attempted to flirt, which was pathetic, and when I told him you'd asked to pay your addresses, he became quite toplofty."

A euphemism for the ages, no doubt. "I promise not to call him out, love."

"Thank you. A lady does worry."

Anwen had male cousins, and thus she still looked worried.

Colin had sisters, and he had Anwen. "I won't even invite him into the ring at Jackson's Salon," he said, stalking closer to her. "I won't provoke him or any of his toadies into calling me out." He came to a halt immediately before her. "I won't disappoint you, Anwen. The children are depending on us."

Her shoulders relaxed and she slipped her arms around him. For a moment, Colin simply held her, telling her without words that she wasn't alone with whatever challenges she faced.

And neither was he. The realization warmed his heart as no drinking party with the fellows ever could.

"Winthrop Montague is a disgrace," Anwen said, resting her cheek against Colin's chest. "He expressed dismay that you'd consider offering for me, not because you have wealth, a title, good looks, and charm in abundance, while I'm the least impressive Windham ever to make her bow. He was wroth with you for poaching on his preserves."

His preserves. To Winthrop Montague, anything he desired was or should be his. Colin's heart belonged to Anwen, but she was very much her own person. How could even Montague not see that?

"Did you laugh at him?" A humiliated Winthrop Montague was a dangerous creature.

"His plan was to inform you that he'd beat you past the post, as it were, and was already courting me. You were to decamp in the interests of gentlemanly honor, and Mr. Montague could congratulate himself on earning my undying gratitude as well as my settlements merely by lifting his eyebrow and waving you off. I found that disgusting rather than amusing, Colin. Is he daft?"

Colin could feel the anger in her, and not a little bewilderment, but worse—why had he promised not to beat the idiot to a pulp?—fear.

Anwen was afraid, and as arrogant as Montague was, as influential as he could be, her fear was understandable.

"Montague is everything detestable about the wealthy aristocrat," Colin said, "writ in a large, sloppy hand. He told me if I persist in courting you, he'll have this building condemned. I'm to run back to Scotland and stay there, lest I make you miserable for the rest of your days. By marrying you, Montague is doing me a favor. He assured me of this, even as he threatened to pitch the boys back into the slums."

Maybe Colin ought not to have shared that last bit, about doing him a favor, because Anwen went ominously still.

"Put out his lights, Colin. Persuade Mrs. Bellingham to serve him the cut direct at the fashionable hour. Break his perfect nose in three places—oh, what am I saying? That would set no kind of example for the boys. Can he have the building condemned?"

Everything in Colin wanted to offer platitudes and reassurances, though Anwen would skewer him for doubting her fortitude.

"His father is an earl, Anwen, and the other wing is in poor condition. We must assume Winthrop's threat is sincere, and be about finding homes for the children."

She shifted, dropping her forehead against his sternum, a posture of weariness, but not defeat. "I was afraid you'd say that. I hate to think of them having to part from each other, and I just promised them their home is secure."

"We'll make our plans, and hope that Winthrop is bluffing. We'll have to say something to Moreland, though." Colin would send a pigeon to Hamish as well.

"Uncle Percy has given *you* permission to court me. What is there to say?"

"Montague will mispresent the situation to your uncle, claim I was toying with your affections, that you'd given him reason to hope, that a woman deserves a choice. He's devious, and I don't put much past him."

Anwen eased away. "I might have ended up married to him, and counted myself pleased to have his notice. I hate that."

Every soldier knew the weak-in-the-knees, cast-up-your-accounts feeling of having dodged a bullet by inches. "You have me, and you always will."

Colin would inscribe that on a ring for her, and give it to her as her morning gift.

Anwen studied the slate hanging at the front of the room. Each Latin verb declension was written out in all six persons, present tense, and of course, the first declension example was *amo, amare.*

I love. Colin loved Anwen, in large part because they could talk like this, honestly, bravely, and create an entire language of love, trust, and loyalty.

"When I met with the boys, I realized something, Colin."

"What did you realize?"

"The great fire yet burns. You said I was a bonfire, but when it comes to those children, I am the sun, Colin. I am a comet, or a meteor, some heavenly body composed entirely of fire. *I am fierce as the devil.*"

"Fierce as an angel, I think you mean."

She smiled at him over her shoulder. "I love you, Colin MacHugh. Winthrop Montague is a spavined, cow-hocked, horse's arse of an idiot."

"And you're being polite." Unfortunately, Montague

was a powerful idiot, despite his relative penury and lack of honor. "Let's find Hitchings and have him show the boys the loot, and then I'll take you home. We can arrange to have an architect look the building over, and plan from there."

Anwen took Colin's hand and kissed his knuckles.

The sight of her head bent over his hand did queer things to his breathing. She was the pirate's treasure, the loot, the prize, the everything. How dare Winthrop Montague presume Anwen should be grateful for his bumbling attentions?

Colin collected the boys and was herding them down the steps with Anwen at his side, when Hitchings came trotting up the corridor.

"Lord Colin! Miss Anwen! We must summon the authorities this instant. The money is gone. Every penny and pound, gone, and nowhere to be found."

Chapter Sixteen

ESTHER PUT PERCIVAL IN mind of a contented lioness, sipping her chocolate and perusing the paper with a victorious gleam in her eyes. Had family been present, she might have taken her usual place at the foot of the breakfast table, but Charlotte and Elizabeth were abovestairs somewhere, and Anwen had already hared off to her orphanage.

Percival thus broke his fast with Her Grace at his elbow, his favorite way to start the day.

"A triumph," the duchess said, putting the paper down. "They've run out of metaphors. My boating party four years ago was a triumph, and now the card party is a triumph as well. I've devised a means of celebrating both the congenial and the compassionate at the lowly altar of the card table, no less. Who writes this drivel?"

Percival's duchess was very pleased.

"There won't be an urchin or wounded veteran left on

the streets of London," Percival said. "I hope you're proud of yourself."

Esther smiled at her chocolate. "This family of ours is a force to be reckoned with, Moreland, but much of the credit must go to Anwen."

"Gracious of you to say so. Would you care for another slice of ham?"

"I'll just have a bite of yours."

The woman pilfered bacon without shame, though not in front of the children. Percival sliced off several bites of perfectly cooked meat from his own serving and put them on her plate.

"Are you up to another wedding so soon?" Percival asked. "Anwen and her Scottish swain won't tolerate a lengthy engagement."

The duchess paused, a bite of ham on the end of her fork. "I thought you had reservations about Lord Colin? He certainly acquitted himself well last night."

"I had reservations, but they've been addressed, or I wouldn't have allowed him the privileges of a suitor. Rosecroft unearthed all manner of debts supposedly run up by Lord Colin in a very short time. That was my toast, you little thief."

"You put just the right amount of butter on yours." She held it up to his mouth for him to take a bite, and abruptly, Percival longed for the peace and privacy of Kent.

"Esther, I miss you."

She gave him a sympathetic look, because they reached this point during every London season. "I miss you too. Maybe it's time to have Westhaven attend some of your parliamentary committee meetings. He's no longer newly wed or new to fatherhood."

"Maybe it's time you had only one at home a week."

For the past several years, they'd been having this argument too.

"Starting in June, I will. Two weddings, a grand ball, and a card party are enough for one season. If Lord Colin is in dun territory, why did you give him permission to court Anwen?"

"Because he's no more indebted than Westhaven or Rosecroft. The clubs are very discreet, but a prank was played, or a series of pranks, and a significant list of expenses was attributed to Lord Colin that he'd not run up. I gather the same dubious brand of juvenile humor resulted in bills all over Mayfair and even at Tatts."

And that was taking things a step too far, or several steps. Accounts at the club could be squared with reciprocal generosity, but glorified horse thievery was the outside of too bold. Greed in young men who'd been born with every privilege was an untenable fault.

Coupling greed with stupidity was intolerable.

Her Grace took another bite of ham and set down her utensils. "I am very glad our sons turned out as sensibly as they did, Moreland. Involving the trades in some puerile jest shows exceedingly bad taste. My future guest lists will reflect my opinion on the matter. I take it Lord Colin paid the bills?"

"Within the week. Even Westhaven would have had difficulty pulling that off. Will you leave me any toast at all?"

Esther smirked, looking about sixteen years old, and bit off a corner of his last piece of toast. "Ring for more. A social triumph always puts me in good appetite."

Percival was an advocate of the love match, within reason, but he did not envy his offspring. No matter their wealth or position—in some regards because of those blessings—they had hard years ahead. Years of parenting, marital discord, heartache, and challenge. Decades of setbacks, joys, sorrows, and readjustments.

If they were very, very lucky, they might acquire the sort of wealth Percival treasured most of all—breakfast with his duchess, her smirking at him over purloined toast while the fire crackled cozily in the hearth, and a dreary day got under way outside.

"Lord Colin's distillery ventures are on quite sound footing," Percival said. "And getting sounder, according to Westhaven. He's heard the talk in the clubs too, and if I were one Winthrop Montague, I might leave early for the house parties."

Esther peered at him. "There's scandal brewing? Does this have to do with Mrs. Bellingham?"

Percival had a sip of her chocolate. "Madam, you shock me. And at the breakfast table. Such talk."

Esther rose and plucked an orange from the bowl on the sideboard. "Let's away to our sitting room, sir. For if you think to withhold good gossip from your devoted wife, you are sadly in error."

She kissed his cheek and swanned off, as only a social triumph pleased with her duke could.

* * *

"I simply hadn't room in the strongbox for the jewels and the cash both," Hitchings said, for the fourth time. "I locked the jewels away and divided the money into the sum we need for each month's expenses. A good eight months' worth too."

Anwen knew exactly how much coin the card party had earned, and now every bit of it was gone.

"We still have the jewels," she said. "We needn't panic."

"We have a thief in our midst," Winthrop Montague retorted from his place at the chairman's desk. "But then, we knew that."

Colin had convinced Hitchings to notify Montague as chairman of the board rather than go directly to the authorities. Montague had taken half the afternoon to bestir himself, and he appeared much the worse for having overindulged the previous night.

Anwen, Colin, and the children had spent the intervening hours searching every drawer and closet of the orphanage for the missing funds. The only place they hadn't searched was the chairman's office, where Hitchings had remained like a martyr keeping vigil over the strongbox.

"Montague, don't leap to conclusions," Colin said. "Moreland himself pointed out that half the pickpockets and thieves in London had to have heard of last night's card party. The usual gawkers were lining the drive and at the ballroom windows. Anybody could have followed the Moreland coach last night."

"I should never have left the money in the drawer," Hitchings said. "The lateness of the hour affected my judgment, but what else was I to do?"

"You are not to blame, Mr. Hitchings," Anwen said. "The money should have been safe enough in the chairman's office. The door does lock after all."

Mr. Montague pinched the bridge of his nose. "Who had a key?"

"You do," Hitchings said. "I do as well, and MacDeever has a set, though to be precisely, entirely honest, I'm not certain I locked the door. I don't usually. The strongbox is locked at all times, but not the various doors."

"Let's establish a sequence of events," Colin said, pacing to the window. "The authorities will start there, and we should as well."

"The money is gone," Montague shot back. "Let's start there. Why shouldn't I have you arrested, MacHugh?"

Anwen was on her feet and leaning over the desk in the next instant. "*I beg your pardon?*"

"MacHugh knew where the money was, knows every inch of this building, and has desperate need of coin," Montague said.

"May I remind you, Mr. Montague, that his lordship has significant independent means, has no more familiarity with the premises than you do, yourself, and *unlike you*, has no key to this room or to the strongbox."

"Miss Anwen." Colin spoke very softly, a warning, though Anwen wasn't sure of the specifics.

"The lady has a point," Hitchings said, mopping his brow. "If opportunity and motive are at issue, I had every opportunity, and my means are very modest, compared to his lordship's."

"As are yours, Montague," Colin said. "You have more financial motive than I do, and greater opportunity. Your social aspirations are beyond your means, and you are passionate about obtaining them. You have a key to the building, the office, and the strongbox, while I have none of those, nor am I frustrated by financial inability to obtain my goals."

Anwen suspected Colin referred to Mrs. Bellingham, and clearly, Montague hadn't been expecting his reasoning to be challenged.

"I want the boy John questioned," Montague shot back. "The little sneak thief has been up to tricks again, and he's probably recruited the other boys to assist him."

Colin leaned back against the windowsill and folded his

arms. "All of the boys should be questioned in case they heard or saw something last night or this morning. Miss Anwen is best equipped to do that. They trust her."

"His lordship has a point," Hitchings said. "The boys love Miss Anwen, and if they were to confide in anybody, it would be her."

"You think a batch of little criminals will confess to Miss Anwen?" Montague snorted. "We fed them, clothed them, housed them, educated them, kept them warm, and that will mean nothing to that lot. They'll protect their own and to blazes with justice. If MacHugh didn't take that money, then the boys did."

For the first time in Anwen's life, she understood the compulsion to do violence, to destroy the source of an offense and render it incapable of offending again. She was about to tell Montague as much, when Colin spoke.

"The children did not take the money. They have had months to steal from this place, and they well know how to turn stolen goods into coin."

Colin didn't mention that the boys were too honorable to steal. He'd resorted to the same argument Anwen had made weeks ago. Montague might listen to him, whereas Anwen would have been dismissed out of hand.

"Any money was carefully secured," Montague retorted, "or was prior to last night. What could they possibly steal?"

"Oh, my goodness," Hitchings said. "They could steal the glass from the windows in the unoccupied wing. They could take door latches, bricks, marble from the fireplaces in the old library, brass fittings, almost anything associated with an intact structure can be sold to the builders. London is mad for new housing, and that takes finished materials."

Anwen hadn't known that, and clearly, Montague hadn't either.

"I'm off to question MacDeever," Colin said. "Miss Anwen, please interview the boys. Hitchings, you'll want to inventory the jewels. Moreland has a list of what should be in the strongbox, and we can compare lists."

Hitchings hoisted the strongbox and bustled out, Colin on his heels. Anwen would have followed him, except Winthrop Montague stopped her with a hand on her arm.

"I'm sorry you've been embroiled in this mess, Miss Anwen. A private discussion between us has become imperative."

Anwen didn't want to be alone with him, much less endure another instant of his posturing and bloviating when the orphanage was imperiled. He'd just threatened Colin and the boys, and she hadn't forgotten his nasty threats to Colin the previous night.

"I can spare you one minute, Mr. Montague, but time is of the essence, and finding that money my priority. It should be yours too."

"Well, it's not. Not exactly."

Then he closed the door.

* * *

The mother of all bilious stomachs plagued Win, along with a pounding head, a few gaps in his recollection of the previous night, and a mood fouler than the London sewers. Everything associated with the damned orphanage became a problem, and yet, he could only pity Anwen Windham.

She genuinely cared about this place, and a corner of Win's heart genuinely cared about her. Mostly he cared about her settlements, though, and her ducal connections. No need to dissemble on that point.

If all went according to plan, Winthrop Montague would soon be invited to the Windham menfolk's Tuesday night card parties, and to hell with the charitable version.

"My dear, your loyalty to Lord Colin as a member of your extended family and to the children here does you credit," Win said, tucking his hands behind his back. A thoughtful pose, if he did say so himself. "And I am aware that to be behind a closed door with you flirts with impropriety, despite our families' long connection. What I have to say is for your ears only, and meant with your best interests in mind."

He paused, as a vicar might, to lock gazes with the object of his discourse. Miss Anwen was agitated, which brought out the color in her cheeks rather unappealingly.

"Please be brief, Mr. Montague. The sooner I speak with the children, the more likely they are to recall something *useful*."

She was trying to make some obscure, righteous point. Logical discourse was beyond most females, though they had all the animal cunning in the world when intent on procuring a new bonnet.

"The orphanage is doomed," Win said. "The infusion of cash effected by your little card party is a temporary measure, and merely perpetrates the cruelty of a false dawn on those who've known enough hardship. The money will run out, the expenses will never end. Trust me on this, for my grasp of economics is thorough. Even if the money were abundant, scandal will be the ruin of this institution and of Lord Colin."

Win would see personally to that last part.

"I will not be made to listen to this." She started for the door on a righteous swish of skirts, but Win had longer legs and a superior male brain. He beat her to the door and held it closed by the simple expedient of leaning on it.

"I wish you didn't have to hear what I must say," Win replied. "But consider the facts. Lord Colin becomes associated with the orphanage, and young John goes badly astray. A few weeks later, our estimable Mr. Hitchings is making noises about stepping down, and we've liquidated valuable assets such as any respectable organization knows are necessary to maintain its dignity."

"Because that rattletrap coach and nasty team were sold?" she said, hands going to her hips. "And Lord Colin hadn't been officially appointed to the board when John faltered."

"You and I know that timing, and you and I know the sale of the coach was a desperate measure, but to those looking on from the outside, appearances outweigh facts. A house is only worth what its equipage is worth, and John stole from an upstanding citizen. None of that matters now, because Lord Colin is very likely to be arrested for stealing a significant amount of cash."

She crossed her arms and strode across the room as if somebody had opened a privy door upwind.

Win had the fleeting thought that he should have started the day chewing a deal of parsley—Rosalyn was a great advocate of parsley—but the thought of fresh greenery aggravated his already troubled digestion.

"You had more motive and opportunity to steal than anybody," Miss Anwen retorted. "Why aren't you worried about being arrested?"

He guffawed, which was terribly ungentlemanly of him. "Because I didn't take the money, of course, and because I am the son of a much respected, titled family, English to the bone, a marvel of good breeding, and esteemed by all. MacHugh is a Scottish upstart, to the distillery born, for God's sake, and I doubt very much he can account for his whereabouts between his departure from the premises last night and his arrival here this morning. I can."

Well, no he couldn't, but doubtless Twilly and Pointy would accommodate that oversight.

"Where were you?"

She was *such* an innocent.

"A gentleman wouldn't say in the presence of a lady, much less in the presence of his intended."

Her expression underwent a curious progression, from indignant, to astonished, to blank. "I am not your intended."

"I can rectify that with a simple call on your uncle, and before you sputter about tender sentiments and other impracticalities, allow me to explain your situation to you. If you agree to accept my proposal, then I will delay speaking to the authorities while we conduct a more thorough search of the premises. Lord Colin will have time to make an expedient trip north, though he'll be regrettably unwelcome in England for the rest of his days."

Miss Anwen turned her back on Win, probably to hide tears. The ladies were prone to such histrionics. Rosalyn could cry over Lady Dremel's missing fan and usually to very good effect.

"Your settlements," Win went on, "will be discreetly modified to replace the funds missing from the orphanage's exchequer, in due course. The Windham family bears some responsibility for the entire situation, after all. But for their connection to MacHugh's ducal brother, your head would never have been turned, MacHugh would never have become involved, and we'd all have been spared that wretched card party."

The future Mrs. Winthrop Montague turned to face him, not a trace of a tear to be seen. If Win had to guess, he'd say she was revising her opinion of Lord Colin, and the rubbishing mushroom had best be making plans to leave the country.

"Are you finished, Mr. Montague? A fortune has gone missing, and while my future concerns me, the future of the children concerns me more."

"Their future concerns me as well, though you should know, the condition of this building is unacceptable. The children aren't safe here, from what I can see. Something must be done and soon. Perhaps you'd like to offer your opinion on that topic?"

She wrapped her arms around her middle. Some ladies did that because it emphasized their bosoms, but Miss Anwen was so modestly attired, a man was hard put to recall she had a bosom.

Though cursory inspection reassured Win that she did, thank God.

"Allow me to summarize your offer," Miss Anwen said. "You will marry me, have the benefit of my settlements, see the missing funds replaced—funds you had motive and opportunity to steal—and likely close the orphanage nonetheless, but you'll allow Lord Colin to flee under a cloud of disgrace entirely of your own manufacturing."

"Well put, though you neglected the sad consequences of the alternative. If you and I wed, then Lord Colin becomes a family connection of mine, hence my willingness to hesitate before contacting the authorities. In the absence of such a connection, my duty to the children means Lord Colin will be arrested by Monday morning."

Win speared her with his best raised eyebrow, lest the lady mistake his point. "I'm not saying he's guilty. That will be for the authorities to decide, and I will defend Lord Colin at every turn. I will also honestly regret that he has no alibi, and that will speak volumes. Finally, I will state my opinion to all and sundry that you, yourself, despite being a somewhat eccentric, difficult woman, would never be so bold as to steal, or to raise funds expressly so you could turn around and appropriate them for yourself. A gently bred lady could never be so devious."

That last part was an inspiration, but it could work, with the right regret sighed into the right ears after the right number of drinks, especially if Rosalyn lent a hand.

It could work marvelously, and the day was quickly coming right—for Win.

Miss Anwen stared over his shoulder as if a lot of dusty old books might start performing the minuet on their dusty old shelves.

"So you'll see Lord Colin condemned in the court of public opinion even if the magistrate finds no evidence to bind him over. Scandal will close the orphanage if a lack of funds doesn't, while you gain a wife, means you did nothing to earn, and commiseration from your many friends for the troubles you've endured."

He hadn't thought about the commiseration. Commiseration was always lovely.

"I am marrying a woman of some discernment," Win said. "I will leave in your graceful hands the delicate matter of explaining particulars to Lord Colin. He has until Monday, no need to thank me. I am a gentleman, after all, and compassion should inform my every decision. I am content that I've prevented a lady I esteem from being ruined by a Scottish rogue."

Miss Anwen said nothing, which boded well for their marital accord. Win kissed her cheek and left her in the empty office. He really ought to have a chat with the magistrate with all due haste, but that would mean locating same, and a trip to Bow Street. Monday was soon enough for those dreary undertakings. The funds were gone, and a day or two's delay wouldn't change that.

A consultation with Win's gold pocket watch assured him the fellows would be gathering at the club to lament the damage done by the infernal card party. Too bad for them. For Win, a celebratory glass or three was in order before he presented himself at his papa's dinner party.

Also some hair of the dog. Rather lot of hair of the dog, for matters could not be turning out any better.

Chapter Seventeen

"MACDEEVER SPENT THE NIGHT with his lady friend," Colin said. "He had his keys with him, so they couldn't have been stolen, but he says the locks in the building are so old they can be forced or opened without a key."

Anwen sat on the chairman's desk where the strongbox was usually to be found, an odd perch for a lady. Her air was distracted, though her calm didn't fool Colin.

"I forced one of the locks when we searched the unused wing," she said. "I used my hairpin, remember? If Win Montague learned of that, he'd be sure to let the magistrate know." Her tone was flat, beyond bitterness, beyond resignation or even despair.

"Has Montague been spreading his foul talk again?" Montague had driven his phaeton out of the mews at a rattling trot, denying Colin even a nod of parting.

"I hate him, Colin. I thought I hated the quadrille, long sermons, serious illness. I don't. I hate Win Montague."

Colin took Anwen in his arms. She remained passive in his embrace, and that troubled him.

Scared him witless, in fact. "Tell me, love. What has Montague done now?"

Anwen felt small and brittle in his embrace. Her fire was down to coals, and Colin would shelter the flame they held with his life if necessary.

"He will have you arrested on Monday morning, and if I were you, I'd be very careful no one has access to your domicile between then and now. Win will put a sack of coin under your pillow or otherwise incriminate you with more than gossip. He can do it too, Colin. You were right not to underestimate him."

For a moment, Colin simply held his beloved, because he needed to stay near her goodness and dearness.

"What's the rest of it?"

"In the alternative, I can marry him, and you will be allowed to slip away quietly as a gentlemanly courtesy extended by Mr. Montague to a distant family connection. You'll be a wanted man, and my family must compensate the orphanage for the missing funds, but nobody will hang for stealing. The House of Urchins will be demolished in any case."

Was there an uglier verb in the language than "to hang"?

"Anwen, I did not take that money."

"Of course you didn't," she said. "Neither did I, but such is Winthrop Montague's honor that he'll intimate from every club and race meet that I planned the entire card party so I could steal the proceeds. I'm withdrawn and eccentric, a difficult woman, much indulged by my family. I had no maid sleeping in my dressing room to attest to the fact that I fell into bed exhausted and barely stirred until I joined you here this morning."

"To accuse you makes no sense," Colin said, holding her more closely. "You love this place, and you have no motive to steal from children. Don't let Win's fancies frighten you into marrying him."

She kissed him, a gesture of faith in a desperate conversation. "I'd kill him before the vows were consummated, Colin, which makes me as bad as he is. I won't blame you if you take ship for Scotland. This situation will sort itself out, and my family will stand behind you. I'll join you in Scotland, and there's nothing Win Montague can say to it."

He kissed her back, a gesture of determination. "What about the boys, Anwen? I've given them and you my word that they'll not be tossed to the elements for Montague's convenience or my own."

She eased away and began a perambulation about the room. "I gave them the same promise, but I won't lose you to Montague's vile games, Colin. The boys had nothing to add to what we know, and they still think you should beat the stuffing out of Montague."

"And be arrested for assault?"

"No, actually." Her smile was wan. "Dickie explained that if you haven't any witnesses, and you say Win fell down the steps, and Win says you pushed him, no arrest can follow. It's a difference of opinion. Quite the little barrister."

"So the trick is to commit my crimes without witnesses. Do you suppose Montague had accomplices when he took that money?"

Anwen left off tidying a shelf of books behind the desk. "*What?*"

"You heard the same evidence I did. Montague had more opportunity than anybody save Hitchings, who has never taken a penny or misstated an expense. Hitchings also has no motive, because if this place closes its doors, he has no job. That leaves Montague, who had motive in the form of designs on Mrs. Bellingham, as well as debts, and endless opportunity."

Win's guilt had been clear to Colin from the moment Win had accused him. Anwen had apparently not reached the same conclusion.

"Your theory makes sense," she said slowly. "In his every pontification and threat, Montague's demeanor supports your version of the events. He'd steal from children, blame others, and think he could get away with it. He's set it up so he'll be the victim of unfortunate associations, while he marries me to save me from scandal. I really do hate him."

And yet, Anwen hadn't wanted to accuse even Winthrop Montague of stealing from the children.

"He hasn't got away with it," Colin said, "not yet. His worse offense is upsetting my lady, and for that, he must be held responsible."

This time when Colin held Anwen, she was with him, she was present, accounted for, and holding him in return.

"You cannot call him out, Colin. He'll cheat, he'll say his gun misfired, he'll find a way to take you from me, and see your reputation the worse for it."

How fierce she was, how protective.

"I won't let it come to that. What was stolen can be retrieved. The banks won't open until Monday, and Win wouldn't trust that much money to any of his dear friends. He'll keep it under his control, and that means I can find it."

"You'll steal from the thief?"

"I'll restore the money to those who are entitled to it."

Anwen sank her fingers into the hair at his nape.

"He's having you arrested on Monday at the latest unless I agree to marry him, and he'll make that agreement public on the instant. I can't marry him, but I can't ask you to risk hanging."

"You don't have to ask me. Honor demands that I put the situation to rights. Fortunately, I've been in Win's rooms many times, and know the entire house well. Then too, I'll have the benefit of expert advice before I attempt this adventure. Your job is to make Montague think you're considering his proposition."

She held Colin desperately tight. "I can do that. You'll consult with the boys?"

"Who better? They know housebreaking, thievery, all manner of useful skills that a gentleman could never claim but I desperately need."

"Be careful," Anwen said, going up on her toes and kissing him at length. "Be quick, and be very, very careful."

* * *

The door to the conference room was unlocked.

In the past three weeks, Anwen had become very aware of when a door was locked or unlocked, when a sister was napping one floor above, and when the footmen came around to trim wicks or clean the ashes from the various hearths. Here at the orphanage, with children underfoot, she was usually even more careful.

Caution was beyond her when Colin planned to embark on nothing less than a hanging offense against the Earl of Monthaven's household.

"I can't stand the thought of you taking such a risk," she murmured. "If you're caught, you could well die. A man who steals from his friends and from orphans, who bullies a woman to the altar, will think nothing of perjuring himself to see you hanged."

The words were the stuff of nightmares, and yet, all of polite society would name pickpockets as a worse threat to the king's peace than Winthrop Montague.

All of polite society would be unforgivably stupid.

"I won't be caught," Colin said. "By Monday morning, the money will be back where it should be, and Montague will look like a fool for going to the magistrate."

How confident Colin sounded, and how solid he felt in her arms. Anwen stroked her hands down his back.

"You don't have that much money in London, do you?"

"Nobody with any sense keeps such a sum in private hands." Colin spoke with his lips against Anwen's temple. "I could likely raise the cash within a week, but I just strained my immediate resources to accommodate Montague's last escapade."

Of course he had. "I'm too muddled to think. Too angry, too frightened, too—"

Colin framed her face in his palms. "Hush. If you weren't worried, I'd fear you failed to grasp the magnitude of the problem. We'll get through this. You are my bonfire, and the harder the gale blows, the more brightly a bonfire's flame roars."

She tugged him over to the desk, scooted back, and pulled him between her knees. "I'm an anxious bonfire. Love me, Colin."

The need to join with him was a confused welter of worry, determination, desire, and hope. Colin could be arrested by this time Monday, the orphanage doomed, Anwen's family embroiled in scandal, but this moment was hers to share with him.

"Lass, there's no need tae—"

"That was your one allotted gesture in the direction of gentlemanly restraint, Colin. Lock the door and make love with me."

His lips quirked, the dimple creasing his left cheek. "When you put it so sweetly, I can only agree."

He twisted the old lock, and as he crossed the room, his walk became a prowl. Anwen's nerves settled, though her heart beat faster.

"This is battle lust," he said. "You're fighting for all you're worth against an enemy who has no honor, and the blood sings."

"The only battle I want to win is the battle for your heart."

He stepped between her knees. "Regarding that conflict, I've long since surrendered, Anwen."

"So did I." And she was desperate to surrender to him again.

Colin had reserves of self-control Anwen lacked. His kisses were deliberate, slow and sweet, then hot. His focus was on her, not scattered in a hundred upsetting directions. Gradually, Anwen let herself be pulled into the loving he wove, despite the dusty shelves, the hard desk, and the missing money.

Despite everything.

Colin made a respite for her, a haven of soft caresses, tender indecencies—he excelled at those—and growing desire. When he eased her skirts up, and moved his sporran to his hip, Anwen was ready.

"You do it," he said, letting his hands fall to his sides. "Bring us together."

She wiggled, she scooted, she took him in her hand, and showed him where she wanted him. Then scooted another half inch, and the joining was begun.

"We've never made love in a bed," she whispered as Colin gently rocked closer. "I want to make love with you in a bed. I want to see your home in Perthshire. I want to learn all about distilling whisky. I want to marry you. I want—"

He surged forward. "You'll have what you want, and you'll have me."

She *had him* until she bit his shoulder to keep from crying out her pleasure; had him until her soul sang with a surfeit of rainbows; had him, until she realized the dampness on her cheeks was tears.

Colin withdrew, and held her close. "None of that now. I'll be careful, and Winthrop Montague will rue the day he trifled with his betters."

Anwen's skirts drifted back down over her ankles. She felt calm, hollow, cherished, and terrified all at once. She stayed close to Colin as he finished in a few deft strokes, and then for a few minutes longer.

"I don't want to let you go."

"You're no' lettin' me go. You're in my heart, and you always will be. I've a few plans to make, and some young gentlemen to consult with, but I should see you home so you can tell your family what's afoot before Montague beats you to it."

The suggestion was like a pail of cold, dirty water tossed on Anwen's fragile sense of peace.

"Uncle Percy will be horrified, not only because the money is missing, but also because scandal threatens to touch his family."

"Then give me one night, and maybe scandal can be averted before Montague spreads his accusations. If Montague comes to call, intercept him, or at least see that his recounting is accurate while you incriminate him with your every question and aside."

Anwen fluffed the folds of Colin's cravat, which had got a bit wrinkled somehow. "I can do that. You're good at this."

He gave her a naughty smile and put his sporran front and center. "We're good at it."

"Not *that*, though you're a very skilled lover. I mean, you're good at seeing what has to be done, assigning tasks to the person best suited to the job, and planning for success."

"Wars are won and lost in preparation as much as battle, and it's the same with the whisky."

Anwen let Colin have the last word, but he didn't realize how naturally talented he was at dealing with responsibility. He was a convivial escort, a charming partner for the waltz, but beneath the polite banter and handsome turnout was a man of substance, brains, and integrity.

She let that thought reassure her as Colin handed her into his coach, but as soon as he'd kissed her farewell, she started praying.

* * *

Colin had arranged to meet with the boys after supper, which meant he had time to consult with one other potential ally first.

Potential being the hopeful version of the facts.

"If it isn't the hero of the card party," the Earl of Rosecroft said as Colin was ushered into the same room where he'd played cards the past three Tuesday evenings. "Have you taken a fancy to my Malcolm? He'll cost you a significant amount of coin."

Rosecroft was the nobleman at his leisure today, no horse slobber on his cravat, no dust on his boots. He did, though, have a curious pink stain on his cuff.

"I've taken more than a fancy to your cousin, Anwen," Colin said, "and I have come to speak with you about coin. In confidence."

"Bollocks. I hate confidential discussions." His lordship sounded very much like Colin's older brother. "Will I need to lend you my matched Mantons anytime soon?"

"You will not. I need the loan of your common sense."

"A paltry item. Shall we sit, or would you rather admire the garden?"

"The garden, if you please."

"This must be very confidential indeed." Rosecroft led the way through French doors to a miniature version of the Moreland House gardens. All was tidy and restful, except for an enormous canine of mixed pedigree, who bounded over to Rosecroft.

"Scout, go away." The earl had never sounded more stern.

The dog licked his hand.

"Bad dog. Begone with you."

This time, the beast insinuated its head under Rosecroft's hand, as if to inspire some petting.

"This is my daughter's dog," Rosecroft said, refusing to oblige. "She pined for him so badly I had him brought down from Yorkshire, and the dratted animal listens only to her."

Oh, right. The girl had pined for her dog. Of course.

Colin gave the sheep-dog whistle for "get out," which meant to give the sheep more space rather than hover at their heels. The dog cocked its massive head, then trotted off a few steps.

"He thinks you're one of his bonnie wee lambs," Colin said. "Must be an English dog."

Rosecroft wrinkled a nose worthy of a ducal firstborn.

"Explain what you just did, and then we can have this confidential discussion."

What self-respecting Yorkshire landowner didn't know his sheep-dog calls? Colin ran through the basic commands as he and Rosecroft wandered a gravel walk, the dog accompanying them. Then Colin explained the situation at the orphanage, and the need to retrieve the funds immediately.

He did not mention that Anwen had been the recipient of a marriage threat, lest Rosecroft put the matched pistols to use himself.

"Montague has you boxed in a corner with no handy windows," Rosecroft said. "If I had the money I'd lend it to you, but I'm a great believer in letting the banks hold my valuables, and most of my coin is York. Have you considered this might be a trap?"

Well, shite. Colin dropped to a plank bench, and the dog sat panting by his side. "I honestly hadn't."

Rosecroft took the other half of the bench, and the dog got up to rest its chin on his knee.

"As devious as Montague has been, as ungentlemanly and even dishonorable, you need to plan on that possibility. You will set your stealthiest foot in his bedroom, and he and four of his friends will leap out from the wardrobe with arrest warrants in hand."

Rosecroft stroked a hand over Scout's head, the caress clearly familiar and dear to the dog.

The boys at the orphanage needed such a companion. Loyal, loving, and full of sharp teeth when the occasion called for it.

"I don't see that I have much choice," Colin said. "The money must be found, or the orphanage will fail amid a storm of scandal. Anwen will be ashamed to have brought trouble to her family's doorstep, and my sisters will not thank me for bringing trouble to my own house."

"And you might spend the rest of your short, handsome, and overly honorable life in Newgate, until such time as you are hanged."

"You Irish are such a cheerful lot."

"You Scots never know when to blow retreat. I can have you on a yacht sailing north before sundown, MacHugh. Don't be an idiot."

The show of support was lovely, the lack of faith was tiresome. Colin had lived his life in the shadow of an overprotective older brother, and one fraternal nanny was one too many.

"A generous offer, Rosecroft, but I must decline. Anwen's good name is at stake, and if I allow Montague to keep the upper hand, he'll have the orphanage condemned, despite the support Anwen was able to garner for the boys. Had I an alternative that allowed me to preserve my honor, I'd take it."

Rosecroft tried the "get out" whistle and the dog dutifully moved a few yards away.

"Your situation has all the earmarks of a Windham courtship," Rosecroft said. "Complicated, full of drama, and undoubtedly a case of true love. Welcome to the family."

"Thank you."

"You're determined to stick your neck in a noose to retrieve this money?"

"Aye, unless you have other ideas?"

The dog sniffed its way back to the earl's side, and as Rosecroft absently scratched canine ears, he shared a few ideas that made Colin glad he'd dropped by for a wee chat with a prospective family member.

"I'll show you more of the sheep-dog signals when this is over," Colin said, rising. "My thanks for your time. I've a housebreaking to plan."

Rosecroft stood as well. "You're not planning on effecting this larceny tonight, are you?"

"I have only until Monday morning to avoid the magistrate's men," Colin said. "And Winthrop will be out with his friends until all hours, toasting Mrs. Bellingham's ankles."

Which meant Win's valet would probably be napping in the dressing room. Ye gods.

"I doubt Montague will be out until all hours. His father is hosting a dinner party tonight, and I can't imagine Montague would be allowed to beg off. If you make the attempt tonight, the house will be crawling with guests, family, and extra staff."

"Bollocks."

* * *

"It ain't stealing if you're just takin' back what's yours in the first place," John explained from his place at the head of the study room table.

Tom didn't think that logic would convince Lord Colin, who slouched by the window in the rays of a weak setting sun.

"I'm not concerned with the morality of reasserting dominion over the funds," Lord Colin replied. "I'm unwilling to let you boys come with me. The risk is too great."

"I'd like to assert some dominion over Mr. Montague's head," Dickie said, smacking one fist into the other palm. "The nervy bastard."

Lord Colin smiled slightly as he gazed down onto the alley.

"Your lordship means well," Tom said, "but if we don't go with you, it would be like letting one of the little boys go down the drainpipe on his own the first time. We can't do it. They go piggyback until they've seen the way of it, and then we watch them the next few times. You going on your own isn't right."

"Miss Anwen would want us to go with you," John said, tipping his chair back on two legs. "Or she should want us to go with you. Proper gent like you trying to toss a whole house on his own?"

John shook his head, looking like old Hitchings at his most despairing.

Joe got up to water the fern, then resumed his place at John's right hand.

"I want your advice," Lord Colin said. "I don't want your deaths or transportation on my conscience. The task will be deuced difficult."

"Now see," John said, "there's a problem right there. You don't go into a job expecting to fail. You do your planning and considering and discussing, and then you march out smartly like you own that house already. If you're skulking along the mews, you'll draw a lot more attention than if you're merely strolling around looking for a private place to piss."

"That was usually my job," Dickie said. "When I got too big to fit down the chimneys, I was the lookout, but I had to drink a fearsome amount of ale to do the job right."

"Good point," Lord Colin said. "What else?"

"Dress the part," Tom said. "None of them pale knees flashing in the moonlight, sir, meaning no disrespect to your kilt. You wear decent clothes, not your Sunday best, but like for calling on your mother, and you wear dark clothes. Everything dark—not a cravat, not cuffs, not gloves, not a silver walking stick that can catch the light. Not cufflinks, even. Dark clothes can save your life."

"Best if there's not much moon," John said. "You need a little moon, enough to see by, not enough to be seen by."

"A reaver's moon," Lord Colin said. "You're describing the best conditions for stealing cattle."

"Wrap your boots in chamois, or go barefoot," Dickie said. "And you need a plan for how we're going to toss the joint."

"*We* are not going to toss anything," Lord Colin said.

Tom was tempted to kick him. "Then stick your handsome head in the noose right now, sir. The other rule you're ignoring is to get in, get the goods, and get out as quick as you can. The longer you're in that house, the more chance some footman, dog, or tippling maid will spot you. By yourself, you'll take all night to toss a fine Mayfair house."

Lord Colin shifted to prop an elbow on the mantel. "I'll be quick, but the house will be occupied until the small hours of the morning. You boys need your sleep."

"We need a *place* to sleep," John shot back. "You're being stupid. Da always said you can't fix stupid."

"Ma said you can't fix arrogant," Dickie added. "She usually said it to Da."

"You have to let us help," Tom said. "You don't know a damned thing about being a thief, and we know everything. Did you try to tell Miss Anwen how to organize her card party?"

"Of course not. She was far better—it's not the same thing."

John let his chair crash back down to four legs. "Right you are, guv. This is serious, not a fancy charity do where nobody could get hurt. Whyn't you take the help we offer, when the stakes are so high? You'll be in Newgate, but we'll have to explain to the wee ones why we weren't allowed to watch over you. And to Miss Anwen."

His lordship ran a hand through his hair and looked exasperated, but Tom couldn't spare him any pity. He was being noble, and a fat lot of good that ever did anybody.

"Joe," Tom said. "Make him listen to us."

Joe rose and came around the table, then extracted a scrap of white fabric from his trouser pocket.

His lordship snatched the square from Joe's hand. "Where did you get my handkerchief?"

"He nicked it," John said, punching Joe on the arm.

"When he watered the fern." Dickie's grin was smug. "Joe's out of practice, or we woulda never seen him do it, but he weren't stealing. We know that. He were saving your bloody neck for Miss Anwen."

Lord Colin slowly folded the white square into a tidy rectangle. He looked at the handkerchief as if answers might be embroidered on it, then studied each boy in turn.

"You can come with me, but nobody else goes in the house."

"Have a seat," John said. "Planning the job is half the battle."

"True in any aspect of warfare," Lord Colin said. "Where do we start?"

Chapter Eighteen

ANWEN MADE IT THROUGH supper without spilling her wine, but Aunt Esther sent her more than one concerned look. Charlotte and Elizabeth—bless them—carried the conversation by recounting anecdotes from the previous night's entertainment. When the fruit and cheese had finally been removed, Anwen nearly fled the dining room.

"Don't run off," Elizabeth said, getting to her feet. "I wanted you to see some sketches I made from last night's gatherings. Immortalizing your triumph, so to speak."

"You haven't shown me these sketches," Charlotte said, joining them at the dining room door. "I hope at least one of them was of Mr. Pierpont's face when Mr. Tresham delivered him a figurative beating at the piquet table."

"Uncharitable," Aunt remarked, "but then, Mr. Pierpont should not have chosen an opponent of so much greater skill. Moreland, I'm of a mind to inspect the roses, now that the garden has had a chance to dry out."

"Of course, my dear." Uncle Percy held Aunt's chair, and they disappeared down the corridor, thank God and old Murray, who supervised the gardens.

"Come along," Elizabeth said. "We'll use the conservatory."

"Why there?" Anwen asked, reluctant to share her sanctuary with anybody.

"Because it's the only place nobody ever disturbs you," Charlotte said. "We realized years ago that when you wanted to be alone, you always went to the conservatory. It's warm, peaceful, quiet, and safe. A perfect haven. As long as we made a great fuss about looking for you in the attics and cellars, you were safe in the conservatory."

"You *guarded* me?"

"The conservatory has glass walls, dearest," Elizabeth said. "Once we knew where you were, we'd make our fuss, and you'd get the nap you needed, or whatever."

Whatever? A memory came to Anwen, of Colin and a delicate, violet blossom.

She stopped outside the conservatory doors. "You *spied* on me?"

"Gracious, no," Charlotte retorted. "We've realized that Lord Colin has taken up the honor of guarding you, and he's a man who knows enough to, erm, lower the shades on occasion when the sun gets too bright."

Not the sun, a bonfire.

Anwen opened the door and led her sisters into the greenery and quiet of the conservatory. "You two are awful and I love you dearly, in case I never told you that before."

"Megan suspected you and Lord Colin would suit," Elizabeth said, pulling a bench over near the sofa. "You must account her awful as well. Now, please explain to us why you had barely two sips of soup, a bite of fish, two bites of ham, and not even one full glass of Uncle Percy's excellent wine."

Charlotte took the sofa and patted the place beside her. "Don't even think of prevaricating. Last night was a roaring success, and now you look as if you're sickening for something. If Lord Colin has misstepped we will instruct him regarding the error of his ways."

Elizabeth settled on the bench and kicked off her slippers. "Or if he hasn't misstepped. Men are easily muddled when matters of matrimony and gentlemanly honor deserve equal weight. You are still planning to marry him, aren't you?"

Anwen considered pleading a headache, considered an early bedtime. She also considered the danger Colin was in.

"You have to promise me something," she said. "Promise me that no matter what happens, you'll help me look after the boys. There are twelve of them, and they're good boys. They can apprentice, foster out, or join the staff here, but I can't break my word to them. I promised them homes—good, safe homes."

"Perhaps we need a bottle of madeira or some cordial to settle our nerves," Elizabeth said. "You are being ridiculous."

"No cordial ever again," Charlotte replied. "Anwen, of course we'll help you look after the boys. Who did you think would keep an eye on them when you went north with Lord Colin? Mama and Aunt Esther would expect no less of us, nor should you. Stop dithering and tell us what the problem is."

They were her sisters, they were worried, and they wanted to help. Anwen took the place on the sofa beside Charlotte, and Elizabeth shifted to sit on her other side.

"There's trouble," Anwen said. "Terribly serious trouble, and scandal, and danger, and Colin is trying to deal with all of it, and I'm so worried, and angry, but I don't dare breathe a word to Uncle Percy."

Elizabeth ordered a bottle of madeira, and Anwen told her sisters everything.

Every single thing.

* * *

Boys who couldn't sit still for fifteen minutes in Latin class could wait in a dark alley for hours without moving. Colin's respect for the children had increased as the minutes had crawled by and the Monthaven townhouse had bustled with activity.

Dinner parties were typically attended by thirty guests, but the ladies often brought a maid along to carry their slippers, touch up their coiffures, tend to shawls, and otherwise ensure the evening went smoothly. The coaches lined the front walkway, and the coachmen, grooms, and footmen whiled away the evening gossiping, dicing, and strolling around the mews to visit with the grooms—or relieve themselves within six inches of Tom's boot.

The boy hadn't stirred, and neither had any of his mates.

Extra staff came and went, relighting the torches in the garden just as Colin hoped the evening was winding down, and most of the male guests at some point took a turn on the terrace to smoke, belch, or pester a passing maid.

Dickie occasionally patrolled the alley, as if impatient to hop up behind some gentleman's phaeton and get home to bed. John idled at the front of the house within earshot of the links boys waiting to escort guests home, and Tom rode dispatch, reporting from all points, while Joe sat beside Colin in the shadows saying nothing.

Colin could not consult anything so shiny as a pocket watch, but the church bells had rung twice when the coaches began filling with laughing, chattering guests. After that interminable exercise concluded, Joe nudged Colin and pointed to the window at one corner of the second floor.

Montague's room, and a lamp had been lit there. Two hours ago, John had gone up a trellis to a balcony and cracked open one bedroom window. Watching the boy scale the building had been both impressive and terrifying.

The children were professionals, and what did it say about London society that their skills had been learned so well and at such a young age?

Windows elsewhere in the mansion went dark, the alley grew quiet, and footmen extinguished the garden torches. The space between Colin's shoulder blades itched, and he sent up a prayer that Anwen was dreaming peacefully in her bed.

Joe touched Colin's sleeve again, and praise be, the lamp in Montague's bedroom had gone out. Colin rose, and Joe yanked hard on his coattail, pulling Colin back into the shadows.

Joe shook his head and pointed to John coming up the alley.

"You're in luck," John whispered. "Montague was too soused to go out to the clubs with the other gents. He's gone to bed, and that means his valet won't be waiting up for him in the dressing room. Give it another ten minutes, though, and recall that some drunks sleep awfully light."

The considered wisdom of the boys was that Montague wouldn't keep the money anywhere but in his own rooms, which sat across a corridor from Lady Rosalyn's apartment. If Colin had to make a quick escape, he was to go through her sitting room—unoccupied in the middle of night—and over her balcony to the balcony below, and thence to the garden.

Any hue and cry from Montague's room would likely start a search on the opposite side of the house from Colin's escape route.

More lights dimmed in more windows, and the grooms wished each other good night.

Joe kept a hand on Colin's sleeve, until Colin was ready to burst from the bushes and stand beneath Montague's window demanding the money.

Silence spread, not simply quiet. Not a carriage passed, not a breeze stirred.

Joe let go of Colin's sleeve and punched his arm.

"Take your time," John warned. "Haste has put many a man in Newgate. If you get in trouble, you know what to do, and we'll make a ruckus, just like we planned."

Colin cuffed John gently on the back of the head. "If there's trouble, you take off like the hounds of hell are after you. You promised."

"Go on with ye," Dickie said. "Damned sun will be up in no time."

Colin wanted to leap over the Montague garden wall and sprint over to the house, but he'd been taught better. Saunter, stroll, blend in, be a footman who couldn't sleep, a groom missing his sweetheart.

Getting into the house was appallingly easy, and the boys had drilled Colin on how to search the room, checking a few obvious locations first—Win's jewelry box, his wardrobe, the table beside his bed, beneath the bed and in the clothespress.

Through it all, Montague lay snoring on the mattress, one pale foot extended from beneath the sheets. He stank of cigar smoke and an excess of spirits, and snuffled occasionally in his sleep.

Some drunks sleep awfully light.

On that remembered admonition, Colin began searching the dressing room, a frustratingly complicated space. Spare boots, hatboxes, slipper boxes, glove boxes—the money could have been anywhere.

The trick, Tom had explained, was to consider the dressing room like a map, and to explore every corner of the map according to a systematic grid, level by level. The money was there somewhere, and finding it was simply a matter of thoroughness and dedication.

An hour later, Colin heard a wagon jingle up the alley—the milkman, possibly.

He was running out of time, and hadn't found the money. Doubts plagued him, for maybe Montague hadn't stashed the money in his room, maybe Montague hadn't taken the money, maybe Montague had enlisted the aid of his friends, and they had the money, or possibly—

Beyond the dressing room, a door clicked open and faint light chased the shadows. Colin dodged behind a rack of tailcoats and silently moved two pairs of tall boots before him—the boys had rehearsed even this scenario with him. Soft footsteps sounded on the bedroom carpet and then the dressing room door opened.

* * *

"He should be out of there by now," Tom said, for the fourth time. "I'm going in."

The urge to storm the house, to see for himself that

Lord Colin hadn't been taken up by the watch, was nearly overwhelming. The money didn't matter, the repairs to the orphanage didn't matter, but that his lordship remained safe mattered very much.

"You sit still," John said, keeping his voice down. "We promised Lord Colin we'd keep a lookout, and not go into the house."

A cat yowled on the garden wall, the sound ugly and loud in the darkness.

"He'll manage well enough," Dickie said. "Taught 'im everything we know, didn't we?"

Dickie sounded worried rather than jocular. A hasty plan and a few warnings wasn't enough education to keep a proper gent safe on his first venture into housebreaking.

"I'm going in," Tom said, rising from among the bushes at the side of the mews. "He's been gone too long. Morning will be here before we—"

Joe hauled him back down into the darkness and pointed to the house. "B-bollocks."

A light, dim but distinct, shone through Montague's window. Somebody was stirring about with a shuttered carrying candle, and Lord Colin was doomed to swing for sure.

* * *

Anwen couldn't sleep, and the two times she'd dozed off, she'd woken with a start, dread making her heart pound.

Colin was searching the Montague household for the money, or possibly he'd already been found out, the watch called, the magistrate's office involved.

Or he might have the money, in which case getting the funds back to the orphanage unobtrusively presented an equal challenge.

She got up, put on her robe and slippers, and made her way through the darkened house to the conservatory, where lovely memories could keep her company. She woke up on her favorite sofa in the world, pink streaking the eastern sky, and her heart once again pounding with dread.

* * *

"You looked inside his boots?" Tom asked.

"Every pair," Lord Colin replied wearily. "After Lady Rosalyn made her little raid for his spare change, I also went through all of Montague's coat pockets, I checked every glove box, under the bed, the wardrobe, everywhere."

"If his lordship says he made a proper job of it," John muttered, "then he made a proper job of it. The money weren't there."

"But Montague took it," Dickie said, sounding whiney. "We know he took it. He's a rotter, and a liar, and he took the money."

They had congregated in the hayloft of the stable behind the orphanage, and light was beginning to fill the eastern sky. Tom had had longer nights, but none more disappointing.

"He's a canny rotter." Lord Colin stood and brushed straw off his breeches. "If he did take the money, he put it somewhere other than his own rooms. He must suspect Lady Rosalyn occasionally helps herself to his loose coins."

"When would he 'ave had time to stash the money any place besides his house?" John asked, flopping back into the straw. "You said he came here with you to drop off the money. Hitchings sent him on his way after you left. He had to have taken the money right after that, and then where would he hide it? We looked all over the orphanage, including the empty wing. The clubs wouldn't have been open that late and you said none of Montague's friends were with him. The money has to be where he lives."

Tom had been over the same sequence of events in his mind, time after time, and had reached the same conclusion. The money had to be at the Montague mansion, which was a bloody damned big place. An army of thieves would need a week to search the house properly, and that assumed it was empty 'round the clock.

Which it bloody well wasn't.

"We're tired," Lord Colin said, "and arguing in circles. I thank you all for your help—I'd be watching the sunrise from the windows of Number Four Bow Street, but for you four. I can try again tonight, assuming Montague hasn't started up a hue and cry."

"He's Montague," Tom said. "He'll be tattling to Miss Anwen's duke, and then the game's up. If a duke starts sniffing about, the newspapers will come trotting along behind him, and we're for the mines."

"Or worse," John said. "I'm scared of the dark myself. Don't fancy a turn in the mines."

He'd never admitted that before, though Tom had long since figured it out. A loathing of being shut up in small dark places all night was part of what sent John on his rambles.

Lord Colin started down the ladder. "Nobody is going down the mines, but you raise a good point. Montague will bestir himself to attend services this morning, and he'll doubtless ask for a moment of Moreland's time. I have never been so frustrated, furious, and ready to do violence in my life, and yet my best course at this point is to show up at services myself, my fine baritone ready to sing praise to my Creator."

Tom went down the ladder next, followed by Dickie and John. Joe came down last, and they stood with Lord Colin in a circle, failure filling the shadowy silence.

"Get some rest," Lord Colin said. "Hitchings will be distracted, but go about your day as normally as you can. I'll make another try tonight, assuming the looming scandal hasn't sent my dearest lady—"

He stopped and scrubbed a hand over his face, an odd expression creasing his tired features.

"What?" John asked. "You look like you seen a ghost up in the rafters."

"Or an angel," Dickie said.

"Bollocks," Lord Colin said softly. "I know where the money is."

"N-now," Joe said. "Get it, n-now. Best time. Services."

Lord Colin left off studying the hay mow. "Break into the house during Sunday services?"

"That's brilliant," John said, shoving Joe's shoulder. "Staff will lay about after being run off their feet last night, family will clear out for a good two hours, and nobody ever looks up. Da always said that."

"Right before the runners got him," Dickie retorted.

"Get up to the balcony now before it's full daylight," Tom said, "and wait until the family leaves for services, then find that money."

His lordship was exhausted, he had a streak of dirt across his cheek, and he was overdue for a shave. He looked like a thief, a bloody worried thief.

"It could work," he said, staring into the shadowed garden. "I know exactly where to look."

Joe's suggestion was his lordship's only chance. John and Dickie's expressions said they thought so too.

"I'll need you to deliver a message to Miss Anwen,"

Lord Colin said, "without being seen, before she leaves for services. Can one of you do that?"

"Aye." All four boys spoke in unison, even Joe.

* * *

Colin's note said Anwen was to detain Montague in the church yard for as long as possible.

She tossed the scrap of paper into the fire, and rejoiced that Colin was at liberty to send notes. She despaired that he hadn't found the money.

"Ready to go?" Charlotte asked, strolling into Anwen's room without knocking.

"I am, and thank heavens the rain hasn't come back. Are we walking?"

"I'd like to, though Aunt and Uncle might want to take the coach."

St. George's was only a few streets over, and most of Mayfair graced its pews. Many a Windham had spoken vows there, and the Montagues were regular fixtures.

"You didn't sleep well," Charlotte said. "Neither did I. Maybe we can catch a nap during the sermon."

"Or maybe I'll see Lord Colin."

Except she didn't. Not Colin, not Rhona or Edana, not a single member of the MacHugh household was in evidence, while Win Montague and Lady Rosalyn were in their customary pew, elegantly attired, and quietly greeting neighbors as the congregation assembled.

Anwen endured. As the service went on and on—why must the hymns have so blessed many verses?—she consoled herself with the thought that every extra verse was another minute when Winthrop Montague had to be dutifully pretending interest in the proceedings, exactly as Colin needed him to do.

As the organ's final notes sounded, and the gossiping began in earnest, Anwen seized her courage with both hands and marched up to Montague.

"Miss Anwen, good day," Montague said. "A most fetching bonnet, don't you agree, Lady Rosalyn?"

His complexion was positively gray, his golden curls lank. Rosalyn, by contrast, was a vision in pink and cream lace, her reticule and bonnet trimmed to match.

"Very becoming," her ladyship said. "Truly it is, but you'll excuse me, for I see Baron Twillinger trying to get my attention."

Rosalyn withdrew on a soft rustle of exquisite fashion, though she'd been very nearly rude.

"You mustn't make anything of it," Montague said. "She's concerned you'll ask her when she'll pay her vowels from your little card party. Dear Roz plays whist with more enthusiasm than skill, I'm afraid. Not much point in collecting the money now, though, is there?"

He was very sure of himself or he was baiting Anwen. Probably both, the varlet.

"That is a decision I am not yet called upon to make," Anwen said. "Shall we step outside, Mr. Montague?"

The church sat directly on the street, with only the front terrace, steps, and walkway separating it from vehicle traffic. The congregation arranged itself along the walkway in twos, threes, or small groups. Others wandered off to the square, where more privacy was to be had.

"My dear, you look fatigued," Montague said. "I hope you were not kept awake by our little contretemps at the orphanage?"

Colin had asked one thing of her: Detain Montague at all costs.

Anwen longed to detain him by doing him a severe injury. "It's about that situation that we must speak. I've had a chance to consider my choices and will want certain assurances written into the settlements."

Montague tipped his hat to the Duchess of Quimbey, who did not appear to recognize him.

"You are planning to be difficult," he said when the duchess was out of earshot. "I stated my position clearly yesterday. You do not dictate terms, you do not bargain, you do not think to manipulate me with conditions and concessions. Time is of the essence."

The church was emptying, congregants filling the walkway, and Anwen refused to lower her voice.

"The welfare of twelve innocent boys must come before our selfish priorities, Mr. Montague, I'm sure you'll agree."

"Them again. If you want urchins to dote on, I will see you well supplied. London has a surfeit of wretched children on offer and always will, though I should hope you'd be more interested in doting on our offspring."

Flora Stanbridge, one of the biggest gossips ever to stumble into her partner's arms on the dance floor, stopped not two yards away.

Anwen patted Montague's cravat—let dear Flora report that public familiarity. "Surely you intend to have a word with my uncle before the topic of offspring becomes appropriate to discuss, Mr. Montague?"

Montague removed a speck of lint from his sleeve and flicked it in Flora Stanbridge's direction. "Where is Moreland? I do need to have a word with him. You're quite correct about that."

Oh, Colin. "If you intend to raise the matter of a

courtship with Moreland, you'd best not do it on a public street."

Montague smiled at that riposte, his expression so doting it made Anwen queasy. "Excellent point, my dear. Let me take Rosalyn home, and I'll drop around directly."

Colin's note hadn't said anything about detaining Lady Rosalyn, and Anwen hadn't the patience to deal with her ladyship in any case.

"Don't tarry at home," Anwen said. "Set her ladyship down, and pay your call straight away, for Uncle has commitments this afternoon."

"Don't worry," Montague said, patting Anwen's cheek with his gloved hand. "My business with Moreland is urgent, and I'm glad you've made the wiser choice."

He bowed and took himself off, while Anwen muttered every curse she knew in Welsh.

Chapter Nineteen

"ONE FEELS SUCH PITY for those not to the manor born," Winthrop Montague said, steering his phaeton out of Hanover Square. "They're bound to encounter difficulties that might have been avoided if they'd kept to their places."

Delightfully serious difficulties in the case of Colin MacHugh.

"You're trying to sound deep again," Rosalyn replied. "I like you better when you're being witty. Do you refer to Lord Colin?"

"The very one. He's about to land in a deal of trouble over the missing money."

Rosalyn shot Win a peevish look, as if he were being simple rather than philosophical. "You should let it drop, Win. Money is vulgar. Orphans are tiresome. Close the place down and get back to making stupid wagers with your stupid friends."

The day was fine, though Rosalyn had always disliked sunny weather. God help the poor dear, she might become afflicted with a freckle.

"How much did you lose?" Win asked. "You can tell me."

"Too much, but I'll come right. I always do."

True enough, and Win never inquired too closely about how she managed it, though Rosalyn's maid was ever busy altering this dress or pawning that one.

"I shall offer for Anwen Windham," he said, "and she'll accept me. Let that brighten your mood, sister dear. First thing tomorrow, I'll have the Scottish bumpkin arrested, though you mustn't mention that to anybody. If Anwen is willing to see reason about a special license, I will ask Papa to plead for Lord Colin to be transported rather than hanged. I think that's being very gracious."

Rosalyn twitched her skirts away from Win's boots. "This isn't a game, Winthrop. A man's life is at stake, and you haven't even proved Lord Colin took the money. Why can't you just let it blow over? You said the orphanage still has the jewels, so the children are better off. Nobody needs to know about a few coins going missing."

Rosalyn wasn't prone to argument when charm would suffice, but she was in a mood about something. But then, her idea of a few coins was most people's idea of a small fortune.

"Do you fancy the Scottish brute? A little longing for the mud, as the French say? I honestly don't think he took the money. Hitchings might have, or that MacDeever fellow. Maybe the brats, or the cook, for all I know. Lord Colin probably won't be convicted, now that I think on the matter."

Rosalyn remained silent, while Win turned the horse onto their street, but her sigh bore the impatience of every sister with every brother, which was a lot of impatience for such a lovely Sabbath.

"Lord Colin's brother is a duke, Winthrop, which means you plan to incarcerate and accuse a duke's heir. No woman with any sense wants scandal to touch her hem. Need I remind you that the money has gone missing on *your* watch and I was on that dratted ladies' committee until yesterday. You are threatening to dump scandal in my very lap."

Gad, she was growing tiresome. "I think it's time you paid a visit to Aunt Margaret in Italy, my dear. You're developing a petulant streak. I'll say something to Papa about it, shall I?"

"Do as you please. You always do."

What Win pleased to do was make passionate, frequent love with Mrs. Bellingham, and to secure such a joy, he was willing to marry even Anwen Windham.

Who wasn't that bad-looking, provided not too many candles were lit.

"If you can't afford to lose at cards, Rosalyn, then you shouldn't play with those who can. I mean that advice kindly, of course. I can think of no other excuse for your poor humor. Perhaps you're jealous of my impending good fortune."

She was probably eaten up with jealousy, but she was the one who'd turned down five offers her first season—and hadn't had a single suitor for the past year.

"Spare me your sermons," she spat, "while you, Twilly, and Pointy live in dun territory from one quarter to the next. Moreland is shrewd, and you'll not be living off Anwen's settlements."

Win brought the phaeton to a halt. "Be off with you. You need a lie down, or a birching, or a good talking to.

I'm marrying into a ducal family, which can only benefit you, and all you can do is complain and carp. Most unattractive, Rosalyn. You should be grateful, and I'm out of patience with you."

She snapped her parasol closed, bounced down from the phaeton on the arm of the waiting footman, and flounced off into the house.

Tiresome woman, which was one of those terms that said the same thing twice. Win clucked to the horse and drove in the direction of the Moreland townhouse, where the first order of business was not discussing marriage settlements, but rather, confiding in the duke about the terrible scandal threatening Miss Anwen as a result of her association with that upstart Scottish rogue.

* * *

"Anwen, I try to have faith that the young people in this family will exercise the good sense and decorum with which they were raised, but your pacing must cease."

Aunt Esther always rebuked gently but firmly, and yet Anwen could not keep still.

"What can they be discussing?" she asked on another circumnavigation of the Windham family parlor. "Mr. Montague has been in there with Uncle Percy for more than a half hour."

Across the corridor, the library door remained closed, and try as she might, Anwen could detect no raised voices, no laughter, nothing.

"What are you afraid they're discussing?" Aunt asked, pulling her needle through a hoop of white silk.

"Me," Anwen said. "My orphans, my future. And I'm not part of the conversation."

"Trust your Uncle Percival," Aunt said, putting the hoop down. "If Montague is presuming to ask permission to court you, Moreland won't reply until he's consulted with you and your parents. Lord Colin's interest in you is already established, as is a connection with the MacHugh family. Mr. Montague might cut a fine figure in his endless procession of new outfits, but that does not recommend him as a husband."

Anwen came to a halt before a portrait of the duchess as a very young wife. She'd not been a classic beauty, and yet she had a loveliness about her, a duchess-ness, that encompassed grace and appearance both.

"You don't like Mr. Montague, Aunt?"

"I cannot approve of a man who makes a jest of considerable sums of money and involves the trades in his prank. As for Lady Rosalyn...Lord Monthaven should have taken her in hand before her come out. The poor girl hasn't a mama, though, and her aunt removed to Italy under questionable circumstances years ago."

Good heavens. "What else don't I know?"

"Much," Aunt Esther said, coming to stand beside Anwen. "I've always liked this picture. The artist was kind but honest."

Another gentle rebuke.

"You and His Grace know about the expenses attributed to Lord Colin by Montague's friends?"

The duchess wrapped an arm around Anwen's waist and gave her a half hug. "Montague instigated the whole business, even if he had accomplices running up the debts. Rosecroft had a protracted discussion with Twillinger and then with Pierpont, and their stories matched in all particulars. Winthrop Montague set Lord Colin up for embarrassment or worse. Montague then tried to shift blame onto the bumbling sycophants who toady to him. Nasty business. His Grace was not impressed."

Anwen shot a nervous glance at the door. "Then what are they discussing?"

In the next instant, the duke strode into the parlor, his expression severe. "Your Grace, Niece, I must accompany Mr. Montague to the House of Urchins, for he claims there's been a theft of valuables, and that all evidence incriminates Lord Colin MacHugh."

Montague followed His Grace right into the family parlor. "I'm so sorry to be the bearer of bad news," he said, bowing to the duchess and then to Anwen. "I wish there were some other explanation."

"There are several other explanations," Anwen retorted. "And you, Mr. Montague—"

"My dear young lady," the duke interjected, "this is a serious matter. I know you care deeply for the children, but that should inspire you to see the situation resolved as quickly and quietly as possible. The worst sort of scandal threatens, and I can only appreciate that Montague alerted me before word reaches the newspapers."

"But Mr. Montague is not—"

"Not now, Anwen." The duke hadn't raised his voice, but he'd raised an eyebrow.

Montague had affixed a sorrowful, resolute expression to his face and was staring straight at Anwen.

"We must go," the duke said, bowing to Aunt Esther.

"Then take me with you," Anwen demanded. "I know that building, the children, the staff, the grounds far better than Mr. Montague does, and I assure you, Your Grace, Mr. Montague's perspective on the situation is not the only one that should carry weight."

"There's time for theorizing later," the duke retorted.

"The first step is to ascertain that the money is in fact missing. Now, if you will please excuse us—"

"Moreland." Aunt Esther had raised neither her voice nor her eyebrow. "Anwen has a point. Take her with you, please."

Montague's expression faltered, revealing exasperation beneath his façade of selfless concern.

The duke and duchess had a silent conversation, which included Aunt Esther flicking a gaze over Montague such as she might have fired off before delivering the cut direct.

"Very well," the duke said. "But delay us at your peril, Anwen."

Anwen kissed her aunt, whirled from the room, and had a cloak and bonnet in her hand in less than a minute.

* * *

"Your expression resembles your mother's when she's made up her mind," Percival said.

Long ago, he'd learned that one did not cross Gladys Windham lightly. One did not cross Gladys Windham at all, if one had sense.

Percival sat beside Anwen on the forward-facing seat of the coach, though the journey to the infernal orphanage could have been made on foot. Montague would have doubtless offered to take Anwen up in his phaeton, and that Percival could not allow.

"Lord Colin did not take that money," Anwen said. "Mr. Montague had more access to the facility, the keys to every door on the premises, more opportunity than Lord Colin, and more motive."

Percival's niece was vibrating with indignation worthy of a duchess. "How come you to know such details, Anwen?" The quiet ones always bore watching. How could a father of ten have forgotten that?

"Because I pay attention, Your Grace. The money turned up missing yesterday, and we've spent the intervening time searching the orphanage. Montague accused Lord Colin from the start, though Hitchings will tell you Lord Colin has no keys to the chairman's office and no need for additional coin."

Percival's niece had found herself smack in the middle of a problem, and had sat at the dinner table last night listening to her sisters babble about whist and piquet until the duchess had worn that "Percival, make them stop" look.

And all the while, Anwen hadn't thought to turn to her uncle—a duke, fifty-third in line for the throne—for aid or advice.

Truly, she was a stubborn, independent, determined, hard-headed... Windham.

"Lord Colin might have a need for coin," Percival said gently. "Montague made him the object of an expensive prank, and even I would have been hard pressed to produce that much blunt on short notice. Lord Colin managed it in less than a week."

"Because his family has means, Your Grace. He borrowed from his brother's London breweries, then reimbursed them from his Edinburgh bank accounts."

Anwen was so casual about a financial transaction that should have been held in closest confidence, that Percival had to reassess his estimation of the situation.

"What else should I know about this imbroglio that you haven't told me?" Doubtless there was more—much more—and Percival would be lucky to pry half the truth from her in the space of a short carriage ride.

Anwen had the grace to cast him one apologetic glance.

"Mr. Montague has been panting after Mrs. Bellingham, but hasn't the funds to afford her."

"Gracious, child. Where do you hear such things?" That *on dit* had been making the rounds in the clubs for weeks, though Percival had forgotten he'd heard it.

The coach clip-clopped along for another few minutes while Percival considered strategy, scandal, and the folly of young love.

"If the money is missing, Anwen, then the authorities must be notified."

"Montague will have Colin arrested tomorrow morning, Uncle. I can't allow that. I'll elope first, and nothing you, Her Grace, or my dear cousins can do will stop me."

He hadn't seen that salvo sailing toward his quarter-deck, but he should have.

"My dear, if Lord Colin hares off, he's all but incriminating himself, and the scandal will be all over Town before you can pack your trunks for Scotland. I don't suppose you know his lordship's present whereabouts?"

When had little Anwen grown so pretty—and so fierce?

"If I did know, I'm not sure I'd tell you, Uncle, but I don't know. I begged his lordship to make a strategic retreat, but he wouldn't listen. He's convinced Montague took the funds, and so am I."

Percival was willing to consider that possibility, and yet, Montague had made a convincing case against not only Lord Colin, but also the old headmaster, the groundskeeper, and even the children.

"Anwen, to some extent, it doesn't matter who took the money. Our friends and acquaintances opened their purses and their hearts on behalf of this orphanage, and their trust has been betrayed. The institution will soon flounder, and I will never hear the end of this from your parents."

Esther would serenely soldier on, despite the discredit to her card party, and Percival would hurt for her on a level he shuddered to contemplate.

"Uncle, I love you and respect you," Anwen said, very calmly, "but I don't care one hearty goddamn for the friends and acquaintances who gave up their eleventh cravat pin or eighth pair of pearl earrings in a public display of generosity.

"I care about the children," she went on, "and so does Lord Colin. If the only result of this thievery were a slight to his honor, he'd have taken me north last night. He's standing against this slander because he gave the children his word they'd be kept safe. Hang the scandal. Let the tabbies and dandies gossip all they please while they squander fortunes on outlandish wagers and new bonnets. You are a duke. *What about the children?*"

The question rang with quiet dignity in the elegant comfort of the town coach.

The only other person who dared confront Percival like this was Esther. She'd been born a commoner, granddaughter to an earl, her family well off and respected, but she'd been beneath consideration when a ducal son had gone in search of a bride.

And yet, when Esther was sufficiently provoked, she'd ring a peal over her husband's head that put the bells of St. Paul's to shame. Truth, honor, integrity, generosity, compassion—she had expectations of her husband and children with regard to each virtue, and became indomitably steadfast in her views.

"The children will be cared for," Percival said, feeling both proud of Anwen...and chastised. "I give you my word on that. I cannot speak as confidently on behalf of the Scotsman you claim has become their champion."

* * *

Where was Colin?

Uncle Percy had asked the only question to which Anwen needed an answer. The money could hang, the scandal could hang with it, and Winthrop Montague...

He paced along at Anwen's side as they made their way from the coach to the front door of the House of Urchins. Uncle Percy marched ahead, leading a charge into God knew what, while Montague's hand rode at the small of Anwen's back.

"You had best not have been telling tales out of school, madam," he said, leaning close. "I purposely did not ask Moreland for permission to court you, because I do not trust you'll honor your word to me. If you make so much as one more peep of protest before your uncle, I'll rethink my resolve to see Lord Colin transported rather than hanged."

Vile, foul, arrogant... Anwen gave up concocting a retort as Montague's hand slipped lower. Because he crowded her so closely, nobody would see him taking liberties.

Nor would they see Anwen driving her elbow hard into his belly, or her heel coming down on the toes of his boots.

"I do beg your pardon," she said, turning on him with mock solitude. "I can be so clumsy. Your Grace, let me take your arm, please."

"Come along, you two," Uncle Percival said, pausing at the front door. "Montague, now is not the time to dawdle about displaying your finery."

"The chairman's office is upstairs," Anwen said. "Mr. Hitchings's office is two doors down and across the corridor."

Would Colin be in Hitchings's office? And where were the boys?

If Colin had failed to find the money, the boys might

well have already left the premises, despite all the promises made to them.

"Anwen," the duke said quietly, "a bit of decorum, please."

She slowed her pace, when she wanted to untangle herself from Uncle Percival and bellow at the top of her lungs. *Colin, where are you?*

Despite this being the Sabbath, Hitchings was at his desk.

"Miss Anwen, Mr. Montague, good day." He rose, his expression both worried and hopeful.

"Alas, I regret we bring no good news," Montague said. "Your Grace, may I make known to you Mr. Wilbur Hitchings, headmaster of this humble establishment. Hitchings, Percival, Duke of Moreland."

Hitchings stood very tall. "Your Grace, I am honored." His bow was stiff and slow.

"Hitchings, good day. Montague relates a distressing tale of thievery, misbehavior, and substantial funds going missing. What can you add?"

"Perhaps we should repair to the conference room, Your Grace? I wouldn't want to keep Miss Anwen standing."

Anwen didn't want to be kept standing either. She wanted to find the boys, find Colin, and make a dash for the docks.

"Very considerate of you," Montague said, gesturing toward the door. "Miss Anwen, after you."

She took a seat across from Montague, lest his hands get to wandering beneath the table.

Hitchings offered a depressingly thorough recounting of the events since the card party, but at least his recitation confirmed that Montague had as much opportunity as anybody to take the funds.

"I suppose that leaves only confirmation that the funds are missing," Uncle Percival said. "You keep the valuables in a strongbox, Hitchings?"

"Yes, Your Grace, though getting both cash and jewels to fit inside the strongbox was a challenge beyond my tired abilities. I am so very sorry, sir."

"As well you should be," Uncle Percival replied. "You have no idea where Lord Colin might be?"

"None, sir. He was here after supper last night and asked to meet with the four oldest boys. Based on their demeanor at final prayers, the encounter was far from cheering."

Montague sat up. "His lordship's absence from services this morning must be regarded as a discouraging development. He's on the board of directors for the orphanage and should be monitoring the situation as closely as I am."

"Balderdash," Anwen retorted. "There are seven directors, Mr. Montague, and you don't impugn the honor of the other five, only Lord Colin. Why is that?"

Uncle Percival remained silent, and a duke's silence could speak volumes.

"The other directors are well known to me, and had no idea the magnitude of the sum resulting from the card party," Montague replied. "They are also from established, respected families, of means, and well connected."

Uncle Percival rose. "Dear me. Do you imply that a man who's heir to a duke lacks connections, Montague? Such admirably high standards you have. Correct me if I'm wrong, but wasn't it you who put Lord Colin's name forth at your club and you who suggested he join the board of directors?"

The duke's pleasant manner was a more satisfying set down than any kick under the table Anwen could have delivered.

"He did," she said, rising as Uncle Percival held her chair. "Mr. Montague implied Lord Colin would take Mr. Montague's place on the board directly. Let's show His Grace the strongbox, shall we? I assume you brought your key, Mr. Montague?"

Hitchings struggled to his feet, his gaze bouncing from Anwen to Montague. "I have my key," he said when Montague maintained an affronted silence.

"Then let's be about it," Uncle Percival said. "If Montague is determined to lay information against Lord Colin, to bring scandal down on this fine institution, and announce his own incompetence as a chairman to all of polite society, I'm not in a position to stop him."

Uncle Percival was trying, and for that Anwen could not love him more. Montague looked far from defeated, however.

"The chairman's office is this way," Hitchings said, "though we don't normally keep it locked. No point locking it now, is there?"

Of course there was a point. Somebody could lift the entire strongbox and walk away with it, though Uncle Percival would figure that out for himself.

Hitchings swung the door open. Anwen was prepared to see the same, dreary, dusty office she'd seen many times before, complete with a strongbox sitting square on the chairman's desk.

Colin sat at the chairman's desk, a sheet of paper before him, a quill pen in his hand, and an ink bottle open on the blotter. Scattered around on the blotter were also neat stacks of bills and piles of coins.

"Good morning," he said, rising. "Your Grace, Miss Anwen, a pleasure. Hitchings, Montague, I'm not quite done with the tally, but my closest estimation is that every penny previously reported missing is present and accounted for."

What on earth?

Colin's demeanor gave away nothing. He was attired all in dark clothing, his face was lined with fatigue, and his blue eyes had the flat, emotionless gaze of a man pushed beyond endurance.

"Montague," His Grace said. "You have apparently developed a taste for brewing tempests in teapots—or strongboxes. I am not amused, and I doubt Her Grace will be either. What have you to say for yourself?"

Uncle Percival was very much on his dignity, so much so that Hitchings shrank back against the door.

"That money was stolen," Montague said. "The money was stolen, all of it gone. Hitchings said so."

"Hitchings was right," Colin said, "but I didn't take it, and neither, it turns out, did you."

Chapter Twenty

COLIN WANTED NOTHING MORE than to scoop Anwen up and spin her around until they fell in a happy, relieved heap, but there stood Moreland, looking like the wrath of Mayfair. Next to him, Winthrop Montague was trying to hold on to an air of outraged dignity.

"Of course I didn't take the money," Montague snapped. "Only the most vile, selfish, outrageous, contemptible excuse for a mongrel cur would steal from a lot of wretched children. I should call you out for the very implication."

Moreland studied the golden lion's head at the top of his walking stick. "Montague, there is a lady present."

"Thank you, Your Grace," Anwen said. "I am pleased to find the money where it belongs, but would like to hear what Lord Colin has to say."

"Nothing he has to say could possibly interest me," Montague said. "I resign from my position as chairman effective immediately, and will take my leave of this dashed place once and for all."

Colin pulled out a chair from the conference table. "Sit, else I will ruin you as you planned so cheerfully to ruin me."

Anwen looked pleased with that threat—except it wasn't a threat, it was a vow.

"Do take a seat, Mr. Montague," she said. "As best I can recall the policies and procedures with my feeble female memory, no resignation is effective unless tendered to two other directors who accept same in writing."

Moreland settled into a chair. "Best do as she says, Montague. Wouldn't want to add rudeness to a lady to your other transgressions."

Montague flounced into a seat, and for half an instant, Colin nearly felt sorry for him. Then he recalled four boys, holding vigil with him through a long and disappointing night, and wished there were no witnesses in the room.

Colin remained on his feet. "The funds were discovered missing yesterday morning. Somebody who had access to the property between about three o'clock and ten o'clock in the morning took them. Those parties included myself, Mr. Montague, Hitchings, MacDeever, the boys, and the staff."

"And Miss Anwen," Montague said. "Don't deny it."

"Mr. Montague, tread lightly," Moreland murmured. "Very, very lightly."

"Montague is right," Colin said. "Anwen was here to inform the boys of the card party's success, and Lady Rosalyn was with her."

Comprehension lit in Anwen's eyes, while Montague fluffed his cravat. "What of it? Poor Rosalyn has cut her ties with this place and not a moment too soon. I rue the day I dragged her onto Miss Anwen's dratted committee."

His Grace sat back. "Young man, I account your father a parliamentary associate, else I should call you out myself."

"If I recall aright," Colin said, "Mr. Montague noted that only the most vile, selfish, outrageous, contemptible excuse for a mongrel cur would steal from a lot of wretched children. The thief is his own sister, Lady Rosalyn Montague."

Colin expected Montague to explode across the table, reel with righteous denials, or otherwise defend his sister's honor. Anwen's expression was merely curious, while Moreland was scowling.

"Explain yourself," His Grace said, "for Mr. Montague's powers of speech seem to have deserted him."

Montague sat unmoving on his side of the table, his expression blank. "*Rosalyn took the money?*"

The poor sod hadn't figured it out, which meant he'd been willing to stick Colin's neck in a noose for the sheer hell of it, not even to keep his sister from going to prison.

"Rosalyn stole every penny," Colin said. "She came here yesterday morning with Anwen, got halfway up the stairs before pleading a headache, and told Anwen she'd wait in the coach. Anwen went in search of the boys, and Rosalyn went to the chairman's office thinking to break into the strongbox. She had the combination, which I've occasion to know has been conveniently jotted down in your daybook."

Anwen's gaze went to the strongbox. "But she didn't even have to open the strongbox, because Hitchings had locked only the office door, if that—Rosalyn would need a mere hairpin if he had—and left the money lying in an unlocked drawer."

"Rosalyn took the money?" Montague said again. "This is terrible."

"Mr. Montague," Anwen said, rising and leaning across the table. "The fate your sister faces for having committed a heinous crime is no worse than the fate you had planned for an innocent man. You are a disgrace and a scoundrel who deserves every bit as much condemnation as your sister."

"Couldn't have said it better myself," Moreland added. "I might call you out after all."

Moreland's duchess would never forgive Colin if a duel ensued, and more to the point, Anwen would never forgive him if the orphanage was associated with a duel.

"I wish you wouldn't, Your Grace," Colin said. "We honestly can't have the scandal, else I would be at Bow Street laying information against her ladyship right now."

"Why aren't you?" Montague asked. "If you can't prove your accusations, you've no business making them."

"Montague," His Grace said, "you are a fool. One cannot repair such a lack with any amount of education, fine fashion, or training. Your father has my deepest pity."

"I have proof," Colin said. "I entered the Montague household and informed the porter I'd forgotten a pair of gloves abovestairs, which as it happens, I did. I was admitted to the premises without protest and invited to retrieve my gloves, and by inadvertence opened the wrong door. The very bag in which the cash had been taken from the Moreland townhouse to the orphanage sat on Lady Rosalyn's escritoire. A cursory examination revealed the missing funds within."

"You have witnesses?" His Grace asked.

Montague had gone as pale as nursery pudding.

"I asked Lord Rosecroft to drive me to the Montague townhouse, Your Grace. He saw me enter the premises without the funds, and exit with them in hand. I then asked him to join me and Lady Rosalyn inside, and he heard her confession with me, as did Lord Monthaven. Montague, your sister has a collection of fans, gloves, even some reticules that do not belong to her. Half of Mayfair's debutantes have probably lost property to her, and they will not be kind should her misdeeds come to light."

"My knitting needles," Anwen said. "She took a pair of my knitting needles, and stashed them into one of those embroidered sacks she carries everywhere. She probably took Lady Dremel's fan, Flora Stanbridge's pearl gloves..."

"She steals?" Montague murmured. "My Rosalyn steals? But she's...she's a paragon, a diamond of the first water, an incomparable, the daughter of the Earl of Monthaven. She wouldn't—"

"She steals from you," Colin said. "All the vowels you've misplaced, the coins that you were sure you left on your vanity. She sneaks into your room, a thief in the night."

"Sounds as if she's a thief at all hours," His Grace said, rising. "I trust, Lord Colin, that you will resolve this matter discreetly and within the requirements of justice. My duchess will want a full report. See Anwen home, please."

"Of course, Your Grace."

"I'll just be getting back to my ledgers," Hitchings said. "Lord Colin, my thanks. On my behalf and on behalf of the boys. My sincere, unending thanks."

Hitchings left the door open, but Colin closed it behind him.

Montague kept to his seat, and even his lips had gone pale. "What are your intentions? My father will not take kindly to you putting yourself above the law, MacHugh."

Colin leaned across the table as Anwen had. "That's *Lord*

Colin to you. I've consulted with those directly affected by Lady Rosalyn's felonious behavior, and they advise me to do unto you as you were prepared to do to me."

"You'll see him hanged?" Anwen said, wrinkling her nose.

"I will give him a choice," Colin said. "The same choice he claimed to be offering me. Escort your sister for an extended stay in Italy with your aunt, or be investigated for forging my signature on bills at the clubs—clubs that are suspending your membership indefinitely, because forgery is a felony. You broke the rules, Montague. The rules of human decency, the rules of law, and even the rules of your silly little clubs. The consequences won't be silly at all, and the scandal, I can assure you, from both your bad behavior and your sister's crimes, will be endless."

"That's what the boys said to do?" Anwen asked. "A vacation in Italy or ruin? They are being far too merciful, if you ask me."

"The boys agreed that I should take one precaution." They'd gone so far as to admit Colin's suggestion was brilliant, for a mere beginner. "A distinctive pair of antique rings have been secreted at the Monthaven townhouse, one ring in Lady Rosalyn's apartments, one in Montague's. I will inform the authorities of the suspected whereabouts of these rings, if Montague should refuse the clemency the boys are showing him and Lady Rosalyn.

"They are gentlemen," Colin went on, "and they show compassion to their inferiors. Have your sister on a ship for Rome by Tuesday, Montague, or prepare to face ruin, prosecution, and scandal. Now get out, and leave me some privacy with my intended."

Montague rose and looked as if he wanted to say something to Anwen.

She pointed to the door. "You heard his lordship. Leave now, and stay permanently gone. I won't be half so forgiving as the children whom you and she have wronged, or as Lord Colin is being."

He bowed—quite low—and left without another word.

* * *

Anwen was in Colin's arms without knowing how she got there. "I was so frightened, and so angry, and I'm so relieved."

"I had some bad moments too," Colin said, "but Montague is a problem solved. His father won't leave him any choice. The earl admitted Lady Rosalyn had been stealing, and said it started when her mother died. This is the first time he's known her to take anything of great value."

Anwen glowered up at her beloved. "Why does she get away without even making an apology to the boys? Her actions could have seen you hanged, and if she'd been anybody but an earl's daughter, she'd be in jail by tomorrow."

Anwen could feel Colin's heartbeat beneath her cheek, could feel the weariness in him.

"I agree, it doesn't sit well to simply banish her to Italy. She knows these boys, knows their stories, and what they've faced for want of coin. Her defense, if you can call it that, is that she took only the cash and left them the jewels."

"That is no defense at all," Anwen retorted, leaving Colin's embrace just long enough to lock the door. "She didn't steal the jewels because trying to open the strongbox meant a greater risk of being caught. The boys had access to the orphanage's funds month after month and never took a penny."

The tenacity of Anwen's rage surprised her. Colin was safe, the money was found, the boys were safe, but still, the Montague siblings would make no reparation for the damage they'd caused, would make no atonement.

"You're sure the boys told you to let her go?" Anwen asked, taking Colin by the hand.

"I'm sure. I asked them to think about what should happen when we found the money. They assumed, as I had, that Win had stolen the money rather than Lady Rosalyn, and they were willing to give him a chance to pull a bunk, as they'd put it. Win was to be given a choice to leave the country and save us all from scandal or face prosecution."

Anwen led Colin to the desk, scooted back amid the piles of bills and coin, and tugged him closer by his waistband.

"So the children simply added clemency for Lady Rosalyn to their offer. Had MacDeever been accused of taking the money, or had he taken it in fact, nobody would have offered him clemency. That is a scandal to me, Colin. An earl's children commit vile wrongs and they go to Italy. That's not justice."

He stepped closer, between her knees. "You are very angry. Now you understand why after a siege, after being fired upon for days, digging all night, and fighting through terrible odds, an army can lose its self-control."

He kissed her and wrapped his arms about her, which did help—some.

"Why didn't you flee, Colin? I wanted you to flee to safety. I would have gone with you." Saying the words let Anwen acknowledge the truth. Much of what she felt wasn't rage so much as lingering terror.

What if Colin hadn't been brilliant enough to find the money?

What if Montague had seen the orphanage condemned? What if Colin had been sentenced to hang?

Maybe this was how Anwen's family had felt when she'd been so ill. They'd been helpless, exhausted, enraged, and determined to fight on even after the foe had been bested.

That thought bore pondering—later—because it had the illuminating feel of a revelation.

Colin stroked her hair as a great sigh went out of her. "I thought about running," he said. "Live to fight another day, aye? I thought about it last night, and again this morning when all seemed lost and nothing to be gained by standing my ground."

"You didn't run, you didn't give up, even when you should have," Anwen said on a shudder. "Why not?"

She loved holding him, *loved him*.

"I love you, Anwen Windham. You are my heart. I could not have fled if it meant leaving you at risk of harm. A few months ago, even weeks ago, I'd have been on a ship, cutting my losses and thanking the Almighty that I'd escaped with life, liberty, and good health. Live and let live, don't dwell on the past."

"The past has lessons for us," Anwen said. "Up to a point. I'm about to cry."

Colin stayed right where he was and kept stroking her hair. "I liked the army because somebody was always giving me orders. Do this, don't do that. March here, camp there. Fix this, replace that. I'd go off on larks and dodge the truly stupid orders, but for the most part, life was simple."

"As long as you stayed alive."

He kissed her again, her right eyelid, then her left. "Maybe that's how badly I didn't want to face making my own choices. I was content to go through life tidying up after others, mending and repairing anything within reach just to feel useful. I'd rather take a bullet than make a wrong choice, but I was mistaken. Choosing the way forward won't be difficult anymore."

"If you choose to risk hanging again, I will make life very difficult for you, Colin MacHugh."

He rubbed Anwen's back, which only made the lump in her throat hurt worse. "Anwen, if I had to choose again, I'd make the same decisions. I was tempted to leave, but then I asked myself: What must I do to protect my Anwen and her respect for me? Then the way became clear. That question will always make the way clear."

Colin was saying he was at peace with how the situation had turned out, pleased even.

"Hold me, Colin."

"Aye, always."

His peace gradually became Anwen's to borrow, to lean on. When her tears came, he held her, and used her handkerchief to dry them.

"I've had some ideas," he said. "I'd like to discuss them with you, and if you approve, we can take them up with the boys and Hitchings. First, though, I'd like to take you home."

Anwen's sisters, and her aunt and uncle would expect a full accounting from her and from Colin. She understood better where their concern came from, and with Colin at her side, would endure the questions with good grace.

"We need to tell the boys what's afoot," she said.

Colin stepped back, shot a look at the door, and regarded her. "I misspoke. Before I take you home, before we talk with the boys, there's something else I'd like to do. Heaven knows when we'll have privacy again, especially if you agree with my plans."

That sounded interesting, and the smile Colin aimed at her was more interesting still.

"We need to set a date soon, Colin MacHugh. There's a tradition in the Windham family of firstborns coming at seven months. We could find ourselves upholding that tradition."

He kissed her with maddening sweetness. "A lovely tradition. I'm happy to do my part."

Anwen fisted her hand in his hair and hiked a leg around his hips. "So am I."

Epilogue

"THE IDEA IS ANWEN'S," Colin said. "She wasn't content to allow Lady Rosalyn and Winthrop Montague to simply holiday in Italy when they'd behaved so badly. Has a fine sense of justice, does my Anwen."

Moreland sent a creditable glower in Colin's direction. "She is, and always will be, *our* Anwen. Just because you married her, don't think you alone have the privilege of loving her."

Sitting behind the massive library desk, surrounded by a wealth of books and expensive art, Moreland looked every inch the duke, just as he had during last week's uncomfortable encounter at the orphanage. At yesterday's wedding in the Moreland House conservatory, His Grace had looked ready to shed a sentimental tear.

"Thank you, Uncle Percival," Anwen said. "I love you too. What do you think of my idea?"

Moreland was many things—patriarch, doting husband,

and devoted uncle. He was also a wily parliamentarian who could produce votes for any worthy bill.

"A parliamentary committee to research the plight of the orphaned poor in London?" Moreland replied. "Any measure hinting of reform faces resistance, but with the Earl of Monthaven to chair the body, it should easily gain approval. Would you like me to approach him about it?"

"No need for you to bother, Uncle," Anwen said. "He was in favor of the notion. I wanted to resent him, to hold him accountable for the actions of his children, but he struck me as a decent fellow."

Colin had been skeptical of Anwen's plan, and surprised when the earl had received them, but—true to Anwen's instincts—his lordship had been relieved to be given a means of putting right what his children had nearly put wrong.

"So I suppose you'll be leaving for Scotland soon?" Moreland asked. "What of the demolition plans for the House of Urchins?"

Colin had used every ounce of his charm, stubbornness, and commonsense to gain Anwen's support for this decision, and then he'd had to convince the other directors, one of whom was now no less person than the ducal heir, the Earl of Westhaven.

"Demolition of the unused wing will begin next week," Colin said. "Every brick, windowpane, door latch, and hinge will be sold. The funds resulting will be used to refurbish the remaining wing, hire a new headmaster, and enhance the endowment. The boys are set to foster in pairs with various MacHugh cousins here in London until the work is complete, though the four oldest will come north with us."

Hitchings's mysterious errands had apparently been necessitated by his courtship of a housekeeper in service two streets over from the orphanage. He and the new Mrs. Hitchings were off to a cottage in Cornwall, where he'd tutor the sons of gentry.

"You have all in hand," Moreland said, looking a bit peevish to have no contribution to make to the plans. "I'll wish you safe journey, and exhort you, Anwen, to write frequently. Your sisters will miss you sorely, as will your parents and cousins. And you, sir"—he came around the desk, hand extended—"get as much rest as you can. If my duchess's predictions have any credibility, you'll need it. Her Grace raised ten children and knows of what she speaks."

As it turned out, the duchess's prognostications were accurate, and while Colin and Anwen did not have ten children, what children they did have were red-haired and, in the opinion of their great-uncle, Windhams, the lot of them, despite a Scottish patronymic to the contrary.

Joseph evidenced a talent for music, having discovered that when singing, his stammer did not afflict him. He eventually toured the Continent as a baritone soloist, and caught the eye of a widowed German princess, by which time he'd lost his stammer—and his shyness.

Dickie became proprietor of a very exclusive tailor's establishment, John a wealthy solicitor, and Tom—who apprenticed with MacHugh the publisher—a journalist, and then a publisher himself.

The House of Urchins—no longer the House of *Wayward* Urchins—thrived, in large part because its successful alumni supported it generously, and also because Lord Colin and Miss Anwen—she would always be Miss Anwen to the orphans—would have it no other way.

Keep reading for a peek at Book 3
in the Windham Brides series.

NO OTHER DUKE WILL DO

Coming in Winter 2017

Chapter One

ELIZABETH WINDHAM WAS ON trial, and she'd done nothing wrong to merit a place in the dock. She perched on the chair behind her father's desk, her back not touching the leather.

"This changes everything," her father said, pacing before her. "Your great-aunt did you no favors by leaving you that money."

"So let me spend it," Elizabeth replied, rising and bracing both hands on the blotter. "Anwen's orphanage, some soldier's relief fund, a lending library for the—"

"You will be engaged by Michaelmas, Elizabeth. Your mother's nerves cannot take another attempt to compromise you, nor can mine. If you have no care for your parents, then consider the damage to Charlotte's reputation when some dashing blade spirits you off to Gretna Green, or worse."

Charlotte, Elizabeth's only unmarried sister, was loyally

pretending to have no interest in marriage, simply so Elizabeth did not face spinsterhood alone. Charlotte was also contrary, stubborn, and—though she might not admit it herself—lonely.

Elizabeth sank back into the chair behind her father's desk. "That is not fair. Allermain behaves like an ass, and I'm the one nearly ruined, but it's my cousins' safety you claim is at risk. I'm not asking them to call anybody out."

Papa took the seat opposite. He was lean, fit, the son of a duke, and nobody to trifle with, for all his charm. Had Elizabeth seen a battle light in his eyes she might have steeled herself to meet his display of temper with one of her own. Instead, Papa's expression was exasperated, and... weary.

Of her, of her unwillingness to marry some mincing fop with clammy hands, merely for the pleasure of risking her life every two years in childbed, to say nothing of how those clammy hands would feel on her person when taking intimate liberties in the dark.

"Elizabeth, have your mother and I set so awful an example that you dread to marry?"

"The example you set is the problem," she replied. "You and Mama are allied in all matters, you are...you love each other, and nothing divides you. Even Uncle Percy and Aunt Esther don't have the same enthralled air."

Aunt and Uncle were devoted partners, Mama and Papa were besotted.

Papa sat back, crossing one booted foot over the opposite knee. "So your objection is not to the institution of marriage, but to the candidates available to share it with you?"

Elizabeth nodded, though she feared she'd given away a critical inch of ground. "I want somebody who, in thirty years, still looks at me the way you look at Mama." That devotion was not merely display. Mama and Papa took holidays together, arrived to and departed from social functions together, and were political allies.

"Then you will be pleased to learn that the Duke of Haverford is having a house party, to which he's invited only gentlemen suitable for consideration by his sister. Haverford is a sober fellow, responsible, and well respected. He will assemble only the best of the best for Lady Glenys, and she will choose no more than one man for herself."

"A house party?" House parties ran the gamut from near orgies to stupefyingly dull rural purgatories.

"At Haverford Castle, not far from where your mother's mother grew up. You and Charlotte have been invited. Your mother sent off an acceptance this morning and your aunt Arabella will chaperone."

Aunt Arabella espoused liberal politics, and had sneaked Elizabeth the occasional sip of Christmas punch before Elizabeth had put up her hair.

"You want me to choose a husband from among a herd of men who're trying to catch the eye of Haverford's sister?"

Like Elizabeth, Lady Glenys St. David was fast approaching spinsterhood, and she appeared to relish the prospect. She'd not come to Town much during the past five years, not even when her ducal brother was voting his seat.

"I want you to consider possibilities," Papa said, "enjoy the Welsh countryside, and avoid the near occasion of kidnapping. If you see a fellow you approve of, then don't rebuff him until you've given the man a chance. Play fair, Elizabeth, for your mother is at the end of her patience."

No sane Windham tempted Mama past the end of her patience. "If I'm to endure marriage, then I'll not put up with some strutting nincompoop who lives at his clubs. I want a sensible man, in good health, honorable, solvent, and sober. A man who will support my interest in worthy charities."

Most importantly, this paragon would have to be the unbothersome sort, once the obvious duties had been tended to. Elizabeth would not approach the marriage bed in ignorance of those duties, but neither would she approach it with any enthusiasm.

Papa pushed to his feet, his movements uncharacteristically stiff and slow. He'd doubtless been up until all hours last night, praying and hoping for Elizabeth's safe return.

Abruptly, she felt like a petulant, ungrateful child, one who'd been rescued from considerable peril.

"I want you happy as well as safe, Elizabeth, and the right man will double your joys and halve your sorrows. You must be willing to double his joys as well, though. You're a fair-minded young lady. Meet the fellows halfway, and see what develops."

Nothing would develop, because the knight in sober armor Elizabeth sought did not exist. "If I meet a man who conforms to my requirements, I will consider him. When do we leave?" she asked, rising.

Papa came around the desk and kissed her forehead, which gesture, Elizabeth had loathed for as long as she could recall. Why did nobody kiss the foreheads of gentlemen or boys?

"The day after tomorrow."

"I'd best start packing, then."

* * *

"You are a horrid brother," Glenys said. "I sought to while away a few weeks of summer in the company of congenial young ladies, and you've turned my gathering into a summons for every solvent bachelor under the age of fifty."

Julian Andreas Cynan Evan St. David, twelfth Duke of Haverford, gave the reins of his horse over to a groom, propped a boot on a pot of salvia, and slapped at his dusty toe with his riding gloves.

"I will be present in all my ducal splendor for the gathering before dinner, Glenys. This party was not my idea, but you are my sister and I would never bring shame upon you."

Glenys was tall and handsomely proportioned, if not exactly pretty. She was also worried, and not very good at hiding it. She glanced around at the bustle of porters lugging trunks to the castle's side entrance, grooms leading teams off to the carriage house, and footmen ordering each other about, then patted Julian's lapel.

"I wish, just once, you'd do something a bit naughty, Haverford. Arrive tipsy to services, forget the words to a verse of hymnody, trip over the fringe of a carpet."

Another baggage wagon rolled around to the side of the castle.

"I went to university, Glenys. I wasn't a saint."

"You went up to university more than half your lifetime ago. But for Radnor, you'd have taken firsts in every subject. One despairs of you."

The moment took on an odd quality, such that Julian knew he would recall it decades into the future, should he live so long. He'd gone up to Oxford at sixteen, the normal age, and indeed, that had somehow become more than *half his lifetime ago*.

Not a few years, not a decade or so, but more than half his lifetime.

Across the crushed shell drive, Haverford Castle sat in its gleaming golden glory, turreted towers swaddled in ivy, massive front door open in welcome. The crunch of carriage wheels, the dust rising behind each conveyance, and the light rose scent of Glenys's perfume blended into an indelible moment.

In the blink of an eye, Julian would become just one more poorly maintained portrait among the many paintings crowding onto the walls of the second floor gallery. Where were the years going, and what legacy would he leave behind?

"Perhaps you ought to find a bit of mischief to get into yourself," Julian said.

"Me? Get into mischief? At my own house party?"

"Yes, you," Julian said, wrapping an arm around Glenys's shoulders and giving her a squeeze. "Be discreet, though, else I'll have to shoot somebody, and dueling is a damned waste of a pretty morning."

An enormous traveling coach went rattling past, making room for yet another arrival to advance up the drive and disgorge its occupants.

"I'd best greet our guests," Glenys said. "You stink of horse, so away with you. Dust off what meager stores of charm you claim, and display them on the back terrace promptly at seven."

She was already smiling, moving in the direction of the coach, when Julian caught her by the arm.

"Don't wait for me to choose a wife before you consider marriage, Glenys. You aren't responsible for looking after me."

She shrugged free, her smile faltering. "Somebody has to look after you. The job falls to me because you won't let anybody else near."

She strode off, a lady very much on her dignity, and thus she could ignore Julian's parting shot.

"If I won't let anybody else near, then why do I have so little solitude, and even less privacy?"

* * *

"Shoot me," Charlotte moaned. "Please, if you have any love for me at all, take out the coach pistol and end my torment."

"I never took you for a coward, Charl," Elizabeth replied from the coach's backward-facing seat. "Other people are fatigued by long journeys."

Charlotte sprawled on the forward-facing seat, one foot braced on the floor, one hand on her middle. "I am not fatigued, I am dying. Why did nobody warn me that the roads in Wales are instruments of torture?"

"It's not the roads serving you ill, it's probably the ale you had at the last inn."

Charlotte was pale, dyspeptic, and had stopped to visit the bushes three times in the last five miles. Thank goodness, bushes were in generous supply in this part of Wales. Aunt had chosen to ride in the next coach back with the ladies' maids, so that "poor Charlotte" had room to stretch out on the bench.

"I stink," Charlotte said. "I hate to stink. A lady isn't supposed to perspire, much less cast up her accounts, much less—dear God, have we arrived?"

The coach had turned up a long drive shaded on both sides by towering oaks. In deference to Charlotte's condition, progress was stately.

The dwelling at the end of the drive was splendidly regal. Crenelated turrets stood at either end of a golden façade five stories tall, and the circular end of the drive curved around a fountain that sprayed water a good twenty feet into the air. Potted flowers adorned a raised front terrace and circled the fountain, creating red, white, and green splashes of color against the stonework.

"Haverford owns all this?" Charlotte asked, sitting up enough to peer out the window. "Moreland isn't half so grand."

"Moreland is probably two centuries more modern. You're at death's door, though, so what do you care?"

"I feel a miraculous revival coming on," Charlotte said, straightening her skirts. "Or I might presently. Ye gods, I shall never drink another drop of ale."

The coach lurched forward, and Charlotte's pallor became more marked.

"Lie back down," Elizabeth said. "The bushes are disobligingly sparse along this drive."

Charlotte subsided to the bench. "I'm to be humiliated before all of society, dragged from the coach in a state of obvious ill health. Perhaps I will die in Mama's homeland, and out of guilt, Papa will grant you the spinsterdom you long for."

"Spinsterdom is not a word. If you die, may I have your mare?" Charlotte's ill health was real, but as long as she responded to sororal teasing, Elizabeth's worry would remain manageable.

"You may have my jewels."

"You have the same pearls and pins I do."

Charlotte put her wrist to her brow. "I yield my entire treasure to you. Elizabeth, can't you have the coach circle around to the back of the house? I truly do not want to appear before the most eligible bachelors in the realm looking like some cupshot tweenie."

Vanity was a reassuring sign when a sister professed to be expiring. "I'll get you up to a bedroom, and nobody will think you're anything but travel weary."

"I will write to Mama of the foul brew served to the unsuspecting in her homeland. Rest assured the Welsh bachelors just lost considerable ground in the race to offer for my hand. Such misery would never befall me in England."

"You speak as an earnest husband-hunter."

"As a dying husband-hunter. No harm in looking over the eligibles as they pay their final respects to one cut down in the full flower of her youth. How long is this dratted drive?"

"We're almost there."

The coach soon swayed to a halt, and Charlotte pressed a wrinkled handkerchief to her lips. The vehicle rocked as a footman climbed down, then the door opened and the steps were unfolded.

"I suppose I must move," Charlotte muttered.

"I can have the footmen carry you," Elizabeth said. Charlotte was nearly gray about the mouth.

"Oh, the ignominy. Dragged to the door like some tomcat's decapitated sparrow—"

"Our hostess approaches," Elizabeth said, rising to accept a footman's hand. "I'll explain, and you'll produce a ladylike swoon."

Technically, Lady Glenys was their host's unmarried sister, though thank a benevolent providence, Elizabeth didn't have to explain Charlotte's bilious stomach to the duke himself. In her experience, dukes did not deal well with life's most unglamorous realities.

A delicate bunch, dukes. Marquesses and earls weren't much sturdier.

"Miss Windham," Lady Glenys said, bobbing a curtsy.

"I've been anticipating the pleasure of your company in particular. Are Lady Pembroke and Miss Charlotte with you?"

Lady Glenys's graciousness might have convinced a younger woman, but Elizabeth had been to enough house parties to know what a nerve-wracking undertaking they could be for the lady in charge. Her ladyship had probably spent the day welcoming all and sundry on the steps, while a thousand tasks went awry in the house.

"Charlotte is somewhat the worse for the journey," Elizabeth said. "Her digestion has grown tentative over these last few miles."

Charlotte peeked her head out of the coach. A decapitated sparrow would have been more attractive than the pale, bedraggled creature blinking in the late afternoon sunshine.

"My heavenly stars," Lady Glenys said. "You poor dear. I am so sorry you're feeling poorly, and will have you up to your rooms in no time."

Charlotte tottered from the coach, a footman assisting on one side, Elizabeth on the other.

"I'd curtsy," Charlotte said, "but I've no desire to end up face down on your cobbles."

"Hush, dear," Elizabeth said as Lady Glenys took a step back. "We'll simply follow her ladyship into the house and find you a nice, soft, *private* place to settle yourself."

The footmen stepped away, hands behind their backs. Lady Glenys looked torn between distress and sympathy, and Charlotte hung heavily on Elizabeth's arm.

"Can you walk to the house?" Elizabeth asked.

Charlotte glanced up at the crenelated façade, her expression grim. "If I must."

Why would nobody offer aid? Grooms held teams for

two coaches and a landau behind the Windham coach, and Lady Glenys wrung her hands.

"Come along," Elizabeth said, tucking an arm around Charlotte's waist. "It's not far, and you're a Windham."

Bootsteps crunched to Elizabeth's left, and then Charlotte's weight was plucked away.

"Allow me to aid the lady," said a tall gentleman in riding attire. "I apologize for presuming, but I'm guessing a bad batch of Merlin Jones's summer ale is to blame. Lady Glenys, which bedroom?"

He smelled of horses and hayfields, his boots were dusty, and his dark hair was less than tidy. Charlotte's rescuer had the steady gaze of a man used to solving problems with common sense and hard work. He held her as if striding about with a full-grown woman in his arms was part of his daily routine.

Charlotte would be utterly safe with this man.

Every woman was safe around this man. That conviction landed in Elizabeth's mind with the same certainty she felt when she picked up a new book and grasped in the very first lines that great treasure lay on the subsequent pages.

Clearly travel had taken a toll on her wits.

"Take her to the Dovecote," Lady Glenys said. "Both Miss Windham and Miss Charlotte are in the Dovecote."

Charlotte looked to be enjoying her first convincing ladylike swoon.

"Miss Windham," the man said. "If you'll come along?"

He had dark auburn hair, green eyes, and his expression held no flirtation, no suggestion of humor at Charlotte's expense. Sober and steady when sober and steady were desperately needed.

"My thanks," Elizabeth said, falling in step beside him. "Who is this Merlin Jones?" *And who are you?*

"He's the innkeeper at the nearest coaching inn, and known to occasionally mix up a bad batch of ale. Because he serves the suspect brew only to those traveling on, he's not held accountable for his mistakes."

Charlotte's rescuer spoke with the lilting diction of the educated Welshman, and his fitness was such that even carrying Charlotte up a grand curved staircase, his strength was not taxed. Something about the angle of his jaw suggested Mr. Jones would be held accountable this time.

"The Dovecote is one of the tower suites," he said. "The views are lovely, and you're close to both the family wing and the guest wing. If the apartment is not to your liking, I'm sure Lady Glenys can see to other arrangements."

He was local, then, a neighbor, cousin, or close friend of the family. Was he a guest at the house party? For all his athleticism, he might also be a well-read man, which was Elizabeth's favorite sort of fellow.

"I'm sure the accommodations will be fine. Charlotte, how are you feeling?"

"A little better," she said, lashes fluttering. "What a magnificent castle."

"It can be cold as the devil's root cellar in winter," the gentleman said. "This is your suite."

He carried Charlotte straight into a circular chamber graced with three windows. The walls were easily two feet thick, the plaster a mellow cream. A single red rose sat in a crystal vase on the sideboard.

The gentleman set Charlotte on a tufted sofa and regarded her, his hands on his hips. In his dusty boots and with a streak of dirt on one sleeve, he might have been a steward assessing a heifer gone off her feed.

"Fresh air, I think," he said, wrestling two of the windows open. The latch screeched in protest, but the breeze was heavenly. He then knelt before the sideboard. "At the risk of being indelicate, you might also need this."

He rose, holding a porcelain basin painted with daffodils.

"At the risk of being pathetic," Elizabeth replied, taking the basin, "we thank you. You are being very kind, sir."

Though not exactly proper. Why didn't the fellow introduce himself?

The gentleman bowed. "I'll leave you, then, ladies. A footman is on duty at all times at the top of the steps and will alert the kitchen should you need anything. Welcome to Haverford."

Elizabeth dipped a curtsy, and then took the place beside Charlotte when the gentleman had quietly closed the door on his way out. He was a handsome specimen, in a mature, un-fancy way.

A bit short on charm, though. "Shall you live, Charl?"

"I've been carried to my boudoir in the arms of a duke," Charlotte said, flopping against the back of the sofa. "I'm not sure I can bear the strain such an honor has put on my maidenly nerves."

"Your color has improved, but do you mean to tell me *that* was His Grace of Haverford?"

ABOUT THE AUTHOR

Grace Burrowes grew up in central Pennsylvania and is the sixth out of seven children. She discovered romance novels when in junior high (back when there was such a thing), and has been reading them voraciously ever since. Grace has a bachelor's degree in political science, a bachelor of music in music history (both from Pennsylvania State University); a master's degree in conflict transformation from Eastern Mennonite University; and a juris doctor from the National Law Center at the George Washington University.

Grace writes Georgian, Regency, Scottish Victorian, and contemporary romances in both novella and novel lengths. She's a member of Romance Writers of America, and enjoys giving workshops and speaking at writers' conferences. She also loves to hear from her readers, and can be reached through her website, graceburrowes.com.

You can learn more at:
GraceBurrowes.com
Twitter: @GraceBurrowes
Facebook.com/GraceBurrowes

Do you love historical fiction?

Want the chance to hear news about your favourite authors (and the chance to win free books)?

Mary Balogh
Charlotte Betts
Jessica Blair
Frances Brody
Gaelen Foley
Elizabeth Hoyt
Eloisa James
Lisa Kleypas
Stephanie Laurens
Claire Lorrimer
Sarah MacLean
Amanda Quick
Julia Quinn

Then visit the Piatkus website and blog
www.piatkus.co.uk | www.piatkusbooks.net

And follow us on Facebook and Twitter
www.facebook.com/piatkusfiction | www.twitter.com/piatkusbooks

piatkus